THE OTHER AMERICANS

A Novel

Navidad Thélamour

To my beloved mother, Patricia. The one who always believed in me, who always rooted for me. I still hear your cheers now. The eternal wind beneath my wings.

THE DESSOMMES
FAMILY TREE

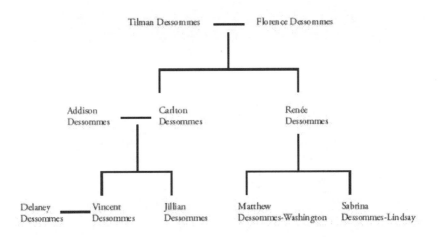

Then it dawned upon me with a certain suddenness that I was different from the others; or like, mayhap, in heart and life and longing, but shut out from their world by a vast veil.
−W.E.B. DuBois, The Souls of Black Folk

PROLOGUE

DELANEY

O f the fabled seven cardinal sins, greed and vanity had always been the real family Achilles' heel, at least for as far back as she could remember being with them. Admittedly, her memory hadn't reached much farther back than her early college days for quite some time, the immersion in their world was so complete. But that was another story in and of itself, wasn't it?

Greed came with the Dessommes territory. One couldn't want the lifestyle that they wanted, continue the legacy they had built, and never feel the cold fingers of self-indulgence at their throat. After a while they forgot about it because those fingers at their throat could be worn like a necklace, plain as day for everyone to see. Why not? Everyone had one and everyone flaunted theirs, the new must-have statement pieces that the tittering Clan members raved about over conference room tables and luncheons out with the girls: what to acquire next and how to get it before anyone else had it. There was no stopping the snowball effect, because having more has always bred needing more.

The Clan belonged to the few. Built on the few, nurtured by the few, entered by the few. Because, as they were all too aware of, this wasn't the television lifestyle of new-money reality stars renting their furs for the cameras. This was real life, true exclusivity. This was money as old as the days of liquor running and prohibition—older. Young investment bankers who could call in big favors in New York and tenured, graying professors who lectured on anthropology and were invited to give pricey speeches at the ritzy, old money schools with ivy clinging to their walls. This is where Laney had found herself.

Among them all, the Dessommes family was one of the oldest legacies in the South. Just ask any one of them. Those people made "passing" an art form in the post-war Reconstruction period, when the rebels were still flying their flags and trying to forget the North had won. There were whispers that the early Dessommes had owned slaves themselves, but those were only whispers, unconfirmed. What was certain was that since the late nineteenth century at least, they'd sat in the opera houses and school houses alike, next to the former slave masters and up-and-coming construction barons who never guessed they were sitting next to Negro blood. From petticoats and corsets to flapper headdresses, the styles morphed marking the generations, but their bloodline stood the test of time. At first it was the underground poker shacks, speakeasies and illegal liquor runs that distinguished the family, though, by the post-World War II era, they'd branched out from their modest New Orleans roots toward a more tangible form of legacy.

The Second World War earned the Dessommes name a Purple Heart, posthumously; the Vietnam War brought about a handful of other service ribbons and decorations, titles and, increasingly, influence. Cultural notoriety abounded with the politically conscious sit-in and protest participation of the Dessommes' younger generation—the self-proclaimed educated, strong-minded early Dessommes Baby Boomers. Of course, the Dessommes teens and twenty-somethings of that day didn't have the support of their elders for sticking their necks out in such a fashion until after the socially conscious trend became vogue, until it began to lend all-the-more deference and respect onto their family name from those other peers in their inner circles—circles of old money social clubs and fraternities, which had begun underground as a networking mechanism for educated Negroes to fraternize with others like them, and who were now emerging, advancing aboveground, collecting power along the way.

And thus, they'd spread from the underground of the French Quarter to a more distinguished air of old money and increasingly social, political and financial influence that, a few generations later, dominated board rooms and stockholdings alike from Georgia to New York. And, it was within this atmosphere that The Dessommes Group was born, under the watchful eye of Tilman Dessommes, and from which their seat of social power began to morph, with ever-mounting gusto following the *Brown* decision, away from its humble roots and toward the financial entity they were to become.

Starting with a single hotel in Atlanta similar to Portland's historic Golden West Hotel, the Dessommes' accommodations offered a haven for people of color—a melting pot of lounge singers and prestigious brown-skinned doctors, cooks and porters, entertainers and politicians. They swirled in and sauntered out for decades before the color lines were redrawn. Then they were—or, rather, slowly blurred—and another hotel opened. Then another.

They were smart those Dessommes, passing the legacy and the money down from generation to generation, keeping the fortune and the secrets of the family's less-than-upstanding past in the pedigree, while keeping the bloodline "pure" as she'd once heard the late matriarch put it. By that she hadn't meant marrying cousins—not in that century anyway. She meant *light, mulatto*, able to pass the Brown Bag Test in a snap, for that was what'd started the family's legacy and what would remain its hallmark: the ability to straddle the line, to fit in with the larger nation while still flaunting their black roots to those of the darker nation. Now that it was fashionably tolerable, of course. It worked out beautifully for them, especially in this twenty-first-century era where the hierarchy of color still existed but so did affirmative action.

With that in mind, the women in the family weren't married in so much as they were vetted in. Their contribution to the gene pool was considered, whether or not that was spoken out loud. They had to talk the erudite talk and walk that poised and fashionable walk to be allowed in, the rules strict and rarely bending. Of course, she hadn't known any of this when she met Vincent that warm day in the campus quad – before it all shifted, before she was changed.

Vincent and his younger sister Jillian were products of Jack and Jill, the Links and all those other assorted black social clubs that let in the few and claimed bragging rights to grooming the brown-skinned elite, clubs that Laney had never even heard of or thought about before meeting them. When they'd first met, it all seemed so outlandish, even laughable, to her: a bunch of folks sitting around forming national cliques and then deciding who was and wasn't good enough to be a part of them.

But that was before her parents died in the car accident on that sweltering summer day. Before she lost her way that fateful semester of college, then finally allowed herself to be sucked into all the pretentiousness of their book clubs and cotillions just so that she'd have somewhere to truly belong, a dark story that she avoided dredging up at all costs but that simultaneously made her the revered enigma of the Clan. After all, even the ancient Greeks had had their fraternities, and the concept had served them well enough to deserve to be mimicked. So, outlandish became the norm until, years after their deaths, it was firmly a part of her everyday life.

Somewhere along the line, she'd become the new sovereign of the South's gaggle of Machiavellian geese without even realizing it.

PART ONE: BEHIND THE VEIL

That's the thing about prejudice: It doesn't just disappear because you're the same color. – Chibundu Onuzo

A HANDFUL OF BLUE MAGIC

Jillian

Seven.

Had there ever been a time of carefree ordinariness in Jillian's childhood, she certainly could not remember it. A time and place that served as the prelude to all adult life's issues waiting just over the horizon but as yet undiscovered. Jillian couldn't picture a time like that in her life having ever existed outside of her imagination, which was never actually encouraged to run freely during her youth anyway. Too much imagination led to originality then individuality, and there was no room for that in the strict traditional institution of elitism in which she was raised. Too much originality rotted the brain and distracted one from the task at hand, from the goal of the larger whole, and that could never be tolerated, could it? Similar to pledging allegiance to a proudly billowing flag, there was a certain amount of indoctrination that could be expected from such an upbringing, its own form of nationalism within a minority group of minorities.

Hers was a clan of backstabbers and gossipmongers, lies and deceit. A place where incest was only taboo if you were caught at it and blood wasn't always thicker than water. The Dessommes couldn't be touched by clichés such as those. They were above them, ask anyone.

She recalled 1999 vaguely and only ever in conjunction with the memory of the funeral. It was the year of new-millennium parties filled with futuristic Tinman-referencing outfits and Britney Spears blaring from the stereos, the year of the frantic checking of computers around the world for the millennium bug. It was a year when gas cost around a dollar and a stamp could be bought for thirty-three cents, when it seemed like every child in America had a Game Boy, even if they didn't have food at home to eat and a year when Jillian Dessommes was seven years old.

Grandpa Tilman died the summer of that year, surrounded by the sound of cicadas and June bugs as he sipped vodka-laced lemonade on the wraparound porch of his summer house down in Savannah. In adulthood, she came to assume that the culture of Porterhouse steaks and brandy is what had finally did him in. Of course, the coroner's report had found it to be a textbook heart attack, but Jillian came to realize that it was excess that'd really killed him. Excess of liquor, excess of cigarettes, excess of time on his hands and loose young women looking for a meal ticket since her daddy, Carlton, had taken over the family business. Grandpa Tilman had achieved his three score and ten years, plus a few months, before he was taken to whatever hell or heaven that lay in wait for him. He died on a balmy night, not far from the beach, with the sound of waves lapping the shore whispering behind him. There was a Benson and Hedges still smoldering in the ashtray beside him when he was found by a neighbor from down the way who, strolling past his house that night, waved to him as he passed and got no wave back. Or so the story goes.

His wake then funeral were ornate affairs attended by every member of the Gold Coast who truly mattered—as expected, nothing less for the patriarch of the Dessommes family, the former CEO of the infamous Dessommes Group, which was busy buying up land all over the South and spreading its reputation "like disease on the Nile." In attendance were a smattering of law professors and judges, media tycoons and their jeweled wives, old debutantes three decades removed who still craved a good reason to bedeck themselves like peacocks and primp around a room like fools.

They, the first family of The Group and, as she was too young to realize at the time, increasingly of the Gold Coast as well, rode in the limousine behind the hearse. Jill's daddy was clean shaven of his usual low-cut beard. He was serious, solemn on that day, and who could blame him? His father had just passed quietly during the night hundreds of miles from home and before either of his children could say goodbye.

Jill's mama played her role brilliantly as she always did, clad in her timeless black Chanel dress and three strands of pearls. Her hair was pulled back from her face in a high bun—that was before she cut it short, you see. She ushered Vince and Jill into the limousine before her and hissed at them to behave when Vince pinched Jill and she, yelping in pain, shoved him.

"Get your heads on straight and act like I've raised you with some damned sense, you two! Don't you know what today is? Now sit down and shut your mouths before I give you something to really holler about."

And sit they did as she scooted in behind them, locking them between her and Daddy who put his arm around Vince's shoulders and pulled him close so that their foreheads touched. Told him to remember that day, that they were putting a great man in the ground, so pay attention.

"You'll remember today for the rest of your life, boy, 'cause now it's just you and me. We're carrying this thing for the next two generations. You got that?"

Whether he got it or not, Vince nodded eagerly. Daddy nodded his approval and released him from the embrace. Jill smoothed her black satin dress, clicked her shiny Mary Janes and waited for her mama to say something to her about marching into the future and their lineage. Addison never did. Instead she scolded her for her fallen curls and turned to stare out the limousine window as the car pulled away from the curb.

They sat in the front row at the funeral in a church where the rows and rows of pews seemed endless and the cathedral ceiling was three stories high. A respectable church where respectable praise took place on Sundays. No, none of that catching of holy ghosts and emotional spirits—nothing so dramatic and violent took place at their church on the few occasions per year that they attended. The grieving was muted, Jill remembered. In fact, she didn't remember seeing many tears at all, not even from Grandma Florence, Tilman's wife of nearly fifty years.

Florence was a true Dessommes woman, married in when she was still young and taut and full of potential for breeding more Dessommes back in '51. She was a tall woman of café-au-lait complexion, a curvy Lena Horne replica back in her day, famous for her elegant sense of style always complemented by a hat or scarf: pillbox hats with demure veils and sun hats with large satin ribbons. Even then, listening to the pastor speak on her husband, she wore one, black as a crow with a large brim that obscured her eyes from nosy rumormongers—those just close enough on the periphery of their family ties to have warranted an invitation to the funeral—who tried to feign that they weren't just that. Her hair was now all white. Jill loved her hair when she was that age. Like waves of snow falling down her grandmother's shoulders.

She'd married in bringing nothing but her winning smile and cunning wits, her beauty and her charisma, an exception to their rules even back in her day. And that was enough, even then fifty years later. She was her husband's right hand, as The Dessommes Group grew from a few scattered real estate transactions for undeveloped land in Atlanta to the hotel empire it was becoming when Jill was in elementary school back in '99. Jill's daddy held Grandma Florence's hand, but she didn't need the comfort. She never even shed a tear.

I I

"Well, they say he went out peacefully. That's all we can ask for him."

"Oh, puhlease. That man probably went out the same way he came in: right between some woman's legs."

That was Aunt Renée, Jill's daddy's younger sister, peeling off her wide-brimmed black hat, similar to her mother's but lacking the luxurious aura of the matriarch's collection. She plopped down in the high-back chair in the kitchen with a sigh, her eyes moving around to take in the five dozen or so friends and mourners, all dressed in various hues of opaqueness, who'd come back to the massive Colonial family home the senior Dessommes had raised their children in. The considerable amount of acreage around the house still existed, of course, though Jill's generation never played in those wide-open spaces. There was the old barn, painted a charming grey and converted into a lofty guest house, behind which Renée and several of her cousins had lost their virginity. There was the pond behind the home, the ducks who lived in it. For, it was the shapes, colors and sounds there that Jill noticed growing up, never knowing the behind-the-barn histories and handed-down wives' tales she was sure to learn later.

There was a layout of finger food in the formal dining hall and people milling around, talking in small huddles and groups from the front porch to the den to the back stoop off the kitchen, and a low hum filling the house. A hum that sounded serious to Jillian. Sounded grown up. Peppered by the occasional twinge of laughter here, a hand rested sympathetically on an arm or the murmur of condolences there, as her grandma and daddy took their places at the front hall greeting the last of the guests. Jillian darted around, playing with Sabrina and Matthew, Aunt Renée's children from her first and second husbands who looked nothing alike but loved each other dearly.

There was Sabrina, mild mannered and sweet. Brown like a paper bag with a round face and pouty mouth. Black buckled shoes and a black silk and lace dress that tied behind her back in a large bow and brushed around her knees as she tagged Jillian and giggled, running out of the den and into the kitchen. Her curls bounced and still gleamed from the hot comb and Blue Magic hair grease she'd endured before the funeral. Grandma Florence had insisted on doing Sabrina's hair herself, sitting her down in one of the dining room chairs dragged over to the stove. The hot comb smoked and crackled over the blue flame of the burner; she reached for it with one hand there in that kitchen with her mourning clothes already on.

"Hold your ear down," Grandma Florence instructed her, blowing the comb to cool it before pulling it through Sabrina's "kitchen," pressing those unruly coils of hair at the nape of her neck. When the searing metal comb raked lightly against Sabrina's skin she winced and squealed, the hair grease on her scalp popping and sizzling as it heated at the touch.

"Hush now. And stop that wiggling." Then over her shoulder, "Jillian, you go find your mama and have her to do something with your hair. This comb here'll burn those fine hairs right off o' your head."

Then there was Matthew, closer to Vince's age, dapper in his creased miniature tux and crisp white bow tie, too serious even then to be bothered by the likes of immature banalities such as a childhood game of tag. He reminded Jill of butter, which always made her titter to herself when she saw him. Whipped butter like the kind her mama left out in the antique coronet for fancy dinners: smooth and light and bland. He sat on the sofa, back straight as a board and feet hovering off the floor, as he read a copy of *As I Lay Dying* and ignored the nattering conversation from the adults around him just as he ignored the girls running around in their black finery.

It was during this game of tag that the girls ran into the kitchen just as eleven-year-old Vince was walking out. Her mama was fixing herself a cup of Earl Grey and Aunt Renée was peeling away her hat and tossing it onto the marble table. Addison pressed her hips forward against the counter as the girls flew by. She rolled her eyes, smiling just a tad despite herself, stirring her tea and skim milk and settling herself at the table.

"Stop that running girls. Before you break something," Renée called over her shoulder when they continued their game, Jillian reaching Sabrina, eyes gleaming as she tagged her with a shout, "You're it!" and scampered off.

"...between some woman's legs." Her aunt ruffled her bobbed cut and leaned her head back over the seat, stretching her arms luxuriously above her head, stretching her legs under the table down to the toes like an old cat. "You know how he was. Always behind Mama's back."

"I know nothing of the slightest," Jill's mama grinned conspiratorially back at her over the rim of her tea cup. "The man was never anything but sweet to me."

"Sweet *on* you more like. Shoulda seen how proud he was when Carl brought you home, Addie. Man's chest was all puffed out like he'd be bedding you himself!" Renée clapped her hand over Addison's and she snickered along with her, shaking her head as if she hadn't known, hadn't suspected he'd felt that way all along.

"Got you! Tag, you're it!"

"Renée, how many times have I told you to take that mind and that mouth out o' the gutter? In front o' the children at least, Heaven forbid all the time. We've got to be the ones to show them how to walk upright, for who else you think will show them such posture?"

Grandma Florence stood in the doorway, giving her daughter and daughter-in-law her disapproving glare. Addison's cheeks colored a shade of red, her face growing warm in a way that had nothing to do with the Earl Grey. She'd appeared as silently as a wraith and now moved into the kitchen, her own hat still firmly on her head, to make herself some coffee, tussling Jill's mane of soft curls as she went.

"Oh, Mama Florence, let me get that for you." Addison stood and moved her way only to be halted by a single raised hand.

"Don't you even bother, girl. You weren't nearly so concerned about my thirst just a moment ago. If you want to make yourself useful, when you're finished here, you can go find that husband o' yours, and tell him come see me when he's done putting on his show for those folks in the corner there. Didn't know Tilman from a can o' paint and over there boo-hooing on his shoulder like they were old chums."

"Mama," Renée sighed with a pout, like a scolded toddler. "You know we didn't mean nothing by it."

"Honey, I know what you meant by it. But you keep your daddy's name good and polished, you hear. And for God's sake don't be airing out dirty laundry in front o' company." There was no question there, only a hard glare that could melt ice masked with practiced politesse. "Both o' you. One day you'll find your name is all you've really got in this world."

Florence poured herself a serving of black coffee out of the pot, one sugar, no cream. And she hardly tossed a glance their way as she left, saying, "And if you think that man ever managed anything behind my back, you're as silly as he was."

She shooed them back to their silly cackling, but neither even cracked a smile, sitting there at the table with warm, red cheeks.

THE SADDEST BUNCH
OF NEGROS

Delaney

There was a wall of books from Delaney's college years on sociology, modern politics and contemporary literature growing layers of dust in her study. Most of them had notes hastily scribbled in the margins on Marcus Garvey or *Roe v. Wade* and the mountain of other dogmatic ideologies and social reform practices that were contained within those pages. There were sticky notes stuck in between chapters and peeping out, quotes scrawled in the end pages in various hues of ink—Toni Morrison this, Doctorow that—from a range of years, all firmly in her past. Before this, of course, there was that phase of Poe before she moved on to the likes of Chopin and Rossetti. She was fascinated with the Gothic because it was like some alternate universe to the world in which she lived and had grown up in: a world of conventional middle-classness. There had been a time when such notions filled Laney's head and consumed her free time with reading. Occasionally, she'd flip through those books now, reading the comments she'd left behind all that while back, the thoughts she'd had in that faraway time before life shifted.

Occasionally.

But now her best friend Aaliyah was admiring them, Cabernet in hand, glancing over her collection and pulling out various books to inspect. She moved slowly, fingers grazing the spines of some, reading the titles. Her locks were pulled back into a chignon, soft and lovely with strands of gold to highlight her smooth ebony skin. She and Delaney were about the same size and height, a fact which proved most helpful when Aaliyah needed to borrow evening attire from her for one of the many events—only a few of which she accepted—Delaney invited her to. Aaliyah was a little taller. Delaney wore her hair long and pressed and was a size six to Aaliyah's size four, which never proved especially troubling when it came to most dresses.

Laney and Liyah.

Yin and yang.

Or something like that.

Laney lounged on the divan in the center of the room watching her, hair up in a ponytail and her polished feet bare. They'd been chatting for hours, since Aaliyah had come over to break bread with her over their usual Thursday night Italian takeout, wine and banter. Aaliyah removed her blazer at the door and her stockings somewhere around the end of bottle number one, going on about the newest marketing account she was hoping to snag at the firm she'd been slaving at since she finished grad school. Then Liyah asked her how things were going with the Dessommes Group transition from father to son.

"Well, they're preoccupied with some acquisition at this point. You know how it goes. They find land in some up-and-coming area or another, do the bidding war thing. Vince and Carl usually win, of course. Or Nate'll stumble upon some chump who's in over his head—or ripe for divorce—and they'll lowball him out of his property, pack him up and move 'em out, then take over. Wash, rinse, repeat. Once that's over, they'll get back to the business of transitioning, I guess."

"Please, honey. None of us ever doubted ethics weren't their forté. Vince's time will come soon enough."

Aaliyah purred and rolled over her consonants, those Trinidadian roots always on display whenever she opened her mouth, though she'd learned to Americanize herself when in the presence of those of the paler nation. But when she was with Laney, it was at times—often when she was especially riled—like listening to another language entirely, a point that never failed to bring a smile to Laney's face.

Laney poured herself a refill. "Pfft, well, Liyah, they say behind every great mogul there's usually a crime or two."

"Oh, do they? I recall some other variation of that phrase."

"Liyah, I swear to God, you're such an asshole sometimes."

They shared in the laugh, Aaliyah leaning against the ultra-modern desk with her feet comfortably out in front of her. They both knew that was meant to slide off like water, Laney's stab at humor that only failed if they both took it too seriously. "That's just who they are. Just dumb luck followed up with greed."

"Oh, and is that gonna be your new career, too? Living off their dumb luck and greed? Closed in behind your gates and fences and security systems away from the real people you were *supposed* to be helping?"

"Nope, I've already got a career. I'm a professional bullshitter, just like the rest of them."

Aaliyah scoffed. "Saddest bunch of negros I've ever seen. All they care about is making it—and making it where? As far away from their roots as they can manage."

"Liyah, don't mistake these gates for lost roots. That'd be your first mistake."

"Is that what we work for now? To move up and away? To separate ourselves from each other? To lock everyone else out and pin yourself in so no one can get to you or your garaged cars or your fancy things behind those doors?"

"Nowadays, I think that's called the American Dream."

"Oh, is that the dream, you sitting around turning into some ole' Addison Dessommes clone?"

That one warranted a stern glare her way. "Liyah, I am *nothing* like Addison Dessommes."

"Is that what you think? Funny thing about mirrors, they don't lie, you know."

Laney felt that warm tingle on her face, that old familiar feeling her inebriating loves always brought her when she needed them most, when she needed to unwind, to be herself, to forget. She was on her fourth glass—or maybe her fifth—while Aaliyah nursed her second.

"Neither do I. And I'm not even in the mood to hobble down this road with you again, I swear. Meanwhile, I don't see you pointing that accusatory finger at yourself or standing in front of any of these magic mirrors you just *love* to reference. You're working at the same sort of place you despise Vince for running. Grossly capitalist. Profit grubbing. Et cetera, et cetera."

"All I'm saying is I see you, Laney. Better than anyone else, I see you. I know you. This here," she gestured around at their surroundings, at the home they sat in in the North Atlanta suburbs and the four-hundred-dollar bottle of wine they were drinking. At the three-foot vases that lined the marble hall and the floor-to-ceiling windows overlooking the guest house. "You're caged in it. The glitter don't make it any less of a cage and ya'know that. Laney Coker knows that, n'matter what Delaney Dessommes doesn't. Just don't sell yourself short, Laney. That's all I'm sayin'. Selling out, forgetting who you are—won't get you anywhere good."

With that ringing in the air between them, Aaliyah watched her friend over the rim of her glass. Laney knew there were questions swirling in her mind, things Aaliyah wanted to say. Yet, she kept them to herself in that way friends do when they sense they may be pushing too hard. Or that the cause is already lost. Laney met her gaze but offered no invitation for her thoughts. Aaliyah offered no objection.

They'd been friends since freshman year of undergrad at Spelman College. Both women understood this was neither the first nor the last of these little exchanges they'd have on the matter and both accepted that fact silently. Even in the beginning, before Laney met Vince and was then forever altered by the death of her parents, they were opposites in every way, and she loved Aaliyah for that. Revered her for that. Aaliyah's roots were obvious, deeply planted in the Caribbean soil and culture, and she'd come a long way from her past in pursuit of some different horizon. She and Vince had long ago perfected their dance around each other, coldly polite yet intolerant of each other's ideologies and broughtupcy.

In the earlier days, when doctrinal ideology and the dark side of history took up her thoughts more than what to wear to the next dinner party or corporate fundraiser, Laney had danced around the idea that maybe it was even Aaliyah's skin that bothered Vince most, equally if not more so than her social ideology and political stance (firmly Democrat, and a liberal one at that). But, of course, he would never ever admit that, not even to her. Aaliyah was easily shades darker than the Dessommes blood would allow for, and Laney knew she'd be kidding herself to believe that the same mentality of three hundred years ago didn't still apply in that ole South. They were still mentally divided into those in the field and those in the house, and Laney could never shake the idea that her locks and accent reminded Vince of how far he was from embracing his own history, how far he had come in assimilating into the mainstream. Aaliyah reminded him every time he saw her, and without ever saying a word, that she wasn't going out of her way to do so. Laney still remembered when she and Aaliyah had joked about it years earlier, tongues loose from the half-empty bottle of rum between them in the dorms. They had remained the best of friends ever since, even after the enjoyment Laney got from infuriating Vince with their friendship had passed, and for that they were both glad.

Laney was happy with him, or some muddied and muddled version of happy, anyways. Happy in the sense of the word that Laney had come to understand with the Dessommes' over the years. Happiness came in different shades within that group than what 'normal folk' aspired to. It held a different meaning. Alluded them for different reasons, and now Laney was just the same.

Aaliyah let the subject drop just as she heard Vince coming in and setting his briefcase down in the foyer as he always did. They both looked up at the clock. Just after ten. They exchanged a glance before Aaliyah gathered her things and shoved her stockings in her purse. She would never take her friend up on an offer to stay over for the night even if Laney asked, so she didn't. Aaliyah didn't like being there when Vince was home, and Laney knew he didn't like it either.

I I

Laney hugged Aaliyah goodbye downstairs then shifted her gaze to Vince as he closed the door behind her, his slate suit and silk twill tie still neat even after a day in the office. He wore his beard low as his father did, when he had one. But even that didn't hide his round face, a smile that had much practice lighting up a room and dark eyes surrounded by long lashes that gave him a pensive look at some times and a playful look at others.

She didn't ask him about his day and he didn't ask her about hers either. They were long past the tedium of such conversations. Questions like that only seemed to enhance the monotony they'd already begun to grow accustomed to, though they were not yet thirty years old and had only been married for the better part of a year. Those other seven years before them had certainly done a number on the couple. But they were already on the green mile by that point, and they knew that. Inching toward the inevitable with every appearance they made together, with every year that passed.

The marriage proposal itself had been a queer mix of anticipated and unexpected, at the semi-annual, ultra-formal gala thrown by Vince's aunt Renée two years before. Cocktails were flowing and, by the time he knelt before her on one knee, in front of everyone who was anyone in their circles, she was already snuggly in the bottle and feeling that warm glow she needed to perform for the people—to smile and dance and chatter mindlessly with the other ladies of the Clan.

Those countless drinks had nearly allowed her to forget the epic argument they'd had the night before, an argument spurred by his comment—

Fuck, Laney, it's my money keeping this lifestyle going without a hitch. That shit in your closet—all this—

—What the hell are you getting at, Vi—

—so won't you show some damn appreciation—

She, feeling bought and paid for by his tactless words, had railed against the feeling—and his accusation—which he insisted was not an accusation at all.

We must not look at goblin men

We must not buy their fruits

Christina Rossetti had warned her of such temptations in some faraway book from college now somewhere on her shelves. She remembered the line then shoved that thought from her mind, turning back to him in time to hear him say, of course, he wanted to take care of her. That was his job, his duty, his role, was it not? He'd chosen her with that understanding, but wasn't there an understanding on her end as well?

The fight had ended with her in tears—typical, she'd thought—and Vince leaving to go to his own place, presumably to lick his wounds as well. She'd vowed that night to be done with it all, to stiffen her back against the backlash she knew would come and leave the infamous Vincent Dessommes and his family behind. She'd stand on her own two feet and follow the path she'd been on before she was derailed by the unexpected turns of life, diverted by the swank, by the promise of heightened influence and the allure of the route that so few others had followed before her.

So, one could imagine her surprise when, in the middle of chatting with Renée and some distant cousin of theirs she'd only met once before, Vince snaked his way through the parting throng and knelt before her with a little box from Tiffany's that held a diamond deserving of its own safety deposit box replete with security guards and alarm codes. She'd stood there in the middle of the growing crowd, grappling with her words and stumbling over what she was trying to say.

An hour.

Had he just waited an hour, she would have been okay. By then she would have already told him she was done. She would have spared herself this shameless act of decadence that made her face color for reasons other than the alcohol, and she would have spared him the embarrassment he would face when she told him no in front of all those people.

But she didn't tell him no.

How could she?

How could she embarrass herself like that, never mind him? She decided, in the few seconds she had to think before she was forced to answer, that she would tell him yes now, then find a way to back out later, a way that would allow them both to save face and go their separate ways respectably. Didn't he remember their fight the night before? Didn't he feel the same way she did: that the jig was up and it was time to face the music; that they'd built a life inside of a house of cards? The smile across his face was so organic, she'd thought to herself, just before saying yes. Too bad there was no way in hell she was going through with the wedding, and he just didn't know it yet.

Only, she did go through with the wedding, eight months of enduring Addison Dessommes later. She'd taken over the wedding as though it were her due and, in retrospect, as mother of the groom, it probably was. She'd swooped in like a vulture on a carcass and started giving orders, booking venues and handing over her credit card for purchases that made Laney's head spin. By the time Addie was done scolding and fluffing and flitting around Laney, she was too exhausted to protest, and what would she do—who would she be—if she did protest anyways? Who was she anymore, was the question that crept up on her at night, eventually lodging into her psyche and staying there, a bothersome companion? She couldn't tell if she was idealizing the idea of some independent future—social work perhaps, or maybe teaching. She wouldn't have minded a PhD and a collegiate role that would really challenge her—or if she'd been idealizing the Dessommes way.

So, the planning carried on and the wedding happened without a hitch and without anyone being any the wiser that Laney had increasingly felt herself becoming, from proposal to wedding, a terrified and dismayed, caged little bird who could feel her wings being clipped with every dress fitting, with every toast raised in the soon-to-be newest Dessommes' honor and with the utterance of those two little words: I do. She soon pushed the proposal to the back of her mind completely, because with every thought she lent to it, the remembrance that she could have avoided it and all of the subsequent experiences after it if she'd only broken it off with Vince when she'd kicked him out of her apartment, if she'd only not shown up at the party at all, haunted her.

Then came the long honeymoon and the five-bedroom, three-car-garage home out in the 'burbs that was waiting for them when they returned. It all happened so fast, and swept her up so completely, that it wasn't until she finally had a moment to look around, to take stock, that she realized how much it had changed her. How much *they* had changed her.

Vincent Dessommes and Delaney Coker had spent two years together at Emory, the same school his near-reclusive sister attended now, after meeting on the Spelhouse campus that had spawned so many Clan marriages before theirs. At graduate school, Laney studied social work, with a focus on counseling and her own personal interest in race relations, with a passion and fervency that surprised her. Vince, of course, got his MBA, as they always knew he would. He was always destined for letters behind his name from some fancy institution.

Vince was amused by Laney's choice of study at first but never—well, hardly ever—tried to persuade her against it. Instead, he assumed that social work was an obvious choice for her, considering all the charity work she'd be doing once she took on the Dessommes name. They were, after all, destined to wed. Everyone knew it, including them. After the dinner, there was no turning back. Back then, it was an unspoken rule that she still had yet to grasp, that she wasn't expected to work once they were married. It was never a concrete conversation between them until after graduation, after the theses had been written and stages had been crossed. Neither of them had thought to have the conversation for very opposing reasons: she'd assumed she would work; he'd assumed she wouldn't.

Now, Laney kissed him on the mouth and he followed her into the sprawling living room, all his mother's choice of vaulted ceilings and furnishings. At the sight of Aaliyah, Vince was immediately annoyed. Not because of her presence in their home— that, he'd grown only too used to over the years—but because Laney had chosen to continue her Thursday evening tradition with the undeserving Aaliyah Walker rather than tend to her duties as a member of The Dessommes Group's First Family.

She, of course, thought the term needlessly patriotic and grandiose and scoffed, at least inwardly, every time she heard it used. By the time she'd claimed a seat next to Vince on the couch and steadied her ears to hear his newest complaint, he'd already launched into a mildly impassioned tirade on how Carmella Greenwood had become more of a fixture at The Group than Laney herself, a disgrace if not embarrassment to the entire family.

"And with the transition so close, Laney? We've got to have our heads on straight."

"Vince, I'm not a Suzy Homemaker, and those events nearly bore me to tears. You know that."

"That's not the point. We're constructing something here. *You* know *that*. This isn't just a corporation. It's a culture. And cultures need leadership."

"Oh, is that what they need?"

"Anyways, Cammy is always there, so she'll be there with you. It's ridiculous she spends more time planning and curating for The Group than you do, Laney." Vince took her small foot in his hand as a gesture of olive branch extension and massaged it in tiny circles. "You like her, don't you? You'd tell me if that was the matter?"

"It's nothing, Vince. Why does it always have to be something?" Laney took her foot back into her own possession and tucked it underneath her on the couch. "Jeez, Master Waller, sometimes I'd just like to get off the plantation, if you don't mind."

A glare his way.

A glare tossed back her way at the *Roots* reference.

Vince shook his head and stood. Laney, uncomfortable with him staring down at her and her back up at him, stood, too.

Some only ever whisper sweet nothings; but Laney and Vince had learned to speak silently through their veiled glares and ten-foot gaps. Both tried to fight against it—against the ravages of time on their relationship and on each other—as most people do. Still, it was their own little language that they understood and could now read fluently in their friends and family around them. A glare hidden by an amiable smile, whispers hidden by a hand.

Laney said nothing. There was a cautious glint in Vince's eyes for such a fleeting moment that she might have imagined it. It came too easily, she realized, arms crossed over her chest as they both refused to back down. Aaliyah had opened the gates with a single idea: sellout.

And now, up against his expectations, which she had neither chosen for herself nor had much of a say in, she couldn't go back. She couldn't back down. Those tensions had been building up long enough to numb that little voice in her head that used to tell her when she was making a fool of herself or when a fight was in futility. Or maybe that was the alcohol. He was suffocating her in that way of his, in that way of his family's, making demands and assumptions in that tone that communicated their overt belief orders would be followed with no further back talk.

Aaliyah had struck a nerve. Plucked on it like a harp to create just the right note replaying itself over and over in Laney's mind.

Sellout.

She told him so, to which he snorted derisively and replied, "And what does she know? Laney, we've had this dialog before. You knew what you were getting when you got me."

Delaney looked him square in the eyes for a matter of seconds that slowly seeped by. There was nothing standing between them— nothing tangible anyway—but she could already feel it in the air, the amiable words and foot rubs shifting into something else entirely. He chewed his bottom lip in that pensive way she used to adore—often still did. In that way that made him look soft and thoughtful, like the Vince she'd met all those years back in the quad. She softened her gaze at that thought and pulled him down to the couch beside her. Laid her hand on his. Squeezed it. Told him that she didn't want to fight. And she didn't. He said he didn't want to either.

"I don't want you to think I'm trying to dominate you or oppress you or whatever other word you pull out of your ass from your Jane Eyre days, but you know how this goes."

There it was again, that sly reference to her duties to the family, to him, to the name, like a contractual obligation that didn't really need to be written out because the rules were already agreed upon and understood. Laney told Vince she wasn't talking to his family, she was talking to him, and that pushing his family's wishes on her was unwelcome. She may have even used the word 'please.' Inside, something in her withered a little more. Those long seconds of silence between them ended too quickly. He stood and so did she, moving into his space. But he never backed down from his stance. He never even retreated an inch, and she shouldn't have expected that he would. But the thing is, she hadn't bargained on this and she hadn't married to sit around twiddling her thumbs and dressing up pretty for parties.

There was a larger world out there, wasn't there? She remembered it, she was sure. A world that she'd once navigated with poise and anticipation, with optimism and buoyancy. But, it was out there, and she was in here.

It was out there, and she was in here.

THIS WOMAN'S WORK

Nigel

Nigel woke up to find a woman in his bed whose name he couldn't remember.

This, he found, had been the case increasingly often, startlingly often. At twenty-nine, the idea of indefinite bachelorhood was more alarming than exciting, and while he understood that he was still a young man, he'd never imagined being one indefinitely unattached, constantly searching and not finding. Now was the time in their lives, he and his counterparts, when homes were being purchased, careers were taking off, and weddings were popping up around him so frequently that he wondered how there were still single people left in his circles. Ten years prior, or even five, the conversations had always veered toward hopes, dreams and the occasional slipped condom. It was a time when everything glinted around them, bright and shiny and ready for the taking. All of those clichés applied and nestled them comfortably throughout their journey to true adulthood. Nearing thirty, the world still held its glimmer, though he'd lived quite long enough to have seen it dimmed on a few occasions, nearly extinguished at others. But serial dating had never held much appeal for him.

He shook his head at himself and looked back over at her. She slept with her back to him, and her brown skin and pixie cut did nothing to remind him of who she was. He rolled out of bed, stepped over the condom wrapper that explained it all and closed the door behind him in the bathroom. Nigel stared at himself in the mirror but saw no sign as to what had been going on with him, what had him hopping from bed to bed, woman to woman. And there was no clue there as to what could calm the nervous energy that was the root of it all.

He splashed cold water on his face to wake himself up, then filled his tumbler and swallowed that down too. He really had no idea why he'd let himself end up there like that again, waking up on a Friday morning faced with the task of removing yet another woman from his bed before he could even get ready for work. This was beyond casual dating. Somewhere along the line, he'd stumbled into the realm of coitus for sport, a domain he'd never been comfortable in and never quite understood either. There was no joy in the union if there was no chemistry. At least, that's what the old Nigel had thought before he'd crossed that line.

He didn't know why he'd even gone through the motions of dating when he knew none of those fish in the endless streams of women were the one for him. He just kept throwing them back to the current and moving on. Nigel couldn't imagine any of them holding a decent conversation, let alone rearing his one-day children, so what was the point, he wondered to himself, standing there in his bathroom? Just boredom and wishful thinking, because they were all the same: over-eager and under-intelligent. Or perhaps, at some point in time he could no longer put his finger on, his tastes had matured; his predilections had shifted without him even noticing, without a single introspective conversation with himself, without a single traumatic love event to set him off.

Well, except for that one...

Nigel went downstairs for a full glass of water and passed by that letter again. It was in a plain white envelope, addressed to him with a return address that simply read *NY, NY.* He glanced at it but left it where it was. Grabbed a glass from the cabinet. Filled it with water from the refrigerator door. Leaned against the counter and tried to pull his thoughts together. No one else had handwriting like that; those loops were unmistakable. He'd known the minute he pulled it from the mail box who'd sent it. But that'd been over four weeks ago, and he still hadn't opened it. Didn't want to open it, if he was being honest with himself. All she brought with her were bad memories and longing, but even he didn't know what the hell he was longing for. What, for the good 'ole days all those years ago or for the days before he'd even met her?

Either way, he wasn't going back down that road again. Not a chance. And, of course, she'd sent a hand-written letter, not an email or a Facebook ping. (He wondered if she'd resisted looking him up all these years as he had resisted searching for her.) No, she had to go back to the days of the past when letters meant something so unaffected, so pure and authentic, to them.

Nigel didn't remember when it had started, but he knew it had gotten to the point where he felt a little tug in his chest every time he got one in the mail from her. He knew she felt the same. So, letters became their favorite way of communication. Sure, she'd call. Yeah, he'd text. But those letters did it for them. They set her apart from all the others. He felt that, standing there in his kitchen. He admitted it, and he hated that she could still have that effect on him at all.

He downed the water. Looked away from the letter and then back at it.

But seeing that envelope with her handwriting on it then, he couldn't stand the damn sight of it. Why had she done it, brought back all that long history with a flick of her damn wrist like she knew it was just that easy? He wouldn't let her pull him back in. Not like that. Not so easy as if she'd always had him by a chain.

Nigel threw a stack of junk mail on top of it, but couldn't bring himself to toss it out. He went upstairs to get rid of the stranger and tried not to think about Paige or her letter. It, like she, could only bring bad things. Bad fucking things.

THAT GREEN-EYED DEVIL

Aaliyah

Scene.

There is a gold envelope on her desk when she comes into her office. The   envelope itself isn't a surprise to her—Laney has had it delivered and told her the night before to look out for it—but the fact that there is a second gold envelope beneath it is. Aaliyah reads the sticky note with the hastily scrawled message from Laney. It's a plus one. Might she find a date to bring along? Wouldn't that be nice? Smiley face. Aaliyah rolls her eyes and tosses the sticky into the trash. It flutters down to the wastepaper basket.

Her office is situated on the thirty-third floor of one of the many glass towers that Atlanta's corporate canton boasts. From her window, she has a view southward toward the Old Downtown district, which means that she mostly has a view of historical if not dilapidated buildings and poverty that at one time had been the essence of black culture, back when Martin was busy marching and sit-ins were the protest of the day. At a good angle, though, she can see the workings of gentrification taking over, shops sprouting up, Yuppieville in the making from the ashes and destruction of what used to be.

After endless years of schooling and over two dozen years of working twice as hard to get half as far as her mama used to say, Aaliyah is safely seated somewhere near the top of the middle of the hierarchy. Not quite to the corner office overlooking the lovely view of Centennial Olympic Park or the sprawling expanse of cement and glass that is the financial district of the South's most bustling city. And, not quite to the level of competing for—or, even better, graciously being handed due to seniority and the payoff of many hours, years, of playing the right cards and schmoozing the right people—the most coveted accounts that reap tens of millions in revenue for the company. No, she is still doing marketing campaigns for middle-brow authors and the occasional up-and-coming software company, but she knows that one day she'll step into the world of Fortune 500 clientele and compensation. She, ambitious through and through, has always longed for the power that a nameplate on a swanky desk yields. See the swanky nameplate? At least she's got the swanky nameplate.

This self-assured composure that is her hallmark arises not from some puerile, if not improbable, American Dream fantasy—no, was sufficiently slaughtered and disposed of at pyre before she even stepped foot on a college campus—but from the knowledge that she, here and now, is right where she is supposed to be, if not yet where she'd like to be, because she has laid the groundwork—the hard part—and can now allow that foundation to help her build her way to the top. Armed with that notion at mind and heart, she lays in wait, biding her time and putting in the hours to be noticed. Armed with that notion, she knows that her due is just on the horizon, not cheapened by nepotism or some benevolent helping hand, but because she, herself, has earned it. Earning it is where she feels most comfortable because that will never fade or go out of style. Earning her due will never leave her indebted. Earning it is how she's learned to survive and thrive. That's what she tells herself every day, anyway.

Aaliyah walks past the nameplate without a second glance. She removes her blazer and takes a seat at her desk, head bent over demographical statistics and commercial B roll.

[End scene]

I I

Scene.

It is after six. Aaliyah's heels click down the empty marble hallway on the way to Micah's office. She lifts her hand to knock on his ajar office door but hears:

MICAH: Come in.

The symbiosis of attaching herself to others who'd already mastered the game of thriving in hostile waters had always been her hope coming in the door, but she was surprised to have so wholly found her match when she found it in Micah Barker. This, their usual ritual founded in camaraderie, mutual respect and the knowledge that there is strength in numbers, has become a staple of her work week, these tête-à-têtes with her jested work husband. After six, she isn't his colleague and de facto underling. After six, there is a certain letting down of hair that is expected and encouraged between them that she too often longs for in the middle of a particularly long or grueling day.

MICAH: I could hear you clicking on the floor from all the way down the hall. *(He looks up from what he is doing and stands to offer her a hug.)*

AALIYAH: *(with a smirk)* Oh, is that so?

MICAH: Not to mention, I don't know anyone who works longer hours than you. If heels are clicking after hours, it's probably you.

At the time of her arrival at Myers & Peterson, Micah had already been there for nearly two years. They bonded, slowly but surely, over being two of only four African Americans on the entire floor—though one of them was a secretary, so she hardly counted in their conversations. Secretly, Aaliyah admires his drive and work ethic but will never tell him, lest he think she condones his after-work proclivities. Still, he's succeeded in the firm much faster than she has, measuring year for year. He was already "one to look out for," as was often said in office meetings and quarterly reviews, when she arrived. No wonder he is now sitting pretty in his grand almost-corner office like the cat who's got the crème. Not too shabby for a native of South Side Chicago, though the Syracuse education doesn't hurt, she's sure, or the fact that the man still smells of spicy Creed even this late in the day.

AALIYAH: Where've you been? I haven't seen you all week.

MICAH: *(Hands her a bottle of water from his mini frig, coiffed locks pulled back from his face.)* In Pittsburg with Peterson for a few days. I meant to text or call you but shit got crazy. The fuckers tried to reject our campaign after agreeing to the mock-ups beforehand. Can you believe that? *(Micah gestures for her to take a seat, standing behind his desk and looking out at the view from that thirty-third-floor wall of glass.)*

41

Unlike in Aaliyah's office, Centennial Olympic, Midtown and the CNN building are within his sightline at varying degrees from one another. We stand at Micah's shoulder watching the view until he turns back to her. During the winter months, when night falls even before the last office meeting of the evening is over, she particularly envies him that shimmering view that speaks volumes. In fact, even now in these early days of October, as the sun sets on Atlanta.

AALIYAH: That's the job: always expect the unexpected. When did he ask you anyway? He's never asked me to come along to his closing deals, and out-of-state at that.

Micah takes her comment as rhetorical and continues examining the view, hands clasped behind his back.

AALIYAH: I'm so annoyed with the Boys' Club round here. It's beyond annoyin'.

Micah turns to hear the last of her usual rant, only answering with a grunt as he's learned to do. Now is not the time to reason with her. Now is the time to stand as still as possible as the wasps swarm about and hope he doesn't get stung himself.

AALIYAH: I'll try not to appear jealous, ya'know, next time you're on the green with him or at some fancy luncheon. I just have to assume one day it'll be me. (*She smiles sardonically and sips her water.*)

She really is jealous, of course, and she knows that he knows it. But envy will get her nowhere fast and is best left jested upon and kicked under the rug once brought to light, a topic to be laughed about over drinks and banter but never harped upon. But Micah steers them out of those waters before they get too choppy with a parting mollification.

MICAH: Aw, that's just office politics, Liyah. Nothing personal, I'm sure. (*Flashing her that white grin and set of dimples that's been his leg up in life, his trusty card to play that always wins the hand.)*

AALIYAH: I *will* take it personally if I don't get one of those accounts I made pitches for, though. It's the freakin' Holy Grail of campaigns, Micah. I need this one. Jeez, I need it.

And Holy Grail it is, complete with Hawks All Stars and millions of dollars to throw about on getting this one right; she sees it as the chance to change the way people see athletics, and Aaliyah knows she is capable of that. More than that—she's ready for that.

MICAH: I know.

AALIYAH: I'm serious.

MICAH: I know. Just pace yourself. Playoffs are still a little way off, so there's still time to get it before we launch into it. You've already invested some crazy time and energy on this one. We all see it; everyone knows it. Just think positive, and keep doing what you've been doing, Liyah. I know you've stayed here a lot of late nights for this one, and Peterson can see it, too. How could he not? You practically live in this joint.

AALIYAH: Oh, you didn't know? I got a closet full of clothes in there and I take baths in the sink.

MICAH: I believe you on that one. By any means necessary, you know. There aren't any easy breaks out here no matter where you come from.

AALIYAH: So, that means you and that woman are still cutting a night on the regular then?

MICAH: (*Eying her as he takes another sip and closes the bottle*) You mean Milla? Yeah, we still get together every now and then.

AALIYAH: Get together implies you're dating, Micah. (*She laughs, keeping it jovial in her prodding.*) Get together implies you do more than just roll in the sheets. Don't lie to me.

He tries to hide that smirk, shaking his head as he fiddles with a folder on his desk, the pen in his hand.

AALIYAH: Sleeping with the boss's assistant. Using that joystick to climb the ladders, are we?

MICAH: (*Shrugging it off and changing the topic, pushing the attention from him onto her*) It's all in good fun, that's all. Anyways, big plans for the weekend?

She takes the cue from him and pulls back. Actually, that's what she's been wanting to talk to him about. How would he like to go to a party with her? It's being thrown by the Dessommes crowd—he's heard of them, right? Yup, them, those 'folks from the hotel empire'—and would he like to go with her? She still hasn't gotten comfortable enough to hob-knob over brandy and laughter as she's seen Laney do and knows Micah will, but she'll try her best, watching and learning from them, the best at it she's ever seen.

She already anticipates his response. An invitation to network with the Dessommes, with urban professionals who've already used their family connects to walk through the doors he is still trying to pry open? Micah knows that snagging the right connection could set him years ahead of his goals, and Aaliyah knows he knows that. Well, there's an invitation he can't refuse if ever he's seen one. So, it's a date.

Now, she just has to find something to wear that'll at least allow her to assimilate with Laney's lot. Aaliyah isn't used to dressing up and playing social, so the last thing she needs is to show up looking as out of place as she already knows she is.

[End scene]

DADDY'S LITTLE GIRL

JILLIAN

The room smelled of stale weed and Dos Equis, but it was the sun glaring through the bare windows that woke her. Jill groaned and rolled over, flicking the guy's hand from around her waist like it was a pesky fly. She shielded her eyes from the sun and grabbed her watch from her jeans on the floor. Twelve thirty. Well, she could kiss making it to class goodbye, as if she'd been planning to go.

Jill leaned over the guy, peering into his face to jog her memory of who he was. Closed eyes, long lashes, goatee, brown skin. Xander. She thought that was his name. The guy who usually sat behind her in her Thursday morning class who always came in with a lopsided smile and smelling like a good time. She called him on it that last time when he flopped down in the seat just as the professor started droning on. She craned her head back to look at him upside-down, her unruly tendrils grazing the top of his flip-down desk, and asked where he'd just rolled in from. He chuckled throatily and said he could show her if she wanted.

45

Twenty-four hours later she was rolling out of his bed and pulling her jeans back over black lace. She grabbed his pack of Marlboros from the dresser, tapped the pack against her hand a few times, which didn't even make him wince, and lit one up. Dragged in long and deep. His loft had once been part of a factory of some kind. It overlooked the old train tracks, graffiti and Atlanta's train line with floor-to-ceiling windows, smooth concrete floors and three-quarter height walls. A view of hipster life right there from his window.

She liked that.

Jill took another drag and stubbed it out, wrote her number on a scrap of paper by the bed and left.

II

Six.

There was a line that had been crossed so long before that Jillian no longer remembered when it had happened. A point when the rift between the two siblings became so wide and so clear that there was no longer any use in denying it, no longer any use in pretending, which said a lot. The Dessommes were pros at pretending, always had been; it was a part of their pedigree. It had started even before the days when Addison pleaded with her husband for a nanny, insisting that everyone had one —*"Hell, even Renée has one!"*— and continued, heightened after he denied her one the final time there on the stairs. Never mind that "everyone had one." They didn't. They were the leading branch of the family. They would raise their own.

Whether or not Addison realized her children could hear her shouts, Jill never knew. Likely, she simply didn't care, trailing behind her husband as he climbed to the second floor, beating at his back when he refused to turn her way.

"I had another baby because *you* wanted one! Now you—"

"What, demand that you raise them? Addie, you'd best go simmer down somewhere, woman. All this I give you, and you complain about *this*? *This* is your job first. Not The Group, not anything else. *This* is!"

The study door slammed shut, Addison standing there on the other side, raising her fist to beat on the door but never doing so. Jillian stared up at her from the first-floor landing, watching her mother's back rise and fall then rounded the corner out of sight before she could be spotted.

The void widened.

Then came the ballet shoes and baseball bats.

There was a painting that hung in the grand hall of the Dessommes family home. Sure, there were several paintings that hung there, really, but this one was special. This one always got to her. This one was the only one that she remembered, that made her wax nostalgic and reach for her Bensons.

Above the marble parquet floors and below the Victorian crown moldings was a painting that had been given to her mother by a portraitist friend from her days at Smith. She didn't think Addie still spoke to the woman, now that she thought of it. Probably too eccentric for her tastes now that she was the crowned jewel of the Gold Coast. But she remembered Addie's surprise when Sara gave it to her. Jittery with the expectation of her old college friend's appreciation, Sara rubbed her hands over and over again against her caftan, smiling nervously, inspecting Addison's every facial twitch as she unwrapped the painting that leaned against the royal blue wall in the sitting room. Those walls were sultry and rich.

Expensive to find that color in such a finish, Addie never hesitated to point out. Jill remembered the heavy painting leaning against it as Addie tore the wrapping paper away, mulled it over and touching the frame with the soft graze of her fingertips. Jill had been in the sitting room, staying out of the way, good at that by then—staying out of grown folks' business, being seen but not heard and seen as little as possible. She was six years old.

Addison stepped back to admire it, or critique it, and Sara waited anxiously in those few hovering, heavy, prolonged seconds to hear approval on her friend's lips.

"It's lovely," Addison finally said, turning her head to one side. "But I thought you painted realism." She'd laughed in that dainty, vaguely condescending manner and touched her friend's shoulder. "What brought this on?"

"Oh, but it is realism. Oh, this is realism at its finest."

And Jillian, unaware of what that word meant still knew that it was, for she knew as soon as she laid eyes on the charcoal watercolor where Sara had gotten her muse.

Ballet shoes and baseball bats.

Specifically, Jillian's ballet shoes—small and prim, dainty in their pink powdery hue—and Vincent's baseball bat, smooth and worn. It was the one Grandpa Tilman had made for their daddy by hand but that had now been given to her brother. The first in a long line of tangible genealogical gifts Vince would receive, not the last of which would be their family's legacy-sake. Jillian realized in a flash what Sara was now explaining to Addie, her voice sounding far away in Jill's ears like she was underwater. She realized because that was the day everything changed. Or perhaps not changed, but became clear, was understood, the fuzzy edges suddenly brought into focus.

Her daddy and Vince had been out in the backyard a few months back. Back when the days were still as hot as they were long and summer vacation was upon them. Addison lounged on an outdoor chaise in her one-piece with a copy of Vanity Fair in hand and a wide-brimmed hat perched on her head. Carl tossed the ball back and forth to Vince who, delighted, relished the opportunity to show off for his daddy, for his mama. For anyone, really. And why shouldn't he? He was "doing so wonderfully!" Addie had exclaimed only half-interested from over the rim of her drink.

"Terrific son, now go long for this one!"

Jillian had just finished her dance lessons in the grand hall used for entertaining guests. Her mama insisted on having a teacher come in on Sundays to help her work on her posture and turn out. She had to be the best when she went to her classes Tuesdays and Thursdays, didn't she know, didn't she care? And so, Jillian had been eager to run outside to play, to free herself of the monotony of *grand plié, rond de jambs, forth position, grand plié* that her teacher incessantly tried to drill into her.

She'd taken her ballet slippers off and tossed them against the wall in the front hall, right next to Vince's new bat that'd been so proudly presented to him by Tilman. Then she ran outside to play in her pink leotard and tights. Could she play, could she play? She jumped up and down, thrilled to be away from the reproachful eye of the instructor, to be outside in the sun.

"Toss it to me, Daddy!"

And he had. Underhanded and delicately so that she could catch it with that grin on his face he usually had, even now. But Vince caught the ball instead, jumping in the way of her outstretched hands and knocking her over into the grass.

"Here, Dad, I got it!" he called back, as though his father weren't a mere ten feet away, and tossed it back to him overhanded, practicing his pitching.

Jillian, fuming, reached out her toes before she realized what she was doing and kicked him. "Why'd you do that! Daddy threw that for me!" She stood and brushed herself off, a fresh grass stain on her leotard and against the thigh of her tights. "Now look, you got me all dirty!"

"That's why you shouldn't even be out here," Vince had spat back, taunting as he waited for their daddy to throw him the ball back. "Girls don't play baseball. And now look, *you're all dirty*," he mocked.

"Go inside now, Jill. Change." Addie raised her sunglasses to peer over them at her daughter disapprovingly. "You know better than to be out here in your leotard, what's the matter with you, simple thing?"

Maybe Sara saw the bat and shoes when she came by for drinks later that evening. For when Jillian returned home from day camp the next day—anything was better than having the kids in the house with her, and day camp lended the excuse of adding culture to their lives—she found her ballet slippers kicked into the corner, a scuff mark on the side of one, and Vince's bat back in his room.

But that painting—that lovely charcoal watercolor of soft pinks and warms browns, of the rich grey of the hall walls and the parquet painted in under the head of the bat and the soles of one slipper as the other slipper rested on its toes leaning against the wall—she'd gotten it all right. It still stood in their hall to this day. That painting made Jillian cringe, and she hated to go near it, made a game of never walking under it.

Step on a crack, break your mama's back.

Walk under those shoes, all day long you'll hear bad news...

And from there it had started, that line. That fissure. That gaping chasm. Perhaps she hadn't known it then, hadn't understood it. But as her mama stood there, regarding the gift and proclaiming she knew just the place to hang it, Jillian remembered.

And that memory never died.

II

The invite was already on the floor inside the front door when she got home weeks back, dropped in through the mail slot. It was obvious what it was and who it was from by the trademark gold envelope and looped *RD* left as the sender's name. That's why she tossed it on the counter and never gave it a second glance. But now Jillian picked it up in the kitchen, dropping her bag down on one of the high-back bar stools as she came in from her late night turned late morning with Xander No Last Name. She glared at it, knowing that tomorrow was the night without even opening it. The grapevine was at work, as usual, so all she needed was a set of ears and the occasional text from Sabrina to remain in the know. She tossed it back down.

Renée had used those same gold envelopes since Jill was a child, announcing her latest dinner party or wedding with flair. Jill grabbed a Heineken from the fridge and popped the top with a bottle opener, leaving it on the marble counter with a *clink*. There it was again. That gold envelope. She reached for it, then pulled her hand back.

Why even open the thing? She and Renée both knew she wasn't going. Couldn't remember the last time she had.

Oh, right. Must've been when Renée's idiot son—really, a near-genius—got into Stanford early decision, their days of childhood tag long behind them. He was two years older than Jill, three inches shorter and had the classic Napoleonic complex to go with his superiority complex of being the son of Renée and the hotshot banker from Manhattan. That marriage had eventually ended, but there was another there waiting to take his place, no surprise. And along had come Sabrina.

That gold envelope had come in the mail then, too, and Jill had dreaded it then just as she did now. She knew exactly what it was when her mother came home and opened it later that evening. Instead of announcing what the special occasion was, Addison charged up to Jill's room and greeted her with, "What the hell has been going on with your grades, young lady? How do you ever expect to get in somewhere decent if you can't –"

"What, Mama? Match Matthew's genius? Or Sabrina's?"

There she went being the problem child again for which she was rewarded with six quick steps across the hardwood floor and a hard smack across the face. It rang throughout the room as her mother stepped back and left her reeling, face beet red on the left side.

"I've told you about that disgusting mouth of yours, Jillian. Take that tone with me again, and I'll knock your teeth out, little girl. Think I won't."

There was a fleeting moment when her eyes watered and her cheek throbbed, but she pushed it back, down, deep down. She shoved it away and kicked it under the rug. They glared at each other, into a pair of honeyed eyes that one had inherited from the other, until Jill swallowed it all down and turned back to what she was doing. Turned the page in her book, though she hadn't yet finished reading it. She was used to it by then. But, she knew that if she didn't care, they couldn't touch her. She hoped that was true anyway.

"So, that's what this is about?" She hoped her mama hadn't heard that crack in her voice but knew she had. Addison Dessommes missed nothing. "Renée is throwing a party because Matthew got into school?"

"Stanford. Early decision."

"Great." Jill turned the page again then rolled over and reached for her notebook. "Call up the nanny and those expensive-ass in-home tutors he's had since God knows when and congratulate them on a job well done, why don't you? 'Cause we both know Aunt Renée had nothing to do with raising that weirdo or his grades, so I don't know what the hell she's taking credit for."

Jill had seen somewhere—National Geographic perhaps—that there really was such a thing as Twin A and Twin B. She'd seen it in reference to some grueling Siamese twin surgery, but she'd always thought the analogy worked just as well for her life. And why not?

She could relate to those twins, laying naked and exposed in front of all those doctors, save for a paper-thin sheet, in front of the world on national television. She could relate.

The doctor explained the concept of Twin A and B to the cameras, to the world, and gave her a name, something that she could finally put her finger on to call what she'd been feeling all her life. He explained that, in essence, one twin had a higher likelihood of survival and success than the other. That was Twin A. They'd do triage on both twins, try to give them both a good chance of survival, but if Twin B started to slip, as they half-expected would happen upon separation, the doctors would throw all of their resources behind the other twin, Twin A. Of course, no one ever told Twin B that they were Twin B, but everyone knew. And that's what'd happened with her and her brother. With her and her cousins. There would always be a Twin A, but she would always be Twin B.

There was always a scale, some caste system within their tribe, just as there was out in the larger world beyond, that wasn't quite unspoken. For instance, Jillian knew that she was considered to be the pretty one between her and Sabrina—Sabrina who'd grown up with soft, dark eyes and course hair that had to be pressed regularly. It wasn't that she was ugly, or even unattractive, but it was still understood that Jill was the pretty one. Jill with her café-au-lait skin and piercing eyes, with the long dancer's legs and wild, mane of hair highlighted with sun-kissed blonde streaks. Jill who had admittedly Eurocentric features.

Jill didn't know when the rift had begun, when the grown-ups had started comparing one child to another like prize horses at the hippodrome; perhaps it had been since birth. But they all knew what their attributes were as if there were labels permanently glued to their foreheads. That was never a secret, no longer debated. It was always Matthew the Smart One, Sabrina the Sweet One, Jillian the Pretty One, Vincent the Destined One. All Jill knew was that she'd embraced it at some point, the fact that being the rebel—the Bohemian, as they liked to dress the term up—was her saving grace as well as her cross to bear. But she'd never chased rebeldom, never once. Never even really thought about it as a complete deliberation. It had happened upon her like a stranger at night, a byproduct of her resentfulness toward Addie's coarseness, her strictness, her iron fist. And once she saw how well that Bohemian armor protected her, she knew she would not be one of them ever again.

Weren't there things to do in life that didn't follow such strict ceremony and custom? Couldn't she be someone not surrounded by such trivial nonsense, of no kin to her toxic mother who'd never developed a single mothering bone in her body in her quest to catch a Dessommes, in her quest to marry well, but had always known nurturing Vince was a role she could not shirk. Jillian was, after all, the abdicated princess of the Clan, forever condemned to be equated to her brother, the messiah. She didn't care. Well, not so much. Not anymore. And those words comforted her at night so that then, by the time she was in her mid-twenties, she'd grown used to that condescending tsk: "Such a pretty girl. It's really too bad. Such a shame." *What a waste*, they might as well have said. Sometimes they did.

Jill pulled the Venetian blinds up over the couch. Grabbed her pack of Hedges and antique lighter. She took a drag and exhaled a cloud of thin, grey smoke. Stared at that gold envelope for a few seconds, cigarette in hand, feet on the floor, elbow to knee. That envelope picked the recesses of her brain with its sharp corners, digging out old memories that left dust in their wake. Memories of him. Of them. All of them.

She'd always found it funny how many sides, how many faces, a person could have. That's what her brother was to her mostly, a chameleon-like memory forever shifting right in front of her face, slick fucker. Just like Renée, just like them all. It was as if no one had ever seen him in his true skin but Jill, gold on the outside and sharp at the edges. Not even Laney, the perfect shadow to his ego he'd caught in college and never released, now a true captive of Stockholm Syndrome. They thought they knew him but they really didn't. Maybe it didn't really matter to them what his true face looked like—what it held behind those soft eyes of his—because he did what he was supposed to do as Jill never had. He conformed and made it look natural as Jill never could. Maybe it was for him. Renée probably would've sold her own fucking daughter to him if marrying cousins wasn't so taboo nowadays and if Laney hadn't gotten there first. Jill stubbed the cigarette out, half-smoked, and reached for the lighter. Lit the corner of the envelope on fire with a flick of her wrist and the *tsss* of the lighter that satisfied her.

She got up and tossed it in the sink, flames licking at her fingers, and poured the rest of the Heineken over it. Probably should have stayed to make sure the fire went out instead of heading upstairs to shower off last night's bender, but what could she say? Self-destructive behavior had always been becoming of her.

I I I

Fourteen.

By this time Bohemia already looked good on her. Jillian had learned the word and it no longer tasted metallic in her mouth each time she thought it, each time she mulled it over, rolling it round and round in her mind during trigonometry or advanced French. There were times when she realized that the taste was actually the result of her chewing the inside of her lip, deep in thought, nibbling it to shreds. She'd roll her pen between her palms as the teacher droned on and on about God knew what. Then the bell would ring and white-haired, blue-eyed Sandi—sorry, *Alessandra* now that she was in high school—would tap her on her shoulder and say, "Girl, wake up. We're outta here," with a little jerk of her thumb toward the door, flipping her phone open to check for messages.

And it was thus that Jillian floated through the halls of the posh private school with her head in the clouds and her escape on her mind. There was cheerleading practice to go to and articles for the school newspaper to write, but none of that interested her because she had figured it all out. When she passed Vince in the halls that last year they were in school together—he a senior, eagerly filling out his early application forms to Morehouse, Purdue, Georgetown, Tulane, Carnegie Mellon and Howard with their mother at his elbow and their father proudly checking for updates on a near quarter-hour basis—neither of them spoke or nodded toward the other.

Ever.

When his friends jostled around him, already part of his one-day collection of aficionados jockeying for his attention, lacrosse sticks in hand and Letterman jackets bearing the proud green and gold of the school colors (screaming, she always thought, to be noticed, those colors), she turned away. When she saw him walking to his car with the saucy Paige Darensbourg, cutting fourth period for an elongated lunch of fast food and making out with the head cheerleader, she pretended she didn't know him. And when Sandi, the daughter of a Superior Court judge who never missed a beat and was always nosing into everyone else's business, asked her, "What's up with you and your brother? Man, you guys are so fucking weird," she closed her locker and kept walking, leaving Sandi prancing to catch up. Likewise, when one of Vince's peripheral friends—for his true friends knew better—commented, "That's your sister? Man, she's hot!" or "Isn't your sister that freshman, that cheerleader?" Vince would give them the eye, allowing it to linger for a least a few seconds, so the message that talking about her was off-limits was clear before he moved on to the next subject.

Jill never really knew why he hated her so much. At first it seemed like a normal brother/sister dynamic as they were growing up. A pinch here, a tattle there. But there came a point when even she realized it was extreme. Then again, there was no room for overshadowing the messiah, and the messiah always needed to make sure she knew that, didn't he? There was only ever enough air for him to breathe in his sphere.

Plié, rond de jambe, plié. Tour jeté, pirouette, tendu.

It was amazing how many times she could rehearse a dance in her head. In class, between classes, on the walk home. (She refused to ride with Vince to and from school in his BMW and preferred to walk the mile home instead. Her parents did not object.) There was a soothing repetitiveness to it, similar to counting sheep, that lulled her. Eventually numbed her when others were talking to her. To her dance principals, this was the hunger, the drive, the thirst to succeed in ballet that one needed to survive. She was praised for always knowing her steps, for her beautiful execution, for her elegance and much-practiced poise. She was the example, and this would have bothered her had she allowed herself to think about it. She was *that girl.*

And she hated *that girl.*

At the school dances, she would've much preferred to be in jeans and her Converses with a beanie pulled low over her unruly curls—or better yet, to not got to those lame ass parties at all—but, of course, that was never an option. So, she was plucked and primped at the spa under her mama's watchful eye. Shoved in a car and deposited at the entrance of the dances with Sandi and the beige-skinned Darensbourg girls. She'd stand on the edges of the crowded dance floor with Pia and Carmella Darensbourg, loud music blaring in her ears, as Pia checked her flawless makeup in a jeweled compact mirror and smacked her lips shamelessly at herself, making pouty faces before she giggled and snapped it shut then marched onto the floor to find her next ex-boyfriend. Pia and Cammy were juniors the year Jill started high school, but all those years of joined family functions and summer vacations with their tribe gave her enough clout to stand next to the Darensbourg girls, though Paige always held herself above it all, even Jill. No matter; being near Paige was always somehow unbearable for Jill anyway, not that Paige ever noticed, her nose permanently aimed at the sky.

Jill remembered her middle school days, watching Paige flounder and flail, all those years ahead of her, to live up to her sister Pilar's reputation at the school, unsure of whether she preferred books or MAC lip gloss. It was painfully comic, though no one else seemed to notice. But by the time Pilar graduated, Paige had slipped comfortably into her Louboutins, found her way, her voice and her favorite shade of lipstick. She'd slipped into the brand of the Darensbourg Three: all bright smiles, luxurious, flat ironed hair and flirty winks. Jill stood in their shadow grateful for the shade.

The days passed faster that way, shaded and busy, by now used to being shuffled back and forth from school to ballet to Jack and Jill, a membership-driven institution established for black families during those precarious years in American history between The Great Depression and the Second World War that was still running strong in plain sight while also managing to be an entity that outsiders had never even heard of. Of this selective establishment, Jill was a firm member and her mother a staunch supporter, filling her free time with volunteering and blithe social gatherings. Admittedly, those were the less troubling years of her life, if not the happiest. And if she hadn't withdrawn so completely from those circles, she may have found that she still had a few friends within those old social cliques of black convention. Days sometimes crept, sometimes flew, by in a whirl and blur of teenage slumber parties at Sandi's and the Three's that were really gab-fests about tea-bagging boys behind the gym or sneaking a smoke from their mothers' purses when they were conked out on benzos and the cleaners, nannies, tutors weren't around. Jillian always chuckled wryly but never added any stories of her own to the mix—even when Sandi prodded, even when Paige scoffed and Carmella tried to hide her blushing face.

This, of course, all came after she'd figured it out. After that moment when all the pieces had clicked in her mind, when she'd stopped trying to really impress them, when she'd gone on autopilot. After she'd decided it was all in vain and numb was better.

When Vince got home that day, he smelled like weed. But then again, he often smelled like weed, leaving a pungent herbal scent in his wake whenever their parents weren't around. By then, the lacrosse stick had replaced the gifted baseball bat in the hall, Grandpa Tilman's bat now hanging in its revered spot above Vince's bed since the man had died.

She didn't even turn her head to acknowledge his presence when he came up the stairs, the same as he did every day of their lives after school, after practice, after smoking a joint with his entourage in the park or going to a study group for one of the extraneous classes he'd opted to take, because maintaining his four-point-O until graduation was more important to his parents than what classes he took in that last semester to achieve it.

When he hovered in her doorway, she didn't even glance up. "What do you want?" she muttered irritably, as she flipped a page in her textbook, stomach down, feet up, on her bed. Her back was to him and she couldn't see him, only felt his presence, heavy and lumbering in her peripheral when she turned her head slightly over her shoulder. "Are you just going to stand there like a fucking idiot? What do you want, Vince?"

Finally, she rolled over and sat up, glaring at him, suspicious because he never volunteered to come into her space. And why should he? There was nothing for him there. Nothing left to take from her, to steal from her. He'd won already, hadn't he? Parental affections and approval, the one-day heir to the throne that became more and more daunting, more and more real every day. He was their chosen one in more ways than one. To her daddy, he was the son he'd always needed, for they were quite the ceremonial family as most were in their Clan. Carrying on traditions—brooms being jumped over, girls being presented at cotillion and given away by proud fathers at weddings—was the basis of their very existence. And so Carl had groomed him, nurtured him, taught him by his own hand. How to tie his shoe, how to tie his tie, how to shave. And to her mama—well, to her mama he was her pride and joy, the continuer of their legacy and the end result of her most important duty in that marriage. Maybe she was just as hard on Vince as she was on Jill. But maybe the reality of his position in the family was his armor against her, so much sturdier than Jill's.

Vince hovered for a moment longer then took a step over the threshold. Jillian stared at that foot slightly in front of the other and frowned. Crossed her arms over her chest. Waited for his sarcastic remark or scathing comment. His eyes were red and glassy she saw, his trademark smirk was somehow awry, but she couldn't put her finger on what it was about it that was so different from usual.

"Calvin thinks you're pretty," he finally said, leering, swaying a little on his feet as he stood in that doorway.

"What?" Irritation rang out in her voice. She heard it, felt it between them. "What did you say?"

"I said, Calvin thinks you're pretty. Said to me, 'Man that sister of yours is something to look at, ain't she?'" Vince wiped the back of his hand across his mouth and chuckled, "Can you believe that?"

Jillian rolled her eyes and went back to reading. "Get out of my room, Vince. Nobody gives a shit about your jackass friends—"

"But then, you know what I told 'em? I guess you are. I'd never really thought about it."

Another glance back over her shoulder. "I'm serious, Vince. Get out."

But he wouldn't go. He wouldn't budge. And she jumped up to shove him out of her room, to slam the door in his smug face and lock it behind her. She pushed him, and he stumbled back a little, just enough to throw him off balance. Vince's eyes flared up, trained on her. Hard. He shoved her back.

"What's the matter with you?"

That untouchable thing in the Dessommes air had made him...entitled. He felt entitlement. That's what she'd seen in his eyes, she realized. And, in retrospect, she supposed he was.

Entitled.

Still, it surprised her when he reached out and grabbed her breast and stunned her into shocked stillness when he caressed it as if leisurely. As if he had all the time in the world. As if he was fondling the petals of a delicate flower to be admired. It wasn't until he said, "You know, you've got a nice set of tits on you. You'd probably be worth more if you stopped covering 'em up like that," that she finally snapped to as if slapped violently in the face and shoved him off. She understood when she heard that heavy exhale in the air, felt her hands pushing against him to push him out of her room, that she hadn't breathed up until that moment.

What had it been, seconds? Maybe four? Four seconds that she'd stood there and allowed her brother to touch her like that. Like she liked it. Like she wanted it. Had it been a feeling of surrealism that'd overtaken her, or had she asked for it? Is that why she'd stood still, stood by? She didn't know. Wasn't sure. But she pressed harder against him, hands to his chest, trying to knock him off kilter, to push him out of her space. He moved his hands in a maneuver so quick she only remembered it as a blur. Tucked his arm on the inside of hers and swatted it away like a bug. Grabbed her by the wrist, angry now by her daring to push him away or excited by the thrill of it. Or both.

One hand was all that it had taken to subdue her. That was the part she always recalled. How he'd pressed her two wrists together so tightly she'd nearly screamed, the joints at the base of her hands crushing each other. He'd held them tightly in one hand, in one of his over-sized bear paws, and used the other hand to grab her by the hair nearly pulling her off her feet. She remembered the brief second that she'd been pulled up on her tip toes before feeling his hand at the V between her legs. But it was the kiss—the wet, groping, bruising press of his lips against hers, of his tongue slithering between her teeth—that had finally made her scream. But then it was too late. His lips covered hers, muffling the sound, pressing it back down into her throat.

He shoved her back onto her bed using the hand encircling her wrists, and she landed with a plop and a fluttering of book pages. And she knew. She knew in that moment that he was going to take something from her—one of the few things he'd not yet managed to get his hands on. Something he had no business taking. Her own brother. And she couldn't fight it. No, resigned wasn't the word. Nor was terrified, meek or weak. But somewhere along the line, somewhere in the midst of the ballet shoes and baseball bats, she'd felt that she'd lost her right and her voice along with it.

Entitled.

He was entitled to everything by right, by ancestry, by convention. And why not this, she imagined he must have thought? Maybe she thought, too.

Except, he didn't make another move. Instead, he sneered down at her. Told her not to be stupid. That there was no way he'd want to fuck a stupid bitch like her anyway. That he just wanted to see if he could, and now he *knew* he could.

And then he was gone, dissolved back into the hallway through the blurriness in her eyes. He was gone. And the sole tear that was allowed to fall was wiped before she'd even felt it on her cheeks. Jill touched her fingers to her tongue and tasted the salt. She'd learned that tears were made up of salt water in one of her slew of science classes, but had realized, there in the second row of a classroom full of second, third and fourth generation snobs, that she'd never known this for herself. Had never tasted her own tears. Well, not in quite a while. Not since she'd resolved to stop crying, to stop fighting, to count the days until she was free.

IV

That night, the cold bathroom tile against Jill's skin sent goosebumps down her arms and legs. The water on her back left a noisy streak as she slid down the wall until she hit the floor, knees to her chest. The only light filtered into the darkness through the window above the bathtub, cutting a milky path through the thick steam that bathed the room in a scented mixture of shampoo and sweat.

There was a razor in her hand. The one that was always stored in the porcelain trinket box in the back of her bathroom cabinet under the towels and bath sponges. A straight razor that could be hidden in the palm of her hand but never needed to be, because no one ever knew to look for it. She tapped her head against the wall, wet curls sticking against it. She felt the water trickling down her body from the shower. Closed her eyes.

There was that familiar sting, followed by the slow trickle of blood that meandered down her hip and started a small pool on the floor. It was the sting that she always waited for, longed for. That sting like a pinch in the night to sober her. Jill watched the blood run for a while, then angled the razor diagonally across that cut and dug it into her skin, pulling downward. There was another familiar sting that radiated through her right leg. It was a liquidless elixir of endorphins. She heard her heart thumping, not faster necessarily but perhaps harder. In her ears, like a drumbeat, like a serenade.

She cut herself and she relaxed. She cut and she breathed easier, found shelter, found solace. But only on her hips. Only ever on her hips, so her parents wouldn't see the marks. So no one would see them. Maybe part of her still thought she'd give in to them one day, that she'd bend to their will and succumb to their ranks —

"Jillian, Margery has a son home from Yale. Wouldn't you like to meet him?"

— Well, today one called that marriage and, in the Dessommes family, marriage was still an art form. Maybe one day she'd let them do it—one day she'd be Florence in her own right, wry and cunning, above it all though still a willing participant—and on that day, she'd need her outward face intact just as Florence had maintained.

You could literally see traces of her soul on the outside, if you looked hard enough. If you looked deep enough. The skin there could tell you a story. The skin there could paint you a picture like Cézanne, all realism with every frill stripped away. Patterns of lines, x's and crisscrosses, as if all of the crossroads she'd ever come to in her life had all converged together and branded themselves on her in one endless mess of regrets and rejoices.

There was a patch of skin on her right hip, just where the bone gave way to meat, where she'd hacked her skin into a tough patch that was thick and bumpy. Where she ran her fingers over it from time to time and remembered. Where the scars had heaped one upon the other for so many years that scar tissue had formed and reformed. Where she tried to resist cutting anymore even now. And this was where Jill's story was told, because she never said it out loud. There was no room for that in the Dessommes way, no room for repentance or lamenting. Only forward movement and conquering.

The doors were shut to the outside, the windows opaque. "Trust me. Anyone not a Dessommes," Jill had once told her best friend Alessandra with a shrug and a chug of her Heineken, "wouldn't understand. You don't get this...long-standing establishment of ...I don't know, crazy solidarity and brick walls. Brick walls crawling with ivy and shit. You don't see it, Sandi." With a snort, "We're the best at hiding shit, ever."

"Jesus, Jill." Alessandra snatched the bottle from her and held it out of reach, setting it under the bed, glancing over her shoulder to listen for a parent at the closed door. "Why do you always have to be such a rebel? It's so...annoying."

Jill rolled her eyes, shook her head. "It has absolutely nothing to do with being some rebel, Sandi. What's rebellious about me? I just want to be myself. I just want to be normal, that's all."

"Get a grip on yourself and look around, girl. What's normal? Who's normal? There's no such thing, or haven't you heard?"

"You're a fucking idiot. Have you ever felt what it feels like to be free? I have. Try it one day."

Being smashed always made her wax existential, made it bubble out of her like a faucet. Sandi used to always get the truth out of her, back in their younger days, the only person on the planet who could, with those blonde-lash-framed ice blues and shiny white hair. The combination often led to long conversations in the middle of the night over shot glasses and the occasional recreational drug.

But that had been years ago. Too many years ago. Now, Sandi was just the occasional Facebook ping, the obligatory birthday text from across the country.

Jill cut again, this time harder, longer, deeper than usual.

More.

Always more for them.

Her muscles relaxed and the tension around her spine lessened as she leaned into the tiled wall because here they couldn't reach her. Here, their voices were silenced and she was not Jillian the letdown; her brother wasn't there to compete with; her sister-in-law wasn't there to overshadow her, smiling and cajoling with the other members of the Gold Coast elite seamlessly as Jill should have been doing, as Jill was raised to do and Delaney was not. Here, she could just be herself and her story was her own. She could wear it on her sleeve, or on her hips as it were, without questions and without condemnation. That's all she could ask for. All she ever asked for.

Jillian reached for the crumpled pack of cigarettes she kept in the porcelain box. Pulled one out. Lit it up with the gold lighter and rested her head back against the tiled wall. The smoke mingled with the thick haze in the air as she exhaled.

She was calm.

HIGH SIDITY

AALIYAH

Scene.

The party is in full swing by the time they arrive. The black town car pulls into the roundabout and waits in a line of others to release their cargo. Aaliyah steps out in a floor-length pumpkin-colored gown of silk chiffon—a gown she would never have bought on her own accord and likely would've been too nervous to wear at all had she seen the price tag it'd come with. But Delaney has come to the rescue again and dressed her herself as though Aaliyah was her life-sized doll. She's woven a velvet ribbon into her locks, and molded them into a sophisticatedly prim chignon as though she's been doing it for years. Delaney steps out beside her donning a simple black satin bateau neckline gown with a crème skirt. Her hair is pulled back into a simple nape-of-the-neck pony that fits her own personal style effortlessly: simple, classic. The night is clear and crisp, a sure sign that fall is finally settling in if the crunching orange and brown leaves littered over the cobblestones aren't enough. A half-moon shines brightly in the night sky.

Renée's home—wait, Aaliyah wonders: can she call Renée by her first name or is there some formal way she should address her?

She laughs to herself at this thought, gripping her clutch. What had she been thinking, Your Majesty? The home is exactly what Delaney has prepared her to expect: enormous and grand with a fountain at the center of the roundabout and the entire west wing dedicated to entertaining alone. Laney loops her arm into Aaliyah's—thankfully Vince is to arrive in another car straight from his office—and leads the way toward the bustling room of fine silks and drapery, mingling patrons and women decked in their finery. We follow them close over their shoulders, the live band inside getting louder as they approach. Before Aaliyah can ask, because she certainly intends to, Laney leans in close as they climb the steps to the ballroom entrance and relays the quick version of how ole Aunt Renée keeps herself wrapped in such a grandiose fashion.

DELANEY: Don't be too impressed. She didn't get this all on her own by any means.

A cacophony of noise overtakes them as they enter the ballroom.

[Fade to white]

I I

Renée was the self-proclaimed belle of the ball, a Wendy Williams clone who would have never fit in with her own surroundings had she not been born into the bloodline that she had been. She was too much of everything, Vince had once complained: too ostentatious, too loud, too unrefined for the crowd in which she traveled, but she was forgiven for her transgressions against convention because of who she was. One would have thought she and her niece, Jillian, would have been kindred spirits, but Renée had retained her elitist snobbishness if nothing else, not to mention her resolutely Republican ideals that made her firmly, in Jillian's mind, "one of them." Her gossipy chatter rubbed her niece the wrong way, and her affinity for "marrying well" to continue building her own wealth was "a disgusting practice of self-prostitution all too befitting that woman's character." You see, Renée Dessommes Washington Lindsay had married into and divorced out of two other fortunes—a banker/investor followed by an engineer with a half-dozen patents—before the age of forty and was now able to live separate from the family money if she pleased, thus her continued eccentricity.

Aaliyah took the story in, nodded it down and opened her mouth to ask a follow-up question that never found its way up to the surface. Laney was pulled away by some prattling acquaintance or another as soon as they stepped foot in the room, offering her friend an apologetic smile as she was whisked away, her narration left hanging in the air. Aaliyah swallowed the question and looked around for Micah, who she thankfully found in the sea of voices and laughter just inside the grand entrance.

She hurried over, navigating chattering attendees as she crossed the bronze marble floor, anxious not to be the only one in the room tragic enough not to have a date to the ball, literally, but slowed herself as she approached when she noticed that he wasn't actually standing alone but with a man who looked to also be an early member of Generation Millennials. She pressed herself to walk even slower still. Over-eagerness was a virtue to no one, and there were still steps to this dance she could easily trip over. Aaliyah took hold of Micah's arm, glad to be near someone she knew. She felt so awkward in her skin there, it had nearly become a palpable itching sensation.

"Oh, there you are. I was just telling him about you." Micah wrapped a strong arm around her, pulling her into a one-armed embrace. She returned it and allowed him to plant a kiss on her cheek. "You look beautiful."

"Thank you. All compliments of Laney Dessommes." She had to raise her voice a notch to be heard over the chatter and clinking of glasses.

"Hope I get to meet her tonight. I'm starting to think she's just a figment of your imagination or something, the way you talk about her."

"Oh, no, she's very real," the man laughed, rubbing his goatee and nursing his amber drink wrapped in a tulip glass. "I'm sure she's around here somewhere."

Aaliyah's ears perked at this. "Oh, do you know her?"

He took a sip and shook his head. "Not well. Know *of* her more like. I only know her as Vince's wife."

Aaliyah started to reply, instantly deflated at the sound of Vince's name from his mouth. Well, if he ran in Vince's crowd, she certainly wanted nothing to do with him. She smiled away her disappointment as Micah rescued her from commenting.

"Well, I gotta say, if she was able to get you out of the house and all dolled up like this, then I'm looking forward to meeting her all the more, whoever the hell's wife she is!"

Aaliyah smirked. She felt the man's eyes on her but couldn't bring herself to match his gaze, though she couldn't tell if this was a pull of attraction that made her shy or a repelling of disgust that made her disinterested. His acquaintance with Vince placed him in a small box automatically, one she wasn't interested in examining any further, like a cat who'd already tired of a ball of yarn.

"Nigel, sorry, that was rude of me. This is my colleague and date for the evening, Aaliyah Walker." She shook his hand.

"So nice to meet you," though now it wasn't really.

"And you as well. Your accent is beautiful."

Nigel smiled her way and held her hand just long enough to be too long. She felt her eyes lowering, though she hadn't told them to, and made herself look him in the eye and remember who he was.

That natural pull her body felt toward him didn't excuse the fact that he was also one of them, so she commanded herself not to fold in front of him, undoubtedly the same mentality she used with those of the paler nation, not allowing them to see her sweat, to see her squirming and aware that she was, on at least some level, misplaced. This thought annoyed her so tremendously that she raised her eyes to his and felt herself returning the grin he flashed her way, almost defiantly.

The live band started up on a platform at the front of the room, drowning out the voices only momentarily. The patrons adjusted their own vociferousness to be heard over the music, energizing the atmosphere in the grand hall with a lively rendition of Ella Fitzgerald's "Fever." They moved in packs, Aaliyah noticed. All back pats and cheek kisses, clones of each other in different variations of overly expensive garbs. These weren't folks who'd get down on the dance floor. Not folks who'd ever hike up their skirts or kick off their heels to feel a groove. These were swayers, moving to the melody of the music as if automatons, as if in a dollhouse. Younger couples added a bit of flair with the occasional twirl or jig, the outright laughter. Those were the ones she watched, flitting her eyes away from Boomers still stuck behind their walls of custom and tradition.

She joined in their chatter: who they knew in common and the office politics in their professions. Two quick flutes of champagne later—the waiters proved efficient at spotting an empty glass in the throngs and quickly materializing to offer another, and Aaliyah was eager to lose the edge that always held her back from fully blossoming in social settings—Nigel signaled a waiter over for another cognac, and Micah spotted someone he knew in the crowd. Before she knew it, the short flurry of events had dissolved Micah into the throng and left her standing alone with Nigel and his tulip of aromatic liquor. She smiled wanly his way and tried to look for a retreat, but there was none because neither of the only two people she knew in the room were within her line of sight.

And then it started: the Who's Who game of black geography that seemed to Aaliyah to be the foundation of their society. It was always the same ole thing, as if the rules had been carved into time and it was just common knowledge to know how to play. They must've learned it in place of schoolyard games, she mused—

Eeny, meny, miny, moe

Catch an impostor by the toe

—There would be, she knew, talk of childhood summer homes in Maine and fishing trips to Rhode Island. The Vineyard. Boothbay Harbor—*oh, and those breathtaking views, didn't you love them!* It was always the assumptions she even knew what they were talking about that both tickled her own superiority complex—*God spare me. How pretentious!*—and made her feel all the more an outsider.

Nigel steered her into it, sipping his drink with a confident stance—one hand in his pocket—that pulled her further in against her will. Aaliyah was acutely aware of what he was doing, where they were headed, and what the end result would and should be but for whatever reason wasn't as annoyed by it as she normally would've been had it come from someone other than him. She finished her champagne and tipped her head to the side, ready for question *numero uno.*

Or in these circles, might it be *numéro un?*

"So, Aaliyah, where are you from originally?"

"Where would you guess?"

He pretended to think about it. "You're an island girl, no doubt. That accent is hard to hide even when you're not loose." He chuckled throatily. "But now you are, and I can hear it like a song."

Aaliyah repressed a grin. "Born and raised in Trinidad. Well, until I was twelve. Then we moved to Queens, so good guess. So, now it's your turn. Where are *you* from?"

He laughed and said, "Well, I'm actually home grown, from right here in Georgia. Little town called Statham, if you've ever heard of it."

"No, I haven't. You're an HBCU man for sure then."

"You guessed it. Morehouse actually."

"Hmm, I can see that," I nodded. "I can see that. I'm surprised we never met on campus if we were there at the same time."

"Spelman?"

"Mmhmm."

That question was a big one, she knew—a deciding factor in the next shift of the conversation. If you couldn't answer that simple question acceptably, the game would be over, and you'd find yourself suddenly standing alone. Oh, well, there'd be the smile, all polite-like of course, followed swiftly by the escape-route polished bow and conversation exit. Never rude. Never overt. But the sentiment was the same. Then they'd be gone before you could even open your mouth to defend yourself. No education was intolerable, hell even offensive. Even if Laney hadn't told her that with a derisive eye roll years earlier, it was obvious by the air and the very aura of that congregation.

"So," she asked him as a peacocked woman in a jeweled red gown brushed and flashed past her, "is that how you and Vince became friends? You went to school together?"

Nigel nearly spit his drink back into the tulip, then wiped his mouth and snickered. "Friends? No, no, Vince and I are hardly that."

He stepped closer so she could hear him, or maybe not for that reason alone. At her questioning gaze he clarified, "We're frat brothers. Alpha Phi Alpha."

She nodded her understanding, not to mention her internal relief that this man didn't see Vince as a comrade of some sort.

"And I *do* use the word 'brothers' loosely. But I was in the class above him and ended up being his big bro when his line crossed, so it just sort of happened that way. We're not close though. But, uh, how about you? Are you another member of the tribe I haven't met yet...?"

"A member of the—no! I mean...no, not at all." Aaliyah glanced around the room then back at Nigel. "I could never have...I mean, being here—these people—it just always feels like I'm in some weird dream when I'm in these situations—at these things—like a bad movie or something. Every time I'm around them I feel like they've rehearsed some script I never got. Like I'm watching myself trying to act it all out with them all out-of-body like. Can't ever get the steps right. I can't believe anyone chooses these...tribes. No offense."

"Offense? I didn't even know these people existed until pretty recently, myself."

Nigel smiled her way. Aaliyah read his face, skimming for signs of jest or affront, but found none. Only then did she smile back.

As the game continued, they slowly closed the chasm in personal space from professional distance to familiar closeness. When Aaliyah reached for another flute of champagne from a passing waiter, she spotted Laney and Vince sitting at one of the round tables in a semi-circle around the room. But Aaliyah no longer felt that urge to run to the comfort of Laney's proximity, too busy learning Nigel's own personal history, which came easier with every sip he took.

When Aaliyah and Laney ended up in each other's line of sight again, Aaliyah gestured for Laney to come over. They kissed each other's cheeks, Laney out of habit and Aaliyah playing along, not wanting to make it obvious to all that she wasn't used to the custom. Aaliyah started to introduce her out of convention, but Laney wrapped Nigel in a hug. Asked him how he'd been doing since they'd last seen him. They should really have him over to the house sometime. He agreed, flashing Aaliyah a conspiratorial glance over Laney's shoulder as if to say *not a chance.*

"So, Liyah," her friend started in, turning her full attention back to her. "I really want to introduce you and that colleague you brought—what's his name?—to Renée. I just saw her a second ago." She looked around the boisterous room trying to spot her again.

"Oh," Aaliyah chuckled, "Micah will just love that. I can see it now."

"Well, I'll leave you ladies to it. Aaliyah, it was great meeting you. I hope to have the pleasure again soon."

Nigel stepped back from them with a gracious bow. He shot her one last smile then melted into the crowd. Aaliyah opened her mouth to get him to stay, but he was already gone.

Laney nudged her in the side, grinning. "What was that about, little miss? Was he flirting with you?"

"Well, if he was, he certainly isn't now, is he?"

Laney swayed to the band's version of Boyz II Men, sipping her 1975 Château D'Yquem, attention elsewhere already. Her swaying was off beat in a way that betrayed her condition. She was pretty close to drunk, Aaliyah judged, eying her closely. Then she smelled the sweet smell of alcohol that let her know Laney wasn't close; she was there. Comfortably drunk but still in control of herself. She'd mastered that, and if Aaliyah didn't know better she'd mistake that glimmer in her eye for delight rather than inebriation.

Micah ambled over in the midst of Aaliyah's musings and Laney's obliviousness and placed his hand on Aaliyah's back. She welcomed him into their space, only to find he'd already started his own introductions to Laney, having seen them together and taken the opportunity to make her acquaintance. He extended his thanks for the plus one that had brought him there; she turned at the sound of his voice, smiled broadly as if on cue and graciously accepted in that way of hers that was all Laney Dessommes: practiced coquette with a discernible blend of seasoned affability.

He had impeccable timing, Laney had grinned. She was just going to introduce Aaliyah to Renée. Silly her for not having done it before. The banter between them continued on jovially—Laney laid her hand on Micah's arm as she asked how he was enjoying the gathering, and he punned his astonishment at her not being exhausted of such festivities after so much storied practice with them—until Laney spotted her mark and waved her over in all of her glittering red finery.

"No, thank you. I'm good on that." Aaliyah stepped away from them in no mood to chatter with the likes of Vince's aunt who, by the looks of her as she approached, would prove to be even more of an irritant than Vince himself. "I'll leave you two to it."

She went in search of her new acquaintance, slowly pressing through the throngs in search of him. But, soon enough Aaliyah was snatched up by Laney once again and introduced around the room against her will, her friend teetering blithely beside her, laughing and jesting with one acquaintance after another.

"But what happened with Renée?" Aaliyah tried to squirm out of it.

"Oh, Micah's more than got her covered. He's quite the mover and shaker, isn't he?"

With another glass of something bubbly she was able to loosen up enough to smile and converse in short spurts that left her feeling dizzy, like a fish flopping on land, as one acquaintance was replaced with another and another at Laney's choosing. After a while they became nameless and faceless, a blur of similitude and homogenous personalities that all amounted to nothing, to little more than white noise over the sound of the band and a headache that would require a prescription dose to relieve.

Carmella, a favorite of the Clan, as Laney explained on their way over to her, proved to be the only one of them who didn't give Aaliyah the haughty once over, the only one who seemed to her like a real person. She wore her hair cut into a layered bob with highlights that paired well with her complexion and light eyes. Aaliyah knew all too well that she was Vince's best friend's wife and his childhood friend to boot, but the champagne allowed her to not hold it against her. And, also because of the few drinks she'd had, she managed to forget to feel threatened in the presence of this woman who thought herself to be Delaney's closest friend. It all felt very schoolyard, despising the pretty girl who wanted to take her friend on the playground yet felt stranger still actually meeting her for the first time.

Aaliyah complimented her on her hair, the only way she could think to strike up a conversation without sounding completely awkward, and Carmella took it from there, asking how she was enjoying the party, recounting the tale of how she'd first met Laney—before Laney's coming out dinner even—when Vince wanted Carmella's opinion of her at the start of it all.

"And this one here's been a dream—the sister I never ever had—ever since."

It was when Carmella said this, latching onto Laney around her waist and pulling her playfully in with a snuggle, that Aaliyah thought to glance around for Nigel. But she couldn't find him anywhere. He'd already gone.

PICKING YOUR BATTLES

NIGEL

The day after Renée's soirée was when Nigel realized he'd stumbled past his eureka moment only to notice after turning the corner that he'd already passed it up.

It was on his mind when he flopped down on the bed, still in dress socks and pants when he got home that night, and still nudged at him when he opened his eyes the next morning. The festivities had amounted to exactly what he'd figured they would when Vince sent him the invitation: an ornate affair that nearly bored him breathless but that'd been wonderful for business nonetheless. That's really why he went to those events when Vince summoned, because their money was just as good as anyone else's, but they had plenty more to spare than most.

So, while he knew the invites continued flowing his way out of polite convention—he and Vince hardly said two words to each other when they saw each other at those things and even fewer words passed between them when they didn't—there was never any reason to turn them down. He wasn't the legacy snob Vince was, but he still enjoyed the titillation of stimulating conversation and new-venture schemes made over Calvados, which he was always sure to stumble upon within those ranks. Over the past few years he'd sold over a dozen houses, condos, and lots of acreage both to and for the acquaintances he'd made at those soirées, the commissions sizeable because no one wanted to be outclassed when it came to parading their level of affluence, feigned or not, with their choice of residence.

Despite the realtor/client relationship he'd established with several members of their tribe, many of whom were present in the room that evening, Nigel was no less surprised when Vince ambled over, embraced him in a brotherly hug and asked if he'd talk with him about consulting with The Group on their next few commercial property acquisitions. A major shift in regime was approaching, he said. Vince's father was being phased out as the holder of The Group's reins and Vince was stepping up. Besides, Carl was even younger than Vince when he'd stepped into his own father's shoes, so it was about time Vince took over.

He needed the best, he'd said, grabbing two more cognacs from a passing waiter and clinking glasses with a still bemused Nigel. And, he'd heard from his cousin, his old college professor and one of Renée's confrères from NYU that he was, indeed, the best among their circles. Would he, perhaps, like to have a sit-down? Maybe they'd be able to work together. After all, they were brothers, so he wouldn't trust anyone more with such a significant undertaking.

Nigel nodded agreeably, plenty of questions on his mind that he promised himself he'd sort through after at least hearing what Vince had to say. Had it been a coincidence his old college acquaintance had sought him out in the crowd—or perhaps simply stumbled upon him and decided to ask—or had his invitation been extended this time for this very purpose? The reasoning was irrelevant, Nigel decided. There was no harm in hearing him out. A quick calculation in his head was all it took to decide that if The Group was as prosperous as it seemed, it was possible that he could make his entire yearly salary just from their business alone. Or more. So, iPhones were extracted, and a date and venue were set for the rendezvous. They toasted again and drank down their liquor, which Nigel already felt in his blood he'd regret in the morning. Then Vince introduced him to their Director of Finance, Nate Greenwood, who Nigel had played badminton with a few times at the Club when invited by clients but had never really had the occasion to converse with beyond that. Small world, they'd laughed, but then again, they'd always known it was in those circles.

Thus, he'd met Carmella and danced with an old college mate from his junior year at Morehouse—what was her name again? — when she came to pull him to the dance floor. He'd reminisced over dinner with his old Econ professor who, now greying, still taught there. And he'd danced again to a lively rendition of "Sway with Me" with an older woman he didn't know at all but who'd been laughing with Renée Dessommes earlier that evening. His evening had been consumed with such conversations and trivialities until, fairly inebriated and considerably talked out, he'd opted to make his departure before the valet situation became a nightmare.

Now, he rubbed his eyes as the sunlight streamed through his blinds and noticed that he hadn't even bothered to pull the covers over himself the night before. His mouth was dry as cotton in that familiar dehydrated way that he'd grown used to in college but seldom experienced nowadays. After his clothes from the night before were tossed in the dry clean hamper, he showered away the drowsiness threatening to pull him back to bed.

Standing under the hot cascade, steam building around him, he thought back on the night before, as morning showers often encouraged him to do, and regretted not making contact with the lovely woman with the accent of silk he'd met the night before.

Surprisingly, he hadn't seen her again as he'd figured he would, the room overrun with chattering consociates and dancing couples that made it hard to search out anyone in the controlled chaos. He'd thought about her in the car on the way home but pushed the thought out of his mind until then, assuming because he hadn't seen her again that all was lost and it was best left alone.

But as Nigel plodded down the stairs of his townhome, bare feet to the runner over hardwood steps, he glanced back at the letter on the island in the kitchen and wondered if he should have put more effort into looking for her rather than assuming fate would intervene on his behalf, at least to see if there really was the spark between them he'd thought he'd felt, because bachelorhood wasn't really turning out to be all that it was cracked up to be. He had no problem with the idea that his bed-hopping days may have been approaching an end. Nigel welcomed that end.

He didn't know what it was, but he was sure he'd felt something between shaking her hand and seeing her with Laney, noticeably uncomfortable but unwilling to make it obvious in a way that set her apart from all those other women in the room. In a way that showed her authenticity, betrayed her lack of pretentiousness. He could relate to that, appreciate it, particularly when surrounded by the alternative. Nigel didn't know if the feeling would amount to much more than that. But, that letter on the counter, coupled with waking up to the nameless and now faceless woman in his bed earlier that week, made him more than willing to find out.

Upstairs, he rifled through his wallet and found the card he'd been searching for. Right, that was his name: *Micah Barker*, he read. He turned that card over in his hand again and again, the happy alternative to contacting Vince and Laney for a social call such as this. He mulled the idea over once more, fingers hesitating over his phone. In the end, he dialed the number. If Micah was as equable as he seemed, maybe he'd be willing to give him Aaliyah's phone number.

BEAUTY AIN'T NOTHING BUT SKIN DEEP

JILLIAN

Fifteen. The heat steamed up from the asphalt and surrounded the four girls as they strode, sandal-clad, from the car.

Somehow, they'd all settled on wearing white for the day without even consulting one another, and they laughed at the coincidence when Paige pulled up at Jill's house to pick her up. Tennis skirts and tight jeans all gleamed with impeccable whiteness, almost blinding them under the hot beam of the sun overhead when they looked at one another for too long. The quartet shimmered like a mirage as they moved from Paige's Infiniti toward the crowded burger joint.

Inside bustled with bodies. Lululemon-clad soccer moms out with their car-fulls of boys and driving-age high schoolers the girls knew from school. Pia slid her curvy body into a dirty booth near a window just as a family slipped out, claiming their spot and motioning a passing worker over to clean the table for them. The guy nodded, tugging on his burger-joint-issued baseball cap, and went to grab a tub for the dirty dishes. Cammy slid in across from Pia, and Jill sat next to her while Paige waited outside the booth, her lean legs crossed at the ankles as she brushed invisible lint from her pleated skirt and waited for the bus boy to finish cleaning. He smiled at her as he finished, a broad, shy smile of picture-perfect teeth against eggshell skin and a dark goatee. Paige raised her brows and pursed her lips impatiently then slid in beside her sister when he took the hint and backed away.

"Ugh, I hate dirty tables. Gives me the heebie jeebies, all those toddlers drooling and licking the tables and touching everything then putting it in their mouths." Paige shuddered dramatically down to her toes. "Pia, you know that. You shoulda waited 'til he came to clean that shit."

"Shut up, Paige. Somebody woulda nabbed the table by then, and then where would you sit your tight little ass?"

Pia and Paige looked almost identical, with the same shiny, dark hair, the same playful eyes. But Pia carried an extra twenty or so pounds around. It curved her body and rounded her face, but Jill couldn't picture her without them. They lit up her visage and gave her a different beauty, a more mature beauty, than her sisters had, though she was the youngest of the Three. She carried it well, Jillian had always thought, and no one had ever said otherwise.

Paige shoved her sister, grinning and mouthing *Whatever*. She ran her fingers through her hair and let it fall over her shoulders. When their server came over with menus, Jill and Cammy shared one, handing the other back.

"Hi, my name's Crystal, and I'll be your—"

Paige handed a menu over to Pia with a flick of her wrist and held her other hand up to halt the smiling server from handing them another.

"We're good. I always order the same thing."

"Yeah, a skinny bitch salad," Pia giggled with her tongue stuck out, leaning over Paige to grin up at Crystal who was putting her notepad back in her apron pocket and fiddling with the forward doobie wrap she'd wrapped her hair up in.

"Hold the croutons, hold the dressing. Hell, hold anything with flavor or calories, will you?" She collapsed into a fit of snickers, and Cammy joined in lightly. Jill rolled her eyes and shook her head, burrowing deeper into the pages of the menu.
"Shut up, Pia!" Paige shoved her hard with a dropped jaw and palms outstretched.

"They don't even serve salads here!"

"Oh, my bad! Never heard you order anything else. You're gonna fall the fuck over with those giant tits if you don't put some meat on them bones." There was another fit of giggles as Paige turned away and back to the server standing over them.

"Ignore her. Bitch wishes she was a size six, *and*," she turned back dramatically her sister's way. "These are only Cs, large Cs, but Cs; I keep telling you that."

"Shiiiit, coulda fooled me. Jugs look like Ds."

"Well, they're not. I fucking wish. Anyways," turning back to Crystal, "as I said, ignore her. I stepped on her head when she was a baby and she's never quite recovered. I'll have a sparkling water, please. With lime."
After the rest of them ordered milkshakes and water, Cammy turned to her cousin with a raised brow over a grin. "That totally sounds like something you'd do, Paige."

"That's because I did. Bitch wouldn't stop crying so I stomped her." She laughed, neck arched back with her hair lapping over the booth seat.

"Yeah, you wish you did. Then I wouldn't be outshining your ass in every subject known to man."

"Only in dick sucking and cum guzzling, Pia. I admit, you got me there."

The girls both erupted into another fit of laughter, jostling each other with their shoulders and kicking each other while Jillian and Carmella watched their antics from across the table.

"I'm not the dick sucker, Paige. Everyone knows you've been having Vince's cock for breakfast, lunch and dinner. Don't try to be coy just 'cause his sister's here, girl! Don't worry, you'll be on the same campus next year, so I'm sure you'll squeeze time for seconds."

Jill froze, her body seizing as if trapped in a cold clamp.

Paige shrugged. "He's a decent enough lay, that brother of yours. For a high school boy, anyway."

She smirked at Jillian from across the table, took a sip of her drink when the server set it down in front of her and wiped the side of her mouth with a perfectly manicured pink fingernail. Jill sat stock still, her eyes widened in her head, feeling his hand clamping over her breast again.

Squeezing it.

"But who has time for recycling like that? I'll be on a new campus, new things to see and do. I'll probably hardly even talk to Vince."

"Paige, you're such a skeez. Don't act like that in front of Cammy; you know you'll traumatize her."

Cammy blushed a little in return and took a sip of her strawberry shake through the straw, ducking her head down to reach it.

His hot breath on her face.

His bear paws wrapped around her wrists until the bones cracked together.

Jill gulped hard, trying to keep it all down. Didn't even try to manage a smile, but instead let the queasiness in her stomach show on her face. Paige looked her in the eye, meeting her gaze as if daring her to turn away. Jill did, lowering her eyes back to the menu though the words blurred in front of her.

Down.

She pressed it all down. That acidic bile raising up in her throat, that cramping in her stomach. She pulled in a deep breath and held it, let it out, leaned in closer to Cammy as if she was studying the menu for a test.

The conversation recommenced around her. Phones were extracted and pictures shown around the table. Paige wrapped in both her sisters' arms at her high school graduation the month before. Cammy at her latest piano recital. She'd played some German composer whose name Jillian let fly into one ear and out the other in the same beat. She was concentrating on that hot cramp in her stomach, feeling it knead around in her lower abdomen as if readying dough.

He's a decent enough lay...

Jillian swallowed again and tried to steady herself in the flow of her friends' voices, in the chaos of the noise all around her – all clinking plates and chattering teens, like she'd found herself in some upscale other version of their school cafeteria. But when she did, she felt a warm flow gush gently between her legs. Jillian pulled her lips in and turned Cammy's way. Watched her lips move on and on about something Jill wouldn't remember five seconds later. She was trying to get lost in the rhythm of her voice, in the bedlam of them jostling and teasing each other instead of reimagining her brother's marijuana breath on her face just a few months earlier, his hand between her legs. The wind in her hair as she fell back on the bed in a flutter of school papers.

...for a high school guy, anyway.

There it was again, a warm swell between her legs that felt somehow sticky. It was a sensation she'd become less used to over the past semester or two. It was hard to even prepare for nowadays, it'd become so temperamental and unexpected over those months she'd waited for Vince to "grow up" and leave the nest. Over those months, she'd tiptoed around him and ate very little and kept her nose pressed into her books. When Sandi told her it was normal, that the stress of school sometimes delayed her period too, Jillian was relieved. She never mentioned to her friend that school had never stressed her out, though.

Jill raised herself from the table when the surprise of the suddenness and force of the flow finally overtook her. And when she stood, she realized she'd just been sitting there, in it, until it was too late.

"Cammy, gimme your cardi."

"Huh?"

"Just—" Jill motioned impatiently for her to remove the white lightweight she wore over her tennis dress, then stood and tied it quickly around her waist. Paige and Pia didn't even notice the abruptness of her movements until she was side-stepping out of the booth and hurrying off to the restroom, the cardigan tied around her hips "like it's 1994 or some shit," she remembered mumbling to herself, weaving in and out of the talking, laughing, buzzing around her.

Chill, she thought, smiling fakely at a mom as she stepped around her. The woman held up her hands, milkshakes in each, and let her pass with an annoyed little glare that said, *Watch out! You almost spilled this all over me!* But it was a perfectly normal style, wasn't it? Some school girl with her cardigan tied around her waist over her jeans? Sure, it was. Perfectly normal. Perfectly normal. *Just walk perfectly normal, Jill. Perfectly normal. No one knows, see? Not even them.*

She nearly collided with two other people on her way across the crowded restaurant to the doors marked HIS and HERS, and even she couldn't tell if it was because of Paige's words still pounding in her ears or because of the growing gush between her legs that propelled her forward, away. Away from them. There was a swell of panic rising up in her throat again. Was that what it was? Panic? No, she decided. Just vomit, of course. She was just suffering from a period same as other girls, probably even in that very room. It was normal. It was all fine. All completely fine.

Jill slammed through the door into the empty bathroom and took a moment to collect herself, bent over the bathroom sink, catching her breath, palms flat on the counter. When she finally raised her face to see her reflection, she remembered why she was in the dimly lit bathroom in the first place. She tore her eyes away from the mirror and pressed her fingers between the legs of her white jeans. When she drew her hand back to her face, there was the unmistakable smear of crimson on her fingers. It smelled like copper pennies left too long in her closed fist under the summer sun. She crinkled her nose and pulled her face away. Stared at herself in the mirror again and turned the water on to wash her hands.

Her eyes darted around for a way out of this mess, deciding between running back out to the table to ask for a pad or tampon and closing herself in the nearest stall to stuff toilet paper in her panties to the catch the flow until she was safely back home. The bathroom door swung open as Jill turned the water off. The server from their table—what was her name? Crystal? —smiled her way, heading toward the nearest stall.

"Hey."

"Hey." She paused, one foot in the stall and turned back to Jill. "Oh, um, you've got some...I mean, it looks like..."

"I know. Do you, um, have a pad or something?"

"Yeah, no problem. Just a sec; I'll go grab one from my bag."

The girl vanished around the corner and the bathroom door swung behind her, but it'd hardly swung shut when Paige charged in a few moments later.

"What's wrong? You just left and—"

The door swung open again and Crystal stepped past Paige, handing Jill a tampon. "Hey, this is all I had. Do you know how to use these?"

Jill started to nod gratefully, reaching for the small package like she was reaching for salvation. Their hands touched lightly, like a warm flow of light to brown chocolate, as the tampon exchanged hands and Jillian smiled appreciatively at her. But Paige stepped between them, scoffing with one side of her mouth pulled into a jeer.

"Jill, do you know her or something?"

"Uh, does she have to know me for me to help her out?" Crystal started to step around Paige and back into the nearest stall, accepting Jill's gratefulness with a small nod of her own.

Paige pivoted to face her again, her index finger in the air already. "Um, yeah, maybe she does." Turning back to Jill, "Why didn't you tell us you were...having trouble?"

Crystal laughed as she turned to close the stall door. "Shocker. I wouldn't come to your ass for help either."

Before she'd even fully closed the stall, Paige's hand was against it, pushing it open. Crystal stumbled back into the stall a little, caught off guard.

"Oh, well, it's nice to see you can conjugate verbs and all, with that shitty-ass public-school education you must have, but I wasn't talking to you, bitch. And if I wasn't talking to you, you don't need to respond."

"Excuse me? Are you fucking serious, girl?"

"Yeah, I am, actually. So, mind your fucking business. We didn't ask for notes from the peanut gallery. Jill, if you weren't feeling well, you coulda told us. We're here for you." Paige's voice lowered an octave, becoming light an airy in its staccato of concern.

"Paige, it's fine. It just...happened so fast." She looked over Paige's shoulder and caught their server's eye. "Thank you, for real. That was really cool of you."

Crystal swung the stall door open a little wider and stepped toward them. "*You're* welcome. But *you*." Her eyes were boring a hole right through Paige. "*You* need to learn some damn manners, girl. I didn't do nothin' to you. Just trying to help your girl out, which, if you were a better person, she mighta asked *you* for. So, check yaself."

"Oh, okay, Aunt Jemima..." Paige rolled her eyes and turned back to Jill, concern glowing through on her face. She reached out a hand to rub Jill's arm. "Get cleaned up, okay, and I'll take you—"

The server touched her doobie-wrapped hair and finally snapped out of her shock. "Excuse me, what the fuck did you just say to me? What, you think you're better than me? You think 'cause you got on some prep girl shit and drove up here in some fancy car I'm supposed to bow down to you or somethin'? Listen, you don't know nothing about me, so don't go judging me or my hustle."

"Yeah, well hustle your ass on outta here. I got it from here, alright? I'm sure our food's up by now, and my folks are out there waiting for you to bring it."

"Oh." The girl chuckled, wiping the corner of her mouth with her thumb, shaking her head. "Oh, I see. You think 'cause I'm serving up in here I'm your beck and call girl. You think that fancy skirt and that proper talk got sway over here, is that it? You don't even know me. You're just another high sidity, bougie bitch I see coming in here all the time. Think you're better than me. Judging me, what, because I work here? At least I know *how* to work for what I want. All you know how to do is sit around with a horse between your legs and silver spoon in your mouth, swiping your daddy's platinum card."

"Oh, you may think you know who I am, but you don't get it *'twisted, sistah.'*" Paige over-pronounced those words and Jill cringed with the weight of it in the air. "I came in here to help my friend, not to argue it up with *you.* If you knew something was wrong with her, you shoulda marched your black ass back out to that table and told us. But no, here you are—"

The bathroom door swung open again and Jill turned, hoping to see Pia or Cammy—anyone who could talk some sense into Paige and pull her away from the unnecessary argument. But it was another server, shoving her cell phone back into the front pocket of her apron.

"Yo, Crystal. You've been double seated again. Been looking for you everywhere, girl."

Before Crystal could respond, the girl pulled her face back through the opening in the door and was gone. Crystal sucked her teeth so hard the sound reverberated in the air and turned her back on them, shaking her head and moving toward the door.

"Oh, and don't worry about your tip, either!" Paige called after her. "I don't mind putting that on my sidity ass platinum card for you either, boo!"

EARNING STRIPES

DELANEY

Delaney had always loved the smell of bookstores and the low drone of activity they emitted. As she walked into the Barnes and Noble, college students huddled in quiet groups on the floor while housewives killed time near du Maurier and the self-help sections. There was a muted humming, a sound just above silence, that Delaney especially enjoyed. The sound of light footsteps and low conversations, the opening and closing of books. It relaxed her, gave her time to reflect and the privacy to complete a thought when life was too busy to permit her to do so otherwise.

This new period of frivolity and pretenses, which she feared would be permanent now that she'd entered into it, hollered out for words of undeniable substance, phrases of grit and perseverance, of struggle and strife—in short, of ordinary life miles away from cotillion and private social circles, away from the snobbery and obliviousness to human strife that made her secretly annoyed in its presence, nauseous at its height. Hence, words of dissension replaced actual dissension in her day to day, and it was those words as reminders, like news constantly playing in the background of her mind, that sparked something within her she often thought she'd forgotten or left behind. She admired them, yes, of course. Not only because they'd stood up when others had stayed seated in the complacency of history, but because they made her feel that she, too, could stand up in the complacency of copiousness.

So, she read on when she was alone, wondering if she was an utterly unappreciative ingrate who should shut her mouth and stop biting the hand that fed her, wondering if those that she most respected and admired would laugh in her face and think her some traitorous apostate, some impostor who'd defected from real "blackness" long ago and forgotten about the struggle she'd spent years studying and being immersed in personally, because she felt she had abandoned the collective struggle that she herself had been so passionate about just a few years prior.

Vince, naturally, found her interests—and her internal struggle, on the few occasions she chose to bring it up to him—to be endearing in a way that was both condescending and revolting. Condescending because he thought it was so "cute" that she had such interests, often kissing her forehead and running his fingers through her hair when he said this, and revolting because he believed himself to be above them. He was more than happy in his obliviousness, she'd realized sometime just before grad school. He was purposely oblivious, seemingly going out of his way to avoid any mention of matters that did not intimately touch their little world.

He'd likely learned this skill from Addison, who'd taken her role as the Jackie Kennedy of the Gold Coast after the passing of Florence Dessommes with a cool air of entitlement that had made her much more of an enigma and societal force than her sister-in-law could ever have been. Delaney could not imagine a single thought of societal reflection or dissent having ever graced

Addison's pretty little mind—and certainly not having ever been taught to her offspring, for that would've been like teaching Darwinism to the Orthodox. At such, Delaney imagined, she would have waved her hand dismissively at the poor, huddled masses and said something shocking like, 'Let them eat cake.'

She'd realized the absurdity of ever assuming that she and Vince—or any member of his family for that matter—could see eye to eye on such matters years before. If voiced, she would only label herself the interloper she often felt she was there. So, she remained silent on the subject, only allowing herself the occasional reflection when both time and her conscience permitted. Deep in these thoughts she found herself, Adele's crooning filling her earbuds, when she heard her name called over the music by a tenor voice from behind.

"Laney? Aaliyah's friend, right?"

She pulled the music from her ears and turned to find Micah Barker standing behind her, tying back his locks. "Oh, my goodness. Where'd you come from?" She tiptoed as he embraced her.

"I thought that was you over here, but I wasn't sure."

"Oh, yeah, I'm not in the get-up today," she laughed, gesturing toward her distressed jeans and ponytail. "Hard to recognize out of costume, I'm sure."

"That was quite a party. Thanks again for the invitation. I really enjoyed myself."

"Good. I'm glad someone did. I usually hate going to those things." Laney laughed and turned back to the book she'd been browsing.

"You do? I thought Liyah said those were your thing."

"Ha! I guess you could say they're my thing as Mrs. Dessommes, but not as Laney Coker."

"Ah," a nod. "Gotcha." Micah stepped closer to her and gently turned the book in her hand to see the cover. "I guess that would explain why you're perusing Tricia Rose. That's remarkable. No, not remarkable—I don't mean to be condescending. That's refreshing. I mean, I wouldn't have imagined—I didn't think...I'm going to stop now while I'm ahead."

Delaney laughed and replaced the book on the shelf. "No, it's fine. I get it." A shrug. "I guess I would be surprised if I didn't know me, too. But I studied social work, you know, so this is kinda my thing."

"Really?" She couldn't miss the surprised raise of his brows, though he tried to hide it, and the lopsided grin that asked her to clarify. "I mean, Liyah never said. She's never mentioned it."

Laney propped her fist against her hip. "How *did* she describe me to you?"

Micah slipped his hands into the pockets of his slacks, dressed in work attire and suspenders that she found to be trendy and endearing, in a casual stance that matched her own.

"She really hasn't told me all that much about you, to be honest. She's mentioned that you've been really close since college, and I've gotten the impression that you spend a lot of time together, but we've never gone into an in-depth conversation about her other friends before." He thought about this for a moment then admitted, "I can hear how weird that may sound when I say it aloud. But, social work, that's really surprising. I'm..."

"Impressed?" They both snickered away the awkwardness, noticing it but not minding and never considering yielding to it. "That's an asshole thing to say, huh? I mean, you're obviously intelligent and all that, and I shouldn't have assumed—yeah, totally asshole. I hear it."

"No. Refreshing."

Laney grinned and he reciprocated. She noticed his awkwardness as he tried to process this unexpected view of her. She, amused, felt his reaction somehow verified why she needed to break away from the image that'd enveloped her somewhere along the years she'd been with Vince. She called him on it, obviously catching him off guard, to which he responded that Aaliyah hadn't prepared him for a real person. She'd prepared him for some faraway monument who he'd never expected to actually meet and who, with all the talk of parties and the infamous family she'd married into, certainly couldn't have been particularly intellectual.

They laughed together at this, the easy rapport effortlessly continued from their first meeting a few nights before. Then it was his turn to surprise her when she pointed out that he wasn't carrying any books, so what had brought him to the bookstore that afternoon, and did he need to go back to the office soon?

"The office? No, no. I'm done for the day."

A glance at her dainty Rolex. "Wow, lucky you. I couldn't pry Liyah from that office before six if I bribed her. You must really have some clout there."

Micah shrugged in a modest way they both knew was probably overly so and shoved his hands further into his pockets. "She could make the time to get out of the office if she tried. It's all about organizing your schedule and prioritizing, really."

"Puh-lease. That woman's life is on the thirty-third floor of that building. She freaks out at even the mention of leaving before five. Says Peterson makes little comments to her about her work ethic when no one's paying attention."

"I don't think he would mind her leaving, and I definitely don't think he'd say anything inappropriate like that. The guy's decent enough. A little egotistical and self-entitled, maybe. But who wouldn't be?"

"Oh, who wouldn't be, huh?"

"I've had my hands full the past few months, so I can guarantee her it's not a race issue."

Laney sucked her teeth. "Sounds like a 'boys will be boys' issue to me."

Micah smiled. "Liyah's the sharpest junior on our floor by far. No way they'd pass her over. I've just been with the firm a little longer than she has. She's still paying dues, but she'll get her shot."

A brunette excused herself and brushed past them on her way to the coffee bar. Micah watched her pass then asked Laney if she'd like to grab a cup themselves. Laney hesitated, glancing from him to the Starbucks, weighing the distance and the unexpected turn this conversation had taken. But it was unexpectedly welcome, this impromptu reunion that'd taken her mind away from heavier things and brought a smile to her face. So, she agreed, and five minutes later the two were sitting in two armchairs, face-to-face, with a small table between them and blonde roast in their hands.

I I

"So, what *are* you doing here anyways? You never said."

"Oh." Her new acquaintance leaned back into his armchair. "I mentor a group of high school boys here on Monday and Thursday evenings. Talk about life issues, help with homework, that sort of thing. Started out trying to mentor with Big Brothers Big Sisters, but there's just so much work that needs to be done. Mentoring just one kid didn't feel like enough for me, if I could do more...but I guess you know that already. You know, from your background."

"I do. I used to volunteer at centers myself." She pretended not to notice the pause and gave a nod, giving permission for him to continue.

"Boys in my group are...just what you'd expect really. No one else to turn to, look up to. Brothers and dads behind bars, mamas making a monthly trip to the welfare line, running scams you wouldn't believe. Most of 'em can work a switchblade better than a pen. Anyways, Mondays and Thursdays are apparently the only days there isn't something on TV or in life good enough to take precedence over their education or future prospects."

He laughed, which created a ripple effect she joined in on.

"Sounds about right. Glad to know there're still people out there willing to do the work in the trenches to really reach these kids. The only social advancement causes the people in my circle contribute to is their own."

"Yeah. Not all that surprising from what I saw the other night. You must be quite the anomaly in your crowd."

"Not really. I think it's assumed I studied out of convention rather than an actual intent to work."

"Oh, really? Is that common where you're from?"

"Where I'm from, no. Where I've ended up, absolutely."

"Sounds like you 'ended up' somewhere before the atom bomb dropped. They know what decade they're in?"

Laney laughed with him, settling back into her own armchair. "I hardly think it matters to them. So, how'd you get started with this mentoring thing? Through Big Brothers?"

"Oh no, actually. No, I can relate to those kids on a personal level for sure. I mean, I wasn't too much different from them a decade or so ago. One day I saw this need and...tried to do something about it. What else can you do, right?"

"You were?"

"Pfft, yeah. I'm basically just a bootstrap kid from Southside Chicago. Some shit went down in my neighborhood sophomore year. Good friend of mine got caught up in some mess, killed. Knew that wasn't the life for me anymore. I mean, I'd always been good in school, but book smarts aren't always most valued in some of those 'hoods. Same story you always hear, you know. Decided to stop pretending I wasn't smart, stopped trying to fit in 'cause fitting in could get me killed. Worked my ass off to get my GPA back up, tried to keep my head down, stay outta trouble. Ended up at Syracuse."

"Ended up, huh? Sounds like you're in the same boat as me: nothing much to complain about so far as 'ending up' goes."

Over the rim of his coffee, "Touché."

"And the group, how'd that come about? You already knew those kids?"

Another slow sip of his coffee. She mimicked him, and they listened to the quiet between them as they did so.

"I actually, ah, met one of them at Wal-Mart while he was trying to shoplift, if you can believe it."

He told her about that day.

About the boy he'd met shoving Ramen down his over-sized jean pockets. How he didn't think he would've stopped to help had it been electronics or something superficial, something trivial. But to see that young teenager risking being caught to eat—as it turned out, to feed three other siblings, too—made it somehow too real to ignore. But once he heard the words spoken out loud, telling the boy to stop, that that wasn't the way he wanted to go, that he actually wasn't some rich Uncle Tom, as the boy had called him, but someone who had been in his very shoes just a few years back, he couldn't take those words back. And he didn't want to. He paid for the food, enough for them to both walk out with bags in each hand, then offered to take the boy home and asked him what his story was.

Then he didn't hear from him again.

It wasn't until the boy—Jordan turned out to be his name—called him a few weeks later that Micah even thought about that night again. He'd assumed the phone number he'd offered would've been flung in the garbage as soon as Jordan stepped out of his car with his loot in hand. But there he was right there on the line, breathing through his mouth like he'd run five miles, saying he was in a scrape. Saying he knew this was a long-shot, but could Micah please help.

'Man, I know I got myself in some shit, and I'm sorry. But I know my mama ain't got no money to get me up outta here so I can even make amends for this shit.'

Micah was surprised at how easily he'd pulled on his sweatpants and how he hadn't been nervous to get in his car and drive it away from his comfortable living in Midtown and into Stone Mountain—an area as known for its roots in white supremacy as it was for its current near poverty—to the jail overlooking the dark highway. How he'd picked Jordan up, paying the meager thousand-dollar bond, and made Jordan tell him how the hell he'd ended up with a disorderly conduct charge—something about drunkenly toilet-papering houses before sex with a white girl whose boyfriend had come looking for her. He was the only one who ended up in jail, and his moms couldn't afford bail like that, Jordan reiterated. In fact, she'd probably be shocked as fuck when he turned up back at home, because she'd told him before if he ever got arrested again, she'd leave his narrow ass in there, 'Cause 'ain't nobody got money for that.' So, he'd called Micah, the number still in his jeans pocket, one of only two pairs that he owned.

And, so, it had started from there, Micah asking if he had any other friends who were in the same situation as him—hard up, without options, but smart and willing. Willing was the key word, he told him. It sounded like an illegal proposition to Jordan, and he wasn't necessarily against that, but Micah assured him it wasn't.

"Meet me at this bookstore on Sunday. Oh, and bring your books."

III

"So, why'd you choose that field of study?" The question came after Laney had sat speechless for a matter of seconds that passed clumsily on until Micah broke the silence with a throaty laugh. She joined in, laughing at herself, really, for her bemused reaction to this man who'd managed to surprise her in more ways than one. They settled back into their chairs as well as into the conversation, the discomfiture of unfamiliarity forgotten, if ever it had existed between them at all.

"That's a whole other story in itself, really."

"I've got the time. How about you?"

There was that lopsided smirk she was beginning to become accustomed to, a smirk that urged her on and lightened the mood. Laney mulled over what she was about to say before she said it, a byproduct of being a Dessommes, even if just a second-hand Dessommes. She'd become accustomed to small margins for error and instant criticism at the slightest blunder. But when she heard herself speaking in the space between them, other customers milling about near them, she realized that she'd opted not to censor herself with him as she was so used to doing.

"I think it was the disdain. There was such...disdain in the community when I was at Spelman. Not all the time, obviously. Sometimes it was great. Sometimes there were those times when I felt, I don't know, like I just belonged there. Like I'd been waiting my whole life to be there. But when I felt it, it was blistering, at least to me."

"What do you mean?"

"I guess I wasn't accustomed to the way of life going on outside the gates of the school, so it staggered me, for sure. Sometimes it felt like...like fingers at my throat. It was suffocating. The poverty, the struggle. Right outside my dorm window. And that area, I mean, it used to be such a bustling area for blacks, you know? But by the time I got there, it was all dilapidated and falling apart. All that was left sturdy was the schools."

Though she'd set those memories aside years earlier, at the nonchalant suggestion of Vince, there was no denying how quickly they flooded back to her at the slightest beckoning.

"Didn't matter I went out into the community, that I wanted to do my part, ladle soup, volunteer, whatever. I'd still get that look, you know? Even from the kids sometimes, like it'd already been engrained in them to think that way, to hate me. I'll never forget that feeling, that...realization. Liyah didn't seem to notice. Rather, she was used to that. You know, she's from Jamaica Queens, so she's no stranger to that kind of street mentality. But I wasn't prepared for a culture clash like that. Not in the slightest."

"You grew up sheltered then?"

A hesitation before she corrected, "Not sheltered. Tolerant. I'd never experienced intolerance like that before."

Laney ran her hand over her hair, looked away from him and then met his gaze again, hearing her words repeated in her head. "Sometimes, when I was outside those gates, they looked at me like I didn't belong. Like I wasn't one of them. Like I wasn't black, too. Like I didn't understand them. One kid even threw some little rocks—you know, like, pebbles? —at me and some girlfriends while we were walking down the block. He just whizzed by on his bike before we'd even really processed what'd happened. Thought it was funny. You remember, that was back when the neighborhood was being gentrified, and, I mean, I guess I wouldn't have liked it either...I remember I raised my hand to throw something back at him. Micah, for years I looked back on it and thought, I *shoulda* grabbed him, threw my drink at him, something. But he was gone too fast anyways."

Micah leaned forward, elbows on his knees. Laney watched his coolness slowly morph into something different, into something more serious and pensive. She sighed and shook her head again, trying to pull herself away from those recollections that she hadn't pulled out from their hiding place in years. Re-focused her eyes on him as he watched her curiously.

"I think I wanted him to be a surrogate for all of them when that happened. Just in that very moment. Maybe I was frustrated with it all—with the culture shock, with that snootiness coming from Vince's folks. You know, with the history of our people I was coming face-to-face with every day but couldn't make them understand. All of it. I just...snapped in that moment. It was too much. Those rocks, they were too much."

Micah met her gaze, searching. Laney squinted, remembering.

"You know, really it was probably those frustrations, that confusion, that drew me in closer to Vince and his family if I'm being honest. It's weird looking back on it now like this, talking out loud...but they were safe. My parents died the summer before my senior year there, about a year after we met, and they were there as easy replacements. Vince was there as an easy replacement. They were civilized," she accented with air quotes, "and polished and opened all these doors I'd never really thought about before. And I...I needed something. Anything. Tangible. Does that make sense? I wanted to knock the hell out of that boy, but he rode away, and I felt..."

Laney let that thought trail off, because she really couldn't put her finger on how she'd felt. A little boy ran past them on the way to his parents, shouting about a puzzle he wanted them to buy for him. Laney welcomed the display of overindulgence from the boy who'd offered her a way out of those thoughts. Who knew what she would have found if she kept overturning those stones of memory?

"You know, black or white or any color or creed in between—suffering separates people. Always has. Earns you your stripes. That's something you gotta understand if you don't already. If you do social work. They see you as some fancy college kid in your designer sunglasses and they aren't gonna necessarily respect you. Where're your stripes, you know? You ain't one of them. Ladling soup is all very well and good for *you*, but they probably saw it as condescending, like you thought you were better than them, like you thought they needed you and your charity. Nobody wants to feel like they need charity. For the boys in my group, respect and that—that shared experience of suffering–those are the difference between authenticity and fraudulence. You can barter and negotiate it like tangible currency in those neighborhoods, really. One of the few truisms you can still find in commercial rap today."

She laughed at that, as he'd meant her to. "They do this self-segregation into hierarchies of misfortune thing—of who's got it worse. What a waste; that's what I thought."

"Maybe that was your problem there: you were still thinking in terms of they versus us. You were segregating too, just in a different way, and that ain't helping nothing. Ever thought about that?"

"I realized exactly that, actually. Funny thing is I didn't learn it from them; I learned it Vince...and from Addison. Vince's mom," she clarified at his raised brows. Delaney shook her head at the thought. "I told Vince about it that same day. Just, you know, casually, in that oh-how-was-your-day talk people do. And he—"

Another shake of the head, another laugh. "He was furious. Not that some kid had thrown rocks at me and not because of what it meant—if he even realized what it meant—but because, 'That's the shit that happens when you're out there where you don't belong.' Can you believe that? He thought, 'Of course something happened to you. You had no business out there with *those* people anyway. Animals. They're animals.'

And I heard it. I heard that crack in his voice—that...fault line between them and us. And it was...just so loud and clear. Too loud and clear. That line. That divide. That gap. Crazy thing is, to this day, Vince doesn't know he's the reason I turned my major around. Doesn't know he's the reason I went into social work at all."

Micah leaned back with a nod and a satisfied leer. He hadn't discounted her as she'd half-expected he would. She'd jumped into that conversation without a life jacket, without even much thought really, not knowing what she was getting into or how deep the depth of his knowledge went. But, there he was, not only maintaining her attention but setting the pace for her. He continued watching her watching him. Watching her wrestling with those thoughts that she'd successfully pushed away for years, because there was no longer any usefulness for them in her life. Those questions that had been hard to ask herself all those years back, and the same questions that had then propelled her forward in her studies while forcing a self-examination of her own every time she was in the presence of those Gold Coast natterers. Perhaps the word 'sellout' had always played at the edges of her mind but had never been called upon until Aaliyah had touched that sore spot a week earlier. Now she wondered what he thought of her.

How had they gotten there, from unacquainted chatter to political reflection and personal histories? What turn had she followed him down only to find herself lost in the rabbit hole, pondering and slightly embarrassed under his tolerant eyes? His eyes relieved some of her fears, erased away her tensions. They gifted her with a softening sense of relaxation, some bond of trust she felt sure of.

"I'm sorry. I didn't mean to, you know, pry."

"You didn't." Delaney paused and watched him observing her once again. "And, even if you did, it's assuring, to say the least, to be able to talk to a real person. Someone I can actually have a conversation with." She laughed a little when she thought about it. "I'm obviously a little rusty. My mind isn't as sharp as it once was, I don't think."

"Too much champagne dulling your senses?" he laughed, once again allowing her an outlet for her apprehension.

"Sometimes, but really I think it's too much of everything else. But it's nice to talk with someone who navigates that gap a little better than I do. It's such a real thing, and I'm out of practice now. Been a long time."

Delaney's cell phone began a vibrating dance against the table top as they sat there and stared into each other's faces, not really sure of what to say next as a follow up to those exposés.

"It's my husband, Vince," she told him. "I should probably take this."

Micah's eyes narrowed, his lips pulled in. "The boy prince himself, huh?"

She paused and tried to read his face, but his eyes revealed nothing. "In the flesh." She reached for the phone midway between them on the table.

"Really, I'm sorry to hear you're so torn up. Discontent. Sounds like you're on a journey, just like the rest of us."

The rattling phone became almost deafening in her ears.

"Discontent? No, I'm not...I mean, I'm just kind of finding my way right now..."

She tried to smile the remark away, make it seem like a joke, but was met only with his seriousness.

"It seems like this isn't the life you really see yourself in. But you're a beautiful, intelligent woman. You're more than you seem, than Aaliyah made you seem, than everyone probably thinks you seem. You're smarter and more thoughtful and honest than you think, than I thought, honestly. It was a pleasure to really meet you today, Laney."

Delaney gazed at the phone as it vibrated, moving slowly across the table's surface. Micah eyed it too.

"You'd probably better get that. I see Jordan and Marcus walking up from the train now anyways."

And so, she did. She gestured that it would only take a second and walked to the next aisle to hear Vince drone on about his day or something like that—her mind was elsewhere. Only, when she returned, Micah was gone. All that remained of their leftover trash was a single, unused Starbucks napkin on the table. In Micah's scrawling handwriting: *To navigating the gap and talking to a real person* accompanied by his phone number.

FOR THE BIRDS

AALIYAH

The traffic was madness, as it usually was on Fridays, but today she welcomed the all-too-expected delays that jammed six lanes of northbound traffic and cluttered the back roads; she needed to put together an outfit in her mind before she got home.

Out of the blue, Nigel had called, thanks to Micah. So, as she opened the curtains in her bedroom and turned Nina Simone up on the stereo, she contemplated the few options for party-wear that she owned. "Blackbird" crooned, lulling her as it always did. She scanned her closet full of slacks and silk tops in search of some overlooked outfit she may have somehow forgotten.

Aaliyah settled on a pair of cigarette pants with a silk top and casual blazer, eying them for wrinkles or imperfections as she laid them out on her sleigh bed. She stared down at those articles, hands on hips, foot tapping on the wood floor as she considered her options, mulling over whether this was the image she wanted to present on this first date since God knew when. Delaney's advice reverberated in her head—something about letting her hair down and a stick up her ass. Nina serenaded her into a comfort that wrapped invisible arms around her and made her drunk on the possibilities of the night ahead.

Blackbird.

That always did it. Because, she told herself, she was no blackbird. She wouldn't be locked in this cage of self-inflicted loneliness. She would have to find a way to fly out, to be free of the emotional baggage that had held her down as far back as her adult memory reached. So, she reached for the pants. But then she pulled her hand back again.

After her shower, Aaliyah sat at her vanity table, her locks bound with a towel like her mother had taught her and *her* mother had taught her mother before that. She rubbed Shea butter into her arms and legs, those of an experienced runner. She stared into the mirror, eyes moving over every inch of her skin. It was perfection, silky and blemish free, because it had to be. There was no room for deficiency of any kind in her eyes. She had enough to make up for already.

Aaliyah had always known she wasn't the sensual, glamourous party girl that men slobbered over shamelessly, predictably. And she'd never been much with charisma either, to put it mildly. What she did have was an accent hard to cover and a natural shyness she often felt made her the weak link between her and Delaney. So, she'd always reasoned, she had to be flawless in everything else if she wanted to compete, whether at work or in life.

She'd been stateside for over sixteen years and, having recovered from quite the whopping tsunami of culture shock born from her first experiences with blatant capitalism, an onslaught of hyper-sexualization, and the clear devaluation of the family unit that these big-city Americans had fostered into their culture, she'd found herself slowly morphed into the mode of cynical realism that marked her unshakably to that day.

Like many of the children of her culture, she'd been sent for after her mother had come ahead of her several years earlier to establish a life stable enough to then send for her child and family. By the time Aaliyah arrived, three years after the departure of her mother that'd left her in the hands of her droll but old-school grandparents, she was nearly a teenager, still steeped in the traditions of communalism and apprehensive about going to The Big Apple, as her Gran had always called it. When she'd first come over, landing in the melting pot of Jamaica Queens, New York, that was supposed to provide some similarity to her former existence back in Trinidad, she'd tried and tried to talk like the girls in her classes, the Beckys and Ashleys of all colors and sizes who sat next to her and passed notes to boys across the room with a wink and a smile.

Her mother knocked her on her shoulder with the back of her hand the first time she heard the altered accent and told her, "Stop trying to be so prim prim, girl! I not bring you here for dat. You be yourself and succeed, not like that mess out there."

So, Aaliyah tried it her way.

There was always going to be a mask she had to wear, and most people with an ounce of melanin in them knew that mask well. They knew what it was meant to be and what it was for and what it covered, what it evolved from and what would happen without it. She had to remember to add the last consonants to the end of her words and to use proper verbiage, because the paler nation always assumed by the accent that she, of course, didn't know how. Sure, she could let that guard down when she was with friends and family, but Aaliyah wouldn't let anyone low fence her because they took her accent or upbringing for weakness or lack of education. By then, so many years and two degrees later, it came like a switch, same as her bilingual friends who could turn a language on and off.

Aaliyah had never been one to straighten her hair. That wasn't to say that they didn't in the islands, of course. People all over the world wanted to look Eurocentric in their own way, and even she had experienced a faltering moment of weakness early in college. She'd unbraided her two curly French braids and studied the kinks in her hair. Studied the curls and crimps that other girls never had to deal with, that her white friends always questioned her about in that way that had always annoyed her to no end, asking if they could touch her hair because it "looked so cool." After seriously contemplating entering mainstream urban culture with that sleek, billowing mane, she'd finally unplugged the flat iron and got her hair locked the very next day. Call it an act of rebellion if you like. For her, it was an act of freedom. Freedom from the stigma. She'd loved her locks ever since.

With that in mind, Aaliyah pushed the silk top and pants to the side and instead reached for a forest green wrap dress and a pair of suede spike-heeled boots she'd loved on sight but never worn. Spiked anything was usually too brazen for her, but what the hell, she reasoned. How many first dates did she have left in her anyway? She dabbed on a little bronzer and gloss and headed out the door before she could question herself any further.

Either it was good enough or it wasn't.

SOUTHERN COMFORT

NIGEL

Nigel stroked Aaliyah's hair as he lay in bed with her and stared up at the ceiling. Her laughter filled the whole room; she snuggled into his chest, and he wrapped his arm around her. It had only taken those weeks to lift the fog of mundane sexual encounters. And all it'd taken was a phone call.

A routine was starting to take shape, and he appreciated that. There was a tranquility in routine, in knowing he'd hear from Aaliyah every day, see her nearly as often, in knowing he'd meet Micah at the gym to annihilate the preppy corporate boys trying to hang with them on the basketball court three times a week. The newness easily morphed into something expected. Something that would be quickly settled with a short text with time and venue. Tailored slacks were traded for t-shirts and shorts, professional clothes shed first then mannerisms.

"Next time?" Micah would call back to him as they separated in the parking lot, pulling cell phones from basketball short pockets and turning them back on.

"Next time," Nigel would call back with a nod and two-finger wave without turning around.

When Nigel told him he'd taken Aaliyah out on the first date—drinks at a pretentious bar in Midtown where Aaliyah's accent had come out like let-down hair and Nigel had lost track of the time until he realized they were sitting alone in the darkened bar area—Micah grinned and said, "I hope it works out, man. That's a good one there, so treat her right, you hear?"

According to the outdated rules of Southern dating, it was somehow still the tradition for the man to make the first move in a relationship. (Imagine the anxiety he'd endured over the years on that rule! Should he kiss her now or not? Would she be offended if he touched her there, or would she think he was a pussy for not making a move at all? The options were endless and all eventually ended in breakups, be it a week or a year down the line.)

So, one could imagine how surprised he was when Aaliyah pulled him to her after their second date in the same week and pressed her lips to his. When she pulled back, Nigel could feel her apprehension, that lingering moment that tended to separate the women concerned about respectability and those who weren't. He was usually just glad that he wasn't the only one feeling the pressure; so that look of nervousness was always endearing to him. It was the ones without that brief twinkle in their eyes who really worried him.

When she kissed him, he could see the questions in her eyes asking if she'd been too forward, if he thought her brazen now, if she'd turned him off. Really, he was completely charmed; she had won him over in every sense of the word. She turned something inside of Nigel that most men wouldn't admit they had. Had he had a woman to make the first move on him before? Sure. But had he felt that feeling all those other times? No, never.

Laying there with her in his arms after their fourth date, Nigel felt like it was actually possible to be content. Maybe that was just the honeymoon high. They'd talked down in the living room for nearly an hour before allowing the wine to lead them, undressing each other all the way, upstairs where they both wanted to be. After glass number three, her heels were kicked off and her feet were in his lap; she'd twirled a lock around her finger, neck back. But Nigel didn't need to touch her to be satisfied. Just hearing that Caribbean lilt could charm the hell out of him, but he'd rubbed her feet, rubbed her leg, then took the glass from her and pulled her to him.

In his arms, Aaliyah laughed. "This is the first time I've been able to get a good look at this place. It's nice, you know. For a man's bedroom," she teased. "No, really, I like the décor. You've got a bit of style about ya, sir."

"Oh, is that right?"

"What's with the easel and piano downstairs? You paint and play, too, and never said anythin' yet?"

It was Nigel's turn to laugh. "No, I most certainly cannot play that piano, and my neighbors would be very upset if I tried, let me tell you. And the easel I got that when I went to Australia with a line brother. Hand-crafted."

"Nice to meet a man with a little culture, you know." Aaliyah nudged him jokingly.

"Culture, me? What gave you that idea?" Nigel nudged her back.

"Well, the artwork, for one. Are they real?"

"Course. Always bring back something when I travel and whatnot. That mask," he pointed to the wall near the master bathroom, "is from Kenya. The beads in that vase are South African and..." he turned to point over the bed, "That piece is Aboriginal."

Aaliyah smiled to herself, and Nigel realized he'd never impressed a woman with his taste in art. Not that he knew of anyways. Most didn't even notice. That made him snigger a little to himself and pull her closer to him. She looked around the room again then back at him.

"Why are you givin' me the eye like that?"

"You're beautiful in the moonlight."

Aaliyah's smile spread after a hesitant moment.

He asked her what that was about. "I felt a flutter." Then she grinned at him again. "I appreciated that little flutter, you know. Every woman needs to feel that once in a blue moon just to know all the peeling and waxing and makeup dabbing aren't in vain."

Nigel rolled over onto his back. "You're stunning anyway, of course. That's what first attracted me to you. I know that's shallow as all hell," he admitted, "but I couldn't even focus when Micah said your name. I just thought you were fucking...stunning."

Nigel traced a line over her skin with his finger. He hoped he hadn't said too much, made it awkward, but knew by instinct that he hadn't.

Aaliyah closed her eyes. Recommenced their stories about their time in college. They'd been on the same campus for three years and somehow never met, though she was only a year behind him.

"You don't think it's strange we know so many of the same people but only just met?"

"Naw, probably happens all the time. That's how socioeconomic stratification works, you know. We all end up in the same circles and stay there."

Their voices overlapped, interrupting each other and finishing the other's sentences. She held his hand; her hair lapped over his shoulders when she kissed his cheek. Aaliyah sighed and looked over at the analog clock. It was almost three in the morning. She started reaching into the darkness, groping around.

"What are you looking for?"

"Kills me to say, my panties. Where'd you put them?"

"There's no telling." Nigel rubbed her leg, sitting up on his side.

"It's three already. I should get home so I can get up in the mornin'."

"Or," he suggested hesitantly, "you could stay here tonight."

"Here?"

"Yeah. I mean, it doesn't have to get all weird just because we had sex for the first time. We're adults. Adults have sex. And I definitely don't want you thinking I think of this as some fling, Aaliyah. You're welcome to stay."

Aaliyah hesitated, one foot over the side of the bed an inch from the floor. Chewed the inside of her cheek. Nigel called her on it, and she laughed quietly in that way women do when they're embarrassed.

"Well, even if I did believe ya, which I want to, I don't know I want to get so close so fast, you know. It's only been a few weeks."

"And...this was our first time having sex..." he urged her to say what she was thinking.

"Yeah, and there's that. But you know, there's a meeting about that campaign I've been aiming for in the mornin', and I didn't expect to come over here and cut a night in your bed—"

Nigel put his finger to her lips, laughing, so she did too. "We're really far past that now, Aaliyah. Or, at least, I hope we are. I want you to stay, if you will. I mean, I don't always like having people in my space. But I like you in my space. I don't know, it's just so—"

"Organic."

"Organic."

"Guess I'll have to be Speedy Gonzales in my closet in the mornin'." And she pulled her foot back over the side.

Work would always be there, wouldn't it? He *did* want her to stay. Maybe if he took a different approach, if he went with his instincts on a woman and shook his usual routine up a bit, things would work out better this time. Loneliness avoided, but with purpose and a future this time rather than only for the moment. Every man eventually went looking for his other half, and he was no different. So, this time, he would just go with it. Fuck the consequences; they always seemed to come anyways, even when he did things just right and followed all the rules, pulling out chairs and being the shoulder to cry on.

Nigel wrapped his arms around her tightly, drawing her in. Maybe she was ready to take a different approach, too.

EMPTY HANDS, IDLE MINDS

DELANEY

For Delaney, those weeks slipped through her fingers with little consequence. Oh, there was the luncheon with Carmella and the curating of décor for The Group's back-patting celebration, but it was mostly a blur, and she knew she wouldn't be able to remember anything in particular about it in hindsight. Then there was the decision, decided by Addison and Renée, that she would host this year's Thanksgiving dinner, an honor Delaney knew she should have been thrilled about but found herself nearly indifferent toward. This, of course, made it all the more difficult for her to explain to Aaliyah what the ceremony even meant when she came over that Thursday for banter and wine, having few real-world applications to reference. In the end, Aaliyah shrugged it off, changing the subject away from baroque Thanksgiving plans that interested her none and back onto the topic of the phone number at the bottom of Delaney's purse.

Her habits and routine remained fixed most days, winding through the motions then releasing the turnkey in her back to do the dance all over again day after day. Of the habits she formed in those weeks leading up to Thanksgiving, her favorite was surely Calvados. She'd learned at Renée's party that it could make her fuzzier around the edges for longer, and so she tried it at home too.

The twisting away of the bottle cap slid comfortably into routine, and the splash of it into her glass became a welcomed sound in those days after seeing Micah at the bookstore and as the pressure of the upcoming acquisition attempt seemed to mount on Vince—Vince, who showed his distractedness with preoccupied little kisses to her cheek, when they encountered each other within the walls of their home, or with absent-minded strokes of her hair when they lay in bed together. Occasionally, those strokes to her hair would lead to petting, sometimes heavily. And when they fell asleep, she'd listen to his breathing until it lulled her to sleep as well, as snippets of old exchanges wafted through her thoughts.

Flowers in his hands, worry in his eyes. *"Laney, you've got to stop this! You're scaring me; this isn't normal."*

Her hand to his face as he sat on the edge of his bed in grad school. She grinned down at him and he tried to return the gesture but settled for nuzzling her hand between his cheek and shoulder. *"Go for what you want, Vince. You're a Dessommes, right? So, go for it..."*

But she always managed to shake those thoughts away and move on with her day. Either in spite of or because of her newfound affection for the heavier stuff, she neither dwelled on the chance meeting nor reached out to Micah as he'd proposed. Instead, she stared at his phone number from time to time, when life felt particularly tedious and her head threatened to spin with the banality of it all, folding and unfolding the paper yet never calling.

What was there to call about? She'd made it, hadn't she? She'd married a "somebody" and lived in comfort. In too much comfort, probably. She had achieved that goal without ever really thinking of it as one, and now that she had she felt her hands emptying. Her own dreams back-burnered, out of her hands. Even her own day-to-day schedule often snatched from her control. Empty hands, idle minds. Hadn't her mama had a saying about that? Something about the devil's playground? Or was it his workshop?

Still, the thought settled nicely in her mind. The fact that Micah made her question herself, her motives, her surroundings, nestled her in sleep and provided a softly urging hand at her back that was more of a comfort than anything else, but also something more—something that she hadn't yet named that felt to her strangely like a catalyst—this understanding that there was someone else out there, now within her circle, who felt what she was trying to express and who already had the words she'd thus far failed to summon on hand.

Aaliyah was off living her own life aside from the occasional Thursday drop in. Despite the fact that the most selfish part of Delaney occasionally begrudged her that—only for a moment, every other missed phone call or so—she knew her friend deserved it. It'd been a long time coming. Laney lounged in a steaming bath with her new friend Calvados when the question came to her. Was she going to storm in on her best friend's love affair, or whatever the hell it was she was currently embroiled in, only to whimper about her own non-action, her own lack of forward motion and feeling of stymie? Was she going to wait around for Aaliyah to once again be available as the springboard for her ideas and her worries, the wall from which she bounced her ball in contemplation? The thought made her tighten her grip around the glass, squeezing until she heard her knuckles *pop*.

What had happened to her that she even needed the comfort of her friend—or, of the glass in her hand for that matter—just to get through one day after the next? Jesus, what had they done to her, she wondered, then balked at then fumed, the bath water slowly fading from steaming to tepid as she did so.

Pop.

The specifics of when, where and how proved far less important than the facts. They'd done it. And she'd let them. They'd smothered her. And she'd let them. Pressed a pillow to the face of the old Laney and snuffed her out. And she had let them. Smiled on as they applied more pressure. Kissed their cheeks as they branded her theirs.

She'd let them.

It wasn't until after the sound of glass fracturing against the wall that Laney realized she'd wound her arm back to hurl it, and it wasn't until shards of glass *plunked* down into the bath water, liquor sprinkling her face, that she realized why she had. What other option remained but to do it herself, to find *herself*, wherever she was, wherever she may have been going? Because one day the Calvados would run dry, and she'd still be there, smothered.

One day she'd look in the mirror and be too far gone to recognize herself.

Snuffed out.

Laney lifted a shard of glass from the rim of the bathtub. She rotated it through her fingers staring into it. She wasn't too settled, was she? And it wasn't too late. This wasn't all there was left, because how bleak and ironic would that be?

II

Delaney hadn't moved from her bed in a few days, probably longer. Not since she'd returned to campus from her parents' double funeral.

A double funeral. The reality of it still slammed into her every day. Though she was the only child, thankfully, her parents were not, and her aunts and uncles had set her gently aside to tend to the funeral arrangements of their suddenly snatched-away siblings.

When she returned from putting her parents in the dirt in Texas, Laney trudged back onto the Spelman campus for the start of the new school year—the final school year. Vince picked her up from the airport in a clumsy silence she appreciated. Thank God he wasn't talking, filling the air with useless words, though she could tell he wanted to. Was fighting the urge to. She stared out the window as rain streaked down the glass, watching anonymous lives blur past her in the mist. Three blocks from campus, the slums closed in on them, the wreckage of cozy historically black neighborhoods now turned to drugs, to shooting, to ash and boarded-up windows. Vince drummed his fingers on the wheel of his new seven series then slid his hand affectionately onto her thigh.

Two little girls ran up the way away from them, ducking from and giggling in the rain, maybe eight or nine. The lighter-skinned girl with the box braids was barefoot and taller. The other one—the dark-skinned girl in the old and faded Ninja Turtles t-shirt, too-big jeans and short pigtails with mismatched barrettes—shoved her and ran off faster, both of them laughing.

"Girl, you better c'mon!" Laney thought she heard one of them yell. "Mama gone trip if we don't get that stuff from the sto'."

She watched them through the sheets of rain and the swipe of the windshield wipers. Ninja Turtle Girl was twirling in the downpour, face up to catch the drops showering her face, her mouth open and her eyes closed, and her sister was splashing in mud puddles. A least, to Laney, they felt like sisters. Laney smiled at their freeness as they passed them, hearing their shrieking laughter.

She didn't hear them whoop as Vince's car passed them, splashing panes of water up from grey puddles and crunching against the gravel. She didn't see the taller girl tap Ninja Turtle, stopping her twirling, or when she pointed at the car and said, "Girl, you see that rich folk car? Imma get me one, one day."

It was the year of graduate applications and enjoying their final steps into adulthood. Or, it was supposed to be anyway. The start of one thing and the end of another. Laney got out of the car and let Vince pull her suitcases from the trunk. But she stopped him short of helping her to her dorm. She registered the torn look in his eyes but didn't respond to it. Let him kiss her cheek and felt him watching her as she meandered through the rain up the walkways to her dorm hall. She couldn't remember any of that journey after, but she knew it must have happened because here she was, in her room, in some old boxer shorts and a t-shirt. She'd sloughed off all her bags and clothes when she arrived, and there they were still by the doorway days later. Other than water, she couldn't recall putting anything in her mouth since walking through that door. Maybe she hadn't.

There was no air conditioning in her dorm. It was broken or non-existent; she wasn't sure of which yet. As the summer rains melted into scorching summer days, a box fan rattled and blew hot air around the room from the window as she lay atop her thin sheets in her twin bed.

There was a knock on the door. Laney didn't move. When it came again, it was followed by the slow pushing of the door open and Vince's head nudging around the corner. She didn't even manage a smile, not even when he came fully into view and closed it behind him, a bouquet of tropical flowers in hand. Vince held the small, petaled fortune out to her. She watched him. When Laney didn't take the flowers, Vince sighed and set them aside on her clean dresser drawer, still empty of her clothes and belongings. With the flowers right by her face, she could smell their sweet perfume, study their unusual shapes and petals. She fixed her eyes on them and studied every thorn, every flower, every stem, unblinking.

Vince crouched by her bed, his knees spread on the balls of his feet, one hand to her face. He kissed her cheek and smoothed her hair back. When Laney still didn't respond, Vince sat next to her and traced a finger down the salt trail meandering down her face.

"Laney. Laney, you've got to stop this. You have to come out of your room." He paused for a response that never came, then pressed on, "I'm worried about you. Your friends are worried about you. Even my mom, she's worried about you."

"Your mom doesn't even know me."

"Yeah, she does. I mean, she knows of you. I talk about you to her all the time."

Nothing.

"Laney, you've got to stop this! You're scaring me; this isn't normal. It's been weeks already. You've been back here for days and you haven't let anyone see you."

"Weeks? Weeks! My mama and daddy—they're—and you're talking about weeks?"

Vince heard his mistake in the air and his face collapsed. He reached for her, pulling her close to his chest, up off the bed. She hung like a rag doll until he cradled her head to his shoulder. Laney breathed him in, smelling the scent of his hair and the faint, crisp aroma emitting from around the collar of his shirt. Her hands crept slowly up his back and around his neck until she clung to him even as he rocked her.

Vince raked his fingers through her loose, now-matted curls and kissed her head, her face, her arms, until her eyes got heavy. He was the last thing she saw as she closed her mascara-rimmed eyes and the first thing she saw when she opened them, hours later.

His position had changed, but the creases in his face had not. He sat on the bed with her, his back against the wall, feet to the floor, her legs thrown over his lap. He didn't smile at her when she opened her eyes. This, he seemed to understand, would be too painful for her. Instead, he touched her hand, squeezed it.

He's still there.

Reading a textbook whose title blurs as he closes the book and tosses it aside.

He's still there for her.

Vince.

Laney felt the hollow ache in her chest, the void left by two fallen parents taken from her in a collision of shattered glass and twisted metal while she was off living her life, probably laughing at some stupid TV show or feeling the warm sun on her face with her girlfriends in the quad, weaving through the throngs of Alpha Kappa Alphas *skee-weeing* and tight lines of sorors and grassroots activists passing out flyers in the crowd. As Vince moved toward her, making room for himself and laying down next to her, caressing her face again, she felt that void opening wider. That was a caress she would never feel from her mother again. Never smell her daddy's spicy cologne when he wrapped her in a hug and lifted her from her feet. *Oh, Laney Bear—there you are!*

She folded into her tears again, but this time Vince's chest was there to catch her sobs. This time, his arms were around her to hold her together, to keep her from puddling into the floor. She swiped the bouquet of flowers violently with her hand in a rattle of shimmering paper and ribbons, in a flurry of petals floating downward. She pulled him closer and he did the same. Kissed her forehead. Her cheeks. Her mouth. He murmured into her hair that she had all the time in the world. All the time she needed.

She's okay.

You're okay.

And she felt herself falling, tumbling, really. Freefalling in the air as her heart sank at the memory of her mama's throaty laughter, her father's wry smile as he doled out the dominos over the card table in the kitchen. But there he was to catch her. To buoy her up.

They laid there like that for hours, until she fell asleep again, woke up again then repeated the cycle. Until the sun was up and burning against her window, the sound of the box fan still lulling in her ears. Her mind was slick with the recentness of her loss, her tongue thick in her mouth. And she clung to him harder still that day and in those days after when he asked her to a family dinner and told her that he could take away the pain.

III

The door was ajar to Vince's downstairs office, and his tenor murmured into the phone as Laney passed it on the way to the kitchen. She'd left the mess of shattered glass upstairs and wrapped herself in a robe, traveling down the stairs leaving wet prints in her wake.

Vince's office had an altered feel from Laney's. While not intentional, it did serve as a mirror to their differing personalities, she'd always felt. Hers, all crèmes, suede, books and glass. Four hundred square feet of calm and ease and intellect overlooking the white stone pool house on their property. His, dark with sharp angles, calfskin leather and hides from cows he liked to brag had never seen barbed wire in their lives. There was a black marble chess table in the corner, which could only have been an antique passed down from somewhere back in their family tree. Every degree, trophy or accolade he'd ever earned, from high school to present day, was proudly on display to himself in his corner office at The Group, but even here he'd displayed photographic memorabilia of past exploits, travels, honors and graduations, as if as a constant reminder of his mastery of all things worldly.

It was while pouring the last bottle of Lecompte Secret Calvados down the kitchen sink that she heard his voice raise above the murmur. She shook out the last of the twenty-four-hundred-dollar bottle—how many of these must they have gone through at the party? —and tossed it in the garbage, the glass clinking against the others discarded there. When she heard it again, Laney paused to listen. He'd put the call on speakerphone, and she recognized Nate's voice before Vince had even cut him off the first time.

"Fuck that. I don't give a shit about that, Nate. You and I both know that place is gonna be a goldmine."

"Naw, I don't think so, man. The numbers just don't support an acquisition like that."

Laney opened both doors of the fridge. Made herself a spinach salad next to the chef-grade stove and served herself water from the faucet. The volley continued, neither man gaining any ground on the other. Nate insisted Vince wait until he'd brought the other partners on—or at least the acquisitions guy. Vince refused; he knew what he was doing. Nate pushed harder, his voice growing sharper, more insistent, more firm, a sure sign of his friendship with Vince that he'd even dared under the circumstances. And yet, Vince pushed back, nevertheless unfazed.

Delaney set her plate down at the bar counter and padded closer to Vince's ajar door. Her bare feet made no sound, and even if they had, it was unlikely Vince's storm would have subsided, so incensed had he become by the checks and balances system that had been a hallmark of The Group since the beginning, first suggested by Florence Dessommes, who knew her husband and his ways with money well.

"No, Vince. Not until we sit down with someone who can give us better insight on this, so let's just wait on the acquisitions guy you're bringing on. I don't have a good feeling in my gut about this one. And, man, we really need to bring Carl in on this anyway."

"Goddamnit, Nate!" A boom thundered throughout the room, but Laney never flinched as she pressed her ear closer. His fist to the desk, a gesture of petulance she'd seen before. "This is not a fucking debate, and Dad has nothing to do with this. You know he's gonna step down soon, so just leave that part to me and stick to the numbers."

"Vince, you need to wait this one out. At least until after the holidays."

"I'm not in the mood for some democracy-type bullshit right now, Nate, man. They're gonna be here for the holidays *today*, and I want everything done. They need to *see* everything done. Numbers, everything. They need to see us ready to take this—you and me, and that's it!"

Laney rolled her eyes and allowed herself an exhale, a sound that was swallowed by Vince's resounding bellowing. She turned on her heels and padded away without another thought or backward glance. Power was something better used than left to get rusty, she'd learned. A Dessommes family trait that never seemed to skip a generation.

Nothing had changed, in that regard, and nothing ever would.

IV

Delaney heard Vince make his way up the stairs and stroll into the room an hour later, munching on a Granny Smith from the fruit basket on the bar. She stood looking out the panes of glass separating the bedroom from their sprawling backyard. He had an expectant gaze in his eyes, and she knew why. The elder Dessommes were back in town, a sure sign, if the calendar didn't suffice, that Thanksgiving was sneaking up on them. Vince asked her why she wasn't dressed yet and she shook her head, pulling herself away from both her inner reflections and the window. Delaney started to pose the question of what exactly the plans were for that evening with his family but bit her lip. She was sure the evening events wouldn't stray from the norm, that his assistant had already ordered something or booked somewhere. The details of their lives were always too trivial to handle themselves.

"Give me ten minutes."

"Try to make it five, babe. They should be here any minute."

This time, they were flying back from Vancouver just in time for the Thanksgiving festivities, having been gone long enough to have missed Renée's semi-annual soirée. Really, Delaney was sure, they'd missed it on purpose at Carl's urging, his taste and patience for flamboyant galas—much less those thrown by his younger sister—waning in his older years. But they would never miss Thanksgiving. Never. Especially as it was Delaney's first year at the helm.

She stood in the presidential walk-in closet contemplating what she should be wearing when she swung the front door open and greeted her in-laws for the millionth time. Now, as petty as it seemed, she thought of how she wanted to appear casual so Addison wouldn't think she was too eager, but not so much so that her mother-in-law would disapprove. All she needed was a fraction of a reason to start in on her, on anyone. At this thought she clucked her tongue, shook her head, sighed. She was too tired of it all to still be playing these games with these people. She was, after all, already one of them. Nothing that crotchety old hag—who had never in life actually been either crotchety or an old hag—could do about it now, so let her pick and flutter as she liked. She started to play it safe, reaching for a pair of dark skinnies and a blazer, but Vince came up behind her and touched her hand.

"I prefer this," he said, holding up a casual dress he'd bought her months before. It was long-sleeved light denim with a denim bow that tied on one side and a rather deeply plunging neckline. "You have beautiful legs. Let's see 'em sometimes."

"Vince, I'm wearing the jeans. It's chilly outside, and you know they'll probably want to go to dinner or something."

"So, put the blazer over it. I want you to look nice for my parents. Don't you?"

He laid the dress over the back of the chaise near the shelf for her sandals, kissed her cheek and walked out. Delaney stood there, holding the pants in one hand as she watched him exit, then grunted irritably and reached for the dress.

V

Downstairs.

Dom Perignon Rose Vintage. And why not? The holidays always called for a little something extra.

Delaney stood in their cavernous kitchen, dressed in the charming little denim dress Vince had picked out for her, complete with four-inch nude heels, turning the glass up to her face and sucking it all down, when she noticed the droning in the background of her mind. Or was it real? She couldn't tell. She poured another splashing fill into the flute, and it sloshed a little around the rim from where she'd carelessly over filled the glass. Thank goodness she'd only thrown out the hard stuff, she thought.

As she stood there working on that second helping of escape, knowing that she'd need it for the upcoming evening, she propped her hand on her hip and leaned back into the motion of drinking it down. That's when she realized that the Charlie Brown-like droning on in the background was coming from none other than Vince himself who must've come in while she was too deep in thought to hear or notice him. Now he was womp womp womping about something or another, leaning against the countertop with his Cole Haan-clad feet out in front of him as he always did. She wiped under her eye where a tear of exertion had welled and steeled herself to shake free from her thoughts and listen, because he assumed, as usual, that she was there to be his listening ear.

"...anyways, I've got it all planned out. I've got something in the works that should come through by tomorrow. Just waiting on contracts to be signed and all that. You know how it goes."

"Oh...yeah, I do."

She set the flute down harder than she'd intended, sending a hollow *thud* sound between them as the glass connected with the counter. Laney swallowed again and gave her head a little shake to clear it.

"Once it's all finalized, you have no idea. Mama knows I can do it, you know. Don't have to worry about her; she trusts me. But Dad. He's the one I need to impress. Just got to..." He made a snatch and grab motion in the air. "Get 'em right where he needs to be. No way he won't hand the reins over to me by the end of the weekend. He's gotta."

The doorbell rang, chiming throughout the house. Laney smiled Vince's way and tilted her cheek up to him when he wrapped his arms around her and kissed her.

"You look beautiful, babe. This's gonna be a Thanksgiving to remember, I bet you that."

VI

That first night the in-laws stayed over, they dined at Michelin-starred restaurant Addison was constantly raving about.

By the time they were seated in the sophisticatedly décored space, all six of Delaney's calls to her sister-in-law had been ignored, and there was really no surprise there. Jillian never cooperated with the flow of their plans, the current of their traditions. Nothing ever ran smoothly when it came to Jill.

Ever.

"You know she doesn't speak to me, and she talks to Vince even less than that, so I don't know what's going on with her, Addie. I don't know."

"Oh, it's not a question what's going on with her," Addison declared as she took her seat at the white-tableclothed table in the tasteful lavender and white room. "Her daddy spoiled the sense out of her letting her carry on as she does, and now she thinks she's gotten away with it. But mark my words, she will come around. She knows where her place is."

Laney ventured a glanced at Vince and Carl, taking their seats around the round table in the middle of quiet chatter that kept them occupied away from the women's. Laney settled in for a dinner of what she used to call 'tiny food' and now had grown accustomed to simply calling 'food.'

"I'm just saying, it doesn't seem like she wants anything to do with The Group, like she even wants to be around."

"And I'm just saying, I don't care."

After dinner, Delaney hugged her in-laws in the foyer of their home and watched as they retired up to bed. Carlton stepped aside so Addison could climb the imperial staircase ahead of him, and she spoke to him over her shoulder—probably about their second-born—as they ascended, one hand daintily sliding up the banister. Jillian's car was still not in the driveway as Delaney had half expected, if not hoped, it would be.

Some part of her had assumed they would come home to Jillian lazily lounging on the lanai, wrapped in an oversized sweater or eating a salad at the breakfast nook, as if she hadn't ignored a half-dozen calls. As if she'd ever actually use the key Vince had begrudgingly given her and she'd begrudgingly accepted at their parents' urging. But there was no sign of her, and to Delaney that was just as well. She kicked off her heels in the front hall and held them in her hand; Vince headed up to bed with a quick kiss to her cheek, and life carried on without Jillian's presence.

In the kitchen, Delaney gulped down a bottle of room temperature water, sidestepping the full bar and resolving to remain clear-headed. Her cell phone rang in her Kelly bag just as she set it down on the counter, and she reached for it only to find that it was Carmella Greenwood calling.

Delaney had always tried to keep Cammy as a just peripheral friend, despite Vince's counseling and Addison's assumption to the contrary. Delaney's resolve to politely ignore her had finally faltered sometime before the wedding. She'd feared it would feel more real, be more absolute, if she really accepted them—his friends, his family, his interpretation of the world—fully into her life. That is, until she'd walked down the aisle, Cammy as one of her bridesmaids that she hadn't really had a say in—and why not? It was a union in matrimony as well as a union for The Group and his Clan. Since then, Cammy always seemed to be in her immediate sphere by default, her sisterly prodding now becoming proverbial in Delaney's life. There she was, in the office chattering and planning, at dinner parties smiling sweetly behind her wine flute. She was everywhere, really. And Delaney came to understand that this was the world she now lived in.

This society of elitists that baffled Aaliyah and had only recently, and accidentally, been surmounted by Delaney had already been conquered by Carmella Greenwood years before, somewhere around her days of cotillion when she was still a Darensbourg, the quiet and demure younger cousin to the Darensbourg Three, whose beauty always seemed to outshine theirs with its quiet luminosity. In a way, she was everything that Delaney was learning to resent. At the same time, Delaney acknowledged that her life was on a crash course to becoming the mirror image of Carmella's if she continued on her current path. If nothing else, she had been an ally and liaison in that glitzy jungle, and for that Delaney was internally thankful.

At the bookstore weeks before, the nervous inkling she'd carried with her for a while had finally scratched its way to the surface and revealed itself: she *was* just like them, but somewhere along the line she'd allowed herself to become blinded to that with denial. She no longer had a secret fascination with those trust fund kids turned adult; she'd become one of them, slowly but surely and without her own consent. The thought of being like them— educated at the best schools, trained to be exquisite, articulate and dignified, but still lacking any valid substance or street smarts— sobered Delaney back to reality. Micah had granted her that, if nothing else, this understanding of her continued disillusionment with it all. And, he'd started opening her eyes to it so effortlessly. There was a whole world of strife and conflict, suffering and real decisions to be made that her counterparts on this side of "the gap," as she'd come to call it in her mind, would never truly understand, never honestly care about. They only prattled about it fashionably—so far removed from the situation that it was distorted in their minds—over their foie gras and framboise petit fours.

Micah's words had flown into her ears and sometimes over her head, forcing her to face that truth. Words that had challenged her in a way she hadn't confronted in years. He reminded Delaney that most of the pedigreed socialites she called friends left something to be desired in the intellectual conversation department. Although they all held a degree, it was the intellectual equivalent of a blank sheet of notebook paper for many of them. He reminded her that deep down she was from a different world. Maybe she resented that, being stuck between the two, never sure of who she was or where to turn. She knew there was a world aside from Prada, cotillions and three-thousand-dollar bottles of champagne. It was the kind of knowledge that could only be embraced.

"I wanted to remind you about our holiday dinner tomorrow night. I'm sure Vince has told you all about it, but tomorrow is a truly special occasion, Laney, so everyone needs to be there on time." Cammy's voice was soft and wispy, like a feather against the cheek, bypassing the unnecessary pleasantries. "He says the in-laws are back in town, so I know they'll be coming, too."

"Right, maybe even Jillian, if my luck runs out the way I think it will. Can you fit that many in at such late notice?"

"You're kidding, of course," Cammy laughed in that way of hers. "Leave it to me, honey, and I'll see you all tomorrow night."

PART TWO: TURKEY AND SMALLPOX BLANKETS

... the Negro is a sort of seventh son, born with a veil, and gifted with second-sight in this American world, --a world which yields him no true self-consciousness, but only lets him see himself through the revelation of the other world. It is a peculiar sensation, this consciousness, this sense of always looking at one's self through the eyes of others, of measuring one by the tape of a world that looks on in amused contempt and pity. One ever feels his two-ness, --an American, a Negro...two thoughts, two unreconciled strivings; two warring ideals in one dark body, whose dogged strength alone keeps it from being torn asunder. The history of the American Negro is the history of this strife, --this longing to attain self-conscious manhood, to merge his double self into a better and truer self. – W.E.B. DuBois, The Souls of Black Folk

NOT IN FRONT OF COMPANY

JILLIAN

Jillian closed her eyes, lying there in her bed next to the sleeping Xander with a Benson & Hedges to her lips, the blind-filtered sun rays leaving criss-crossing patterns over her face and throwing mid-day shadows into the corners of the room. A shaky exhale surfaced from her lips, from somewhere deep inside of her. From somewhere she tried to push away and forget about but that resurfaced on occasion like a salty wave lapping at her feet. She turned her head toward those hats because the sight always calmed her. Made her remember it could all be conquered. Someone had.

The shelves in her room held not the typical books or knickknacks she saw on others' walls but her grandmother's prized hats still in their hat boxes. One of them held the jewels she'd left for Jill. There were moments when should would—on rarer and rarer occasions now—pull one down and try it on. Tip the brim forward in the mirror and turn her head to admire herself in it.

Florence's hats gave her an odd source of strength, the kind founded in memory and respected tradition.

It was the morning before Thanksgiving Day and that was why, she knew, the musings had resurfaced. Today, she would have to go to them. She'd have to answer them. She couldn't hold off on it any longer.

The alarm went off on her phone, and Jillian sat up in bed. Sleep had overtaken her, she realized. The cigarette had burned itself out in the ashtray. Xander on his back, still asleep beside her, a hand flung over his head. The comforter covered one leg but exposed a patch of pubic hair. Fuck, it was moments like this when her mind really wrapped around the idea of leaving her family in the wind for good. Moments like this that, thankfully only came around on major holidays, leaving her yearly calendar bottom-heavy with the obligation of family.

And Laney.

There was always Laney.

II

Eighteen.

When she first met Laney at the dinner party arranged for that very occasion—the Dessommes did everything with flair, including welcoming new members to their household—she wasn't surprised. If nothing else, her brother was the quintessential Dessommes son. He was the malleable one, the pleaser, the one who fed into the Dessommes legacy bullshit. So, he would conform, she knew. She'd always known.

So, after years of skirt raising, serial dating and sexual mischief across his undergrad campus, he'd met Laney and lured her in. Perhaps it was the approach of graduation and true adulthood that egged him to do it. Maybe he'd always been aware of the ticking clock above his head, like a woman's biological timer, letting him know time was winding down, that his family would expect him to get serious with someone soon. Or, perhaps, he'd always had his eye on Delaney Coker and finally decided it was time to step up to the responsibilities of their surname and settle down with her specifically. Jillian didn't know. She hardly cared either, for that matter, but Sabrina had proved to be a constant and accurate stream of gossip and knowledge in that respect. That was a trait she must've inherited from her mother.

Vince had talked about Delaney before her coming out dinner, of course. But nothing was ever final, nothing ever mattered, until that dinner. So, when he brought her home, just weeks into his senior year of college, Jillian couldn't help but to think how perfect the timing was; he'd gotten it just right. What a girl he'd become, she'd laughed inwardly. Wanting everything to be so picture perfect and bow-tied.

When Vince came home from campus that night, Jillian was on her last night at home before flying back to campus to start her own semester. Vince announced that he was bringing Laney home to meet them all, right there over the squash blossoms and green pea purée. Her parents nodded, Addison with her flute of Viognier turned up to her lips and Carl with his knife and fork poised over his accompanying Porterhouse. They smiled and sighed a collective *finally* under their breaths. Or maybe Jill had imagined that part.

So, she's aware of the need for the dinner then?

Are you sure about this one?

Have you given her a lot of thought?

Because you know what this means...

The dinner party itself was a relatively intimate affair. Thirty or so immediate family members gathered over refreshments, mingling and chattering until Vince entered with his girlfriend in tow, hand-in-hand. Jillian was curious to meet her for the same reasons that Addie and Carl had been: he hadn't picked one of the

clan as they'd assumed he would. He hadn't picked Carmella or
Paige or one of the other Darensbourg sisters. He'd found an
outsider, Tilman style. And it was that fact that made Laney an
instant enigma and source of intrigue.

Her entry was quiet and graceful. Jillian remembered leaning
against the wall with Sabrina, fruit punch in hand, gazing at her.
From that perch in the corner, just to the side of the pianist hired to
play for the evening, the girls could examine her from afar. Jillian
was ready to attack like a hyena; anyone in love with her brother
was the enemy, surely. But there was nothing scary, nothing
menacing, nothing Addie-like about Delaney Coker. She was sweet,
smiling behind her hand and giving polite nods to those introduced
to her. She'd chosen a simple but accentuating little black brocade
dress for the evening, one that cut just below her knee but allowed
for the heart-shaped display of modest cleavage. Pearl combs in her
hair. Muted but porcelain makeup. Classic. Addie would love that.
So would Carl.

"She's not so bad, right?" Sabrina asked. "I mean, he could do
worse. You could be sisters with Pia or Paige Darensbourg."

Jill snorted at that one. "Oh, God, no! Jesus, I couldn't deal with
one of those cunts. Ma and Renée are bad enough as it is."

Sabrina never got the chance to respond. Laney approached the
girls head on, cutting Sabrina's retort short. Somehow, Jill hadn't
expected that. She was used to her wallflower routine (that Addie
loathed and always rolled her eyes at). No one ever came up to her.
All she ever had to muster at these functions was the occasional
polite nod and mindless chatter about her schoolwork, her choice of
major, her summer vacation plans. And that's what she'd expected
here; then she'd be back on a plane back to school never to think of
this event again. But here Laney was, smiling wide, strutting with
demure confidence her way. She hadn't expected her to walk right
up to her, without the chaperoning of Vince at her side, and say,

"You're Jill, aren't you?" Jill didn't know what to say, so she just nodded dumbly when Laney extended her hand and said, "It's really great to meet you. I'm so glad Vince has a sister."

It wasn't until Laney was whisked away by Renée and Sabrina jabbed her hard in her side that she realized she hadn't managed to utter a word during the entire exchange.

But the bathroom is what changed it all.

After the duck breast and Napoleons, the bathroom called Jill's name. She'd stashed a tin box of razors there, under the lid of the toilet, just in case, but even just a breath of air away from everyone would do her some good. She rushed in that direction, once the dinner plates were cleared away and guests had started mingling again. Her heels clicked across the parquet as the voices from the formal dining hall faded behind her with each hurried step. At the end of the hall, she turned the knob and stumbled into the bathroom, tripping over the rug that'd been pushed in front of the door. Laney was at the vanity, breathing deeply, fingers to the bridge of her nose, eyes closed until they flew open at the sound of the door being forced open.

A fleeting second passed where they stood there five yards apart, Jill's hand on the knob, Laney's dropped to her side. They stared at each other, surprised and unsure of next steps.

"I'm sorry, I—"

"No, I shouldn't be in here. I—"

Their voices overlapped then quickly subsided. Jill gestured toward the door. "You didn't lock it."

"Yeah, yeah I see that."

"You'll learn. You *always* lock the doors in this house."

Laney frowned, unsure of how to respond.

I'm so glad Vince has a sister.

Jill would've, could've, should've said something to her, asked her what she meant by that. An ally had likely been so close at hand without her even knowing it. But Renée ducked her head into the bathroom, gestured toward Laney and moments later she was gone, back in the flurry of well-wishers and gossipmongers.

III

Jill drove through the gate and continued up the long driveway toward her brother's house. There were gardeners blowing leaves down the manicured lawn and one still shaping the hedges. The lawn was freshly mowed, lined and rippling like a sea of green. The sweeping expanse was dotted with landscapers in the trees, lacing white lights into the branches up the length of the driveway and hanging Christmas reefs and twinkling lights on the doors and awnings of the house. The commercialism of the holiday season was now fully upon them. Jill drove past it all and parked in the circle in front of their home in no hurry to get out. She'd held off for as long as she possibly could, procrastinating on packing her bag and ignoring all six of her mother's insistent calls just that day.

Vince's black Bentley faced her, but there was no sign of Laney's car, and Jill wondered if she'd be forced to endure her brother alone for any period of time. She decided that she wouldn't—couldn't—and that they'd have to at least allow her the peace of mind of avoiding that displeasure. So, she lit a cigarette, reclined her driver's seat and enjoyed the calming inhale of nicotine and exhale of anxiety with the steady roaring of leaf blowers in the near distance. She didn't hear the massive oak door open, so Laney's knocking on her window startled her into dropping the cigarette, which rolled between the seat and the door after burning her fingertips enough to warrant a yelp.

She pressed the button to roll down the window. "What the fuck, Laney!"

Jill wiped her hands on her jeans and swung the car door open, narrowly missing her sister-in-law who jumped out of the way. She didn't notice the eye cutting Laney tossed her direction, because she was busy feeling under the seat for the butt and, finding it, flicking it into their driveway. Laney watched it hit the cobblestone and seemed to be resisting picking it up, closing her eyes and pulling her lips as if she was counting to some undisclosed number.

"Where's the asshole?"

"Not here."

"But that's his car there," she gestured toward it, as she popped the trunk and reached for her bag.

Laney pressed her loafer against the car door and pushed it closed, leaving an outline of dust near the bottom. "Yeah, he went with your parents to—"

"You can stop right there. I'd be lying if I said I cared."

Laney followed her toward the house, toward the four stone steps that led up to the front door and into the stone foyer. Past the mud room and into the main hall. From cobblestone to marble flooring.

Inside, Jill headed straight for the staircase and up to her guest bedroom. She'd only been to her brother's home twice since they'd bought it, but she'd stayed in the same room, The Wheat Room, both times. It was the room directly to the left of the landing of the staircase. A whitewashed oak ceiling capped the bedroom, the beams overhead towering, making the room feel cavernous. The walls were painted a tint of gold that reminded Jill of wheat billowing under the sun, hence, the silly name her sister-in-law had dubbed it. There were crème linens on the bed so soft they could only feel like home and a settee in the corner with an oversized throw pillow tossed onto it. The chandelier and floor lamp were both designs of some vogueish artist of the moment, as if anyone noticed or cared, Jill had thought when Laney had shown her to the room for the first time. The silk curtains floated airily away from the raised windows. Jill loved that room, but she'd never admit it to Laney.

"You know," Laney called up the stairs after her, "you don't have to wait for some big occasion to come visit, Jill. The 'prodigal daughter returneth' act is getting a little old, and, like it or not, we're family. You're always welcome here, and your room will always be there."

"Prodigal, my ass, Laney." She paused on the stairs, hoisting her satchel further up on her shoulder, and glared down at her sister-in-law. "By the way, you're looking nice and spry. Glad you finally got your head outta the bottle for once in your life."

UNCLE TOM'S CABIN

AALIYAH

She couldn't have known, but she should have.

Yet, until that moment there was buoyancy in her step walking into that boardroom, notepad in hand. It was one of those new-millennium boardrooms, the kind that was glass on all four sides and hinted at both money and a new-age work environment. Hipness, an open mind. The staff didn't really fit that bill, though, creating a disparity of environment that would have been puzzling had she ever lended time to trying to figure it out. Instead of eager and innovating Millennials, the office was flooded with die-hard Republicans still young enough for after-work hipster jeans but old enough to want to follow in their conservative parents' footsteps. They golfed on the weekends, chaffed about the new boats they'd taken out on Lake Lanier the week before and were midway to the right in their ideologies.

Sunlight flooded the room through the wall of windows on one side. She chose a seat across from Micah who smiled at her as she pulled her chair in under her. Aaliyah waved back at him then, smoothing her skirt with her hands, turned to the woman on her right to ask what account she was working on. It was a reflex move, really. Something to do with her attention until the jitters subsided, until the meeting started, until she had something else to turn her attention toward to avoid feeling like the only one at the party without a friend. But she stopped short, mouth still forming the words, when she saw that foolish grin spread across the woman's face. She hardly even seemed to register Aaliyah's existence, that there was anyone sitting next to her at all. Aaliyah followed her eyes until they fell on...Micah.

Micah?

The man was grinning like the Cheshire cat and flirting with the woman from across the table in that discreet way adults do when the possibility of getting caught is all in the thrill of it. She was eating it all up, smirking, lashes fluttering. And, if she was being honest, Aaliyah could understand why she would; the woman wasn't all that much to look at by any means, a mousy-looking something. Dishwater brown hair and grey eyes that'd lost their shine. Thin like a rail but not very tall. Well-dressed enough to fit in with her surroundings but nothing bordering on fashionable. A person who could easily go without notice.

So, she concluded, rolling her eyes and touching her chignon of locks, that must've been *her*, the assistant to the vice president three floors above them. The one Micah had been cutting a night with after hours for a little career boost if nothing else. He'd told Aaliyah about her; Milla she thought her name was. The one who kept all the V.P.'s records and schedules. The one who Micah was pretty sure was giving it to her boss, too. No one but Aaliyah even noticed their antics. Or nobody but Aaliyah cared. Poor fool had probably never had so much attention in her frumpy little life.

Aaliyah sat back in her seat and crossed her legs, glaring at her old friend in a disapproving manner that could've passed for sisterly, but certainly conveyed disgust. The Micah she met in her office every day—the one who'd sat with her friend in the bookstore—was the one she knew, inside and out. She knew his mama's name and where he'd grown up; she knew of the boys he mentored and that he had the better free throw between he and Nigel. Only, this man, the leering alter ego across the table from her, wasn't anyone she knew at all.

When Micah caught her eye, he straightened up and shrugged as if to ask her, what's the big deal? She glanced away, out the window. Micah straightened his tie and reached for a raisin bagel from the platter at the center of the long table.

When John Peterson and David Myers came in, their voices boomed with a confidence that reminded them all they were there thanks to their good graces. They greeted the room, shaking hands like dirty politicians. Aaliyah wiped her hand on her skirt after Peterson passed her, resolving not to even think about where on Milla, or anyone else for that matter, the man's hands had been that day. Because, she decided in that moment, head raised just a few degrees higher with a defiant jerk, she wasn't there for their antics; she was there for her campaign.

When they took their seats at either end of the conference table, Aaliyah knew the moment of truth was coming. She didn't need their sweeping gestures and polite little applause. She just needed to know that the long days and sacrificed nights would be acknowledged and repaid. That her mother hadn't been right, hovering over her stove as she made *plantainos* with her hand on her hip and tsks ready on her tongue. That she wasn't better off "making her own way." She *was* making her own way. She was trekking a path through uncharted waters, for her lineage anyway. She was a pioneer; she was determined and aware they thought her a bit of a maverick at the family reunions. She was the cousin whose head they petted, whose arm they stroked sympathetically when they asked her if she was still at it at the ole' company. And when she nodded, they'd say, "Alright, chile. Well, we hope it works out for ya, you know."

But she was ready for this. Ready for the career Renaissance explosion she knew was just around the corner. She felt it in her bones like elderly aches on rainy days. It was right there. Micah had it, and she, too, would get it.

She almost didn't hear Myers when the campaign leads were announced. Really, it wasn't until Aaliyah noticed the pleased smiles and quiet congratulatory pats on the back, none of them for her, that she started to replay his words in her head. That confidence she'd put on when she walked in the room started to fall away quietly. There was a hand raised at the head of the table followed by Myers' booming, overly self-assured voice calling for a settling down. There was still a fourth person to be announced, the team lead.

But, of course, she must've thought to herself. He hadn't said who the group director would be at all. This was exactly what she'd been waiting for. No way with all she'd done, the hours she'd labored on and reviewed all those drafts of proposals to be presented, that chair wouldn't be hers. Naturally, she wouldn't just be *on* the team. The more she thought about it, the more obvious it became. That chair was hers. The Renaissance was poised at the tips of her fingers.

Except, then Peterson took over and announced that the project director would be "none other than our Micah Barker," and the buzz of chatter recommenced around the table. Hands were shaken and jovial banter filled the room, the important business now over, the climax having been achieved before she'd had the chance to get hers.

Everyone was moving but her.

It took Aaliyah several seconds to realize this, to feel the chair underneath her and the slightest of breezes as colleagues rushed to Micah to congratulate him and flanked Myers and Peterson to brown nose them. She was still in the clamor around her. She'd heard the wind in her throat at the sound of Micah's name and never quite got round to breathing normal again. She blinked. And blinked again. Yet nothing had changed.

Now Myers was clapping Micah on the back. Milla was smirking an impish leer that truly made Aaliyah's stomach lurch. She still couldn't grasp all that was happening. Weeks later, thinking back in retrospection, she wouldn't be able to remember half of it.

She wouldn't remember the moment she'd finally stood to her feet, pushing her chair back and away from her. She wouldn't recall the glance Micah tossed her way or the quickening of her pulse. Yet, she would remember thinking, *What about those late nights? The proposals, the mock-ups, the pitches?*

When her eyes did meet Micah's, she noticed he wore the same expression she did. Myers shook his hand, but there was limpness in Micah's. Could it have been that he hadn't anticipated this outcome, that he hadn't engineered it himself?

No.

Hell no.

There was a ring of finality when that thought swept across her mind, knocking all other possibilities aside. He had to have known. He was, after all, bedding that little leering imp, spreading her legs to reap the professional spoils in between, sullying her because she so foolishly let him, so naïvely believed in him. Aaliyah gathered herself. Her thoughts. Her words.

"Micah?" Her voice came out a weak little whisper. She tried again. "But that's ridiculous. There must have been some mistake."

The room quieted, as they noticed her standing there at its center. Her voice raised a decibel or two. There was a tremor in her hands she hid in closed fists. Peterson took a cautious step toward her as though he was approaching a skittish horse.

"I'm sorry, Ms. Walker. What do you mean?"

"I mean just what I said: there has to be a mistake. Micah didn't even work on the pitch for this account. I did. I made the presentation and everything."

A hush fell over the room again like a blanket accented by the click of a pen, the rustle of papers from somewhere to her left. It was mind blowing that she could be the only one in the room realizing what was happening there. Peterson proceeded cautiously, but it was too late for silly pacifications. She heard careful words of appreciation for her contributions, maybes and next times. She wasn't what they were looking for "on this occasion."

Aaliyah muttered something she wouldn't remember later. Something incredulous and incensed, though her mask remained in place, her accent neatly tucked away. Micah stepped forward and spoke up on her behalf, abdicating, announcing her the rightful victor of this opportunity. His words were waved off, and Aaliyah heard herself speaking but sounding small, her voice hardly carrying over the hushed murmurs in the room. Then she found her spine again and put her hand on her hip.

"I'm not even on the team?"

She could hear her own thundering heartbeat pounding in her head, louder now, harder. The heels pinched her feet and cut at the back of her ankles, and she thought she felt the start of a headache coming on.

"Micah, giving up your spot on this team would not be wise. You earned it."

"Earned it? He didn't earn it!"

Aaliyah hadn't realized she was shouting until she was. Control was slipping away from her, and she heard herself pointing out that the only woman assigned to the team had been Peterson's niece.

Nepotism.

Preferential treatment.

Condoning.

Incestuous.

Those words tumbled out of her like a firehose. She heard Micah trying to interject again but didn't really process it.

"Ms. Walker I really must insist you calm down. Do you understand? I can't think of a less appropriate time or place for such a discussion, and I really don't appreciate your tone of voice or these aggressive accusations. So, if you want to keep *your* office here—"

"Maybe I don't."

"I'm sorry?" Peterson eyed her suspiciously, as if she were up to no good.

"I said," she spoke up, finding her voice, squaring her shoulders just a touch, "maybe I don't want to retain my office here."

"Take a seat, Ms. Walker," he advised with a stern edge cutting a new tone in his voice. "And you might be able to avoid major reprimand."

It was the way he dismissed her that did it. The way he turned his back on her and reclaimed his seat at the head of the table without so much as another glance her way, like he just knew she'd fall in line and slip quietly back into her place as sheep. She didn't even pick up her notebook and pen but turned and put one foot in front of the other.

I I

Scene.

Aaliyah walks down the empty corridor, no one else in sight, heels clicking and echoing as she hurries. The clicks grow closer together as she approaches her office at the end of the hall. She bursts through her office door breathing heavily, slamming the door behind her with a bang. Her heavy breathing echoes. The generic, framed artwork hanging rattles. She isn't entirely sure of where to start the packing or of what to do first, and the fluster shows on her face. She supposes the letter needs to be written. Maybe that should be the first step. Looking around the room, she understands that this will be her last time stepping foot in this box of sheetrock and glass she's worked so hard to earn in the first place.

There are half a dozen boxes of files stacked against the wall. Aaliyah pours the contents out and it all hits the carpet with a whoosh. Graphs and tables flutter down. She tosses her own belongings in and keeps moving as fast as she can.

Aaliyah finishes with the first box and turns the second upside down, spilling its contents into a satisfying heap on the floor. But that high only lasts momentarily.

Micah pushes into the room and closes the door behind him. His eyes smolder, and his jaw is set firmly, but Aaliyah ignores him.

MICAH: Are you crazy? You can't just quit like that!

AALIYAH: *(without turning to face him)* Watch me.

MICAH: Aaliyah, I didn't have anything to do with their decision. You gotta believe me.

AALIYAH: Do I?

MICAH: Seriously, you can't think that—

AALIYAH: Oh, but I do, Micah. I really do.

She twists to face him, feeling some tangible ire rising in her. If he doesn't play his cards right, he'll face an Aaliyah he's never seen before. Or, perhaps, she'll meet a side of him she hasn't either.

MICAH: Aaliyah, that's fucked up. We're friends, remember? And not some bullshit office friends; real fucking friends.

AALIYAH: No, I don't think so. A friend would never do some shit like this to me, Micah. You and I both know a friend would never've let that situation in there go down like that.

MICAH: What else did you want me to do, Liyah? (*His finger jabs the air.*) You thought I saw that coming; I didn't.

AALIYAH: Micah, you've been screwing that woman for months, and she's too simple to even act cool about it. Anyone with common sense could see!

MICAH: Shh, Liyah, don't try to throw that shit in my face now. (*He advances into her space, hushing her, more aggressive now. Yet, her feet never move, never retreat an inch.*)

AALIYAH: That's low. Can't succeed on your own, Micah? Gotta screw your way to the top like some two-dollar whore, huh? (*She shakes her head, turning away.*) No one ever gives men flack for that, do they? But a woman? (*a derisive scoff*) Her whole career is on the line if she sleeps her way up the ladder. Hypocritical bullshit. And that's what you are Micah: you're a hypocritical bull-shitter.

MICAH: Keep your voice down.

AALIYAH: Fuck you!

His head rocks on his neck as if she's struck him. In a way, she has. There's never been a moment of harshness between them before that second, and even Aaliyah is feeling shaky after the lick she's thrown at him. This is the man who's been her comrade, her ally, since the day she stepped foot in that megacorporation of money-hungry capitalist sharks, unsure in her low heels and in her own skin.

MICAH: Look, maybe you can still make this right with the partners. It's not like they haven't seen their share of drama in this joint.

AALIYAH: *(shaking her head)* I don't want to. There isn't a fiber in my bones that wants to work in this cesspool another second.

Her mouth feels comfortable around those syllables, around the long vowel sounds and clipped word ends that come so naturally to her. Sloughing it all off somehow feels natural to her, like a motion she's been waiting to do, expecting to do somewhere deep in her core. But, it also feels terrifying. The kind of terrifying that has also always been waiting on the periphery for her and that she senses closing in on her, its jaws opening around her.

AALIYAH: They can hand the token black girl spot to someone with more endurance for the bullshit politics or more desperation to belong. They wanted to fill their minority quota and they did that, but they never had any intentions of promoting me or respecting me. You and I both know that. We see that.

MICAH: Damnit, be rational! You know that's not how it is.

AALIYAH: What now, Micah? You think I just fell from a tree, that I was born yesterday? Don't go playing the Uncle Tom role on me now, love. Not after claiming to tap dance to your own beat for all this time.

MICAH: Get off it, Liyah! You always go spouting that shit, but it's not even like that, and you know it. I've got the skin and the locks just like you, but I made a name for myself here. You know why? Because I didn't throw some fucking tantrum like you are now when I didn't get my way!

AALIYAH: Yeah, 'cause you've always gotten your way here. Let's not try to pretend like we're on some even playing field. Like being a woman in this damn boys' club isn't relevant to the matter. Like all black is the same black. And don't even go there like we've got the same skin, okay? Like we've had the same experiences here, like we're up against the same odds. You and I both know there's a difference. We're in the South after all, no? You can skip up the highway to the 'burbs where they still got a Jim Crow Road. It's still real here. So, you and I both know they just don't see you as a threat because you're so willing to assimilate with them. You shake the hands and kiss the ass, that woman on your arm and in your bed all the while!

MICAH: That's not 'assimilation.' That's working the system, playing the fucking game.

AALIYAH: It's all the same thing, Micah! They can't see you for the conniving bastard you are 'cause they've already got some preconceived little notion of what they think you are in their heads. (she taps her head to illustrate the point) They think you're that faithful servant, so they're willing to pat you on the head and throw you the bones. I'm not saying you aren't great at your job. You are. You're a fucking rock star; I get it. But it's not just that either, and you gotta see it. It's sexism and every other 'ism' in the book up in here. You can't see that? You can't see what's happenin'?

The boom of her fist connecting with her desk fills the room. The sound of her frustration becomes literal, and they both take a moment to gather themselves as they hear it reverberating between them. Aaliyah rubs the side of her hand that has connected with the wood. Micah shifts on his feet.

MICAH: Look, you're gonna throw away everything you've worked for over this? Over some silly, backwards notions from your HBCU days?

AALIYAH: *(walks past him and sets the two boxes at the door)* You don't have to worry about me, Mister Syracuse. This is the most rational I've been in a long while. I never gained a single ounce a weight here. And I'm not gonna either. I'm done.

The resignation letter is cursory and concise: one sentence stating she is no longer an employee at Myers & Peterson. Aaliyah signs the bottom when the printer spits it out and folds it three ways. She hands it to Micah with a roll of her wrist.

AALIYAH: You'll see this makes it to the right hands, I trust?

MICAH: Aaliyah...

AALIYAH: There's nothing else to say.

MICAH: But there is. I...I told Milla to make sure you got it. The campaign director position. I told her to suggest to Peterson that he hand it to you. I didn't want it. I don't want it. I—I've been thinking of taking another position anyway.

Aaliyah leans against her desk, regarding Micah with a calculating slowness.

AALIYAH: So, I was right. There was never any shot a me gettin' it myself. You were gonna use your pussy connections to get me a job I deserved on my own merit in the first place? What's worse, you knew—you *knew*— the whole time they didn't want me to have it, and you...you didn't say anything to me? Didn't tell me about this other job—that you were thinkin' of jumpin' ship. Were just gonna leave me here without a damn word? Just let me sit in your office talking my head off like an idiot.

MICAH: That's not what I meant. It's just complicated because—

AALIYAH: They were never gonna give it to me. After all I did? After all...God, I knew it.

MICAH: Liyah, I tried to get it for you. I wanted *you* to have it. You deserve this chance more than anyone on this entire floor; I know that! And I know we have to look out for each other. But Milla—stupid bitch thinks if she pushes me to the top I'll automatically take her with me. Entitled. Stupid.

AALIYAH: You knew she was that before and didn't mind, now did you?

MICAH: Look, Liyah, I'm done with this. What happened in there today—I'm done. I'm not doing this anymore.

AALIYAH: Oh, shut it, Micah. You and I both know you're not done with anythin', not going anywhere. You're not leavin' your little girlfriend behind.

Aaliyah cuts her eyes at Micah and walks right by him, grabbing her sweater from the coat rack.

MICAH: You know she isn't my girlfriend, and you know even better than that I'd never have a serious relationship with that woman, so stop with the pettiness, will you?

AALIYAH: But you'll let her think you will, as long as she gives you what you want.

MICAH: Isn't that your very argument, that it's been happening to our women for years, that I should look at what happened to you? The tables can be turned both ways, Liyah, and that's what the hell I did. What did you think? I was gonna let some expectation of—what, good manners?—get in my way? Let me tell you something: the negro who does that—plays 'Good Manners' and lets them walk all over him—is the *real* Uncle Tom, and you can best believe I ain't that. Best believe *they* didn't worry about what anybody thought of their manners when they were climbing to the top, and that's how you need to be now.

AALIYAH: You're no better than they are, Micah. Just the same as that trash out there in that conference room.

MICAH: *(lowers his voice and takes a step toward her)* Listen, I tried to get it for you. I told her I wanted *you* to have it if she could pull that string. I can't help it if she had her own agenda—

AALIYAH: Did you really expect anything different? Of course, she has her own agenda. Guess those nights in bed hurt me as much as they helped you—

MICAH: —she thinks I'll take her with me. But I didn't plan this for you. I didn't even it. My hands are full as it is!

AALIYAH: *(sucks her teeth and turns back to the boxes)* There's irony in those words, ya know? Got some swanky new job you didn't care enough to even mention, when you already got your hands so full with everythin' else they've given you, you can't even receive what you stole from me.

MICAH: Damnit, Liyah. Get your head out of your ass and listen to what I'm saying to you.

AALIYAH: I'm done just listening. I want to be heard now! You can go fuck yourself. This firm can fuck itself, which it seems to be doing a pretty damn good job at, I might add.

She pulls the foldable dolly from behind the desk and loads her boxes onto it.

AALIYAH: Just give them the damn letter, Micah. That's all I want from you.

MICAH: Let me take you home. I've never seen you this upset before.

AALIYAH: I'm fine. Not that it matters to you.

MICAH: Shit, Aaliyah! It does matter to me. You're like a fucking sister to me, and don't act like you didn't know that. What're you going home to do anyway? All you do is work.

AALIYAH: You're right. (*Now it is her turn to turn on him, to jab the air indignantly.*) All I do *is* work. But I never caught up, did I? I never got wherever the hell it was I thought I was going. So, maybe I need this break. I need...this.

He's pulled her proper mask down and pushed her to the edge, over it. She feels a near-palpable sensation of free falling through the air, a dizzying effect that leaves her breathless and internally flailing.

AALIYAH: I thought I had it right, you know. Thought I knew what no one else did. But I didn't, did I? I didn't know shit. And now I see.

Aaliyah is greeted by the familiar clicking of her heels when she heads back down the hall, boxes in tow on the dolly. She presses the button to call the elevator and we see Micah leaning against the wall, shaking his head in one hand, her letter gripped tightly in the other. The elevator dings. Aaliyah steps on and avoids eye contact with him until the doors shut, creating a steel barrier between them. It is then that she finally allows herself the luxury of tears.

[End scene.]

HEARD IT THROUGH
THE GRAPEVINE

DELANEY

Delaney pulled up at the Greenwoods' home later that evening and parked her car on the curb a few houses away. Night had set in, and most of the homes were illuminated and merry, preparing for their own renditions of Thanksgiving the following day. The Greenwoods' roundabout was flooded with foreign cars and the occasional joy-ride convertible with their tops let up. A chill had descended upon the South unusually early, the prickle on her arms told her.

White shutters accented the grey exterior of the six-bedroom house. Cammy had decorated each room herself—well, with the help of an interior designer who'd come highly recommended from one of her cousins, but who was judging?—and they were each fit for an Architectural Digest spread. Laney often felt self-conscious within those rooms, like she'd be the one to spill tea on the plush carpet or knock over a Ming vase in the stone foyer, betraying her own lack of experience with such settings. Yet, that never happened, and she tended to breathe just a little easier now whenever she was within the homes of her friends and now-family. Those days were all behind her, she rarely hesitated to remind herself nowadays. She was one of them; in fact, she was near the top of the hierarchy. Only she could smell her angst. And then that angst would subside altogether.

Carmella had once told Laney that when she and Nathan had first bought the house, he'd given her free rein to decorate it as she liked. With that, Laney assumed, must've also come free reign of his wallet, though Cammy had brought her own money into the union. All he asked was for a room of his own—his own man cave—that he could embellish how he pleased. She relented, and he promptly turned the room at the end of their grand hall into a miniature frat house: all brandy, cigars, flat screen televisions and Lay-Z-Boys. A playroom for big boys. Or so she assumed. Carmella herself hadn't gone in there since he chose it as his own and had only seen the movers hauling in item after item into that room down the hall.

Initially, she'd stopped to wonder why Cammy would proffer such personal information, such a glimpse into the inner workings of her marriage, but then realized this to be her version of girl chat, an extension of their sisterly bond that was to everyone else a given, and so she'd responded accordingly. In those small moments, their friendship was constructed and solidified, their ally status silently understood between them.

Now as she made her way toward their double front doors, she recognized Vince's car in the driveway but not the elder Dessommes', an indication that he'd driven them there, always the dutiful son. There was Jillian's black Audi far to the end of the opposite street, away from all the other cars that deluged the thoroughfare, as if she was already poised to flee in the night, not having to deal with pesky block-ins and walking-to-the-car conversations.

Vincent greeted her at the door before she could even push it open herself. Laney could hear the clinking of glasses and laughter from within the house, even over the contemporary piano descants wafting through the air.

"What took you so long? Everyone's been asking about you. Why didn't you just ride with us? Or with Jill?"

"Jill, Vince? As if."

Laney adjusted his tie in appeasement and fed him a quick line about having to check on the caterers for their Thanksgiving dinner, a whispered mollification she'd forgotten as soon as she'd said it. The stone foyer clicked hollowly under her shoes, as they entered the home, mingling with the noise from the other guests. There was an intimacy to this affair that Laney appreciated. Here she'd found herself at a no-tie dinner party where the gentlemen loosened their top buttons and the ladies donned short cocktail dresses.

Cammy had invited only twenty to her shindig, many of whom stood in the parlor around the black piano, which surprisingly was being played by none other than Nate himself. Laney had assumed her friend had hired a pianist for the evening, ever the social snob, but no, it was her husband, comfortably drunk. He, built like a linebacker and dressed like sophisticated money, was showing off his own rendition of an old Corinne Bailey Rae song to the intimate crowd of onlookers.

"You look fabulous," Cammy whispered to Laney, pressing a cheek to hers. She stepped back to admire Laney's leather pencil, her sky-high dainty heels with the band of soft feathers across the toes.

Laney reciprocated, which is how their conversations generally began, with one of them complimenting the other as if not acknowledging the other's sheer excellence was more an insult than not saying anything at all. So, she commented on Cammy's cocktail dress, fittingly the shade of freshly popped Brut Rosé. Still, Laney didn't mind. There was some kind of comfort with Cammy, like the severity of the tribe was somehow lessened when in her orbit.

"I was afraid you weren't going to show."

No, Laney wanted to tell her but wouldn't dare. *I was only delaying the headache.*

Over her shoulder, Laney thought she'd caught a glimpse of Nigel Cavanaugh standing in the corner near the tall bookcase, cognac in hand. But by the time she started to voice this thought, Cammy stepped back and recommenced her banter with Vince. Laney craned her neck to see who Nigel was standing with, but there were too many people milling about near him, pressing in closer and closer to Nathan who was now tickling the ivories one-handed, reaching for his brown liquor with the other. Carl laughed along with him and clapped him on his back good-naturedly, Addison smiling widely beside him.

Laney tapped her husband, grabbing his attention away from the menial conversation about how Cammy had just loved the cappuccino cakes the caterers had done for The Group's corporate fundraiser, so she'd hired them for the evening. Vince was smiling her way, his typical vodka tonic in hand, and hadn't even noticed that Laney hadn't joined their conversation, simply content that she was snugly at his arm.

"What's Nigel doing here? I mean—" she caught herself, a little dismayed with the pretentiousness that her tone had implied. "Not that he's not welcome, of course, but it's just unusual."

"Not really, honey." Carmella followed her gaze to see that Nigel was also now one of Nate's onlookers, the crowd becoming more boisterous. Then a playful glance back at Vince as she slapped him on the arm. "You sly dog, you still hadn't told her, had you?"

"Told me what?"

"No," Vince chuckled, patting Laney's hand and raising his voice a notch to be heard over the melodies. "You know I was going to announce it tonight, so I hadn't told her yet. Laney thinks I'm too predictable, so I wanted to see that shocked look she gets on her face when I do the atypical." Vince dropped his jaw and raised his brows in a mock version of shock and awe. Carmella fell into a fit of laughter; Laney rolled her eyes.

"Oh, atypical, huh? And what might that be?"

"Honey, part of the reason we're even having this dinner is because Vince brought Nigel in as a partner with The Group. Surprise! We wanted the family all here to hear it first—Nate's idea. And there's another guy...Micah's his name, right?" She looked up at Vince for confirmation. "I told the boys they should both bring someone, but neither of them did. Shame."

"Micah?"

Micah Barker?

Laney started to open her mouth to ask—feeling a little asinine as she did so, because what other Micah was there—but she didn't get the chance. The small crowd shifted, and she saw that it was indeed Micah who was standing next to Nigel, his amber drink placed on the piano as he laughed along with Nate and drummed his hands to a make-shift complementary beat. His locks had been twisted and pulled back. He wore a vest over his casual slacks and looked, as usual, like he'd been tailored to fit the evening.

Addison had always quoted Florence as saying, "There are only a hundred or so black people who matter in this country, and they all know each other quite well." A bit of snobbery from decades before that still seemed to ring true in some ways, certainly true enough of their circle.

Cammy and Vince were still laughing together over their antics, ever the pseudo-siblings they were known to be.

"...Yeah, well, that's all done now. Not that Laney noticed or contributed. If she spent half as much time at The Group as she does—"

"Vince, don't give me that look. It seems Cammy was there to contribute enough for the both of us, wasn't she? As you always are, honey."

Cammy smiled unsurely. Laney tossed her a smile and wink to soothe the sting of that verbal dagger, then turned back to look for them again in the piano pack, only for her eyes to skim over Jillian then land back on her again. She stood near the entrance to the piano room, leaning against the door jamb chatting with Virginia Darensbourg who, having come from Charleston for this dinner at her daughter's home, nursed her Martini in one hand, her other resting on Jillian's arm.

Jill had done herself up for the occasion, Laney noted with a small heave of relief. Her hair was piled neatly atop her head in a tight chignon that revealed the full loveliness of her features— unlike all those other times when it was draped around her face like a weird kid in the corner who chewed her own hair. Tonight, her eyes shone brightly, practically dazzling. And, though she slouched against the entryway, leaning against her shoulder with one heeled foot grazing her other calf, she was social and dressed impeccably in a black lace cocktail dress with three-quarter length lace sleeves and a charming flow from an empire waste. Her heels were strappy and high, but appropriate.

Laney thought back on her sigh of relief with a snicker. It was as if she always waited on bated breath for her sister-in-law to do something embarrassing, to say something crass, to bring the entire affair down with one sweeping crash of her hand. Sure, she was a raging bitch, as Laney had been reminded of just hours before, but there was no reason to care about that any more. Hell, she was glad to be relieved of the burden of caring, reminded of what her life could be like without it. Laney glanced at Jill for a moment longer then turned away.

The music ended to a raucous applause. Nate was bowing dramatically for his guests, gesturing for Carmella to join him at his side. When she was gone, Laney turned back to Vince just long enough to ask him what had brought about the aggressive advance on Nigel. And what did Micah have to do with anything?

"The last time we spoke it was just some idea. And I didn't know you even knew Micah."

"Uh, I didn't know you did either."

"Well, I mean, he's Aaliyah's friend, you know, from work."

Vince's eye lingered on her before he carried on, "Right, well, it's not quite as theatrical as Cammy made it out to be. Nigel's not a partner, but I did make him an offer to be our new director of acquisitions. Plenty of space in the budget, so I moved some things around, created a few new positions. Shit, looked like they hadn't done any repositioning in twenty fucking years. It was time for a little switch up if you ask me."

"Well, Carl's never been much of a trendsetter or boat rocker. But Nigel? You hardly even talk to the guy."

"Yeah, but I know I can trust him if nothing else. Keeping it in the family, so to speak. Just 'cause we don't talk every day doesn't mean he wasn't the best choice. Far more trust-worthy than some joker I could interview and bring in off the street, right? He knows us, and he for damn sure knows what he's doing. So, it's done. I feel pretty good about it. Now, Micah," he sipped again, "was a real find! I see him talking to Renée that night at her social, right? They're conversing it up like old college buds and whatnot, and she waves me over when she sees me. So, I go on over and it turns out he works for Myers and Peterson. Get this—as a marketing executive! Can you believe it? What are the odds, right?"

Pretty damn high since it seems like I initiated this whole disaster.

"Hmm, but I still don't see what his job has to do with anything."

"Well, I guess you wouldn't, babe, but with an acquisitions director and a marketing director we can expand into new areas; Nate and I can focus on other things instead of trying to be a two-man show. Delegating. Progress. That's what it's about."

"And...Carl should be less nervous about stepping down now, I suppose."

Vince tossed a look her way. "I suppose, you're right."

"So, what about Myers?"

"Don't know. He just called me up today and accepted the offer. Did all that negotiating and hadn't heard from him in over a week then, boom. Contract signed, so the rest is between him and them. But, listen, this guy's portfolio is amazing. I mean, he's done some really phenomenal stuff—and, anyway, I think he's been hanging out with Nigel since the social, so it just all makes sense to seal this thing up. Make it a four-man show."

"Oh, well, good." Really, Aaliyah's cryptic voicemail was on her mind, and whether or not Micah's contract signing had been coincidental. She couldn't yet tell. Laney caught Micah's eye for the first time that night ever so briefly, and then it was over and Vince was waiting for her to speak.

"You know I've always liked Nigel, said we should have him over more often."

"Well, now, I guess we will, huh?"

Vince took her hand again and escorted her into the den, hugging Nate and teasing with words that Laney could not hear. The piano preening at an end, the stereo had been turned on and played throughout, keeping the party lively and the chatter going.

Carmella was back at Laney's side humming to the Adele ballad, fresh flute of wine in hand. She nudged Laney's shoulder with her own and nodded toward Jill.

"How'd you manage to get her out of the house all dolled up? I haven't seen her looking so good since, heck, since cotillion, probably!"

"That's probably because you haven't seen her since cotillion, period."

Cammy laughed, "Likely true but of no design of my own, by all means. She's always welcome wherever I am. You know we all grew up together—" She caught herself rambling and pulled back with a salute before sipping. "Still, compliments to you!"

"No, I wish I could say I had something to do with dressing up ole Stalin over there, but it wasn't me."

She glanced back at their subject over her shoulder. Jill was now chatting with Nigel—had she ever met him before? Laney couldn't recall—still yards away from her parents. In fact, Laney realized that she hadn't yet seen them so much as glance at one another so far that evening.

"Still, she does clean up well. No shock there." Laney turned back to her friend remembering that this brought up another good point she'd yet to address. "So, I saw your mom, but where're The Three? I know you invited them."

"No, I didn't." Cammy shook her head conspiratorially. "For what? They weren't going to drop their melodramatic little lives to come sit at my meager table for twenty."

"It's sort of a big thing, you know, them moving back."

"Not really," Cammy scoffed with a slight raise at the corner of her mouth. "Not if you've been raised with those girls your whole life. Then it's just cause for a sigh as you realize how much of your time will now be spent talking about them."

Addie and Carl were now in the corner chatting up Ginny Darensbourg and a small circle of Gen X Republicans, her arm intertwined affectionately with his. Laney could see their lips moving though she couldn't hear their conversation over the others mingling around them. Addie smiled, rubbing her husband's arm. He kissed her cheek, grinning as their group laughed, clinking their drinks together. Carl had made a joke.

Carmella finished off her drink, signaling to Nigel and Micah who were in the middle of breezy repartee with Nate, complete with back claps and near-raucous laughter. The men walked their way, and only Laney noticed when Micah stopped beside her, Cammy joining the others as they breezed past, chatting on.

"That was quite the sly move. Where'd you learn that one?"

"Oh, you know. Here and there." Micah grinned at her. Laney laughed it off with a shake of the head. "I saw you when you came in with your boy prince—I mean, my new boss. But, uh, you're a hard one to get next to."

"Oh, that. That's a thing he does, hovering."

"Not without good reason, I bet, so we'll forgive him that, huh? Anyway, I guess you've heard the news through the grapevine by now."

"I have, a whole five minutes ago. Congratulations—though, you could've said something...um, before."

"Oh, I didn't know before. It all just kinda happened. And, I wasn't even sure about taking it at first. I was rising fast at Myers and all, but then, you know—seemed like a move I needed to make."

"Hmm, Vince does tend to have that effect on folks once he gets all charged up and going. Starts talking about The Group like some damn motivational speaker. Like he's bringing folks into the Holy Land."

"Yeah, he pretty much had that effect on me, too." Laney leaned against the wall, smirking up at him and he down at her. "Anyway, I'm more interested in how you've been, how you're holding up since our, uh, last encounter."

"Oh, you know." Laney gestured at their surroundings. "Some things've changed. Some things haven't. Plenty to give thanks for, though, your wildly unexpected presence here being one of them."

"Well, I guess we both have a lot to give thanks for this holiday, then, don't we?"

"I guess so. But, what I want to know is how he got you to do it. Never thought I'd see *you* on this side of the gap, Micah. And I know Liyah must've given you *all* kinds of flack for it!"

"Oh, I'm not worried. I'm not that far over, and we're navigating this gap thing together, right? You didn't know he was offering me the job, though?"

"Course not. Fella doesn't tell me anything. Not about plans like that anyway. And, usually, I prefer not to even know. Still, can't imagine today's a bad day for you. Can't imagine it's a bad day for Vince, either."

A scoff, "Can I speak candidly?"

"Always."

"Vince seems like a nice enough guy, but he's used to having good days, so I didn't come here for him, actually. I could've taken the job just as easily without the last-minute dinner invite."

"Ah, came for Cammy's rabbit cacciatore, did you? A little secret: the woman can't dice an onion let alone cook a meal. So, don't be too impressed. It's all catered, I assure you."

"Can't say I was too interested in Carmella's culinary skills, either. But I do know by now, wherever she is, you can't be too far." Micah brought his glass to his lips and tossed her a wink. "Makes you pretty easy to find."

"Only if you're looking."

Carmella passed them on the way out of the room, gliding her fingers across Micah's shoulders and peeking around his back.

"Yoohoo, dinner is served, darlings. Shall we? You know how Mom insists on doing things on time."

Laney shot Micah another glance and pushed off the wall, following Carmella out of the den. And she pretended she didn't feel the graze of his fingertips to her arm as she walked by, just as he pretended he hadn't done it.

MOVING ON UP TO THE EASTSIDE

NIGEL

There was something about it all that felt different to Nigel. Felt different. Smelled different. Like the very charge in the air had altered somehow. He laughed to himself, there in the middle of the Greenwoods' den while Nate drummed away at the ivories. "Would you look at this guy?" Vince was elbowing him out of his reveries, sipping his vodka tonic. "What a showoff, huh?"

They both laughed in agreement together. That's when it really hit him, because, Nigel realized, he couldn't recall the last time he and Vince had ever laughed in agreement over anything.

Here he was, having rabbit at Nathan Greenwood's dinner table, sitting in his opulent home next to his exquisite wife, who Nigel thought he recognized from somewhere long ago, before Renée's soirée, but he couldn't be sure of from where. She was now brushing Nigel's shoulder with her own and asking if the rabbit ate too tough. This was somehow different than the social he'd met them all at weeks before and the previous events that had passed by him in a whirl of brandy and business cards. No, this time it was that he belonged.

That's what it was.

They'd cleared way and made space for him. A space that he'd never asked for or championed. A space he'd never cared to occupy before. And it felt strange. But why, he couldn't put his finger on until he could.

Because he hadn't asked for it. But also because, simultaneously, it felt so right. Too right.

Vince was surprised when he offered Nigel the position over hibachi and neat gin, just days before, and Nigel hadn't immediately taken it, leapt at it, been honored. Oh, he'd covered it well, wiping his mouth with his napkin and placing it next to his finished plate.

"You mean, you need to think about it?"

"Yeah." Nigel took the offer in his hands and glanced it over. "Let me sit with it for a second and let you know."

"Well, what's the matter? Is it the salary?"

The salary? No, Nigel couldn't help but think to himself, though he'd never utter it out loud. The salary was more than generous, almost as if Vince was showing off, peacocking to ensure he caught the hen he was after. No, it wasn't the money that made Nigel pause. It was that feeling of his toes at a line that he hadn't felt before. Some imaginary line that'd sprung up palpably during Vince's pompously sure speech about what The Group meant and where it was surely headed with him at the helm. Vince had rattled off sales figures, ratings and occupancy rates as he watched the hibachi knives dance in the air. He'd given this speech before, Nigel could tell, and knew it like the back of his hand. When their food was served, Vince raked up a forkful and, bringing it to his mouth, laid out the offer to Nigel. That's when he felt it, when he just as suddenly as surprisingly felt acutely aware of that line between him and them. Between their kind and his kind. And now it felt as if he was being offered some apple he knew better than to take. Because he didn't like them and their pompous sureness. Didn't get them and their legacy of customs and fluff. Didn't particularly want to.

So, what would it say about him if he took those papers home and put wet ink to that signature line? He'd read the tale of Doctor Faustus somewhere back in the depths of college and resisted the urge to compare himself to that cautionary tale now. Yet here was the devil, self-important and self-assured, and there was the deal; all of the necessary players were present right here at the table. That must have been that foreboding feeling he'd felt while admittedly toeing that invisible line. Of course, he wanted to resist the cliché of selling his soul, but was he? Or—he had to stop himself from snowballing into melodrama—was this all completely logical, just the next step in his own forward progression? A role that he'd earned, deserved, because he *was* the best one for the job?

Nigel glanced back up at Vince and gave him a broad smile. Clapped him on the back good-naturedly. "Yeah, man. No worries. Just let me take it home and marinate on it for a second."

"It's a big step, huh?"

Nigel shirked off that hint of condescension. "Bigger than you know."

II

"So, how high *are* you right now?"

"Mmm," Jillian pretended to think about it, brushing her heel against the inner calf of her other leg.

Nathan's piano preening had been replaced by a soulful mix of pop artists crooning out of the mounted speakers in every room. There were people he'd not yet met peppered throughout the common areas of the Greenwood home, new associates he was sure he'd meet again, possible liaisons he'd now have to somehow explain to Aaliyah who hadn't answered her phone all night. Delaney and Carmella were shifting to his right, yards away, watching as he spoke with Jillian then converging into two separate groups. Delaney turned away from them to speak to Micah; Nigel turned back to Vince's sister.

"Pretty fucking high."

"Is that how you always get through these things then? Some lesson I should be picking up on?"

A smile. "It doesn't hurt."

"Funny, I thought you were supposed to be one of the nice girls of the bunch."

Jillian grinned at Nigel over her empty glass then placed it on the tray of a passing waiter. "I'm well mannered, not nice. Those are two very different things."

He grinned back at her, bemused at this second meeting of Vince's notorious little sister who seemed to laugh in the face of her own notoriety. She motioned for Nigel to hand over his drink, and he, surprised, raised a brow and his tulip as if to say, *You mean this?* Jillian nodded and laughed out loud, mouth open, revealing beautiful, straight teeth and a glimmer in her eyes. He handed it over and laughed with her as she raised the drink to him in thanks.

"So, how'd you get an invite to this little shindig? I didn't know you and the bro were cool like that."

"Um, yeah." Nigel heard the hesitation and tripping of one word over the other as he said this. "We've come to a few agreements."

"Agreements. You must be talking about The Group." A gesture with her chin his way, her eyes twinkling. "He recruited you?"

"Well, he made me an offer."

"One you couldn't refuse, as the saying goes?"

"Mmm, no need to refuse, I guess."

There went his hands casually into his pockets. Adele wrapped up and Birdy followed her act.

Nigel had only met Jill once before, at a holiday party less intimate than this one the year prior, during a conversation even briefer than the one they were having then. She'd mentioned returning to Atlanta for grad school and didn't seem happy about it, then insisted on calling him "bro" over and over again, punctuating every sentence with it, until he realized that she meant it as an insult, a reference to his link to Vince. Then she was gone, her back to him walking away until he couldn't see her in the throngs anymore. Now, he watched her sip his drink and pucker distastefully. That warranted a chuckle from him and an echo from her as she passed the brandy back to him shaking her head.

"Bad move on your part, bro. You shouldn't have taken the deal," she said. "You should never take his deals."

GROWN FOLKS' BUSINESS

DELANEY

Delaney woke up to list of missed calls and texts so long she had to scroll it. She turned her phone off, opening not a single message, and shoved it aside. If the world wouldn't offer her a disconnect before the Thanksgiving madness began, she'd steal one for herself.

Vince was in the kitchen, whistling of all things. But then again, the announcement of his big success the night before was bound to have given him some expresso-like charge to start Thanksgiving morning out right. The smell of dark coffee permeated the air, wafting up the imperial staircase and through the open bedroom doors. Downstairs, Laney wrapped her arms around him from behind, barefoot and on tip toe. He smiled and wrapped an arm backwards around her then went back to cleaning his mug in the sink.

"Can I pour you a cup, babe?"

"Of course, you can, kind sir." Laney took a seat at one of the barstools facing into the kitchen and leaned on the island. "Is the Grinch up yet?"

Vince placed a mug of coffee—two sugars and a splash of skim milk—in front her and leaned into the island facing her. "Uh, I think she bolted. Her car's gone. And before you start going into some worried panic over her," he chuckled, "don't. I'm sure she'll wash back up on the doorstep before dinner."

"I wasn't the least bit concerned either way." Laney held her mug in both hands and sipped.

"I'm gonna head to the club with my dad and Nate in a bit. But you've got the caterers all set up and—?"

"Relax, Vince. This isn't my first rodeo."

"I know, but we can never let 'em see us sweat with it being your first time leading the dinner and—"

"Mmmhmm."

"Anyway," he kissed her forehead. "I'm leaving it all to you. I know you've got it handled."

A note in his voice raised her spidey senses like a dog's ears lifted to sounds in the wind. "Well, thanks for the vote of confidence."

Vince leaned in, rubbing his forehead to hers. Laney flinched away slightly then laughed it off when she realized she'd done so. Vince paused, his forehead to hers, before he kissed her on the mouth. She let him. She felt when he started to pull away, to continue on with his day, then changed his mind and instead parted her lips gently with his tongue. Laney inhaled the smell of his light cologne when he nuzzled his face to hers, and she heard herself laugh again. Light, airy, almost an unrecognizable timbre.

His hand was on hers, his fingers replacing her mug of coffee. He still smelled the same as he always had in those intimate spaces, at the fold of his ears, at the nape of his neck.

Familiar.

Both her past and her present. Everything about him was like second nature to her, like the comfortable routine of his fingers mixing her morning coffee. The sound of his voice, the feel of his body near hers in bed, even as they turned away from each other. It had all slipped into a recurring pattern that made moments such as this, their mouths opening to each other, almost foreign. And even with such patterns at play, deeply entrenched in their day-to-day lives, standing there in that kitchen Laney could at least see why they'd lasted together for so long. Maybe *this* was her world and running from it was only a futile notion. Even with her apprehensions and doubts.

When he kissed her forehead again, she felt his fingers wrap tighter into hers and she did not pull away. When Vince wrapped his arms around her, she didn't flinch away. She let him press his lips to hers, trying to ignore the awkwardness between them until it slid away completely. It was like doing the waltz for the first time in years, and the steps did not come readily without beckoning.

Laney sighed, relaxing into his arms just a little. Just enough. Then his hands were in her hair pulling gently at the roots, and the echo of the stool scraping the floor signaled insistency, fierceness, urgency in their affection. Vince breathed her in as if starved for it.

He lifted Laney from the floor and wrapped her legs around his waist. Laney appreciated the maleness, the power, the feeling of self-confidence she'd nurtured in him and fueled way back when. That self-confidence that had first turned her head his way and allowed his personality to swell until it filled every room he ever entered. She'd often marveled at that confidence, that bravado. It had once excited and seduced her. Primally. When Vince lifted her from the floor like she was his, it reminded her of those grad school days when she would encourage him in his aggressiveness, taking up where Addison had left off without ever missing a beat, without ever noticing the shoes she filled.

"Go for what you want, Vince!"

There was a certain sensation it inspired between her legs back in those days. Perhaps even in these days. She heard him murmur something, perhaps her name. Perhaps any number of other things that slid right by her. Vince traced his fingers under her shirt then raised it over her head and let it fall to the kitchen floor. Squeezed her breast through her bra. Pulled her even closer to him when she tried to pull away for air.

So, she stopped trying to pull away. Leaned into it instead. Ran her fingernails over his scalp, through his curls. Pressed her thumbs into his neck and she squeezed her legs tighter around him and bit into his kiss. Vince sucked her ear mischievously—imagine that, his boyhood mischievousness renewed and returned to her!— and Laney suppressed a smile, her head rolling back. She floated back up the stairs as if on a cloud instead of in his arms. The abandon of it shocked her. She didn't know what her feet off the floor felt like anymore. Vince put her down and he was murmuring again and she was shhing him until she heard words of love stumbling from his mouth.

Laney paused, unable to react or respond at all, briefly wondering how they'd even moved from coffee to this unrecalled place. How long had it been since she'd heard those words from him, in that way, with that hush? Laney thought about the words 'I love you' and was surprised to find she wanted to say them to him, whether by knee-jerk or not she could not be sure yet. When she said the words back, Vince pulled her onto the bed with him and she clutched on to him. Laney whispered his name and he kissed the name away, tasting it as it melted between them.

She fell asleep in Vince's arms, exhausted, content. And it never escaped her how long it'd been since they'd fallen asleep at the same time and in the same bed.

II

By the time she rolled out of bed, less than half an hour after closing her eyes, Vince was already dressed and gone. Real life awaited. There was Thanksgiving dinner to be curated and overseen, if not cooked herself, clothes for the evening to be picked, hair to be pressed and guests to be greeted.

She parked near the entrance of the caterer's, a one-story semi-Grecian-inspired building with sweeping windows and ionic columns.

That warranted a wry snicker from her as she parked her car, maneuvering through the sheets of rain that drenched Atlanta and left flashing streams of rainwater rushing through the streets. Laney's umbrella was, stupidly, in the trunk, and she would've gotten just as wet trying to retrieve and open it in the high winds as she would have simply making a run for it.

So, she ran through the downpour and grey puddles toward the front entrance of the building, as thunder rumbled and growled overhead. There was a server in pressed black pants and a starched white collared shirt, bowtie loosely draped around her neck, smoking a cigarette and looking out into the rain from under the stone awning. Laney hurried past her. Shook her feet and ran her fingers through her hair, regrouping like a wet dog, feeling her hair curling at the roots from the rain. Out came the phone that had to be turned back on. It lit up and vibrated in her hand with a jaunty little chime that told her she was back in touch with the real world.

It was in the middle of the feet stomping and regrouping that she noticed a woman in jeans, a black turtleneck and ballet flats leaning against one of the columns. She pulled out a pack of cigarettes and tapped them against her hand absentmindedly before pulling one out and bringing it to her lips. Laney started to walk past her then paused. Turned on her heels and eyed her more closely. It was none other than Jillian Dessommes, standing under the protection of the awning, shielded from the rain but staring out into it, her hair feathered around her face and shoulders frizzy from the humidity. Laney tapped her shoulder and Jill whirled around, furrowed brow creased hard.

"I wouldn't have pegged you for a smoker, Jill. You know, before that little stunt you pulled in my driveway."

Jill's eyes stretched big and wide, tinged with alarm, then fell with a simper. "Yeah, well, there's plenty you don't know about me, Laney, so don't go getting all warm and fuzzy in your moist places like you know shit about me." Jill lit the tip with a gold lighter then started to shove it and the pack into the back pocket of her jeans.

Laney stopped her before the thought had even crossed her mind that she was doing it, distracted by something she was sure she'd seen. From the flash of skin when Jill's shirt raised. She moved Jill's hand when she saw the lines of scars on her hip. There were red, jagged lines that touched and crossed each other, tripping and falling over themselves to create some sick pattern of old and new wounds in her skin. Covered in scar tissue, almost as thick as if she'd been burned and it'd healed over. Laney met her gaze and didn't know what to say. She felt herself wincing as she ran her fingers over the lines, and she didn't even fathom she was still holding Jill's shirt up until Jill recovered from her own shock and pushed her away, pulling it back down into place. It all happened so fast, Laney staggered back under the force of Jill's glare.

The waiter headed back into the building without so much as a glance their way. The downpour enveloped them in a constant roaring, like a howl in the night that never subsided, only ebbed and returned. Rain peppered their faces, left by the wind, and neither of them moved for more seconds than they realized until Jillian opened her mouth and spat, "Jesus, Laney, I didn't mean literally. How long have you been fucking standing there, anyway?"

"I, um, just need to check on the caterers. Saw you when I was coming in. What are *you* doing here?"

Jill jerked her chin toward Laney's phone. "You need to check on the caterers is right. Your fucking phone isn't on. Ma started freaking out and called me to come down here and do *your* job. I'm the fucking guest, remember?"

"A guest you are not. Anyway, I'm here now, so you can go back to..." Laney tried not to let her eyes wander back to what she'd seen on Jill's hips. "Whatever it is you do."

Jill turned back toward the rainy city, shaking her head. She folded her arms over her chest. "So, I guess you're gonna go run and tell my mom and brother, right? Jill the smoker!" she laughed bitterly, shaking her hands around her face with mock exaggeration. "Jill the fucking loser." She shook her head again and took another pull. "Whatever."

"Why would I do that?"

Jillian raised a brow and pushed her hair from her face, pulling it up into a ponytail, knotting it around her hand and then letting it fall back to her shoulders. "Why wouldn't you? You're all up my mom's ass, so I can just imagine what you'd tell her to make me look bad."

Laney started to say, *You do a good enough job making yourself look* bad, but she bit her tongue.

"Are you serious? That's what you really think of me? You think I'm trying to take your family from you or something?" That one made her laugh at the sheer absurdity of it all, but Jill didn't think it was so funny.

"Trust me, I don't even want my family, so have at it. God, you're like some kind of cancer, you know that? You just spread everywhere, touching everything, 'til I can't get rid of you."

"Oh, get a grip on reality, Jillian! You're the one staying in my house. Here to check on the food that *I* ordered. I'm not at your place, not following you or touching you or smothering you in any way. Can count on one hand how many times I've even thought of you."

"Don't look at me with that silly little smirk. That fucking good-girl façade is getting old, Laney. Jesus, I knew this is why she dragged me back to Atlanta. But it's not gonna work. I don't want to be you! I don't want to go to dinner at Carmella's or sleep in your pretentious ass house or be anything like you! Run tell her that, won't you?"

"Well, Jill, guess what? I don't want to be like me either, so I don't see any reason why you should be. Get your head out of your ass and grow up. You're not the only one under some microscope, okay, so let's not bring out the violins. You're not the only one feeling it. Addie judges me, picks at me. They all judge me, expect shit of me. Same as you. I'm measured on the same tape you are."

Jill shook her head with a grin that stung Laney, exhaling toward the awning above them. "Get the fuck outta here. We're not on the same tape—nowhere near it. *We*," Jill motioned back and forth between them, "aren't even on the same planet. She's grooming you to be like her *because* she cares—nepotism at its finest like only we Dessommes can do, right? But you don't even have your eyes open enough to see it. Must be nice," she huffed, "to be able to afford to be so fucking comfortable, so fucking blind."

"Believe me, Jillian. I'm neither comfortable nor blind. So how about you just figure your own shit out and I'll figure out mine?"

Laney could hardly meet her gaze after seeing those criss-crossing lines. Jill's words brushed up against her like a shadow but never fully seeped in, the memory of those scars like a film of grease on her mind, allowing nothing else to bleed past it. They spoke volumes about her while making her all the more a paradox at the same time. Instead, Laney crossed her arms over her chest the way Jill had just moments before, just to have something to do with her hands.

Another pull. "If you've got anything else to figure out—if any of this shit isn't already clear as day to you, Laney—then I suggest you get on that ASAP, huh. But I've had mine figured out since before you even showed up. I've known. I know that woman tolerates me because I'm her daughter. I'm the one who anchored her down. The one she didn't want. And if I know it, then you know it. So, don't pretend. Don't do that thing where you pretend like you don't pity me, and I won't do that thing where I pretend like I care."

"I don't pity you at all," Laney started, taking a step back when thunder clapped above them. "I don't pity myself; I don't pity you. We've all got choices to make. I've made mine." A gesture at her half-smoked cigarette. "Looks like you've made yours. I'm...not always what I seem. Neither are you, apparently. Nothing is. Nothing in this messed-up kaleidoscope world of y'alls is as it seems! But same way it squeezes you, Jill, it squeezes me."

Laney reached out and gripped Jill's arm to illustrate her point. She gripped it harder, then harder still. "It *squeezed* me. You should damn well know that. None of this shit around you should fool you in the slightest. You see right through it, Jill. I know you do. And if you see right through it, then you know that nothing is perfect. You know. So, don't hold me up to some tape you don't want held up to you, because I'm done with that shit, Jill. I'm done."

Jill said nothing and made no move, other than the leer that pulled at the corner of her mouth. Laney could smell the tendrils of smoke drifting up around them, felt the spray of rain hitting her face.

"Look, I'm sorry if you think I've done something to you, because I haven't. I don't have a problem with you, but let's be honest here, okay? You're a complete, raving bitch to me any time you get the chance, which is often, and it's been that way since the day I first met you! Since that fucking dinner when...when..."

"When what?" But Laney shook her head and started to turn on her heels to go into the building. "When what?" Jill insisted again, grabbing Laney's arm and spinning her back around.

"When I should've known fucking better! When I could've still turned back or just taken that road with different shoes on. In that bathroom, when I could have said something to you—or asked you—or something. Anyways," she nodded toward Jill stomping the butt into the ground. "I'm not going to tell anyone about your bad habits or your...masochism. So, calm down." Jill chewed the inside of her cheek, the glare in her eyes hard, set. "I don't give a shit what you do to yourself when no one's looking, because, frankly, it's none of my business. I don't know you, and you don't know me. So, what is there to say?"

Laney turned and stepped toward the entrance to Chef-D'Oeuvre.

"Wait!"

It was the reluctance in Jill's voice that made Laney pause. That catch in the back of her throat usually hidden by the false bravado in her tone. She'd never heard that from her before, hinting at a pain she'd never seen Jill let her guard down enough to express. Their eyes locked with ten feet between them. Jill fidgeted with her hair again. Laney waited for the other shoe to drop.

"I know you, Laney. I know you just as well as I know myself, because we're the same. The same. But I thought—I thought you were them. Something I've fucking itched to get away from for God knows how long. Someone I've hated since I can remember. I thought you were one of them. But I know you now."

"No, you don't."

"Yes, I do. Because you're just like me."

Laney shoved her hands into her back pockets and watched those words coming out of Jill's mouth. Saw her sister-in-law grappling with the same truths she was, having already shirked them off years before Laney had realized to do so. And she didn't step away when Jill took a step toward her. She didn't wave her off when Jill looked her in the face and told her, "Laney, I can't apologize to you. I'll just be honest. All that time I was feeling that way—seeing it all that way—I just don't have it in me to apologize for that or pretend like I didn't mean every fucking second of it. Because I felt it too long, and it cut too deep. It left its mark already."

"I don't need any apologies. List one time they've ever solved a damn thing anyway."

"There's just so much shit you don't know. Shit you couldn't even imagine. And I just saw you flitting around in a field full of bombs and mistaking them for sunflowers. Pressing your nose right up to it, but never seeing. Like, Jesus—it was disgusting. I don't know if you've finally seen it, or when you finally saw it, but I can show you. I can show you the way out of the minefield if you're looking for that out."

"Out of the minefield, huh? Then why haven't you taken that route yourself, Jill?"

Jill glanced up at the skies and made a face. "If you get me at all, you know the answer to that one. One more semester, and I'm outta here. But, 'til then, I'm here, in it. And while we're both here, in it, if I can trust you, Laney, then you can trust me. Sometimes...sometimes it's just that that makes all the difference."

Laney still felt those scars against her fingertips, marks of a serious cutter. New layers of Jillian that she'd never known or suspected existed in the two-dimensional view she'd had of her for years. Really, she'd never cared. It was almost too much to swallow all at once after years of seeing her in just one light. She'd seen Jill sullen and cranky, sharp-toned and spiteful enough to take away from the incredible physical beauty that she had, but never forthcoming and honest, never searching for a friend and wanting to share. It made Laney wonder why and how many more secrets she still might have. Those scars said Laney had less of a reason to hate Jill than Jill had to hate her. So, she nodded. Offered a conciliatory smile that felt so genuine on her lips she knew it could only be that.

"Fuck it. We *are* sisters. Even if it is in the Dessommes tradition."

"That we are."

Those three words finalized the deal. Neither Jill nor Laney knew what to do next—hug, shake hands, say something profound—so they did nothing. It was Laney who finally offered them an escape from the awkward silence their new alliance had left in its wake.

"It's raining cats and dogs out here. Let's see what's going on with this food, and get this weekend done, huh?"

To which Jillian readily obliged.

And the rain continued pouring.

A CLOSED MOUTH
DON'T GET FED

JILLIAN

Theirs were never dinners of cooking together barefoot in the kitchen. There was never blithe taunting as they chopped tomatoes, never the sound of children running around between their legs. They weren't that kind of family, never had been. What you would see were children playing primly in the den, sitting with their dolls or reading their novels. That was, of course, back before this in-between period when the children were now adults with no offspring of their own. In those days, you'd hear seemingly constant decanting and pouring, bottle after bottle being emptied and tossed nonchalantly into the trash, the clink of glass hitting glass announcing the end of one and the start of another, glass shards scraping against each other as bottles burst and shattered.

And then, of course, there was always the setting of the table.

This was one of the traditions, along with a woman's coming-out dinner to the family, that had crept up into their familial fabric at some point—probably by accident—that no one could pinpoint exactly but that had become a staple of the Dessommes convention. Jillian remembered Florence setting their heavy oak table with Addison, their hair pulled high up into buns or big in large, fluffy curls. Then Addison passed the tradition down to Delaney. And now...well now, here they were.

The flatware and dinnerware would be laid out on the sideboard by the host, so polished that they glinted and gleamed under the dining room lights. She'd done so well. Jill wouldn't have expected less of her. It was all laid out so beautifully, the neat little groups of salad, shrimp and dinner forks. The careful rows of crystal stemware. The saber and magnum of champagne.

Jill was in the Wheat Room. After coming to the top of the staircase and peering over the side, she found Laney chatting with Addie, both with wine in hand, and Vince and her father in the den watching football. The grandfather clock in the hall told her it was just after five o'clock, so she knew the setting of the table would commence any minute. But maybe that was enough time, that minute. Jill had decided she wasn't ready after all and gone back into the room. She closed the solid oak door behind her, turning the knob to quiet the lock. She leaned there for a few seconds, swiping a few loose coils from her face with the back of a hand.

II

Sharp words from her mother greeted Jill when she ambled down the stairs and into the open dining room. She wouldn't have expected anything less from Addison's mouth, her tongue sharpened by whatever liquid she had in hand. Jillian hardly tossed a glance her way, expecting her mother's reaction before she'd even stepped foot out of the room upstairs. She ignored that piercing glare she'd grown up with and somewhere along the line learned to shrink from a little less, sidestepped her mother and started helping Laney at the sideboard.

The table would be set for eight—the five of them, of course, but they would be joined by Renée with her two offspring. By the time Jill had gotten downstairs in her long-sleeved turtleneck dress and suede boots—after a quick line of blow and a backward glance at the mirror—Renée had poured brown liquor for both her and her sister-in-law, Matthew was chatting with Vince and Sabrina had managed to keep away from it all with her phone inches from her face and absorbing all of her attention on a couch, no doubt texting or chatting her Carolina beau.

Laney's formal dining room was dressed up for show, just as they all were, a perfect reflection of the tradition at hand. The servers were in the kitchen, out of sight but offering soft clinking and sliding sounds as they prepared to serve the Thanksgiving meal. It was a large, open room, separated from the front hall and staircase by Doric columns and no walls. For the occasion, Laney had opened the plush curtains to the floor-to-ceiling windows wrapping around the dining room and overlooking the infinity pool and lanai. The dinner table, all bleached wood and marble, was bare save for the three glass centerpieces. She'd done it all up to perfection, even omitting the place mats, which Addison always griped were "tacky and pick-nicky." She did it just as Addison would have done, and that, Jill was sure, was no mistake.

Laney started, as was the tradition for the host of the dinner, at the head of the table where Matthew handed her the first plate. She smiled out at her guests ceremoniously and placed the first charger down. It had begun. Sabrina and Matthew followed behind her, placing the remaining seven chargers at their places, a perfect two inches from the edge of the table. Vince bent down and kissed Laney lovingly on the mouth as he placed the pressed and folded napkins and she followed behind him with the salad forks and dinner knives.

Carl and Renée stood to the side, watching, grinning over their drinks and commenting. Something about the good ole days. Then, "Sabrina, that plate's off-center."

"Matthew, don't just stand there. Where are the water goblets?"

Always used to giving orders, those two, and them always used to taking them.

Addison placed the butter plates, butter knives lying diagonally over them. She arranged them with delicate care that Jill needn't have noticed, because she remembered it perfectly from when Addison oversaw the set. She'd run her fingers over the porcelain china and sterling silver cutlery. She'd make sure it was placed just so, then move along. Renée came up behind her—bumping her playfully on the hip with her own, to which they both threw back their heads and laughed—with the white wine glasses and champagne flutes, which she placed next to Matthew's water goblets.

Sabrina came up to Jill and laid her head on her shoulder. Like old times, Jill remembered thinking. They both stood there for a few long seconds before Jill placed the fish forks and Sabrina followed her with the oyster forks.

With the table now set, the sounds of the servers preparing their first course in the background, Laney pulled the magnum of champagne from the wine bucket. Water droplets rolled down the side of the bottle and plunked onto the floor. Jill watched as they fell, trying to find herself somewhere far away but not succeeding. Then Laney's left hand was on the sabre, a charming grin on her face as she slid it along the bottle and broke the top of the neck away. The biting of her lip in that vaguely determined way of hers gave way to a delighted laugh. She tossed her head back and reveled in the round of whoops and cheers, as the sound of the saber breaking the glass finished the ceremony and congratulatory squeezes, pats and kisses flowed her way. The champagne was poured for all by her steady and practiced hand. It flowed, some lapping decadently onto fingers as salutes with flute in hand were spiritedly made. Glass clinked on glass in unison, "Happy Thanksgiving" being toasted, laughed and murmured all around. Jill watched as Laney accepted a kiss from her daddy and a hug from her mama.

She'd done it; they'd witnessed it. Or maybe only Jill had noticed her full crossover into the family, into their world, with that swipe of the saber in her sturdy hand. And yet, there was that grin on her sister's face. That effortless, carefree grin that didn't smell of liquor, that didn't feel contrived. Jill heard Laney's words in her head from earlier in the day and smiled. Raised her glass and clinked it with all the others. And so, she stood back to watch it all, as the dimmed light from the overhead chandeliers grazed their skin and the soft rays of the day outside turned to dusk behind them.

III

"So, what'd you decide about the benefit ball, Jill? Are you going? Do you have a dress yet?"

Sabrina was sitting to her left, at the middle of the table, whispering toward her ear. The table was complete and animated. Carl sat at the head with his wife fittingly on his right side, his son on his left. Laney, of course, was seated next to her husband with Jill then Sabrina to her left. Renée had seated herself at the other head of the table, fitting of her perceived role in the Dessommes clan.

It was after the oyster course had been cleared and the chowder was on its way that Sabrina leaned over and asked her this. Laney sat to Jill's right, chatting with Matthew over the table about absolutely nothing. Occasionally, Laney would nudge Jill with her elbow when Renée said something asinine or Vince went on about his new recruits, fishing for compliments and back-pats, which they always offered up. Later, Jill would nudge her back. This went on even after Jill excused herself to the restroom for another line and a splash of water to her face. But, it made her laugh—it made her forget—so, she didn't mind.

"Everyone's going, so I've been told."

"Yeah, but I asked if *you* are going."

Jill never answered her cousin's tittering question. There was no need because, aside from the fact that her inebriated mind wouldn't even allow her to think that far out at the moment, of course, she was going. She was going to avoid the otherwise inevitable. To elude her brother's condescendingly unsurprised reaction to the alternative, her father's dismissive nonchalance, her mother's melodrama. She was going because she still had another semester of graduate school to finish for which their checkbooks were needed—she never having been a recipient of any scholarship for academia and the offspring of parents too far outside the bell curve to merit financial aid. She was to be their prisoner for at least that while longer, bought and paid for in exchange for a framed piece of paper and a lifetime of being debt-free she felt they owed her. Yet, it was a calculated submission to captive status. While she always remembered this, it never made it easier. So, yes, she planned to don a gown, perhaps even a trinket of her grandmother's jewelry handed down to her, and appear there that one last time. That last—

Jill felt herself giving Sabrina a little nod, picking up her glass and sipping from it. She noticed when the servers brought out her chowder and placed it in front of her but never lifted a spoon, hardly gave it a glance. The conversation rewound and replayed in her mind two or three times, a nearly palpable screeching of rewound VHS tape audible in her ears each time.

Because, she hated them.

God, how she hated them all.

Not Sabrina, maybe —or maybe even Sabrina too, her indoctrination completed long ago—and not Laney, whose playful nudging hinted back to their words of mutual understanding before. But for the rest of them, it bubbled up inside of her like hot lava as she listened to Renée prattle on about upcoming vacations to her left and her father debate with Vince about the new arrangement of position at The Group to her right.

She hated them.

It burned up her esophagus and scratched at her throat. It wasn't until she physically started choking on it, reaching again for her wine, that she noticed it was not only in her head but somewhere deep inside of her, too. And they were all the same, weren't they? Sabrina preparing to wed some clown from the Charlotte circles and pompous little Matthew sitting across from her with his pinched nose in the air and his nasally tone assaulting her ears. She wasn't one of them.

She neither joined in the chatter nor truly heard it. It melted into some bubbling cacophony of noise around her. Not a single word of it would she remember the next day, and that was only half because of the drugs she'd ingested through her nose. Likewise, her head was swimming, but it was only half because of the Thanksgiving chatter around her, the soft nudge from Sabrina, the wide smile from Laney.

Laney.

She watched her, neglecting her polite upbringing and turning her head to stare at her full on. She let go of their faces streaking around her, the clamor of their lively dinner-table voices churning, and watched Delaney Dessommes as though she were the only person in the room. Her shallow breath in her own ears, the room around her shifting between slow motion and hyper speed, as she tried to swim her way back to the surface of reality.

They aren't yours. They aren't mine either...

And yet, she'd known that all along, hadn't she? She'd been dropped into their family by chance, nurtured at the witch's breast by some command of Carl's that Addie had resented ever since. And she was now too old to blame it on some sick freak accident on the part of the stupid stork who'd gotten her mixed up with some other honey-eyed little girl. Even still, in a way, the Dessommes had taken her home by mistake, and they knew it just as well as she did. They could feel it just like she could in her veins.

But, no. She wasn't the only mismatched case of mistaken identity at that dinner table. For, there was Laney right there next to her, now smiling, having figured something out that'd changed her entire persona. Altered the very hue around her. Nodding pleasantly at whatever Vince's twisted, laughing mouth was spewing. Saintly and all things good, all things Dessommes, but somehow distorted at the edges. What was that Laney had said? Like a kaleidoscope?

Kaleidoscope...squeezes me...

They're not mine, and I'm not theirs...

Chatter.

Stop it, Jill. God, you're fucking tweaking...

But that only made her laugh out loud, loud and boisterous enough to warrant clamping her hand over her mouth. But she didn't. Laughed out loud because in her head it came out sounding just like her mother.

Stop it, Jill.

She laughed harder, hardly noticing when the rest of the table slowly ground to a halt to take her in, to stare, to wipe their mouths politely on their dinner napkins and wait for her to reveal the big fucking joke.

Jesus, I fucking hate these people. I fucking hate—

Tweaking...

Stop it, Jill.

She laughed harder, doubling over at the table. Jill felt the quartet of tears running down her cheeks and the clenching of her abdomen. Laughter.

Stop it...

There was no need, she realized there and then, in ever scolding herself again. No need in admonishing herself for cutting or reproaching herself for shirking off her studies, failing a class, fucking some guy in the back seat of his car. No need.

No need.

Because there was her mama in her head to do it for her. Ground in there from birth, ready to swoop in and finger wag at any given moment for the slightest offense. There they were all around her. Everywhere. In her thoughts. She didn't even need them anymore because there they were, ingrained.

Admonishing.

Shit.

Staring.

Except for Laney. Laney turned her head to the left as Jill heard her laughter so loud in the air around her, as she started to scold herself on behalf of her mother, then stopped, repulsed at herself for even thinking to do so. Laney turned. Her laughter stopped, because Laney's gaze was on her, their elbows lightly brushing. Laney caught her eye and there was no smile. There was neither admonishment nor joy.

There was only concern. Concern and alarm. Jill saw those register on Laney's face before she heard her say Jill's name over the sound of noise in her head.

"Jill! Jill, what's wrong?"

And Jill knew she'd crossed her own line. A line she'd continue to blur too many times over as long as she was there.

She needed air.

She needed to get away.

She needed to never lay eyes on them again.

Jill dropped her napkin and pushed away from the table before she even felt herself doing it, her head moving too quickly in front of her body out of step. She was almost to the front door before her mother's voice yelled out her name and already outside in the crisp night air before she registered that she'd even heard it.

LIFE IS A BUNCH OF LITTLE TRAPS AND IF YOU LISTEN YOU CAN HEAR THEM SNAPPING SHUT BEHIND YOU

DELANEY

There was a palpable quiet in the air with Jill gone and the in-laws dispersed. It was heavy, and it pressed down on Delaney like some oppressive hand. She was neck deep in a steaming bath, sinking deeper and deeper into the water until it grazed her nose, warming her lips and causing beads of perspiration to prickle on her forehead.

Silence.

No bubbles and no frills.

She could hear him downstairs the entire time. Whistling in the kitchen, sliding the lanai door shut. Popping the tab on a Coke in the hall. It was his casualness toward the matter that made her pulse thump at her temples the way that it was, the reason why she heard her breath like a harsh wind in the still air of the master bathroom around her.

For Vince, the night continued on into oblivion in the typical Thursday-night-in-suburbia fashion. As though the Thanksgiving ham and turkey weren't still warm on the kitchen counter. As though he hadn't heard the awkward family pleasantries from Renée and the cousins when they wiped their mouths, stood from the table, slipped on their coats at the door.

She stood up from the bath when she heard him enter the room, the hot water sloshing around her shins.

"Is she back?"

"Don't know. Don't think so."

He was untucking his collared shirt and peeling it off. It found its way onto a chaise, but his eyes still had not found their way to hers.

"Vince, I know you know what's wrong with her. You know something. Don't play stupid."

A scoff melted into a chortle. "I never play stupid."

"I wouldn't say never."

Vince turned to face her, the slightest sneer sneaking up the left side of his mouth. Laney was dripping. She could feel it. But it was the first time she could remember feeling the breath of wind between her legs cooling her hot skin in a long while. Steam wafted from her as they glared at each other. Vince ran water in the sink. Started brushing his teeth.

"What the fuck is with you today? You're all up Jill's ass?" He spit into the sink, filled his cupped hand with water and sloshed it around his mouth. Spit again.

"Really, when did we start talking to each other like that?" She stepped out of the tub and felt the thick bath rug cradling her toes then the slate floor cooling her feet. "Like we actually gave a damn, right?" Laney was behind him, her bare breasts grazing his back. A puddle pooled beneath her. "That girl is fucked up—barely hanging on by a thread—and none of you even bat an eye."

Vince pushed past her, turning off the lights in the bathroom. Laney wrapped the terry cloth bathrobe around herself, tying it as she strode into the room after him. The sight of Vince sipping the Coke in the dark scratched at her nerves. What a pompous asshole. But hadn't she known what she was getting? Hadn't she encouraged it?

He was silhouetted in the moonlight spilling into their bedroom, but he'd left the lights off. Sitting on the edge of the bed, peeling off his trouser socks, he watched her.

"Laney, I'm sorry you're so upset. But I don't know what you want me to do. We had a good morning today. Thought we were getting back on track. Getting back to us. Like you've been saying you wanted. Now this?" He switched on the lamp at the bedside table.

"I want you to care about something or someone other than yourself. Can you do that? Do you even know how?"

"Don't do that. You know I care. And I hardly even know Jill for all intents and purposes. I don't know what's up with her."

"What did you do to her?"

"Me? Fuck has this got to do with me? It's not my fault Jill's a loon. I don't have any idea what the hell she was thinking tonight."

"Oh, please! That's a mighty fine high horse you got there, Vince. Why don't you go ahead and climb down before you catch a nose bleed! For Christ's sake, that act is old as dirt already!"

"I'm too tired to even shower. I'm going to bed."

"No, you aren't. We're gonna to talk about this." Vince pulled back the covers and reached for the switch to turn the lamp off, but Laney swatted his hand away. "This conversation is not over."

"So you think. Babe, it was over before it even began. If you care about the girl so much, why don't you go check on her? Cradle her? Rock her? Do whatever the hell it is you women do when one of you's in hysterics."

"Fuck, Vince. What the hell happened to you? To us?"

"Nothing. It's still us. If you didn't feel that this morning—like I felt it this morning—then..." Vince reached for her hand and tried to pull her to him. She resisted, pulling back against him. Vince sighed, let her go.

"You keep talking all that junk about before. For weeks. About college. Living in the past like that's gonna help anything. Like I know what the fuck is wrong with Jill. But, Laney, we're still us. Don't worry about her. We're still us."

Laney registered the pleading look in his eyes but didn't trust it. She didn't move closer to him in the dimness between them. Instead, she stood there staring. Who was this man sitting on the bed in front of her, some sly smirk on his face and no remorse on his conscience?

"Damnit, Vince. I must've been delusional. Somehow, I thought you were some other guy. Some other man."

"Don't do this shit tonight. We've got a whole weekend ahead of us and...I can't do this shit without you. I need you to get off Jill's back and get your head back in the game. I need you to jump in and do your part. We're a team, remember?"

"Oh, the shenanigans tonight weren't my part? This whole weekend?" *Our whole existence?* But she couldn't bring herself to say it.

Jill was the safer bet. Jill was the perfect distractor, the mirror to their faces, the one she could turn toward him to make him see what they'd become, what they were doing to each other.

"Now, come to bed and let me show you again just how much of a team we are." He patted the covers next to him, that smirk growing wider.

"Vince, Jesus."

"Time for us to start making babies anyway. The Group is mine. It's happening."

Laney shook her head and felt herself swaying on her feet. Rubbed her forehead and looked back up at him. He grabbed her wrist again and pulled her toward him, but Laney rocked back, pulled away.

"No!"

"Fuck, Laney!" He was on his feet now, but the gap between them hadn't narrowed an inch. Vince stood his ground watching Laney stand hers. "I'm not gonna do this shit with you tonight. I don't know what the fuck is up with my fucked-up sister. I haven't done shit to her. Haven't laid a finger on her. Haven't even looked her way this whole weekend! I don't give a shit about her—not this weekend—and you shouldn't either. Let that big girl take care of herself. I don't want to hear anything else about her. Do you understand?"

"If you don't give a damn about your own sister, then how the hell can you say you give a damn about me? Don't feed me that bullshit, Vince. All you care about today, this weekend, maybe ever, is that Group. That empire of snakes you and your dad have built."

There was silence between them for a long while as the words oozed between them and Vince stood there across from her in the dark.

When he did finally speak, it was with a loud exhale and both hands rubbed over his head. "Laney, goddamnit—sometimes you can be such a bitch."

"Yeah, well a 'bitch' is just a woman who won't bend to a man's will. Isn't that what they say?"

"Oh, stop it with the literary, psycho-babble bull, will you? I thought you left that feminist crap behind in grad school. This is the real world here."

Left it behind. As if the very act of a woman speaking up or asserting her rights was a phase to be passed over with age and sensibility.

Laney stepped away from him. "I don't want to do this with you anymore, Vince. I really don't. It's getting...too hard." She sighed, dropping her head into her hands then ran them over her face.

"Do what?"

"Do you not see how messed up this is? Your sister just had some mental break at our dinner table and you're gung ho about the rest of the weekend? Girl either had a complete breakdown or was on something serious. Addie's just reeming her. Your dad's just silent? You don't see what's wrong here?"

"I haven't heard you spit Jill's name without disdain more than twice in the past year. This morning, you didn't care if she'd fled town or not, and now you're on my back about some crack up she had outta God knows where? Get a grip on yourself! Focus on what's in front of us, on what matters."

"This is what matters!"

Laney's voice rattled the room around them. Vince flopped down on the bed, as if it had blown him over. Laney held one shaking hand in the other to calm them.

"I'm tired of arguing with you, Vince. I'm tired of pretending everything is okay. With us. With your family. I'm tired of your fucking superiority complex and this messiah-walk-on-water bullshit. I'm tired of it all. Years. I'm just...just...tired."

"Yeah, Laney, years. And all I've ever wanted is to be with you! To do *this*—accomplish this—with you! What's happening *this* weekend has *always* been the plan. Why the fuck can't you see that and just...cooperate?"

"Cooperate, huh? Like some well-trained fucking pet—"

"We both have a part to play in this, and you knew what you were getting when you got me. I made it clear. You knew everything you needed to know before I walked you in my mom's house and showed you off at that dinner. You held off, fine. Wanted to finish school first. Fine. I've given you everything you've ever wanted, played by your rules. Now it's time for me to get what I want for once and for you to play by my rules."

"Barefoot and pregnant, huh? Curating bone china while the whole world just—while we all just—"

"You knew. And now you're reneging." He shook his head disgustedly. Stared at her like he didn't even know her. At her. Through her. "The world, Laney? My sister? I don't give a shit about the world or my fucking sister! This is about us! This is about what we want, what we deserve!"

"What you want. What you deserve."

Seconds passed before he said, "They're one in the same, aren't they?"

"No, Vince. They've never been one in the same."

"Look, you keep acting like you're lost or some shit. Like you're trying to find yourself on some coming-of-age bullshit." He was right in front of her before she completed a blink, and suddenly his bear-sized hands were cupping her cheeks and his scentless breath was on her face. "But you aren't lost and there's nothing to find. I've given it all to you. Everything. It's all right here. Just take it and enjoy."

"And be grateful. Right? That's the next thing out of your mouth?"

"Gratefulness never hurt anybody either."

Laney shook him off and stepped back from him. "I just need something to myself, Vince. Something. But you won't even let me have that."

"What do you need to yourself, Laney? Your mini bar?" Leaning back in her face. "Your Beaujolais? Calvados?" Closer. Closer. "To unravel right before my eyes? Glass shards all over the fucking bathroom floor. That's what you want? Don't kid your fucking self—you know I won't let you do that."

A scoff. "Didn't know you cared so much. But then I guess you don't, because if you did you'd know I haven't been drinking anymore. You'd have noticed."

"I take care of you. I care *for* you. You can't even deny that, despite what I may say when I'm angry and—"

"It's what you say when you're angry that really counts, Vince! That's what tells me who you really are! I know you know. I know you know what happened at that table."

"—now I'm trying to do just that, and you're giving me a headache with this bullshit. We all have eyes on us. You have eyes on you—Jill does, too. It's not on us if she cracks. Just you don't crack up, too!"

"I don't need any more eyes on me!"

"This weekend is a marathon even without Jill's bullshit—"

"It's fucking suffocating, Vince!"

For a while, the space between them was only filled with the sound of Laney's breathing. Those words rang out in the air like a slap to both of their faces. Vince realized his mistake, heard the words he'd just said still lingering in the air, and reached out to her. Laney stepped back and held her hand up to stop him. To give herself a second. Vince walked away from her, pacing then coming back. Laney squeezed her arms across her chest, a stance meant to fend him of as much as it was meant to steady herself.

He reached for the lamp switch again, pushing Laney over the edge. Dismissing her and her feelings once again. Once again pushing her to the side.

"Get out of the bed, Vince. We are going to talk about this."

"I told you. I'm done talking. Goodnight."

Laney angrily grabbed his hand. He pushed her away, grumbling something about her being crazy. Furious and at the edge of her sanity, Laney grabbed the lamp and ripped the cord from the wall, hurling it into the wall. She heard it smash and fall to the floor as the darkness enveloped them. Debris of the ceramic lamp ricocheted off the wall.

"Are you fucking crazy?" Vince leapt from the bed. Laney could barely make out his shadow as he scurried toward the wall to turn the room lights on, the remote to their bedroom's features lost in the darkness. He fumbled around, trying to find the switch but couldn't. "That's your thing now? Temper tantrum glass throwing?"

"Get out. Get out!" she screamed before she even knew what she was doing. She pushed him as hard as she could, shoving him against the wall as he, surprised, lost his balance.

"Get out! Get out of here!"

Vince threw up his arm to shield himself from the blows. Laney hit him again, punching his arm, screaming. Dizzy.

"What the hell do you mean 'get out'? This is *my* house. My room."

"Our house. Our room! And I want you out of here." She hit him over and over again until he finally got a grasp on her.

"Are you clean out of your fucking mind, Laney?" He yelled again, grabbing her wrists, pinning her against the wall. "Are you fucking crazy?"

"Let go of me."

Their yelling shook the room. Her wedding ring cut into her finger as he pressed her against the wall. His wedding band reflected the moonlight in the darkness.

"You need to calm your ass down!"

"Get out of here. I don't want to see your face. I don't know who. You. Are."

"Yeah, well I'm beginning to feel the exact same damn way about you."

Laney struggled to get free of his grasp, pushing against him as hard as she could, trying to shake him off her, but he squeezed her wrists even harder. Shook her. Laney's head hit the wall, then again, and she grimaced. She could hardly make out the outline of his face with the weak light through the thin curtains. He finally released her roughly. Her husband panted for breath. She did the same, rubbing her wrists then the back of her head.

"I can't believe you're acting like this, attacking me like you're crazy. Over her? What's the matter with you? I don't know who the hell *you* are because you're just her shell. And I don't wanna be anywhere near your crazy ass right now. I'm gonna take the guest room. You'd best to sit here and get your fucking shit together before I start thinking that marrying you was a mistake. I didn't sign up to marry some Jill clone."

Vince slammed the bedroom door behind him, rattling the artwork and memories dotting the wall. Laney ran her fingers over her scalp, breathless. Buried her face into one of the pillows that hadn't fallen to the floor with their movements. There were tears but no sobs.

No sobs, because she was too busy focusing on the words, that inkling at the edge of her mind. Some words scratching there trying to get out. What were they? Where had she heard them?

Then she knew.

211

II

Jill's townhouse had existed only as a random address in Delaney's phone for the nearly two years Jill had been back in town. An obligatory series of letters and numbers that had to be somewhere in her phone for when it was time to send out stationary and plan for holiday get-togethers. But that night, as Laney hastily pulled on a pair of sweatpants and a t-shirt and brushed the hair and moisture out of her eyes, it was something else. Some kind of beacon.

In Jill's driveway, she parked. And at her door, she knocked.

She knocked again.

And it was when Laney raised her fist to pound on the door a third time, to throw all her weight into it and maybe shout Jillian's name, that the door swung open. And there she was.

Jill was in some ratty sweatshirt with her hair in a mane around her head and feet bare against the floorboards. Her eyes glistened but were otherwise blank, until they focused on Laney and recognition ignited. There was a trail of blood trickling from her hand down her right index finger. Laney pushed passed her and refused to look at it. There were textbooks laying open on the coffee table and a cigarette billowing soft tendrils of smoke in the ashtray beside them, the straight razor on top of some still-smoldering cigarette butts.

Laney dropped her keys on the table by the door and continued into the kitchen. There were no walls between them with the open floorplan, and Jill watched her as she went. There was Patron in the freezer and Guinness in the fridge, right next to the bullet of blended vegetable smoothie, cheap Pinot Grigio on the counter and a glass of water in the sink. Laney bypassed the shot glasses in the frosted-glass cabinets and reached for a tumbler instead. She filled it with tap water and took it all down.

Jillian collapsed back onto the sofa. She leaned over her books as though she was about to continue studying, then thought better of it and reached for the cigarette instead. Laney took a seat in one of the barstools. Swiveled to face Jill.

"Jesus, Jill, how many of those do you go through a day, huh?"

"About as many of those as you go through." She gestured toward the bottle of wine on the counter and blew smoke out of the side of her mouth. "But it's cool. We're cool. Aren't we?"

"Christ, Jill." Laney ran both of her hands through her hair at the roots. "You're a fucking mess."

"Me? Nah." Jillian laughed, took another drag and stubbed the cigarette out. "What are you doing here, anyway?"

"I–I don't know, really. The table. What happened?"

Jill didn't answer right away. Instead, she seemed to catch a glimpse of the blood in her hand out of the corner of her eye then brought it closer to her face to examine it.

"You didn't come here because of some table, Laney. You came here because of those bruises on your arms." Jill jerked her chin toward Laney. No, not toward Laney; toward her wrists. "Looks like you had a run-in with the other side of Janus."

Laney didn't respond.

"So, what happened?"

"You know what happened. All those stories, they're all the same." She rubbed her wrists instinctively, holding one in hand while rolling the other hand until it popped. She was silent for several long seconds, watching her sister close her eyes and slump even further back into the couch.

"Jill, what did he do to you? What did *they* do to you? You don't so much as look at each other anytime you're in the same room. That's not some coincidence. It's not. And if I'm in it now—if I've married in it—"

Jill opened her eyes and settled them on Laney. Focused them. "You're the first person to ever ask me that." Laney let that hang in the air around them, waiting for an answer that Jill never offered. "But what do you really want? You didn't come over here for me."

"Yeah, I did. Someone had to come over here. For you. But, also, it was something you said. Look, back at the caterer's you said something to me. You said there was a time when I played in a field full of bombs and mistook them for sunflowers."

"Yeah, so?"

"Well, I definitely see the bombs now."

Jillian laughed and collapsed back into the couch again. "You don't see shit, Laney. Those pretty little eyes can't see four inches in front of its own face. It's," she giggled to herself, then louder, her laughter rolling as if over Georgia hills. "It's comical really."

"I see—"

"You don't see shit, Laney! Because if you *did*, you'd be angry. *Really* fucking angry! If you *did*, you'd stop that good-girl fucking Dessommes act with the traditions and the sabers because you'd *know* that you were trapped in this shit from the beginning. You'd *know* what I've known all along—that you didn't want any of this. You didn't want to marry Vince and you didn't want to sit in some house on a hill with a calendar full of Group events. You'd *know* that Vince trapped you into this shit because he *does* know. He knew you wouldn't resist, wouldn't back out. Wouldn't leave. And wouldn't say no in front of all those people. Not...if he did it just right. Oh, and he did it just right, Laney, because here you are."

Laney watched on and heard her while not hearing her. Jillian's voice had shoved her somewhere far away—not underwater necessarily. No, that wasn't the feeling, but under sand. Completely buried and suffocated, her lungs filling with hot, sharp grit.

"Ah, now you're getting it." Jillian smirked up at her, raising and lowering her eyebrows as it sunk it. "You let that fucker cage you like a rat in a maze, just like," *snap*, "that.

"Florence once told me, 'Life is one big trap filled with a bunch of little traps. And if you pay attention—if you listen hard enough—you can hear them as they snap shut around you.'" Jill leaned forward and rubbed the column of ashes along the rim of the ashtray then brought it back to her lips. "You weren't paying attention, Laney. Because if you were, you'd see that Sabrina is a mini Renée. She'll leak your business like a faucet, smiling in your face all the while. If you haven't seen that yet, you're more than blind to the traps; you're a fool. And if you never realized the timing of your engagement was just one of the many ways he's manipulated you, controlled you, caged you—you're more than a fool; you're done."

SHOOTING CRAPS

AALIYAH

Aaliyah pulled herself out of bed late the next afternoon and realized she'd slept and deliberated all of Thanksgiving away. No matter; she'd never been one for the hypocrisy of the holiday. For some reason, people had been cultivated to think of turkeys when Thanksgiving rolled around; she always thought of smallpox blankets. And, what did she have to be thankful for on that day anyway? Well, she reasoned, she shouldn't take it that far. There were starving children and the homeless and the abandoned to think of, and all those other truisms out there that sounded cliché on the tongue but still rang so true. There were, she told herself, countless reasons to count her blessings, and so she resisted the urge to pout and complain as she'd always resisted such an urge. Instead, shoulders were squared, still chewing her lip as she did so. What would pouting and complaining get her anyway? *Where* would they get her? Well, nothing, of course. And nowhere.

Aaliyah stood in the shower for half an hour with Billie Holiday playing in the background. Most of the time, she just stood there, water streaming down on her head, hardly bothering to even wipe it from her eyes. Sleeping most of the day before away hadn't helped her mental space as much as it had helped her exhausted body. She'd needed it for that reason and hadn't realized just how in need of rest she was until she finally had the opportunity, more bitter than sweet though it was, to get that rest. Turning off her cell phone had helped too; who knew what Laney and Nigel—oh, Nigel, she hadn't considered him—were thinking, how many times they'd called? Burrowing in some emotional hole was obviously the selfish thing to do. People out there would be worried about her, wouldn't they? But she needed it.

She needed that quiet bubble more than anything that weekend. She needed to ruminate and ponder. She needed to rethink every decision, every move she'd made at Myers and Peterson to figure out where it had all gone wrong, where she'd turned down the wrong path, where she'd let it all slip through her fingers without ever even noticing. But then she understood— somewhere around the time that most families were slicing into their turkeys and hams—that what had happened at the firm hadn't been for fault of her own. She ought to have anticipated it, yes. But she herself hadn't caused the slight, hadn't merited it. That she'd truly given every fiber within herself to that delusion—to that fanciful notion of feeling her foot on the final rung of that metaphorical corporate ladder in the greatest country on the planet—made her cringe. Yes, she'd fed into that too, but she hadn't been to blame for the slight. Once she took that thought in and let it marinate, once she gave it time to work its way through her system until she could feel it in her very bones—well, that's when she moved on to contemplating her next move.

Aaliyah grabbed the bucket from the pantry and set to work. She needed something, anything, for distraction. Something she could take her frustrations out on. She needed routine because that's what she was used to. So, the scrubbing ensued, a nervous habit Aaliyah had adopted somewhere around undergrad when her family wasn't at hand, wasn't just in the next room or in the basement apartment below, to consult with and console her. When pressures were mounting and life was precarious, cleaning always balanced the scales, helped her plant her feet solidly on the ground. Her safe version of nicotine. She scrubbed until the entire place sparkled. Until the oven had been cleaned of every crumb—as though any had ever existed—her head in the oven like Sylvia Plath, depressed but coming out of it slowly. Then the wood floors had been polished, the granite counters shined, the bathtub scoured.

It was after the counters that she felt ready enough to turn her cell back on, and it was while she was leaned into the bathtub, scrubbing with determined strokes, that the phone rang.

II

Scene.
An hour later.
Aaliyah steps aside to let Delaney in and closes the front door behind her.
AALIYAH: Laney, please don't launch into some tirade. *(stopping Laney short with her mouth poised to do just that)* I just needed some time to myself.
DELANEY: Time to yourself for what? I don't even know what the hell happened. Meanwhile, if you knew the kind of week I've had, you'd know why I was worried your phone wasn't answered. Not the best weekend to be out of the loop, Liyah.
Aaliyah steps aside as Delaney walks around her and into her home without so much as a backward glance. She drops her

purse and pea coat on the sofa, resembling some retro artist with her black turtle neck top, skinny black pants and black cowhide loafers. She continues into the kitchen, grabbing a bottle of water for herself and Aaliyah.

Delaney offers it to her, and Aaliyah chuckles.

AALIYAH: Water, huh?

DELANEY: You don't even want to know.

At Aaliyah's glance to the contrary, Laney shakes her head.

DELANEY: Later. I can't even...I can't even go into it right now. I came over to see what was up with you. So, here, take your water and give me a break, too, will you?

Aaliyah eyes her friend and takes the water. Delaney reaches over to brush a lock from Aaliyah's face, but Aaliyah pushes her hand away and gives her a look.

AALIYAH: Just sit down, girl! Your fidgeting is making me nervous.

Laney sits next to her on the other end of the sofa.

DELANEY: Sorry. My nerves are fried to shit.

They sit there like this drinking their water until Delaney caps hers and turns back to Aaliyah.

DELANEY: So, are you going to tell me what happened? You sent some cryptic, *Twilight Zone* message and expected me to just, what, telepathically know that you weren't suicidal and that everything was A-okay?

And yet, the fuss and exaggeration Delaney would usually spew out of her gregarious alter ego is mute, her features serious and pensive as she eyes Aaliyah. Aaliyah resists the urge to tease her, What, no, joke about how I had you so worried? Why the house is so clean—how I'm such a selfish bitch? *She senses that the joke won't be met well, that there is something simmering under Delaney's surface. So, she recounts the tale with no further jesting, matching Delaney's unusual seriousness.*

219

The story tumbles out of her, picking up steam as she goes, as she remembers pieces she forgot during her hours-long musings the previous day.

DELANEY: (*when Aaliyah finishes and looks up*) What did Nigel say? Have you talked to him?

AALIYAH: Nigel? I don't know. No, I haven't talked to him.

DELANEY: At all? So, he doesn't know you quit your job, and you don't know...

AALIYAH: What? Oh, that stupid Carmella dinner he was going on about? I told him I didn't wanna go.

DELANEY: No, that he... (*Delaney's hesitation isn't unwarranted, of course, but still she feels silly for not just telling her*) You know, Nigel took a job with Vince at The Group. (*So, she does.*)

[Cut to black.]

THE ONLY THING CONSTANT IS CHANGE ITSELF

NIGEL

There was no reason to call her again after all the direct-to-voicemail outcomes he'd gotten thus far, so he opted to drive to her instead.

It wasn't the easiest thing to do. There was some self-doubt there and plenty of nervousness. There was that all-too-familiar mental nag asking if he was moving too fast, if she would think it odd that he just showed up at her place. But then he remembered his previous resolution, the resolution to not heed the ridiculous rules of dating that had become all-too commonplace. To do as he felt, not as social cues dictated.

Within an hour of hanging up the phone with Micah—whom he'd asked several times in the past twenty-four hours whether or not he should just drop it all and check on her—he was in his car on the way to Aaliyah. When she opened the door for him, Nigel stood there with his shirt untucked over jeans, a bouquet of lilies in one hand and the other in his pocket. He noticed she didn't step out of the way and gesture for him to enter immediately. She stood there for a few fleeting moments, watching him watching her.

"Well, come on in then. You can leave those here." He pressed the stems of the flowers down into the pebble bed in a silver vase in the entryway with a *crunch* and was already admonishing, "So what the hell?" as she turned to head into the living room.

"What the hell, you, I'd say."

"I'm not the one who went MIA on Thanksgiving, Aaliyah. What's been going on with you?"

"Nigel, enough with the drama. I left your place Wednesday morning and the rest of the day was absolute shit. Yesterday wasn't much better. I don't even wanna talk about it."

He plopped down where Laney had sat less than an hour earlier, arm resting on the arm of the chair. "Lucky for you, you don't have to 'cause Micah already told me what—"

An angry sigh, "Micah, huh? Strange talk for the basketball court, don't you think?"

"Didn't see him on the courts. Saw him at dinner. The dinner you were supposed to be at."

"Oh, Nigel. I didn't go to the dinner because—"

"I know why you didn't go to the dinner, Liyah." Nigel tossed her a knowing glance and let it linger. "And, not just because you don't like Cammy and Nate and whoever else you've decided you don't like today—"

"Hmm, Cammy and Nate." Aaliyah tossed his knowing gaze back at him. "Like you're old chums, huh?" Her glance melted into a glower, but Nigel's softened enough to let her know he volunteered to back down from the defensive. "What'd he say, eh? That I just up and quit? That I'm crazy, and I—"

"He said you were hurt, that you weren't taking his calls. Told him you hadn't answered mine either. You didn't have to quit like that."

"You didn't have to sell out like that, but you did, and I did, so let's just move on."

"Sell...oh, you must've talked to Laney."

"Well, you know I ain't talk to Vince."

"So, she told you about Micah."

"She told me about Micah."

"And how they were flirting with each other in the corner like none of those Gold Coast fools would notice?"

"Flir—what? It's not like that between them. They had some— I don't know—convo at some book store, that's it. Laney wouldn't flirt with that man if you paid her—"

"So, pay her, then, Liyah. Look, I don't care who Laney's giggling it up with. I really don't give a fuck, because, honestly, Vince's ass probably has it coming. But I saw them. I saw the way he brushed her arm, the way they laughed together like you and me do. Do I give a fuck that Laney might have a thing with Micah? No. My point is that Laney didn't tell you the whole story. You don't *see* the whole story. You know I took a job 'cause she told you. You know Micah took a job, 'cause she told you. But that's just her perspective. Just what *she* wants you to know. Why don't you get your own perspective, Liyah?"

"Oh, just join in and sit at the table with them? With you?"

"It's not about some metaphorical table."

"No, it's about the fact those people are like a vortex, Nigel. Sucking up anyone and everyone I love, anything I care about. They throw some money at 'em—a nice, fat check—and then they're gone, whatever—whoever—it is. And that just leaves me. By myself. Over here. You took that job, Nigel, and now you're one of *them*—all of a sudden! And I'm still not."

It seemed like the time to give her a speech, something profound and formulaic. To tell her there were no sides, that they were all friends. But there was no need to lie to her because she already knew. If it was a matter of fitting in, Aaliyah would never even give it a shot because she didn't want to fit in with them. And Nigel wouldn't counsel her to do so, because he didn't really feel the need to fit in with them either. Still, it was the discomfort he wanted to alleviate for her. It was the feeling of left out, a feeling of less than, that he wanted to cure her of and shield her from if and when it ever existed.

"Aaliyah, you're not 'over here.' Anywhere you are, I am. Do you understand? Anywhere you are, Laney is. We're not leaving you anywhere. *I'm* not leaving you anywhere."

"And wherever you are, I am, right? But what if *I* don't want to be there? I mean, we're too different now, Nigel. We're too different."

"I know you're not gonna act like this over some job I took. You know how I feel about Vince, and you know how I feel about you. I never even considered we'd end up here, me and him. I ran into the guy at that Renée shindig and he started talking business. Asked if I wanted to sit down and talk over some idea he had. I didn't think it would go this far this fast. Couple months ago, it'd never even crossed my mind to call him let alone work for him and you know that. But if someone makes the right offer, you have to at least consider it. I had to at least give it a shot."

"It's not about some job you took. It's about *the* job you took. I don't expect you to come tell me every job you might take. I'm not your mama and I'm not your wife. But I *do* expect you to come tell me when I'm being blindsided. When I might wake up one day to find everyone I know is on one side—and it ain't my side."

Still, this wasn't about being like them or blending into their world. And when he told her, Aaliyah gave him an eye roll as he'd expected she would, but he continued on. For him, Nigel explained, it was about finances. It was about career opportunity and she should understand that better than anyone, shouldn't she? Vince was nothing more than a door, a way to ingress a stratosphere of deals that was previously inaccessible to him, that he'd previously only been able to touch on its periphery. Yet, with that deal, with his new corner office at The Group and all the trappings that accompanied that title, that station, he'd embarked on a new path, one he hadn't even given thought to before. It wasn't about being chums with them; it was about a means to quite the self-serving end.

"Why didn't you say something about this deal with the devil before?"

"Say something like what? What would you have said, 'Take the job?'"

Aaliyah glared at him. "You know I wouldn't have."

"Which is why I didn't tell you. I was going to tell you before we went to the dinner, but you said you didn't want to go, and then you disappeared. I had to decide for myself—make my own decision independent of whatever this thing is you got going on with Vince. That's probably why Micah didn't tell you either. We just had to decide for ourselves."

"Nigel, Micah is a snake. Not some play snake, neither. I mean, a true snake. How the hell did the man go from stealing my campaign to sitting in Vince's lap anyway? All in one night, one fell damn swoop?"

Nigel pushed himself to the edge of his seat, elbows to knees, glancing over at her. "It wasn't all in one night. We'd been talking to Vince about The Group for a couple weeks. There were NDAs and offers and back and forth and—it wasn't a fly-by-night thing. He'd already been offered the job by then. He just hadn't made a decision yet. Hadn't told Vince yet—"

"Hadn't told *me* yet!"

"He wanted out—needed away from that chick Milla. You *know* that. She was smothering him, trying to control him. And then with what happened Wednesday—"

"He asked for it. What'd the man expect?"

"And, I mean, why wouldn't he take it? You said you invited him to Renée's to network. This is the Gig Economy at its finest, and now you're mad he did just that?"

"No, I—I'm mad because—because...that man always comes out top of the heap! The whole time he's being back-patted and congratulated, he already had another move in his pocket, Nigel. He'd already beat me."

"Liyah." Nigel sighed and held out his hand to her. She refused to take it, shaking her head annoyedly, pulling her legs to her chest on the sofa. "Liyah." He moved next to her on the couch and wrapped his arms around her. "You've got to stop making everything a competition. It's not all some race."

"It wasn't supposed to be a race, Nigel. He was supposed to be my friend. We were gonna get there together." Aaliyah allowed him to pull her to him, to rest her head against his chest. She breathed him in in deep breaths and felt him rubbing his hands over her shoulders. "But we were never gonna get anywhere together. He was already too far ahead."

Nigel prepared himself to comfort her. He readied his hand to wipe her tears away and pulled her close to lend her support when she sobbed, but she never did any of that. Aaliyah allowed him to caress her; she even held his hand, but she never crumbled.

After a few minutes of silence, she looked up at him and snickered, "You and Micah. You and Vince." A disgusted little shake of her head. "I shouldn't even be surprised. Micah and Vince are two of a kind. And they'll turn you. I know they will. Slugs leave residue as they pass, ya'know. On you and on her."

"Not on me, Liyah. Not on me. And now's your chance to see that. I want you to see that everything is fine, and you and me are still you and me. You and Micah can still be you and Micah."

"Trust me, we'll never be that again."

"Come to the benefit with me this weekend, and you'll see. Get your own perspective and see for yourself. This isn't some new thing. This is you and me the same as we were the night we met. The same as it's been since then. Now I've got a new job, and you've got some down time, but nothing else has changed."

"And if it has changed?"

"Nothing has changed, Aaliyah. You'll see."

PART THREE: BLOOD IS THICKER THAN NOTHING

Black don't crack and brown don't frown. —*African American Proverb*

THE CAGED BIRD SINGS

JILLIAN

en.

Alessandra lived in a sprawling ranch-style home in the northern suburbs of Atlanta. A community of golf courses and swanky country clubs, their home was one of many idyllic erections situated in a grand cul-de-sac. Crème adobe walls with mixed stone accents complemented the high beams crossing the vaulted ceilings in the grand room and several of the bedrooms. Bear skins covered large expanses of gleaming hardwood floors, freshly polished by immigrant workers who never spoke but bowed often. And the kitchen—where the girls had just run giggling from, requisite oatmeal cookies and milk in hand—was a cavernous behemoth of granite counters and exposed wood trim that tossed an elegant nod toward the Maine summer cabin Sandi's family also owned.

There were blankets covering the floor and draped over the couches to form a makeshift fort in the den, where inside could be found two American Girl dolls—with corresponding hair and skin colors to the two friends—with various outfit options strewn haphazardly around the mouth of the fort, an empty plate, which had just an hour before held sugar cookies, and one of Dante's remote-control Corvettes, which the girls had snuck into his room and snatched at the start of the evening. Across the room, in front of the crackling fire was a lavender hula hoop, a V.C. Andrews book, colored pencils.

The girls settled back into the den, claiming it as their own. The various hues of blankets didn't do a bad job at playing the planted flag either. Jill crawled into their tent on her hands and knees and felt Sandi army crawling in behind her. She felt her ankle being grabbed and yanked backwards to which she laughed out loud and pulled her foot back into her own possession. They set up shop inside, Sandi's blonde ringlets messy and half covering her eyes as she lit her flashlight and held it under her face. A ghost story was started, as promised before their cookie-refill run, but was halted when the roof of the makeshift tent was snatched from overhead and the light from the den and the bay windows flooded into their once-dim hideaway.

"What the hell are you doing with my freakin' car, yo? Thought I told you to keep your paws to yourself and stop stealing my stuff."

Sandi shielded her eyes against the intrusion of light. When she looked up and saw that it was Dante, her fourteen-year-old brother, her reaction did not mirror Jill's in the slightest. Jill, hearing the threatening voice with just enough adolescent bass in it as to be reminiscently off-putting, shrunk away, her hands and feet scurrying her backwards until her back hit one of the sofas in a move that was not meant to be a crab walk but was strikingly close to being so. She heard her breath catch in her throat and held it there, waiting, watching, hyperaware of the new presence in the room and mindful that danger may be on the horizon. Jill's eyes darted back and forth between her friend and this older brother for a few quick seconds that flashed by faster than she could grab, a cat whose back was now rounded in readiness.

And yet, Alessandra did not react in the same manner, Jill noticed. Sandi grabbed one of the dolls by the arm and hurled it Dante's way, scrunching her nose and smacking her lips annoyedly.

"Ugh, get out of here, Dante! It's not your turn in here. It's me and Jill's turn!"

"I told you not to be borrowing my shit, girl! Hell's wrong wit' you?"

Dante shoved his dark hair off his forehead with a nonchalant little flick of the head meant to be cool, only for the bang to fall back over his eye. He stood there over them in his baggy patchwork jeans and football jersey with a colorful high-top sneaker.

"God, Dante," Sandi laughed behind her hand, lunging to grab for her brother's ankle but missing as he stepped back and away from her. "You're such a wigger!"

"Oh, I'm a what? Huh? Say it again; I dare you!"

Before Sandi could react, Dante lunged and fell on top of her, his hands grabbing for her. Jill watched, terrified, shaking as her friend tried to fight off her brother, until she noticed that they were laughing instead of yelling.

Then she noticed that Dante wasn't even assaulting his sister, certainly not in the way Jill had expected, that she'd braced for in that moment his body had jerked forward toward them. No, he was pulling Sandi into a loose headlock. Ruffling her hair. Pressing his knuckles into the crown of her head. A noogie, from which Sandi freed herself, pushed him off and then speed crawled to him and jumped on him so her body weight pinned him down. She proved to be less than a match for him. He was able to easily flip her over and off him. Sandi laughed her head off; Dante gave her a shove then stood to his feet, pushing off the sofa next to Jill's head, and grabbed his Corvette.

"Hey, you little booger, stop touching my freakin' shit, alright!"

Sandi laughed harder, then harder still as he pretended to lunge at her again but only tussled her hair.

"I'm so not the booger. You're the booger! Now get outta here!" She kicked toward him, but Dante jumped out of the way again. Flicked his hair again. Grinned.

"Yeah, whatever, little monster."

"You're the little monster!"

"Hey!" an adult voice called from outside of the room. Jill looked up to see Sandi's mom, Chelsea, gliding past the opening to the den and disappearing around a corner, the cordless phone pressed to her ear. "Both of you little monsters behave yourself. Jill's gonna think you were raised by wolves," she laughed, already out of sight.

"We were raised by wolves!" Dante called back, laughing too. He pulled Sandi to her feet and shot Jill a smile. "We really were," he nodded at her, tossing her a conspiratorial glance as if he were letting her in on their family secret.

"You were maybe. But I'm a little lady. Daddy says so. Now get out of here!" Sandi shoved him toward the doorway, her hands pressed to his back, Jill's eyes pressed to the siblings, observing.

"Yeah, yeah. Yack, yack."

Dante picked up the comforter he'd pulled from over their heads and started arranging it back over the arms of the furniture. Sandi scooted back over toward Jill and giggled as the cover was lowered over them and the makeshift fort made whole again.

"There, I'm out. Peace in the Middle East. Chunking up the deuce to y'all homies. And stay outta my stuff, yo!"

"Stupid head. Kid thinks Eminem is the best thing since My Little Pony."

Sandi shook her head, grinning, and reached for the flashlight again. Turned it on. Held it under her face. And though Sandi had not yet opened her mouth to continue the story, Jill's face already reflected shock and dismay. Sandi lowered the flashlight a little and regarded her friend curiously.

"What's the matter, Jillie? Don't you and Vince play, too?"

The evening continued for Jillian and Alessandra in the same manner it'd begun: cheerful antics. Dante nodded that they could come in his room when they rapped at his door and taught them a slew of inappropriate words from his rap collection and rated-R movie stash. Sandi laughed when Jill tripped over the word *motherfucker*, having scarcely ever heard it and never said it. Dante corrected her pronunciation, grinned when she got it right and gave her a little shoulder punch in lieu of a high five. The girls both erupted into a fit of titters at the sound of it successfully falling off Jill's tongue.

Chelsea swooped in later that evening, clad in white pajama pants and an old men's tank top, to help the girls with finger painting and molding clay sculptures from purple and yellow mounds of Play-Doh. She had been an art history major at Vassar before meeting her then public defender attorney husband and settling down to start making a family somewhere around his first year on the bench. Out had come Dante, destined to be tall, dark and handsome like his father—everyone said so—followed by a slew of miscarriages, which nearly broke her and began the philandering eye of her husband, only to finally give birth to the healthy Grace Alessandra—her *prénom* so fittingly given to her at birth because she was so blond and so blue, pure, her father called her, an angel. She was the spitting image of her mother, only fitting since her husband had gotten a clone of himself, and the apple of her parents' eyes. For her father, this was because Alessandra had ended his wife's suffering. For Chelsea, it was because Alessandra had ended her husband's affairs.

Chelsea stayed up all night with them baking another batch of cookies, which she burned. Sandi whispered to Jill that their nanny had made the first two batches and left them out for their sleepover. Jill nodded her understanding. She'd never had a nanny, because her daddy would not permit it. But she knew of the second-mother set up that most of her friends had—the nannies doing most of the domestic work to set the mothers up for the façade of perfection. Neither of the girls minded the burnt cookies in the slightest and nibbled at them anyway because it brought a blushing smile to Chelsea's late-thirties face and a pinch from her to both of their cheeks. They fell asleep with a Disney animated movie playing in the background, surrounded by their colored pencils, notebooks and dolls. Neither girl heard or felt when Dante stood in the doorway to check on them and, leaning against the door jam, shook his head with a snort at the disaster they'd turned the grand den into. Nor did they feel when Chelsea came in to pull the covers up to their chins and kiss each of their cheeks.

The next day, her mama arrived at eleven o'clock sharp, pulling into their driveway in her stylish Lincoln Navigator. She stepped down from the car, beige heel first, and flicked the door shut with a turn of her wrist. Chelsea answered the door in the same pair of pajama pants she'd worn the night before. Flecks of flour and a smudge of egg yolk on her top from where she'd managed to make a few respectable omelets and biscuits for the children that morning. Her hair was pulled back into a ponytail still damp from her early morning shower, and that was how she greeted Addison when she arrived. Jill watched as her mama accepted Chelsea's hug, resisting the urge to titter, for she'd seen that strained look on her mother's pretty face before: the politely agreeable strain that said Addie did not really want the hug. She was probably concerned about getting flour on her pink tweed skirt suit or upsetting her French roll.

Jill had already placed her overnight bag at the front door, so all she had to do was receive the goodbye hugs from her friend and friend's mother while Addison thanked Chelsea for allowing Jill over for the evening. Maybe she didn't mean to be stiff; for she did smile and wave her fingers at Sandi, who was standing to the right of Chelsea. But Jill heard the falter in her mother's voice. She knew it. Knew Addie's nuances like a captive knew those of their captor.

"Addie, Jill is such a joy to have over. You know she's welcome back anytime. And you too, my love. We still haven't had that lunch we've been yakking about. Next week maybe, one day you're at the club?"

"Of course, honey." Addison tossed her a radiant smile, accepting Jill's overnight bag and hoisting it onto her shoulder. "Just ring me up. There's nothing like a nice, quiet lunch with an old friend."

Chelsea accepted that open invitation and waved them off, never closing the heavy oak door until Addison had closed the car door on Jill and Jill had buckled up her seat belt.

In the car, Addison asked about her day and commented on how well Jill had kept her hair. At a light, Addie made a note in her calendar book to link up with Chelsea then, shutting it and pitching it back into her Vuitton, pressed her prettily heeled foot to the accelerator prematurely on reflex. The Lincoln jerked out into the middle of the busy intersection before she realized that the light was still red.

"Oh, shit!"

Her mama slammed on the brakes and the car jerked to a stop. A Mercedes blew past them laying on the horn. Addie, breath ragged from a touch of fear, waved her apologies to the driver and reversed back toward the line at her red light. It wasn't until then she realized that the curse had not only come from her mouth, but from that of her ten-year-old as well. Jill sat in the back seat, mouth ajar but slammed shut with both of her hands clamped over it, eyes wide. The word had flown off her tongue so easily, too easily, thanks to Dante. If she hadn't seen the look on her mother's face when she turned around, Jill would have laughed out loud. Instead, she was greeted with a sharp slap across the face that rocked her in her seat and lit her cheek on fire.

"Ow!"

Addie glared at her from over her right shoulder. "Jill! Watch that mouth of yours, young lady! Jesus, you're turning into a vulgar little street girl right before my eyes, aren't you?" Addie pulled herself together, touching her unchanged hairdo and taking a deep breath. "Jillian, you keep that up and you'll fit right in with the derelicts and juvenile delinquents. Is that what you want? To be wasted goods?"

The light turned green.

Jill dared not speak and tried to force the water collecting in her eyes from submitting to the laws of gravity and falling down her cheeks.

Addison took another deep breath and ignored the blaring horn from behind her when she turned back to Jill and said, "And don't tell your father about this, about the light. You know how he is about this car."

Jill nodded her head that she wouldn't, and Addie accelerated away from the intersection.

II

Twelve.

Florence's hats were still some of her most prized possessions. Not monetarily, of course. But if sentimentality was a currency all its own, they would've been priceless to her. Tiny black boxes with pill box hats and veils. Large boxes wide enough for Jill to wrap her entire arms around sheltering elaborate headpieces with feathers and satin bows. As far as Jill was concerned, they were part of her grandmother's legacy, more so than her winning smile or her cunning business savvy. For a twelve-year-old, faced with the demise of the woman she'd watched her entire life—the woman who'd maintained a straight back and a raised head throughout it all—they were the true currency of her life. The truth behind her wit and personality, her flair, the enigma that had always been her. Under some, she'd tucked away her lovely white hair, knotted into tight, crisp chignons. Under others, her mane had flown freely, elegantly, without inhibition.

After her death—liver cancer had taken the old girl, painful but quick—after the dirt had been shoveled onto her pearly white casket, after the mourners had gone, after the will had been probated, Renée and Addison had been charged with sifting through the remainder of her possessions, the ones that'd gone unclaimed and ungifted in the final will and testament. For, with her husband gone five years preceding her, Carlton concerned himself with the dispersal of his parents' estate, with the business that a death left in its wake. It was the expectation that the women would see to her things. Jill could not recall ever even hearing the adults talk about it. It had been simply understood.

And so it happened that Jillian and Sabrina had been in the next room when the women went through Florence's remaining possessions. Renée wore her pearls. Addison claimed a half-dozen lovely shawls from Hermès, which she complained about under her breath to Carlton, and a diamond and sapphire tennis bracelet. While the girls gabbed and shared their phone screens with each other, laughing at this or that in the next room, their mothers sifted through nine oil paintings, the remainder of her less-prized—though not necessarily less expensive jewels—four furs, and whatever other finery they divided amongst themselves under the guise of continuing Florence's memory.

In the end, there were only four hat boxes left unclaimed, still on the top shelf in the closet. Jill noticed as they were ushered from the room and reflected back on them as her mama said her farewells to her sister-in-law in the driveway. They hugged Jill's daddy and patted their handkerchiefs to their mascaraed eyes. Vincent, always the little novice, stood by his father's side and consoled his aunt and mother, who dutifully let him do so. He patted their backs and leaned his forehead to theirs, at sixteen already taller than they.

Jillian touched her mother's hand. Referenced the hats that had gone unclaimed. Asked if she could have them.

"Your nanna's old hats? But, why?"

"Because, I want something of hers. I wanna remember her, Mama."

"You have something of hers, Jill. Several very lovely pieces, which she gave to you instead of your cousin, I might add. You'll get them when you come of age. It's been willed. You'll get them. What's the matter with you anyway, thinking about a thing like that when your aunt and father are—"

"Mama, they're fine." She ignored her mother's piercing gaze, her annoyed twitching at the corner of her mouth, and pressed on. "And I know about what she left me. But it's not about that. I want something of *hers*."

Addison dismissively waved her hand in Jill's direction, her tire with the conversation already evident on her face.

"Do as you please, Jill. Get the key from your father. Sentimental little thing." And then she was back to consoling and hugging, nodding and dabbing her eyes with Renée.

Her father chuckled at her request, digging into his pocket for the key as if it were a piece of wrapped candy for her. "That's my girl. My Little Florence," he laughed before sending Jill on her way.

Back inside of the half-empty house and up the stairs to her grandmother's room, Jill side stepped the divans and elegant vanity stools that still smelled of her grandmother's Chanel. It had not yet been decided whether the home would be sold, only that the willed possessions would be removed and properly dispersed per the final documents, the rest to be dealt with later. Of course, the home was eventually sold and no other word was ever spoken about it. The family had little need for the reality of the remaining items and even less need of the sentimentality of the home itself.

Downstairs, Jill marched to the Navigator with her arms full, ignoring Vince's sneers and her mother's glances. Because there in her arms she held the true essence of who her grandmother was. Under the name and the perfume, she was in these boxes, and Jill would never let them go.

III

Seventeen.

Charades had never been a Dessommes family pastime, but the one night that it was welcomed into the house Jill made her exit.

It was easy enough to say that she was headed out to Sandi's house to study, though she hadn't seen Sandi in over a week and hadn't spoken to her in nearly as long. She would again, she was sure, likely later on that week, but there was no rush. By then, it was clear as crystal that she and the blonde phenom had had their day and that day had passed. This, of course, was not only because Jillian had been accepted at Northeastern and Sandi was headed off to the sunny beaches at UCLA, but because somewhere in the midst of ballet shoes and baseball bats, sleepovers and cheer practice, Jillian had outgrown her. For Sandi—oh, dear, sweet Sandi—was a true believer, fully plugged in to the hype of their class, their clean and prim socioeconomic setting, and bound to be the willing next generation of WASP nation one day baking cookies and ordering a nanny of her own employ around. Jill had been past that since the early days of high school at least, earlier, surely. And, thus, the rift between her and Sandi had slowly widened, noticed only by Jillian herself.

With Vince off sowing his royal oats or studying hard to be the next Dessommes leader or scratching his balls or whatever off at Morehouse, the house had been quieter for a couple of years. Of course, he often came home on the weekends, and, of course, this quiet meant that all immediate eyes were on Jill, she being the only minor left under any of the Dessommes' roofs. Sabrina and Matthew had flown the coop. Even the Darensbourgs were scattered around the country at universities that all invited an impressed raise of the eyebrows at the mention of their names. Sabrina had left only the year before, away at Clemson, which was close enough for a weekend drive, but only rarely could Jill get relief from the house long enough to make it. Usually her mama deterred her, scolding her for distracting Sabrina from her studies, as if Sabrina was going to school to be some master cardiothoracic surgeon or something instead of earning a requisite Humanities degree to check off the mandatory education column obligatory to belonging to their tribe.

It was ole Aunt Renée who saved the evening though. Downstairs, pouring their first glasses of Chardonnay before the evening guests were to arrive for a night of jovially—if not primly—letting their hair down. It was Renée who patted Addison's hand dismissively and waved a hand at Jill telling her, "Yes, honey, go, go! Because you don't want to see what's gonna happen here next!"

Renée laughed behind the back of her hand, nearly choking on her drink. As though she planned to streak naked through the house or jump into an orgy once the other adults arrived. Jill had no reason to believe she wouldn't, aside from the fact that her mama was there. Still, it was Renée's banter and lifting of her glass to Jill from across the kitchen that sent her upstairs to grab her bag—full of a more party-worthy change of clothes from the current jeans and sweatshirt she wore and a single can of Red Bull.

She crept down the stairs so as not to remind the women she was still there, lest Addison need another reason to call her over and further interrogate here. It was upon reaching the third to last step that she heard Renée say, "Oh, I know. Always commenting on my tight little sweaters. Mama must've known; she was a sharp ole' tack."

"Your mama didn't know shit, and if she did she didn't much care. He was the money. You don't upset the money. Lord knows she walked in on Tilman trying to hand his way up my skirt a few times. Never said a word."

Renée snickered in that way that told Jill she was shaking her head. "Dirty old man. Dirty old good-for-nothing good-for-everything man."

"And cheers to that," Addie agreed to the sound of clinking glasses. Jill's mother's laughter filled the air, throaty and free, uninhibited. Someone who only peeped around Addie's edges in rare, sporadic moments that sometimes frightened and sometimes awed Jill. "Fuck that dirty old man, and God bless him. God bless him."

IV

That night, there was nose candy and Target Practice.

Jill walked into the loft apartment with an air about her not typical of the Jillian Dessommes she knew and longed to shed. That, obviously, was because she was neither that girl nor anyone she'd ever been associated with. That night—with her hair a wild mane of curls, her heels high and blocky, her skirt short copper leather—she'd never heard of Jill Dessommes—who was that? She was Joss Lindsay, a name she'd half made up half stolen from her aunt, having just been in her presence an hour before and in need of a quick substitute last name on the spot. She'd never told her date, a wide receiver from Georgia Tech, what her last name was when they'd met weeks earlier in the Old Fourth Ward section of town where she was nosing around for trouble and he was all too willing to hand her some.

When he, Carson she thought his name was, strolled over to her with a nonchalant swagger that could only be real and opened his mouth, she knew she couldn't be Jillian the high schooler. She had to be...someone else. And she was only too happy to oblige.

Now, the week before her eighteenth birthday, just weeks away from high school graduation, she was getting used to this Joss. Carson's arm was around her, Black Eyed Peas blaring from the speakers in the corner, next to the Scandinavian-looking blond girls who were jumping around to it and swagger-filled ball players—only a couple of whom she even remotely recognized but figured they must be all part of the same circle from the easy way they jabbed and punched at each other. They were busy playing foosball and knocking back whatever was in the red plastic cups that girls kept bringing them, winking and tossing their hair.

The party was themed, Carson explained, walking her in with a hand at her back. He grinned and nodded toward the group of guys rowdily racking up wins and losses at the foosball table.

"Shit's sick, right? Listen, this kid Noel—you'll meet him—parents got mad loot, right. Third year running he's thrown some shit like this right before finals."

Jill nodded how cool it was, hardly able to even hear him over the clash of the loud music and nearly as loud voices around them. She couldn't hear the heels of her pumps clomping on the floor, but she felt the vibrations of the brushed concrete flooring meeting the bottoms of her feet. It was a loft—likely some converted old factory or warehouse that now came with a trendy price tag to match the ultra-trendy aura of the neighbored. The ceilings were aluminum and concrete, rough with pipes visibly running in and out of the walls. A long metal and copper bar area was covered in cases of Moet.

"What was the theme last year?" Jill yelled over the music, maybe a little too loud.

"Cristal. This year," he gestured around them, "Moet."

It was then that Jill noticed not only the cases of Moet near the counter, but the twenty some-odd bottles being held around the room too. Over the patio door leading out onto the balcony overlooking the Beltline, a huge bull's eye had been hung. Co-eds grabbed one bottle after the next shaking them vigorously, on beat with the music sometimes, then popping the tops from them, the white foam pouring out onto their feet.

"What are they doing?"

"Oh, Target Practice," he called back.

They were at the bar area now, surrounding by other late teens and early twenty-somethings—being legal wasn't a requisite to getting into the party, but no one cared. He grabbed a plastic cup and handed it to her. Grabbed the nearest bottle of open Moet and filled her cup to the brim, then did the same for his own. Tapped his cup to hers and spilled the chilled, gold liquid down the sides of her fingers.

"Yeah, see. You shake the bottle up like this—" He put his cup down and grabbed a new bottle from the case at his feet. "Then pop that shit. You hit that target up there, right in the fuckin' bull's eye, and you win the bet. Here, wanna try it?"

"Oh, no! No, not yet." Jill tried to back-peddle what had probably sounded to his ears like childish fear and held up her cup instead. Gestured she wanted to finish it first.

"Well, fuck it, I'll give it a shot."

He flashed her that grin between a stubble chin and dimpled cheeks and crossed the room toward Noel, raising his arm to gesture to Jill that this was the guy he'd been telling her about. Accepted Noel's embrace and clap on the back. Tried his hand at Target Practice.

Carson's cork flew off into the night on his first try, but there were four young co-eds there ready to turn the bottle up to their faces, splashing the champagne down their throats. One of the girls held up her phone and they all posed for the picture, grinning with sparkly liquid running out of their mouths. On his second try, he got close enough to the center to warrant whoops from the guys and two ass slaps from the girls. Jill smirked to herself and chugged down the rest.

By the time he came back for her, she'd danced to one song with a group of black girls who used words like, "Girl, stop!" and "Ugh, boy bye!" They slapped her ass and whooped with encouragement when she popped her ass just right, so, she did it again. Then some guy grabbed her and pulled her into his lap, but when she looked to the girls for reassurance, one flashed her thumbs up, another tossed her a wink. So, she went with it.

Jill gyrated in his lap until the song went off, then a little longer. Excused herself when she felt a hazy dizziness settling in and his dick hard against her ass. There was a line at the bathroom. Two girls with knotted Tech tees on checked their makeup in their compacts while they waited then went in together when the last girl came out. When they tottered out, balancing themselves on high heels, the girl in front of Jill grabbed her hand and pulled her in with her.

"No point waiting out there, right?"

Jill shrugged her feigned indifference. The girl pulled her panties down and flopped down on the toilet, running her fingers through her hair while watching Jill in the mirror.

"You came with Carson, huh? You his girl?"

"No, we just met, like, a few weeks ago?"

"Oh, he's cool. He'll get ya in the *best* parties, him and Noel. Shit, outta paper. Look under that sink, will ya? Any down there?"

Jill pulled out a new roll and handed it to her, fending off her own unsureness with the unusual arrangement by fixing her face like she did this all the time. Pouted her lips. Looked herself over in the mirror and fluffed her hair. The girl wiped herself and flushed. Nodded with her head that Jill could go. They switched places and the girl washed her hands, then leaned against the sink shouting, "Oh, my God! I *love* this fucking song!" as Jill relieved herself. Her long, brown hair brushed the walls and slapped her back as she bobbed her head, her teeth exposed in some show of exhilaration. "I'll see you out there, girl! I gotta go dance!"

And Jill was alone in the tiny bathroom with toilet paper in her hand and her panties at her ankles.

The second she stepped out another girl took her place, and Carson wasn't too far away. He raised his hand to her, and when she was by his side, he kissed the side of her face with his fingers in her hair.

"Noel brought some other party favors. You want in?" He licked her ear.

"Party favors?"

"Yeah, you know. Nose candy."

"Oh, umm, yeah, sure."

Carson chuckled to himself, finishing rolling his white paper into a joint, bobbing his head to the beat of Atlanta rappers.

"Never tried it before, huh? Well, there's a first time for everything if you want to. Don't have to, though."

Jill mulled it over, pulling her lips to one side. "Whatever. Let's do it."

Noel showed her how when Carson refused. Football. Random drug tests, he'd explained, handing the joint he'd rolled to some other guy. Jill said she understood.

Noel put his hand to her back; she leaned into him to hear what he was saying. A girl from her dance circle hopped up on the counter and laid herself down on the countertop in front of them, raising her shirt. Cackled and grabbed Jill's wrist.

"Hey, Light Skinned, do it offa me. I love a nose virgin!"

When Jill heard Noel's voice over the girl on the counter, she heard him say to, "...just swallow it down, Joss."

"Huh?"

"Swallow it down!" Over the music. "It's nasty as all shit when it comes down the first time, but it's worth it!" Noel pulled the little baggie out and poured a line out over the girl's stomach. It lit up like snow on a dark night road against her skin.

Was there something she should have said first? She glanced over at Carson, bobbing to the beat, cheering her on. Of course not. This wasn't some toast at a wedding. This was drugs—wild and crazy off some girl's abdomen with the guy with the hard dick and her faux beau fists pumping the air behind her. This was something she wanted. Something she'd seen done before on TV but had never done herself. This was goodbye to cheerleading, green-and-gold-wearing Jill. God, where had she come from in the first place? This was someone new. This was Joss. This was adulthood on the horizon and college around the corner. Maybe, this was freedom. So, what was there to do but hold one nostril closed and inhale?

And again.

After, when she felt the dregs running down her throat and the high rushing to her brain, Carson wrapped an arm around her shoulders. "Now, *that's* how you do it! You're a natural!" he joked, pulling her close and brushing his nose against hers.

Noel took his turn off the girl. Threw his head back. Felt it take hold. Held up his cup of Moet and nodded to the cheers that raised up around him. It was all there. Tangible. Right in front of her, so she knew it existed somewhere out there.

And when Carson climbed on top of her later that night, tangled up in Noel's cool sheets, she didn't mind. She pulled him closer, because she'd found it. She reveled in it, because she'd found it. She was out of her mind, head thrown back, eyes wide, the corner of his mouth brushing her cheek.

But...she'd found it.

Freedom.

SUCKING TEETH

AALIYAH

She'd never thought of using tweezers for cooking before, but now it was really growing on her. In the days since she'd started her mental makeover, she'd dove into the cookbooks with the same enthusiasm and fervor that she had the paint samples and fabric swatches. One day, she was loafing on the couch, flicking past some cooking show with Padma Lakshmi sultrily smiling on screen, the next she was fully invested in learning to elevate her down-home, Caribbean cooking to something with more flair and finesse. At first, it was like a puzzle, something new to fix her mind on now that she'd worn herself out with Sudoku around day three. Something new to master, to hone. A new avenue to follow that would surely lead her away from the corporate monotony she now sought to permanently escape. With that in mind, she still had not so much as glanced her at her résumé, yet, to her surprise, she felt neither idle nor evading.

She would ride this out.

She would find herself, she knew, though not how. And, if that uncomfortable moment came when her nest egg ran out, when she'd have to ask her friend's help or go to Nigel for assistance, she would muster it within her. She told herself this more than once. She would do it if need be. And they would be there for her. Yet, this thought never settled into fear in her mind. Something would come to her. In its own time, maybe, but it would come. For, the alternative was to remain unfulfilled, to remain a hamster on the endless wheel of corporate monotony, of corporate politics she'd never been one to play. And that was simply unthinkable.

In the days leading away from Thanksgiving, Aaliyah painted the master bedroom and living room, finally settling on warm earth tones. From the taping to the mixing of paints to the rolling of the very last dab, she'd insisted on doing it alone, busying herself while Nigel was at work, was away, was at The Group with those two slugs.

There was something in Aaliyah that had always been drawn to color. Large swatches of burnt red and deep orange, earth tones, jewel tones. This was probably inherited from her long-ago life in Trinidad where color had been an emotion all its own, where each hue told a story on wall murals and painstakingly executed graffiti. Then, of course, there had been her mother and grandmother who had donned sarongs and bangled bracelets, who'd decorated their Jamaica, Queens home with West Indian art and deep red rugs. Aaliyah had watched as her mother would re-paint a wall in their home or buy new paintings at the swap, from which she would step back and gaze at admiringly. Whereas Aaliyah had developed the emotional defense mechanism of cleaning away her woes, literally scrubbing and scouring until she felt whole again, her mother had done the same with décor, rearranging and redecorating the house to get her mind off whatever ailed her.

It wasn't just that Aaliyah wondered if this method could also work for her. It was also her mother's gentle voice in her ear telling her to remember *you're roots, girl...make your own way...*that had Aaliyah now reimagining what her life could look like if she simply...let go.

Let go of the need to control her life and her direction in it. Release the workplace pedagogy and ladder-climbing ambitions. Liberate herself from her role in someone else's rat race, in someone else's company, a cog in someone else's journey to the top.

Her mind was active while she worked, almost galloping ahead so she could hardly grasp her thoughts as they flew through her head. She loved this sensation, this awakening of her senses and stimulation of her mind. The flow of her creative juices had spurred some mechanism within her she hadn't felt in a long time, years at least. Her mind felt more nimble, her laughter easier to come by. A bounce in her step, a lightness atop her shoulders. She stretched her arms over her head and wiggled down to her toes in bed at the start of every morning, this ritual becoming more and more ingrained in her every day, as she realized that she'd never taken even so much as a simple moment to enjoy the basic pleasures of stretching, relaxing, preparing before a new day. No more did she swing the covers off her the moment she opened her eyes. No more did she reach for her work outfit, already picked out and hanging from the door handle the night before. No more.

When she awoke those mornings, the smell of Burnt Tundra paint filled her nostrils; later, papier mâché covered her hands. And when her home smelled of harissa seasoning and ras el hanout, she reveled in it rather than hurrying to scrub it all away and restore it all to neutral.

When Aaliyah burned the casserole, she laughed and tried it again. And the next day, when she nailed the handmade pasta, she cheered, surprising herself more than Nigel with her little fist pump. Nigel glanced up from the blueprints in his hand—sitting there at her bar, half watching her work, half working himself—chuckled and shook his head. Accepted the kiss she planted on his cheek and tried to hide his smirk when he went back to the work in front of him.

"I guess this would be a good time to tell you," Nigel started, never glancing. He scribbled a note in the margins then said, "Micah invited me to come to his group, see what I can do to help with those boys. I'm gonna head over there to their meeting tomorrow after hoops."

"Okay..." Aaliyah continued stirring her pasta sauce. She glanced up, but not at him. "I didn't even know you knew about that outreach group."

"How could I not? I see the man every day."

"Mmhmm."

"Which you would know if you ever came to my office."

"Mmhmm."

"Anyway, sounds to me like he needs a little help reeling them in, so we all volunteered to go on alternating weeks. Try to set an example. Let them see a few successful black men who came from their communities."

"Wait." Now she did turn toward him. "Vince is going, too?"

"Well, not tomorrow, but next week, I think. So he said."

An unsure nod then back to her simmering pasta sauce. "Hmm. They *do* know he isn't *from* their 'communities,' right? The only 'hood Vince is from has a country club 'round the corner, so I know he ain't going 'less he can use it for a tax write off."

"Chill. Anyways, I'm headed over there to see what I can do, how I can help."

Aaliyah kissed her teeth.

"Liyah, don't do that now. You know I hang out with that guy almost every day now, so one thing I do know is he didn't mean any of this to happen. I keep telling you that."

"Yup."

"I've asked you a hundred times to sit down with him and iron this shit out. So things can go back to normal. So we can all just move on."

"Now a hundred and one then."

"You know this is silly, don't you? I know you do. You're more sensible than this."

"Really, Nigel, I don't think I've been sensible since the day I left Myers." She tossed her head back and laughed throatily at this. "Or, couldn't you tell?" with a gesture at her new surroundings.

"Alright, alright, I know. But, you still won't just lay this thing to rest, even if I say it'll make me happy, that it's what *I* want?"

"Never happen, Nigel. I've still got my dignity if not my job. Plus, I've already agreed to go to that thing—that, that benefit—with you this weekend. Already snagged a dress from Laney and everything, so you're already ahead of the game if you ask me. And, there are other things on my mind now than that sneaky fool. Other, more important, things."

II

Aaliyah thought to herself the minute they stepped foot in that ballroom that many of the folks at this fête had been at Renée Dessommes' shindig weeks before, too. Really, it wasn't a traditional ballroom at all, so much as it was a converted industrial art gallery off downtown. Walls of glass and brushed cement flooring. Holiday décor and white lights lit the space into its own rendition of a winter wonderland. A twenty-foot Christmas tree towered over them all as they entered, covered in silver right down to the branches. And, as with every other black- or white-tie event she'd been summoned to by her friend—and this time, by Nigel, go figure—everyone was coskel up, peacocking their money. That didn't surprise Aaliyah at all. Birds of a feather, you know.

She'd gone simple for this event, as simple as Laney's wardrobe would allow. That night, she found herself in Laney's black, fitted gown by someone she'd never heard of. Long sleeves, cutout back and a high neckline. She was covered up and that somehow added to her confidence, her fine locks pulled to the nape of the neck. Nigel's tux was also black; only the teal pocket square and tie kept them from resembling Gomez and Morticia Addams, but this didn't bother Aaliyah in the slightest. Black was discreet and not showy, both traits she respected in all aspects, even clothing.

Up-tempo jazz played loudly from a live band. There were drinks being sipped and dancing in the middle of the floor. Couples talking, whirling. Aaliyah wondered how Laney tolerated it all. The social concern and giving of money was all a joke to her, some cosmic one they all seemed to be in on. It was crawling with hypocrisy and superiority, because she figured they'd certainly skin up their noses at real people in poverty. Pull out their fancy wet wipes from their clutches and tastefully wipe their hands if touched by one. Do-gooding from afar was all very well and good, but Aaliyah was hyperaware of the fact that no one in that room really wanted equality. Nobody wanted to pull the impoverished up to their level. Only so far, perhaps hip level, so that there was still room for jeering superiority when necessary. Anything otherwise would be to collapse the power structure and level the playing field. And who, really, wanted that?

They'd never seen suffering like what they were there to help do away with. Back home and even up in Queens, Aaliyah had seen it—touched it—daily. People living hand to mouth, belly in hand. Those there had never gone hungry or been deprived of education, had to fight for their own rights or, figure out where next meals may materialize from. Had probably never met anyone from the Congo or any of the neighboring countries. Probably couldn't even find them on a blank map. But their money would spend there just the same.

Laney broke off from them when she saw Carmella and her husband near the back by the bar. Since they'd arrived, Aaliyah had been looking for a way to ask Laney about Micah face to face, but the opportunity melted away when Laney waved and walked away. Nigel nodded their way, and Nathan waved back, grinning. Aaliyah did neither but watched them as they exchanged kisses on the cheeks with Laney. Then she looked away.

A short flurry of events separated Nigel and Aaliyah as he found his way to the layout of finger foods and Aaliyah stopped a passing waiter for whatever champagne-colored liquid it was that he was peddling. She nodded graciously to him as he handed her one off the tray and moved on. She brought it to her lips as Nigel found his way back over to her. Nigel bit into his crab cake and beamed her way, pulling her to him by the hand just as the voice materialized in their direction from somewhere in the crowd, drawing nearer.

It was that grin that would always be somehow emblazoned in her mind. It would flash across her thoughts at the least expected time, sepia, time somehow slowing as it replayed in her head. She would always remember that grin on his face, the wiping of his hands on his tiny paper napkin, as the moment that marked Before. Aaliyah would also never be able to forget the sound of that voice, try though she might. It matched that supercilious little persona that it preceded. It, like she, was hauntingly superior and unshakable.

III

Scene.
The live band blares around them. Aaliyah and Nigel are in a sea of benefit-goers, laughing as he bites into his crab cake.
VOICE IN THE CROWD: Nigel. Nigel Cavanaugh, is that you?
Nigel turns, glancing over his shoulder. Aaliyah's eyes are on him as he nearly chokes on his crab cake. He holds the napkin to his mouth, coughing up the food he's inhaled down the wrong pipe. Aaliyah sees the shock on his face before she sees its cause emerge from the crowd. One second she is only a voice, and the next she is right in front of them, in their space.
NIGEL: My God, Paige, I wasn't expecting to see you here.

The woman hardly seems to register Aaliyah's presence at all and barely lends it any acknowledgement. Her eyes find Aaliyah, shifting to Nigel's left, but linger there only momentarily. She never so much as twitches a nod or glance of greeting, but takes Aaliyah in, then moves on, dismissive. She stands there in front of them, her eyes on Nigel again. The look that passes between them says more than words can, because Aaliyah can feel it. What the sensation is, she cannot yet tell, but her senses perk in those few initial moments of their apparent reunion. This woman—Paige he calls her—knows that, too, and offers neither a smile nor a word for several long seconds, until finally she does.

PAIGE: You're surprised to see me. Shame. You give yourself away about the letter, then.

NIGEL: Um, yeah, I didn't...I mean, I never...

Aaliyah clears her throat politely and steps closer to Nigel, as he stares at the porcelain doll and it stares back at him. Though her disregard for Aaliyah's presence and ostensible interest in Nigel are brazen, her expression is difficult for Aaliyah to read, though she tries. There is neither a smile nor a glower, merely an upward twitch in one brow and a slight pull at one corner of the mouth. She reaches out and touches him, her hazelnut skin brushing against his hand then lingering there, like a splash of crème in his coffee. Loose, near-platinum blonde ringlets brush her shoulders, grazing perky but only modestly exposed bust, which assumes no implants for her, but just enough to see that her emerald green dress compliments her body well, covering her lovely, supple little figure, which curves and dips in all the right places. Her gown moves with her when she takes another step into their space. Her glittering, nude heels peep out from beneath the fabric of silk charmeuse as she does so, then disappear beneath the dress again as she closes the space between them.

Only, it is her eyes that grab Aaliyah's attention and hold it the longest. She weighs this in her mind, for they are what will plague her later. Paige's lashes are certainly false but tastefully, expensively so—you see them. Paige smiles at Nigel. She laughs, her finger grazing her nose. They frame her face in a way that Aaliyah finds off-putting, but can't yet put her finger on why, not directly. Wide and innocent like a child's, those brown windows to her soul almost make Aaliyah apologize for thinking she wishes her harm. Almost.

PAIGE: ...and Pia.

Time lurches forward for Aaliyah. She shakes her head to steady herself. The clinking of glasses and chatter of acquaintances refills Aaliyah's ears, and she wonders where all the sound in the room had been sucked into moments before. How long had Paige's mouth been moving? How long had Aaliyah zoned out and away, watching her?

A finger taps Paige on the shoulder, interrupting Paige's sentence and pulling her attention away from Nigel. We see the hand in the frame before we see the owner of it. When Paige turns, the hand it belongs to wraps her in a hug. Paige stands back from the acquaintance just long enough to identify her, then lets herself be pulled back into the embrace. A spell of words is exchanged about how long it's been and how they must reconnect, get together. The intruder waves a quick apology toward Nigel and Aaliyah, then the woman is gone, smiling over her shoulder and wiggling her fingers as a goodbye gesture at Paige as she finds her way back into the crowd. Sabrina, Aaliyah thinks she hears her called. Paige watches Sabrina melt into the throng, turning her graceful neck to watch her admirer leave, as though she doesn't want to lose her to the crowd just yet. When she is gone, Paige turns her eyes back to Nigel, that slight smirk playing just at the edges of her mouth. She watches him like that, out of the side of her eye, then turns her head to face him head on once again.

She giggles, and Aaliyah realizes that she is being playful. The sound is so pure, so clean in Aaliyah's ears. Like tiny bells in the winter air. Aaliyah watches this interaction, her face pensive, curious, figuring out this new situation and surroundings.

So, Paige is one of them. That much Aaliyah gathers by her cool demeanor, her offhand mannerisms, as if she knows she is entitled to everything and everyone in that room. And, by Sabrina's warm embrace, perhaps she is. She is known here within these ranks, someone long lost, Aaliyah can tell. But how she relates to Nigel, a man who is nearly as standoffish from these crowds as Aaliyah is, she still cannot determine.

Paige has still yet to glance her way. Aaliyah holds out her hand to Paige and watches her glance down at it. Paige looks back at Aaliyah, her expression hardly changing, with a mild regard of curiosity, as if she's just been presented with a new person she's never seen before and didn't know was standing there.

NIGEL: Oh, I apologize for my rudeness. (*Nigel saves Aaliyah from the awkwardness of standing there with her hand out, unaccepted, floating in the air. He wipes his goateed mouth with the napkin again then crumbles it and stuffs it in his pocket.*) Aaliyah, this is an old friend of mine, Paige Darensbourg. We go way back to, what, sophomore year?

PAIGE: At least.

NIGEL: Paige, this is my girlfriend, Aaliyah Walker.

Nigel gently pulls her to him, and she does not outwardly betray her surprise when he kisses the side of her forehead and gives her waist a proud little squeeze. Not outwardly, no, but inwardly the gesture does ring somehow false to her. It rattles her momentarily, this woman holding her within her unsettling gaze, Nigel holding her within his arms. She tries not to focus on his words but on

Paige's expression after he says them. It is unchanged, still cool and unconcerned, peppered with such a mild touch of interest that it nearly does not exist at all.

PAIGE: Aaliyah. I don't believe I've ever met anyone by that name? Is it tribal or something?

AALIYAH: Excuse me?

Paige shrugs coolly. Her eyes are a pair of liars. That's what it is Aaliyah detected before. The hint of playfulness disguises her intent, but her dagger-sharp words more than make up it.

[The band changes tunes. A ballad plays.]

Aaliyah tries to phony smile away her aggravation, but it is a skill she's not yet mastered. She glances around the room quickly, taking it all in, searching for an ally—Delaney, Micah, anyone who she can pull into their uncomfortable sphere—but finds no one.

PAIGE: (*Her eyes linger over Nigel for a moment longer. Then it passes, and she again touches his arm.*) We have a lot to catch up on. But, I suppose, there's plenty of time for that, isn't there?

Had she said something about a letter before? Aaliyah remembers seeing an unopened envelope with a handwritten address in his kitchen weeks before, but it hadn't even crossed her mind again until now. Had that been her? Had she been right under Aaliyah's nose all the while?

Aaliyah can't bring herself to ask with her there, or at all, and Paige is gone before she can speak again anyway, swallowed up into the boisterous revel around them.

Gone, as if she'd never been there at all, that quickly, that cleanly. But she had been there, and they can both feel it in the air between them, Nigel's arm now unwound from Aaliyah's waist, with nothing but an old Chaka Khan ballad to now fill the space between them.

[Cut to black.]

STRANGE FRUIT

DELANEY

Airing out had its advantages.

Two hours into the Congolese Benefit Ball Laney had only consumed a small tart and a half flute of champagne. She nursed it throughout the night just to maintain the appearance of social interaction, because she knew that if her hands were empty, drink after drink would be offered up to her on a silver platter. Literally. And so, after hugging and light banter with Sabrina and Matthew—as if they didn't all remember the dinner-table fiasco a few days before—chatting them up about Sabrina's impending tribe wedding and Matthew's pursuit of his Ph.D. in some arcane subject that would leave him teaching at an Ivy, Laney still held the same glass in her hand.

No one from their Thanksgiving table mentioned Jill, and Laney did not bring her up. She didn't tell them she'd slept on Jill's couch that night, Jill's own guest bedroom a messy storage closet with no furniture whatsoever. She didn't talk about the straight razors she'd run her fingers over when Jill fell asleep on the couch opposite her. Didn't tell them Jill was poised to flee, that she secretly despised them.

When she'd arrived home the next morning, Vince hadn't even noticed her absence. She could have told herself this was because she got home before he'd awakened, not long after the sun had come sloping up onto the horizon, but she no longer had the desire or the need to tell herself pretty little lies. They lived separately under their roof until the party loomed over them.

She and Vince had arrived in separate cars that evening, a new trademark for them, she realized. There was no need to go over it all again, to rehash it, to reargue it on the way there or any time before. She wouldn't fall on his side, and he wouldn't fall on hers. Laney progressed through the evening just on the periphery of his line of sight. In that way, she managed not to bring up questions about their proximity to one another while still maintaining a safe enough distance from him and the elder Dessommes as to enjoy the evening on her own accord, without the nagging pestering of duty.

Laney's bronze evening gown offered a suitable nod to the fall holiday season, while also functioning as a cover up for her wrists, which still presented like bruised peaches, the strangest of fruits. Silk sleeves ballooned and billowed, cuffed at the wrist with Swarovski topaz buttons. The open back cowled into a deep V, showing off her bare back and offering her trademark flirty wink. That was enough for them. No one wondered what was happening beneath the fabric, beneath her skin. No one wondered, and no one cared. And this, strangely, did not surprise her.

As she stood in the middle of the crowded floor with Sabrina, Matthew and Carmella, Cammy's cheeks flushed from the wine, she spotted Micah in the crowd. Brother and sister chatted among themselves and dissolved away from the group into the sea of chatter and moving bodies. Cammy waved over Laney's shoulder, the siblings forgotten just that quickly.

"Look who we have here! The handsome devil himself!"

Cammy opened her arms to him and accepted his embrace and kiss on the cheek. Had she even known him from a can of paint the month before? Likely not, Laney mused to herself as she watched them banter together. And yet, a pass from one warranted a pass from all.

"I figured you'd be around here somewhere. And you remember Laney, I presume?"

"Oh, of course. She's not one I'd easily forget." He was shooting her that signature smirk. "I'd have known I could find her here even if Vince hadn't told me she was coming," he laughed.

"Of course, you could! It wouldn't be a party without her!"

"Cammy, have you seen Addison around? I think she was looking for you earlier."

"Oh, probably something about The Three. And she's been dying to tell me how your dinner went. Anyway, I'll go have a look and see if I can find her."

Micah turned back to Laney when Cammy was gone. "Well played."

"Thank you. Probably wasn't a complete lie, though. Addie'll see her and they'll strike it up about something or other. She'll forget I even told her to look."

"Probably true."

Micah shoved his hands into his pockets. No drink, she noticed but did not comment on. He was also dressed impeccably, but something in her had grown used to this trait about of him. Tailored tuxedo, satin facings and a waistcoat under his peaked lapels. A black ribbon held his shoulder-length locks back.

"I assume you've talked to Aaliyah by now."

"I have. Something you want to tell me?"

"There are a lot of things I want to tell you, actually, but where would I even start?"

"At the beginning typically works best, so I've heard. Something about a little birdy named Milla?"

The benefit chairpersons took their place on the platform at the head of the room, greeting the guests on the microphone. Laney watched on but heard not a word. She stared ahead, her ears closed to the noise around them, and felt Micah's eyes on her. Some quip graced the audience with a wave of laughter. Dinner was announced, and those around her began drifting toward their seats, picking tables to sit at and friends and colleagues to sit with. Laney started to walk toward her table, toward Vince and Addie and Carl, who were chatting with a few of the lower execs at The Group. Micah walked with her, moving through the throngs of prettily dressed people who were still hovering in groups, dancing to smooth rhythms or slowly finding tables.

"You didn't strike me as the type, Micah."

He maneuvered just behind her, his hands still casually shoved into both pockets. "What type is that?"

"You know, the kind to fuck a woman to get to the top." She glanced over her shoulder at him. "Is that what you teach your boys Mondays and Thursdays?"

"Laney." He grabbed her arm and forced her to stop. She turned to him, a one-sided simper crossing her face. "Oh no, don't cheapen it with that. Don't smile that way like you didn't mean it. Like I'm just someone you do the Laney tap dance for. We're too far beyond that now, right?"

She didn't pull her arm away and he didn't release it.

Laney found that she could no longer see Vince and the in-laws in her immediate line of sight, even as the crowd thinned and tables filled. Perhaps they'd taken their seats or gone to wash their hands. Perhaps Vince was busy concocting some new backroom scheme for

The Group, full of deceitfulness and the hint of corruption. Maybe the in-laws were busy arguing around a corner. But, as she checked the crowd for a glimpse of them, Micah's hand on her arm, his eyes set firmly on her, she acknowledged she didn't care where they were. There was a customary weight that pressed down upon her she no longer felt, not in that moment, not in days. The weight of continuously checking her peripheral, painting on a disguise and adhering to the rules that surrounded her day and night. And, she noticed, now that she didn't have it, wasn't soaked in it, that the alcohol had only ever dulled her senses to this feeling but had never completely taken it away.

Sharp eyes made for better views and, as Micah stood there watching her for her next move, waiting for her to excuse herself to her own table or walk away, blending into the crowd around them, she understood that the anxiety of their opinion had lifted. Her cuffed wrists hid her bruises, the same as they hid the truth. They allowed for the painting of another lovely façade, but cuffed Laney tightly enough for her to still feel the chains at her wrists. She shirked them off then with a thin smile and gestured for Micah to instead follow her outside.

II

She felt the crispness of the air around them sharper than she'd felt it all season.

As she and Micah emerged from the gallery, she realized it wasn't that the evening was colder than most. It was that she was neither too distracted nor too lubricated to feel it. The moon was almost full, clouds covering then uncovering it, throwing shadows over the pair. The farther they walked from the building, through the parking lot and toward the field on the other side, the more the building twinkled and glowed. She glanced over her shoulder to see it bathed in a warm aura of soft light, the sheets of glass on its exterior reflecting it in a way that nearly rivaled the sight before them: downtown Atlanta glinting on the night horizon.

They were in there, all of them. Sitting down to their dinner. She wondered if they missed her yet. If they would say she'd embarrassed them. Then that idea slid aside. Laney lifted the hem of her gown as she walked over the pavement out of habit, though she did not really care what happened to it. She wasn't even sure of where it had come from really, aside from the label that was stitched into the neck of it. She'd found it lying on her bed months before, with the glittering pair of shoes, an unexplained gift from Vince that she'd thanked him for half-heartedly but had neither asked about nor ever gotten an explanation for.

"Pretty ballsy of you."

"Oh, you noticed that, huh? We have a tendency of doing that, you and I."

Micah didn't respond but offered her a smile. They walked in between the parked cars, Laney in the lead. She didn't know where she was going, but it didn't matter. They were away from that cramped atmosphere, away from the expectant eyes.

"I could lie to you," Micah said, following her toward the metal benches on the periphery of the property. "But you know I won't."

"I certainly hope you won't."

"I didn't need her like Liyah thought I needed her. That's the truth of the matter."

Laney settled herself on the bench, feeling the cold seep through the material of her dress. She crossed her legs into him. Her foot brushed his leg when he leaned forward on his elbows, turning her way.

"Aaliyah had it in her mind that I'd tricked some poor, defenseless woman. Used her against her will to get to the top. That I...needed her. Depended on her. But I didn't. Milla was just a bonus, and that's the truth. By the time I met her—by the time she first started brushing up against me in the elevator and dropping by my desk on the way out of the office—I'd already made a name for myself at Myers. She was attracted to that, not the other way around."

Laney shook her head. "Liyah described her as mousy. A mousy woman isn't brushing up against some guy—a black guy—she doesn't know in an elevator just for kicks. I call bullshit on that one."

Micah sniggered. "Of course, she wouldn't. Not in a million years. But Liyah's descriptions of the folks around her've been off lately. See, the problem with Aaliyah's theory is that Milla isn't mousy. She's innocuous. Inconspicuous. And what an innocuous, inconspicuous woman *would* do is rub her arm against yours in a crowded elevator. She'd drop her pencil when bringing you files from her boss and touch your hand when going over a draft with you. Then, after the seventh or eighth time when you finally called her on it, asked her out, she'd look at you and say, 'What took you so long?' And is there anything wrong with that? Probably depends on who you ask. But I saw the same thing in her she saw in me: an opportunity. She took that opportunity, and so did I. There was a gap. She was the bridge."

"What would she get out of that, though?"

"A good time. A meal ticket, or so she thought. Don't act like this is some shocking, new thing. Like it hasn't been the way of the world since before Jesus turned water to wine. We know how this goes. Why does there have to be some contrived reason for her at all? Why can't it simply be that she was attracted, thought she could turn it into something more, and I saw a door?"

Laney sighed, toying with the sling back of her shoe. "So, did crossing the gap end up being worth it?"

"It usually is. This time was no different."

"Did you know that campaign was yours? Tell the truth, Micah. Did you have...some inkling?"

"Look at me. Laney, I've never lied to you. I know we haven't known each other long, but I will *never* lie to you. I didn't know she did that until the very second Liyah knew it. Not a millisecond before. But, because she did that—because she made that move—I made my move. And if I'd never met Vince, if I didn't have that offer already sitting on my desk, I *still* would've made a move. Because she started thinking she owned me, that I owed her, that it was something more than it was. She started thinking she had the upper hand and that I *needed* her. That was her mistake, but it wasn't gonna be my mistake. Either I would've had to go, or I would've had to get rid of her—make her go. What I'm saying is, it was mutual. And she isn't crying any tears over me tonight."

"Vince said you had that offer for over a week before you accepted it."

Micah let out a hearty laugh and shook his head. "Because I don't trust your guy. But Nigel does, and I trust Nigel."

Laney glanced his way, somehow stunned that he'd said it out loud, so quickly, with hardly any prompting. She'd heard so few people speak an ill word about Vince with such flagrancy, with so little regard for who might hear.

"Why not?"

"Why should I? You don't even trust him."

Laney played with the sling strap of her heel again and only paused for a moment when he said this. She did not turn his way. But neither did she continue playing with her shoe.

"Micah, you need to go and tell her that." Laney brushed her foot against his leg again to pull his pensive eyes from the ground, to make him look at her this time. "You need to tell her."

"You think I don't wanna tell her? She isn't trying to hear that, not in the slightest. I'll give her some space. One day, we'll talk about it. I'm not playing the blind man role here; I know it looks fucked up. It is fucked up. But I would never intentionally take anything from Aaliyah. Never. From someone like me trying to make it like I am. Never. From my friend. Not. Ever. I just wouldn't. And I never thought she'd take a fucking stab at me like that."

"Guess you think you know someone…"

"Yeah, you think you know someone."

"No, I mean that's what she's saying about you. You think you know someone. You think you know how they'll treat you. How they'll take care of you. How they'll look out for you. But then they turn around and back you against a wall. Make you bleed. Take it all before you even see it being taken…"

Laney heard her voice trail away.

Micah's eyes were on her, glued to the side of her face, but she refused to turn to him, to acknowledge it. She'd forgotten what she was saying. What she was addressing. Somehow, she'd started talking to herself. Laney shook those thoughts from her head and settled into the few seconds of crisp silence between them when Micah did not reply and she heard their breath between them.

"Did she say that, or did you?"

"Why? Doesn't that sound like something she'd say?"

"Not really. Sounds like you and Vince are the strangest couple I've ever met."

"Really?" She focused her attention on that non-offending strap. "Most people think we fit pretty well together."

Laney's phone chimed in her clutch. She nearly jumped out of her skin, having gotten used to the distant sound of cars passing by, of an owl in a nearby tree. The trill of the phone screamed at them in the night, and she hurried to find the source and shut it off.

"Vince."

She said his name out loud as she read it on her phone, saw the smiling picture of the two of them across the screen. Vince and Laney on the couch in his dorm seven years before.

"He has impeccable timing, doesn't he? He always seems to know when you are where you shouldn't be."

Laney scoffed that away and turned the ringer off. The silence of the night was welcome. Micah's company was welcome.

"How about you? Do you think you fit pretty well together?"

Laney snapped her clutch shut and settled back into her seat. Tuned her ears, listening for the sounds of before to wrap themselves around her again. There they were. Cars meandering by, Micah's breathing out of step with hers. The sound of her foot when she brushed it against the leg of his pant.

Laney never answered, and Micah never pressed it. She wondered if her phone had gone off again and was glad she'd put it on silent, so she'd never have to know if she didn't want to. She wondered if they'd started looking for her, craning their necks around, pretending to be participants in the inane conversations around them while they were really thinking, *where is she?* This thought made her smile, and it wasn't until that moment she really understood that she was sober.

The night was crisp, and she felt free.

Her wrists were bruised, but she felt free.

They were likely looking for her, and she didn't care.

Micah was beside her, talking to her, listening to her, and she was sober.

When had that happened?

"I mean no offense, but you're beautiful. You know that? Really," he continued, when he had her full attention, "I hate that word—beautiful. It always sounds stupid when I say it. It's overused, oversaturated, so when you see something truly beautiful, it no longer seems like a fitting enough word, you know? But you are. You're a beautiful person, Laney."

"See..." Where had that shakiness in her breath come from? "That's the thing. After a while, you don't see yourself anymore. You see them. You see...yourself through their eyes, through others' eyes. You adjust to fit what they expect, pluck and mold yourself to fit into that little glass case. And, you know, I don't really think it's about losing yourself either. Well, maybe it is a little bit; maybe that's the end result. But, really, it all just starts from this little idea—this idea that you can do both, can *have* both. And it causes this separation inside you after a while. It's an odd feeling, honestly. It's like, being you gets put on the back burner for one night, just a few hours, while you host a party or go to some thing. For just one night, you pretty yourself up; you slip on your airs like some silk gown, from head to toe. You become this object, this item, this...entity that even you don't recognize, but that's okay, because it's only for one night. It's only to get you through that one night."

Laney stared into him, never flinching. Did he hear her? Did he understand? Or would she just find that dismissive flicker in his eyes, betraying his thoughts? She searched his face, waiting to see it, looking for it.

"And so, you do it. You pretend. You erect this monumental façade around you meant to portray someone you really aren't." A snort. "Someone you yourself hardly recognize. And then you go home. You get in your car and slip off your shoes and turn to your guy and say, 'Whew, that was something wasn't it!' He'll rub your leg or kiss your cheek, laughing with you, and you know that he understands. You know that he gets it, what you just went through, what you just did, the performance you just gave. And he'll take you home and tell you to relax, help you get ready for bed. You feel safe. You feel safe, Micah, because you're still you, and you can just laugh about that other you, joke about her like she's not even real, because she isn't. Not really. But then, it happens again. There's another party, another function, another appearance. And so, out comes your gown of airs and your winning smile, and you do it again. And each time, you come home and think, 'Whew, that was something,' until one day it doesn't really occur to you to think that anymore. You see, you've gone from switching it on and off like a light to forgetting where the switch is in the first place. And you know why, don't you?"

He shook his head, perhaps afraid, as she was, to even blink for fear of breaking the crystalline of that moment.

"Because you decide you like this new you better."

"No, because to do otherwise would draw contempt."

Laney waited as that settled between them. Watched as Micah nodded his head slowly, a pensiveness overtaking the creases around his eyes, the furrow in his brow. Then she told him, "Because to do otherwise would be to continue juggling two personas, two different people with two different sets of needs, expectations...desires. So, you try to reconcile them. To merge them. Convince yourself they can be one in the same. Until...until you look up and realize your best friend has described you to her colleague in a way you don't even recognize. In a way that surprises him when he meets the real you. In a way...that you have to apologize for when he meets the real you."

Micah said nothing, his eyes squaring with hers.

"But you're not so different from me, are you?" After a beat, "Because the man who worked with Aaliyah is not the same man who mentors those boys."

"Sometimes, he's not. That man might not've had an office at Myers. That man couldn't always be..." Micah sighed and shook his head again. Looked up, chuckled just a little. Then met her gaze again. "Couldn't be some Southside boy with a juvenile rap sheet.

Can't still belong to or identify with that. He's gotta be Syracuse all the way. Cum Laude. Polished. Another kind of aggressive."

"Two sides at war for the both of us, huh?"

"Seems so. That why you didn't answer his call?"

"Yes, there's that. There's that and...too much of everything. Too much liquor. Too many cigarettes. Too many razors."

Laney neither reacted nor responded to Micah's raised brows, his silent press for her to elaborate. She waited for him to say something. Waited for the judgement, the reasoning, the correction. With the sounds of the night around them and the chill on their skin, she waited for him to betray himself. Yet, he never did.

"You're not so bad, Micah. You're a nice guy. I can see why Aaliyah was so close to you."

Micah chuckled throatily, nudging her with his shoulder. "You're not so bad yourself, Laney. I can see why these geese all flock to you." He gestured around at their surroundings. "There's something about you."

A tilt of her head away from him. "Really? Is there something about *me*...or is there something about Laney Dessommes?"

"They aren't one in the same now?"

"You know they aren't one in the same." Micah narrowed his eyes, chewed his bottom lip. Laney turned her head to face him full on. "Or do you not agree?"

"No, no. I didn't say anything like that. I'm just trying to say—"

Laney kicked off her shoe. Then then the other one.

"Tell me what you see."

He said nothing.

"I'm serious. Tell me what you see, Micah."

Laney unbuttoned the neck of her dress and felt it peel away, exposing a sliver of each shoulder.

"Laney—"

"Do you see me? Or, do you see her?" She pulled the bronze fabric from each shoulder, pressed her bare feet into the gravel and stood.

"Laney, you *know* I see you. Stop, really, it's freezing out here."

Laney felt the pinch of pebbles at the arch of her foot, pressing in between her toes. Then there was that nip in the air, that crispness she'd marveled at minutes before cutting at her skin. Her nipples hardened in response when she pulled the fabric past them and peeled off each of the sticky cups cradling her breasts. She dropped them to the ground, staring down at him, neither pulling their eyes away from the other. It was when she tried to slide her gaze away from his, to divert her eyes, that the first tear welled and fell, sliding down one cheek in the cold night air.

"Lane—"

"See. Me. Micah."

Laney uncuffed the buttons at each wrist and watched him. Something caught in her throat when she unclasped the second button, and she realized it was her breath, her words, stuck. It grew ragged in the night air, goosebumps prickling on her arms and hips. Water sliding down her face, one and then two.

"They don't see me, Micah. But you say you do. Do you?"

The dress slipped away, down to the gravel and clay beneath her feet, and her arms were exposed for the first time since that night. Since she'd looked a stranger in the eye and realized he was the one she'd married. It all slipped away, and his eyes were on her wrists.

"So...what do you see, Micah? Do you see me? Do you *really* see me?" Laney wiped the moisture from her cheek and dared him to look at her. "All of me?"

Micah's hand was on her bruises, then he was on his feet. He wrapped his arms around her and pulled her body into his. The heat of his breath whispered across her forehead.

"Laney, Jesus. Come here."

She felt her body stiffen at this unexpected contact—though more so at the fact that his actions had so completely opposed her expectations, amplifying her feeling of vulnerability but, too, throwing up her walled veneer with a speed that nearly knocked her off balance. But, as the seconds slipped away and he removed his jacket, wrapping it and then his arms around her, she saw her mistake, her error so glaring it ought to have embarrassed her rightly. For, it wasn't pity that Micah offered, not in the slightest. It was the stripping away of her vulnerability, her doubts, her posturing. It was the piercing of realization through that mirror in which she viewed herself—one half of self on one side, one half of self simply following, mirroring, on the other.

She leaned into him then and felt him encircle her. And for that she felt—though she could hardly believe it—tranquil, still. She felt the shelter around her. Warmth around her. Another welled and fell. Laney closed her eyes against it and pulled him closer, wrapping her own arms around him. She squeezed her eyes shut harder and heard her own panting. It never occurred to her the chill on her skin came from the night air, that she'd exposed herself on the edge of a downtown parking lot in the middle of the night to a man she should've considered a stranger.

Because, "I see you," he said. "Laney, I see you."

THE ROAD LESS
TRAVELED

NIGEL

John Coltrane's horn sent its melodies up the stairs and into his bedroom. Lights were out all over the townhouse. Only the upstairs hallway light lit the room through the open bedroom door.

Aaliyah was quiet—so quiet that she'd yet to say a word to him since stepping foot inside the threshold. And even before that, even the casual jesting and light conversation they'd shared before sinking into the seats of his car and riding back to his home had been strained at best, awkward at worst. Aaliyah made little attempt to mask her annoyance, her bewilderment, her hurt. And Nigel couldn't blame her. He wouldn't.

He kept wondering if he'd opened that letter, would he have been prepared for this. There was no way to know without reading it, a fact he knew but circumvented. Didn't matter now anyways. He'd been too chicken-shit to open it, hoping it'd go away if he ignored it. But Paige never went away when ignored. Nigel knew that better than anyone.

Even without his knowledge, she'd been lingering in the periphery. And it wasn't until Nigel saw her later that evening, standing with her cousin in their finery near the bar, that he grasped just how many times he'd brushed up against her in the past weeks. She'd been right there; close enough to touch, to ask after. For, it was her cousin Carmella's dinner party he'd attended and her longtime friends he now worked for. That feeling of déjà vu evaporated away into recognition when he saw them standing together. Cammy and Paige. That's where he knew Cammy from: he'd met her some faraway time ago. So long ago that Cammy herself seemed not to have placed him. Yet that moment of recognition was broken just as it flared. He felt Aaliyah's gaze on him, questioning—*Why are you staring at her still!*—and averted his eyes from the memory.

When they got back to his house, there were too many unanswered questions hanging in the air, questions he knew Aaliyah wanted answered. He wanted to be frank with her, but they were questions he honestly wasn't ready to answer yet. What better to do then but to avoid them?

Nigel turned the music on and poured a glass of viognier for her and cognac for himself. He wanted to just let that dizzy haze take them upstairs where they could forget it all. Maybe even start over, the evening anyway if nothing else. Aaliyah gulped hers down and fell onto the couch with a huff. Nigel hadn't even started on his. He set his glass next to hers and kneeled at her feet. Aaliyah stared down at him.

"You said nothing had changed."

Nigel rested his head in her lap and heard her exhale. "Nothing has changed, Liyah."

Her only response was a snort in the dark. Her hair fell onto the back of the couch when she pulled it down, her fingers playing in it. He pulled her shoes off one by one.

"And now you're going on this stupid trip. With Vince. With them." Another sigh. "Hell, they've got you now. They've got you."

"Come here."

Nigel caressed her. Sat next to her on the couch. He wrapped that woman in his arms like he'd never let her go and tried to kiss all her doubts away. He reached for her dress. For Delaney's dress. She reached for his shirt. He lost his shoes and shirt on the way upstairs. Aaliyah was down to black lace by the time Nigel pushed the bedroom door open, her arms wrapped around him tripping over each other's feet. Aaliyah pulled him onto the bed on top of her. Nigel complied, happy to please her into tranquility. She was brewing; he could feel it. Heat at the crevice of her collar bone, an urgency in her fingertips as they brushed his skin. She had to have been wondering who the woman was who'd breezed in and fucked up their night, bringing this two-foot wall of brick between them even as he kissed her face and then her neck. Paige was good for that. But he didn't want Aaliyah to think about that. Instead, he wanted to bottle those questions up, at least until morning, until he figured out a way to tell her all his history with that woman.

Nigel touched her breasts, squeezing them, wanting to fall into their softness. He fingered the space between her chin and her chest, her sigh telling him that it tickled her. He kissed between her thighs, her back against the pillows, legs ajar just for him. Nigel traced a trail from her knees to the crease of her pelvis, but she pushed him away, grunting. He tried again until she scooted away from such intimacy, pressing herself harder against the headboard. Instead, Nigel gave her what she wanted. He kissed her mouth, the taste of the wine still on her lips, the effects of countless glasses throughout the night between them. She pulled him close but wouldn't look at him. Never met his gaze, her attention always turning somewhere just out of his periphery. She never whispered to him in the way that made him feel he'd never come down. Only her grabbing hands invited him in, and her urgency worried Nigel just beneath the surface.

He gave her the distraction she was looking for that night, bypassing their usual passion at the insistence of her hands, guiding him away from that, toward this. Maneuvering his body to do this, not caress that. She wanted to be far away from that evening—maybe even far away from him—and Nigel was ready to accommodate if it would make her happy. He was ready to push her sexual limit if it would calm her, erase her doubts in him and relieve her self-consciousness.

Afterward, she rolled over to her side of the bed and fell asleep almost immediately, sleeping silently. Nigel lay in bed listening to Coltrane until the playlist ended. In the darkness, he reminisced on the past. In the shadows of his bedroom, under the covers next to the woman he'd called his girlfriend for the first time out loud. She was his now, officially his. But still, Nigel reminisced.

II

Nigel met Paige Darensbourg when he was in undergrad at Morehouse. She was a sight for sore eyes even then, the kind of girl a regular guy like him wouldn't have a chance getting near. Not that he was bad-looking or without his own share of late-night female companionship, but she was definitely more of a challenge than he was willing to take on. She wanted the guys in the shiny new cars, the ones with Roman numerals behind their names.

So, life carried on.

He saw her sometimes on campus but always from afar, he with his friends and her with hers. They'd make eye contact then look away. See each other at Hump Wednesday or in the library.

She'd AP tested out of a handful of classes years before and was on track to graduate with his class instead of her own, a year below. Back in those days, she was still a natural brunette wearing dark ponytails that bounced. One night at a mixer they were formally introduced through a mutual friend and even shared a few dances. But that was as far as it went. Another brush up against each other with no real contact.

The next year, she pledged Alpha Kappa Alpha and Nigel pledged Alpha Phi Alpha. Once they crossed it was a whole other story. Suddenly they were on even playing fields. They were equals and slowly became friends. Study dates, combining their separate groups to hit late-night mixers together, volunteering for the same community service projects.

She found a box of trophy panties under her boyfriend's bed junior year. It was to Nigel's room that she'd ventured to cry, and by then it was only natural because then she was just Paige. All those thoughts of undressing her and conquering her like the others faded away after a while. He'd never so much as kissed the girl until a couple months before graduation. SoCo and lime got the best of them at a party, her long ponytail bouncing as she threw her head back and laughed. Their comfortable friendship evolved into something more. Drunken liquid courage led to sex in her off-campus apartment that night. Then again and again the next day, minus the excuse of alcohol to forgive them. That went on for a few weeks. Nigel guessed, in a way, that he'd suddenly attained some goal without even really trying to, but it didn't feel that way. To him it felt like something natural was falling into place.

When graduation finally came, she was already seven weeks pregnant, but they didn't know it yet.

It wasn't until the next weekend, on a celebratory trip with their friends to Cancun, that she finally figured out the constant nausea wasn't the effect of an ongoing hangover. When they got back to Atlanta, she peed on at least half a dozen sticks, as if the one before and the one before had been lying to her just to taunt her. They all came out positive.

Nigel found her crying on the floor and kneeled beside her.

"Oh, my God, Nigel. I was pregnant on my graduation day!" she wept into his arms. "How fucking trashy is that? My parents will never forgive me if they find out. And Pia! Oh God, and Pia! I'm supposed to be the example for her, Nigel. I'm supposed to be..."

"Shh, it'll be fine. Come here."

But she pulled away from him. "It will not be fine! You don't know my people. You don't know."

"It's okay, babe. We can have it aborted if you want."

"Aborted? Aborted! Nigel, I don't fucking *believe* in abortion! I'm a fucking Catholic, you asshole! Creole. Catholic. Ringing any bells? Otherwise, this wouldn't even be an issue, now would it? I'd just throw my baby away without a thought. Let them flush it like a dead goldfish."

"I–I'm sorry—"

"Stop being sorry! That won't help us now," she cried, and it ripped his heart out. "What the fuck am I going to do?"

And Nigel didn't know what to tell her.

So, he tried to play the soothing role, to tell her that he'd be there no matter what. But she was too seasoned for that. Paige shook her head and pushed him away.

"You say that now, but you're a man. You'll walk."

"Paige, I'm not going anywhere."

"I just need to think. I need to think..."

For weeks, she cried and slept. He thinks she actually lost weight in those weeks. She couldn't bring herself to call the clinic, but she couldn't bring herself to tell her parents either, trapped in some mental and emotional limbo. Nigel comforted her the best he could, but he didn't think it did much good. In fact, he was sure it didn't, even as he was attempting it. He always felt clumsy and clunky with that kind of thing.

Paige covered her windows with heavy drapes and stayed secluded in the dark apartment for those weeks, ate a lot of junk food, drank beers like they were bottled water and slept sprawled in front of the television. Nigel was helpless, a fucking helpless young idiot who had accomplished so much so quickly but didn't know how to help her with this. By then, he was already buying and flipping cheap houses in the neighborhood, nearly done paying off his student loans already with the money he'd made. Paige's entire family had graduated college and grad school and doctoral programs at universities with fancy reputations, then gone on to be successful adults without staining their own reputations or that of their family. She and Pia were the last ones of their generation; she carried the burden of all eyes now turned expectedly on her. But, mostly, he thought, she was wrestling with the idea of letting them down. With the idea of being that black sheep. Nigel had never experienced anything like that before. He was the first in his family to finish anything other than community college, so he didn't really understand the onus on her shoulders that she was talking about. Their differences were more apparent than ever in those days, really. Made him sit back and wonder how the hell he hadn't seen it before. But that answer came easily: her brilliant smile and feisty taunting were enough to blind most men of anything.

Eventually, she had it terminated.

She was a few days from her second trimester before she realized self-loathing wasn't going to get her out of that mess and that time was ticking for a decision to be made. She'd avoided seeing her family for those endless days and weeks, but she couldn't hide forever. Nigel was happy to have her back to her old self, even if it was just a shell of her old self. After the procedure, he took her back home to rest. She held his hand as she lay there in bed. When given the choice between her unborn child and her family's esteem, she chose the latter. Nigel reassured her that she'd made the right decision, but he knew it had shattered her. That glaze over her eyes lingered for weeks. She moved slowly for days.

"Did I?" She closed her eyes, shook her head. "I guess you're right. I won't be disowned now. And all I had to do was betray my morality. Damn, what a price to pay. There ain't enough Hail Marys for that one, are there? Not for me anyway."

They parted ways when she left for grad school.

She went to Columbia but called Nigel regularly. He flew her back to see him, and she flew him up to see her. A romance started again, and one day he kneeled down on one knee.

Shortly into their engagement, Nigel went to visit Paige at Columbia. Something had changed in her. She'd turned into this shallow, callous thing; she was nothing like the woman he'd fallen in love with over the years. She'd become some arrogant woman— bleached and waxed and wearing thousands of dollars' worth of Dolce. She wanted to live the life of a socialite, joining the ranks of her revered family, and she looked down on everyone not level with her pocketbook. Had she always been that way and he hadn't noticed? Had she been morphing right under his nose, right under the blind eye he'd turned?

Beautiful though she still was, and so very intelligent, it wasn't enough to hold his attention anymore and it never could've been. Going away had changed her into something Nigel didn't like, someone he couldn't even respect. Trying to live up to her sister's legacy and her mother's expectations had turned her into some insecure narcissist. Or maybe it was the pregnancy that had changed her. He knew about that embarrassing chapter in her life that no one else even suspected. That made her tense and uneasy, even while bonding them together. She wanted to get away from all of that and blend in with people she could more easily fool with those antics and Southern charms that made her such a success in the Big Apple.

Paige eventually picked up on his sudden change in emotions and started dating other men. Soon after, he received the engagement ring he'd given her in the mail. Their favorite form of communication had been sullied just like that. It was loose, in a plain white envelope addressed to him with no return address. Nigel didn't ask any questions or even try to find her, mostly content with the outcome of their failed romance but disappointed to have lost that woman who'd been his friend. He got over it with time.

So much time.

Now, years later, he was in bed with another woman, a woman who'd put an end to years' worth of sleeping around and serial dating. A woman who was the complete opposite of Paige, and maybe that's what he'd been looking for. She was the first person he'd even become official with since Paige, but neither of them knew that. And Nigel wondered how long he could keep that from them or if he should even tell Aaliyah about that past at all. He decided to wait it out, see where the relationship would lead before he went exposing all his dirty laundry at once. He dove into the cozy warmth of that decision and hoped he was right. Wrapped it around himself, used it as a shield. To think, they'd been on the same campus for years and never met, but maybe it wasn't meant to be then. Maybe they both had to go through the hardships they'd had before they were compatible enough to unite and fall for one another. The wait had been well worth it.

Aaliyah sighed and rolled over, wrapped her arm around him and Nigel pulled her to him. He hadn't expected Paige to be so jealous and vicious. He hadn't expected her at all. Women like that were unpredictable, and Paige, Nigel knew, could be a hellion if provoked. Spoiled and entitled. Their history was so far back in the past it was long buried and mostly forgotten about. There was no reason for her to act that way in the first place, but simple rationales wouldn't work with her.

And yet, that letter.

The reality of it toyed with his mind. The tangibility of it he could feel in his hands.

Nigel slipped out of bed and pulled on his boxers. Downstairs, retrieving the letter was only too easy, as though it had been there waiting for him all along. As though it knew he'd come for it eventually. He knew exactly where it was, though he'd tried to hide it even from himself. Underneath the old Black Friday ads and a copy of a listing agreement from months back, there it was, still in the crème envelope, still sealed. He unsealed it with his finger and unfolded the single sheet of unlined paper. Thick, also crème. Stationary paper. Just like she'd always used, too far above lowering herself to some pedestrian form of lined notebook sheets, torn from a spiral notepad or some such.

Before he even started reading, he ran his fingers over the lines. She felt so close there in front of him on that paper where he could see her thoughts unfolding and her hesitations tripping her up in the form of ink blots, where her pen had rested for too long, and the slightest changes in her scrawl. Maybe her fingers had cramped, she'd shook her hand the way he'd seen her do, then continued on. Or maybe she'd run out of words or ways to say them and set the letter aside for a time only to pick up the pen and return to it later. Nigel could see it all there, could envision her in the act.

The first ink blot came in the comma after his name. Her first hesitation; her first emotional pause.

Nigel,

I hope this letter finds you well. I know, I know, it's terrible, ridiculous, of me to write this way, but I couldn't think of any other way to reach out to you. Nothing that felt right, you know, after so long. Nothing but this. So, here it goes.

A lot has changed since I last saw you. All for the better, I suppose, but I have a feeling that life is going to put us on the same path again. Pilar is married and living out in Bumfuck, Egypt, Connecticut somewhere, raising little Pilars like we always knew she would. Our parents have fled the Gold Coast hubbub for warm winters in Boca Raton. I know, they just can't resist being the cliché. So, Pia and I are leaving New York and coming back home. Since it's just sitting there empty. Since we both need a change and since New York has...I don't know, has scarred us both in its own ways. I guess this city has a tendency of doing that to people. So, what better place to lick wounds than at home, where it all started? Anyway, I'll be back soon, in Atlanta. And while I wouldn't presume to think you'd still think of me, that you'd still...long for me...I still think of you.

Anyways, I suppose I'll see you soon. I hope I'll see you soon. I'm sure Vince still knows where to find you...Because we have a lot to catch up on. But, I guess, there's still plenty of time for that.

Yours Always,
Paige Darensbourg

WADE IN THE WATER, CHILDREN

DELANEY

S he hadn't left the upstairs shower running, but she was sure she heard it.

A mere seventy-two hours after the Congolese Benefit Ball, life under the Dessommes roof had gone back to normal as if nothing had ever happened. As if their holiday season had been completely ordinary. As if Delaney and Vincent weren't avoiding each other just as they had at the ball. Their way, the antidote to everything. The in-laws were gone again, back out of her hair.

Of course, that hadn't come easily—it hadn't come without, say, a five-minute lecture/interrogation from Addison, whereby Laney had been adequately scolded and questioned on her departure from the benefit dinner table. She, utterly unbothered, had chalked it up to, "lady troubles, Addie," and sauntered out of the room with n'ere a backward glance. Not two days later, Laney's husband had departed on his way to Charleston with none other than Nigel

Cavanaugh in tow. There were properties to be acquired. Life moved on, and there were loose ends to be tied tight before Christmas descended upon them. Laney didn't mind that she hadn't spoken two full sentences to her husband between the minute they'd returned home from the benefit and the moment she'd awakened to find his guest room empty. A quickly scribbled note on the pillow reminded her where he'd gone. She crumpled the note and tossed it in the wastepaper basket.

Which was why, now, Laney narrowed her eyes, hearing the shower on in the room above her head. Not Vince's room, no. The room he'd chosen since their late-night Thanksgiving skirmish was farther down the hall. Laney was up the stairs and at the door a minute later, wondering if one of the cleaners had foolishly left the water running while cleaning the garden tub or scouring the wall-length shower. She turned the door knob, half ready to redress whichever of them responsible for the oversight out of habit, half indifferent because she no longer cared about such trivialities.

She stepped into the Wheat Room and hurried into the bathroom to turn the water off. Only, the water hadn't been left on carelessly and there was no member of the staff in the room. Instead, she walked into a fog of mist, the glass door to the stone-tiled shower closed but no match for the hot steam that poured out over the top of it. A mane of curly brown hair bent over a pair of knees, the shower water pelting down. Once her eyes adjusted to the dimness, only the sunlight from outside streaming in through the bathroom's window to brighten the room, she noticed the blood on the floor. A trail of bright red spots lit the copper tiles and splattered on the white rug. A trail that led from under Laney's toe to the closed shower door.

Laney threw the door open, the sliding glass slamming against the wall and ricocheting off with a clamor. She pressed it back as it rolled slowly back toward her and felt her throat clenching at the sight of her sister in the shower. Jill raised her head as the shower door opened, but otherwise never moved an inch to cover or protect herself, to pretend she wasn't cutting into her own flesh right there in front of Laney. Her hair was tousled, wet ringlets that dripped water onto her naked shoulders, into her eyes. Or maybe it was not only shower water running down her face. Laney could not be sure. Jill held her gaze, never turning away, never moving to hide her bare breasts or close her knees that were pulled up to her chest. She swallowed. Bit her lip. Dragged the straight razor poised over her hip into her skin. Closed her eyes. Rested her head back against the shower. Laney was wet before she knew it, soaked through within a matter of seconds that scalded her skin through her jeans and assailed her face and bare feet when she crouched next to Jill. The shower ran the length of the wall with three shower heads. Jill had turned them all on.

"Get out of here, Laney."

"Jill." Laney touched her shoulder, resisting the urge to look down at the blood pooling and running into the shower drain, red streams merging between Laney's toes and under Jill's hips. "Jill. Stop."

She didn't so much as open an eye. Not even when Laney moved her hair and turned Jill's face toward hers. It was hard to ignore the near-scalding water and terrifying that Jill neither noticed nor reacted to it as it pelted her skin, raining down on them from above so that Laney's hair plastered to her cheeks, her t-shirt to her skin.

"Jill, please, stop."

There were questions swirling in Laney's head, none appropriate to utter out loud in such a moment. It didn't matter then why Jillian was there or how she'd gotten in or how long she'd been there. It didn't matter why she was hacking into her flesh or how many times she'd broken her own skin in that shower. Laney laid her hand on her sister's shoulder again, and she realized it was a maneuver as much to steady herself as it was to steady Jill. She felt the fluid downward motion of Jill's arm as she pulled the razor down again. Laney grabbed her face, slapping her hands against her cheeks and shaking her until she opened her eyes, squinting against the water. Until she maintained eye contact and wouldn't look away.

"Jill, I'm here. Listen to me. I'm here." Laney's hand covered Jill's, feeling the hot razor between Jill's fingers, between hers. "I'm here."

Jill shook her head, snickering and shrugging her off. She shoved Laney, putting all her weight behind it in one angry motion that sent Laney on her ass, the side of her head rocking against the stone wall.

"I don't need that bullshit, Laney. You're not here. You're. Not. Here!"

Laney scrambled back to her haunches, kneeling beside her, noticing the girl etched in ink to Jill's skin, into her side between her breast and waist, and grabbed Jill's hand. Obviously not a new addition; no, this had been with her for a while, was comfortably settled into the pigment of her skin: a girl with darkly shaded sunglasses over her eyes, a single tear trailing down one cheek. Laney ran her fingers over it, tracing the inked-on tear, looking into the eyes of the those hidden by sunglasses. But Jill cut again, and Laney felt herself shrinking away disgusted at the sensation, because with Jill's hand in hers it had felt like she was cutting Jill. Like she was the one running the sharp edge into her skin and drawing the blood that trickled down her hip and into the stream of water around them. She shrunk away just enough, kneeling there on her knees beside Jill. Just enough that Jill felt her cringe and recoil. Just enough to warrant a sad little smirk on Jill's face.

"I told you, Laney. You're not here."

Laney's hands were on Jill's again, trying to rip the razor from her grasp. Jill tried to shove her again, barking at Laney to let her be, but Laney steeled herself against the expected blow and moved not an inch. She wrapped her arms around Jill's shoulders and pulled Jill to her. Smoothed her unruly, dripping curls back and pressed cheek to forehead, noticing the hot water pelting her face but no longer caring, feeling her lungs contract in the stifling steam, her breath coming shorter now that it was harder to breath. But she ignored it.

"Jill."

Jillian struggled against her, pushing, shoving off with her shoulder, grunting and shaking her head. The cast off from her hair hit Laney's cheek, her shoulder. But she grabbed for her sister again and pulled her back into the embrace. She didn't even yelp when Jill scratched her hands, trying to shirk her off, or when she felt the blade of the razor dig into the inside of her finger and down her palm when Jill used her cutting hand to try to pry Laney's away from her. The gash was deep; she could feel the meat of her hand pulsating, throbbing, oozing. Yet she didn't pull away while Jill continued to struggle. Nor did she pull away when she heard those struggles morph into groans then melt into tears. Laney felt the racking sobs in her chest when Jill finally let them out. She absorbed them like they were her own. Laid her head on Jill's, felt their tresses mingling and knocked the razor away.

Neither of them reached for it when it clattered in the drain, too large to be pulled down out of sight, but small enough that it clattered around under the rhythm of the water above and beneath it. She threaded her fingers into Jill's hand and squeezed, once, again. And it didn't matter that she felt a biting sting with each flex of her hand or that she could no longer tell whose blood was whose as it pooled, rippled and drained around them. She pressed her free hand into Jill's curls and laid her head on her shoulder. Listened to her sob. Felt the water pelting then trickling down her own face. Again, Laney resisted entertaining all the questions in her head. Resisted putting her cut finger and palm into her mouth to mute the stinging. She resisted being the first one to say another word.

But she did cry.

As she stroked Jill's hair and laid her head over hers, as she squeezed her hand and felt every shudder from Jill, heard every sigh of resignation and groan of contempt, she cried. It was difficult to tell that that's what was happening at first. Her eyes had stung from the moment she'd crouched next to Jill and the hot spray from above hit her in the eyes. She'd felt the water running down her cheeks since she'd stepped into the shower, her feet against the warm stone floor. And she'd felt Jill's shudders since the moment she'd finally surrendered herself into Laney's touch. So, she couldn't tell when her own tears had started, when they'd ceased being a reaction to the water and started being a reaction to Jill. But it happened. And even if she'd wanted to wipe the water from her face she wouldn't have. Her own breath came in even shorter and shorter spurts now, the hot haze filling her lungs with every intake of breath as she fought the battle to steady herself, to not let the tears fall.

But she let it happen, and that she didn't resist.

II

Laney didn't shut off the water until Jill was ready. She didn't know how much time had gone by but knew that it'd been long enough for the scalding water to turn cool and for her joints in her knees to lock up a little. When she shut the water off, their hair dripped heavy, echoing drops onto the shower floor. Jill wouldn't look at her but shoved off from the wall and stood without even acknowledging Laney. Or so Laney thought until Jill paused, turned and held her hand out, pulling Laney from the floor. Jill reached up and grabbed the towel hanging over the shower door and handed it to her, stepping her nakedness out of the shower without so much as a glance at her leg, which screamed with open, red gashes and still bled slowly. Laney toweled her hair, wincing at having to move muscles that protested as she stood on two legs again. She pressed the towel into her hand, wrapping it around as a makeshift compress. Jill took a towel from the linen closet and rubbed it over her own hair, watching Laney with red-rimmed, golden eyes.

"You might want to take those off."

She jerked her chin toward Laney's dripping jeans and t-shirt. Laney thought she saw the faintest pull of a smirk at Jill's lips. What was there to hide now, that leer seemed to say. Or maybe Laney'd imagined it, for Jill was already sauntering into the Wheat Room—her room—still towel drying her hair.

Jill pressed the towel to her injured hip without so much as a flinch and left it around her leg when she sat her wet body on the bed and eyed Laney, still in the bathroom. Laney stripped away her shirt and jeans and another wrapped the towel around herself.

"How long have you been here?"

"That's the question on your mind right now?"

When Laney didn't answer, acknowledging to herself what Jill had already figured out—that she'd deliberately sidestepped the hard questions for whatever reason mistaking Jillian for vulnerable—Jill went ahead and answered that throwaway inquiry.

"Since early this morning." She pressed the towel to her hip again, adding pressure, but casually, almost as a second thought. Like she'd done this before and knew it needed to be done but otherwise was uninterested in the task. "Knew Vince would be gone. Needed a place to think."

"So that key did come in handy then?"

Another smirk. "Yeah, I guess so. Car's in the garage. Figured the longer you didn't see it, the longer I'd have to sort shit out. So much for that."

"What's wrong with your place?"

"Nothing. Just too much emotional noise."

Laney settled into the silence around them but finally stepped into the room. Moved the throw pillows from the chaise and took a seat there. Jill turned her head to watch Laney as she went, then met her gaze when she offered it.

"So, I guess I'll go ahead and ask the million-dollar question."

"Do you have to?"

"Do you want me to?"

"Go ahead."

"Why? Why do you do this?"

Somehow, this seemed not to be the question that Jill was expecting. She blinked a few times and looked down at her feet then Laney's. "I don't know. In some fucked-up way, it makes me feel better."

"Cutting yourself makes you *feel* better?"

"Something like that. I just—just have all this shit going on in my head, Laney. Anyways, I thought you didn't care what I did to myself. Remember that, just a few weeks ago?"

"Oh, come on, Jill. Don't be an idiot. That was before."

"Before I snuck in your house and started damaging myself?" A wry chuckle.

"Before you were my sister."

"Don't kid yourself, Laney. I'm no one's sister. Not to hear them tell it. I'm nothing. Worthless. Or, haven't you heard?"

"You and I both know that's bullshit, okay? And we both know we aren't the fucked-up parties here."

"Speak for yourself. We're definitely fucked up enough."

Jill pulled the towel away from her skin and checked underneath. Decided it was okay to remove it. Laney grimaced when she saw the jagged red lines reaching toward Jill's upper thigh.

"Ah, don't get all sensitive on me. It's not that bad."

"Jill, what the hell? Where the hell have you been? I don't see or hear from you for days—you don't go to the benefit—"

"No shocker. You and I both knew I wasn't going to that thing. Not after…"

"—And now you pop up here? I called you."

"I saw." Laney ran the towel over her hair again, narrowed her eyes Jill's way. "Told you there was shit you didn't know. Plenty of shit you don't know. I've just been dealing with it all. And school. School. I mean, Jesus, Laney, I'm about to get a degree to be a counselor. A *family* counselor. A problem solver!" Jill's laughter rang out harshly and biting, throaty and unnerving. "Can you believe that shit? I mean, who am *I* to counsel *anyone*? It's all a big fucking joke! I'm a joke. This whole thing…is a joke."

She continued patting her leg with the towel, sliding her eyes from Laney's but not off her. Down, to her bruised arms, the marks fading away as though they'd been left by a ghost. "I mean, what the hell? They just…" her voice trailed off so that Laney could barely hear her say, "give these pieces of paper to just anyone, I guess."

"Jill, don't do that. Don't…belittle what you've accomplished. You think Emory lets just 'anybody' in and gives just 'anybody' a fucking master's degree? If you didn't have it in you, you would have quit running that race a long time ago."

"I think I did quit running that race a long time ago. A lot of me quit a long time ago." Jill rubbed her hands over her eyes, inhaled and exhaled deeply as if releasing something too heavy to hold in. "So, I've got this cushy family money to get a degree in family counseling and it just became too much. Like, too comical. It's all a joke, Laney. And I don't know who the hell I am if after all this I'm just a joke. So now what, huh? I graduate in a few months with this shiny new diploma and then what? *Then* what?

"Anyway, my head's just been fucked up about it for a few weeks. I don't know what I'm doing or where I'm going or, hell, what I even am. Do you know how that feels?"

"You have no idea." Laney wrapped the towel tighter around her and met Jill's gaze head on. "So, in other words, you've been sky high out of your mind since Thanksgiving."

Jill's sharp glance her way was enough to ask the question to which Laney simply responded, "You left your drugs out all over the table when I came over. I saw it. I know you were high at Thanksgiving."

Jillian tossed her towel aside then rummaged through her duffle bag and pulled on a pair of black panties. No bra. Wrapped the towel around her breasts and wore it like a dress.

"You said you saw the bombs, Laney. So, you know what this feels like. Your wrists—they know what this feels like. Why do you always need shit spelled out for you? You're better than that. So, you know what happened at the Thanksgiving table. Good, you *should* know."

"Jillian, you came here to my house to reach out to *me*. To talk to *me*. So drop your macho act and let's talk then. You wanted me to find you."

Jill chuckled derisively, sitting on the side of the bed. "I don't know if you noticed, Laney, but I'm not the cry-out-for-help kinda girl."

"Yeah, well, you were today, Jill. You were today.

III

Laney doubted her invitation would be accepted when she extended it, even if it was more than sensible. Jill, she knew, wasn't often one for sensible.

There were nights that could be passed in the company of one another, with Vince out of the house for a few more days and Jill unable to hear her own thoughts in her own space, right? They could—

"—What? Braid each other's hair, Laney? Gab about boys and—"

"—Sing Christmas carols if you're up to that, too! You know, if you're down for that sadistic sorta thing like I am."

The laugh that passed between them was enough to seal the deal, a new entry to add to their glossary of body language linguistics they'd amassed over the years. Laney readjusted the towel wrapped around her body, water droplets still trailing down her calves and neck.

"Go grab some things and come back, huh? We'll talk, figure some things out." The lightest of laughs. "I know we could both use that."

She took the duffle bag from Jill's room with her. Jill watched her as she pulled out a handful of clothes and tossed them on the bed.

"If you need more clothes, grab 'em from home or just go in my drawers and get it. But this bag," she held it up and shook it, wincing at the stab of pain from her hand, "comes with me. Jesus knows what you've got in here to do yourself more harm. And it ain't gonna be that kinda week."

Laney closed the door behind her and followed the runner down the stairs, her bare feet drying on it as she went. In the kitchen, she allowed herself a single glass of wine and left the room to avoid going for another. She grabbed her phone from the counter and found fourteen missed calls and texts. One from Vince to say simply that they'd seen three sites so far that day and everything was So far, so good.

No other words or frills included.

No apology or affection offered.

Sterile.

Clinical.

Business-like.

She guessed he was still playing the victim, his favorite pastime, and decided not to take the bait. If he wanted to simmer, she'd let him. She ignored the call from Carmella, two calls from Addison and the text from her that started with the word "Jill." For, it was the urgency of the two missed calls from Micah and four missed calls from Aaliyah that were wholly atypical.

First call first.

Laney brushed a limp lock of hair behind her ear with her hand holding the wine glass and tapped the phone screen to call Micah back. She could feel the dampness of her feet creating a tiny suction against the marble floor as she padded across it toward Vince's cave of an office. Inside, her feet were swallowed up by plush pools of animal hide rugs, as the phone rang once, twice, three times.

Water meandered down her back from her hair. She was adjusting the towel around herself when the ringing stopped and she realized there he was. Right there, on the other end of the line as, she also realized, he'd never been before. Laney never dreamed he'd actually call her when he asked for her phone number that night. After her puddle of fabric had been lifted like melted bronze from the gravel. After her bruised peach wrists were covered again and he insisted on staying with her while she calmed, on walking her back inside to ensure her safety, on taking her number to ensure she'd be alright.

But here he was. She took a slow seat down into Vince's black leather chair. Swiveled around to face the desk. Leaned her head into her hands and heard his voice come over the speakerphone.

"Hey, how are you?"

Laney chuckled despite herself. "That's quite the question, considering."

"I know," he guffawed back. "Heard it as soon as it left my mouth. Stupid thing to say. I'm good at those around you, you know."

"Oh, I don't know about that. Your way with words tends toward impressive most of the time."

"Yeah, not then. Not that night, I mean." He blew air into the phone, heaving a sigh. She pictured his cheeks expanding then deflating with the effort of it. "I didn't—I mean, you caught me so off guard. I was terrible that night. I keep thinking back, kicking myself in the ass for not knowing what to say or how to help you. I'm—"

Laney stopped him before he could even say the word that would follow. There was simply nothing to be sorry about. Nothing that he'd done anyway. Nothing that was his fault. She didn't say those words but hope her shushing of him still vibrating in the air between them communicated that particular notion.

They sat in silence for a few moments that lingered then drifted away. Laney felt the phone vibrate against the table, but didn't check to see who the message was from this time. There was no need. They were all trivial, all petty, all so enveloped in themselves that she couldn't stand the thought of them. Addison. Carmella. The rest of them.

"So anyway, I'm sure you know why I called. To—"

"Check on me. I know."

"To check on you. Yes. And, to hear your voice." Micah laughed quietly into the phone, but in her ears that nearly inaudible sound echoed in the air of Vince's office. "God, man. Is that crazy? I called to hear the sound of my boss's wife's voice. I don't know. I've been uneasy the past few days from not having heard it. And I know Nigel and Vince are out on that run. Don't know. Guess I was worried about you there by yourself after...I'm surprised he left you there like that, really."

"Why would you be? You know I didn't tell him. Anything. Why would I?" After a shake of the head and a sip of her spirits, "Our ships don't pass that closely in the night."

Micah did not respond to this and, in the seconds following her saying it, she found that she was grateful for that.

"You never really know who's behind the mask, do you?"

"Naw, I suppose that's the point of the mask all along."

She heard Jill when she exited through the garage, cranked up her car, raised the carriage house door and backed out. There was a silence between them as she listened, a silence that did not feel strained or uncomfortable. Her phone vibrated again then again. Laney furrowed a brow, wrinkling her nose, and swiped the screen down to investigate the cause of urgency.

Aaliyah.

This piqued her interest while filling her core with guilt. With Aaliyah permanently wrapped ever so tightly in her cloak of self-sufficiency, she couldn't remember the last time she'd seen such urgency from Aaliyah directed at her. Buckets of bleach-filled water, hours of scouring her home, dismissing and downplaying need: these things she'd seen from her friend in spades over the years. But never this.

The last two: Hey, r u busy? I need to talk.

Where r u, Laney? Fuck it. I'm headed over.

Laney stood and picked up the phone, leaving the wine on the desk. Told Micah she had to go, that something was wrong with their once-mutual friend, Aaliyah. As they hung up, she told Micah she'd call him again soon. Or maybe it was he who told her. Later, she would not be able to remember which came first, in retrospect. Him. Or her. Eventually, it would all fuse together into routine. For now, Laney texted her back, fingers flying as fast as they could.

Sorry about that, I'm here. Yeah, come. There's someone I want you to meet.

But that text couldn't fly fast enough to be received.

BRICK HOUSE

NIGEL

Nigel glanced out the car window at the passing monuments and Christmas décor glinting in the falling sun around them. Vince was at the helm of their rented Porsche Cayenne, navigating downtown Charleston like he'd been there too many times before. In with hindsight, he probably had been. Carmella and her family were from there. Originally, Paige was from there.

They'd passed a day in the city, feeling the icy chill in the air through their coats, viewing four potential acquisitions and starting gentle negotiations over two of them. That was the way Vince typically started, Nigel was beginning to notice. He started gently, almost playfully, as he had over hibachi and pre-signed contracts. Clap a few backs, share a few anecdotes over Scotch, perhaps, and grease the way to a smooth purchase—or blindsiding lowball, whichever the occasion called for. That was the dirty politician side of him, but Nigel had to admit Vince wore it well. It was just his size and tailored to fit him like everything else in his world. He played the good-ole-boy, "oh, don't we go so far back" routine whenever his preceding reputation would allow for it. He even had his assistant to research potential ties between he and his next prey—the six degrees of separation and such—before agreeing to the first meeting, just to ensure he had his ducks in a row, his gun poised to fire. When it wouldn't work, he tended toward the opposite route.

Nigel had seen this act in Atlanta, on his first acquisitions outing with Vince, when he'd damn near played arm wrestling with the building owner—also old money, probably older money than Vince's, the quintessential WASP. There, there had been no laughter, no back-clapping, only intimidation and veiled threats when it looked like the negotiations may not go his way. Nate had warned him about this—some old score that needed settling, some building Nate wasn't convinced they should buy so he wanted Nigel's eyes and ears on this one now that he was on the team. Nigel wouldn't have advised such antics, himself. Yet, when they worked—the following week, the contract was signed and delivered to them via the WASP's commercial broker—he, somehow, was not surprised. Vince had done this too many times. Had seen his father and his father before that do this too many times. These were acts that he could slip on and off, change with the weather of his temperament or current circumstance. If nothing else, Nigel trusted that Vince knew what he was doing, that he was well trained and well oiled. A machine with so many moving parts, so many gears he could switch into to accommodate whatever the situation called for. Nigel watched, listened, noticed, learned.

They were on their way to a steak dinner at the downtown hotel where they were laying their heads for the next couple days. Vince joshed about how he was starving and couldn't wait to get back, turning up the heat in the car. Nigel only tossed him a preoccupied smile and looked back out the window. Bonding with him wasn't necessary, he'd decided on their way out of town. He didn't need to partake in locker room banter or stroke this guy's ego or say any more to him than was professionally polite. Armed with this idea in mind and at heart, he'd felt comfortable boarding the plane with him, looking over blueprints and inspection reports and going over notes from their contractor on possible remodel options. Nigel felt relief that the plan was working so easily, coming together so flawlessly, and that he'd be back home to Aaliyah and his normal life within a few days, in time for the first days of December.

Aaliyah was why he felt especially guilty going on this trip. Of course, she'd agreed that he had to go—his first out-of-town trip with the new company—but it hadn't alluded him that she'd done so lacklusterly and with a sigh. He'd left her home with a mountain of design catalogues, paint samples and fabric swatches. There were more rooms to be painted. More recipes to be discovered. More to do. Always more to do.

"Anyways," her hand at his back, "you go. Your flight with the devil's taking off soon enough. Just don't let 'im sink his hooks in ya."

The reality of Paige Darensbourg still lingered between them, that conversation hovering in the air around them for days now, heavy like a sopping wet blanket. So, he didn't comment. He was still gathering his thoughts; maybe she was too. He didn't ask her what she intended to do for a job, how long she planned to sit out on the bench. He didn't ask her. She wasn't ready. Neither of them was ready.

Nigel pulled out his phone to text her now that she was on his mind again, but Vince pulled into the roundabout of the hotel and got out of the car before he'd even typed the first word. The valet guy slid Nigel an apologetic look for rushing him, and he noticed that Vince had already grabbed his calf-leather briefcase from the backseat and was waiting on Nigel to get out of the car. He did so, shoving his phone back into this pocket and grabbing his own coat and briefcase from the floor of the car. A chill ran down between his shoulder blades. He rubbed his gloved hands together and walked with Vince inside.

In the bar, waiting for their drinks to be served and their table to be ready, Nigel again thought of texting Aaliyah and moved to do so. Their drinks were served, pushed politely their way by a buxom Latina at whom both men politely nodded and turned away.

"Calling your old lady?"

"Yeah, I probably should." Nigel sipped his Hennessy neat and leaned against the bar. "She was up to her neck in a new project at home when I left."

"On a work day? Doesn't she work, uh, downtown somewhere?" A dismissive flick of his wrist when he couldn't remember where she was employed though he'd only just recruited Micah from the same company.

Nigel peered Vince's way, a question on his tongue, until he realized by the blank stare on his old frat brother's face how futile that question would've been. "You and Laney don't talk much, do you?"

Vince laughed that one off, raising his vodka tonic in salute to Nigel. "Oh, is there something she should've told me? We've been, you know, not at our best lately, so I wouldn't have any idea."

"Oh, trouble in paradise?" It was the first thing he could think to say to such an honest admission and kicked himself inwardly for how lame it sounded.

"Mmm, no more than usual. Women issues, really. She'll get over it. But you see, that's what happens when you get settled in and married, man. Get the house and start thinking about the kids and all. Not like you. You've still got options!" Vince clinked his glass to Nigel's in an annoying way that said they were in on the same joke. Nigel didn't get it though.

"Options?"

"Options. Like a pretty little thing named Paige Marie Darensbourg." Nigel opened his mouth to protest laughingly, shaking his head, but Vince cut him off. "You know she got Cammy to call and ask me about you? Wanted to know how you'd been, what you were up to. I told her you'd be at the charity ball, and I haven't heard from her again. I guess she got in touch with you?"

"Uh, yeah. Yeah, she found me. Didn't, uh, didn't go so well."

The hostess came over to let them know their table was ready. Vince nodded and gathered his things, gesturing for Nigel to lead the way. They passed several open tables in the middle of the floor and headed over to the booth in the back Vince had requested.

"Too many listening ears," he'd explained simply when Nigel tossed him a questioning glance at the request. Vince took the booth seat with his back to the wall, facing out into the restaurant. Nigel sat across from him.

"So, you were saying it didn't go so well?" Vince nodded at the hostess as she handed them their menus, then his attention was right back on Nigel.

"Naw, it didn't. But, I mean, nothing big. Nothing worth mentioning."

"Ah, naw, don't go doing that! You know you've gotta spill and tell me what happened. I mean, you know Paige's family and my family—they go way back." A playful finger wagging at Nigel. "But then, I know, you and Paige go *way* back, too."

Nigel grinned it off, suddenly feeling itchy like he was wearing an old tweed suit from his attic instead of the fine tailored garb he had on. The salesman effect, he laughed inwardly. That feeling that made him want to wipe his hand on his pants after interacting with the shadiest of characters. And yet, Vince prodded him on, not taking no for an answer—never taking no for an answer. Momentarily, Nigel calculated the risks of offending his new boss, his old schoolmate, then calculated the risks of giving in to him, of opening up to him. Of letting him in.

Just don't let 'im sink his hooks in ya.

When Vince's knowingly mischievous glance told him never in a million years could he weasel his way out of this one, he caved but only slightly. Figured he'd give the guy enough to keep him off his scent, but not enough to truly involve him in his business.

"She found me at the benefit, but I was with Aaliyah. It was, uh, awkward, to say the least."

Vince glanced over his menu with a raised brow saying, "She and Pia are moving back I heard."

"Yeah, I got the gist of that."

"How do you feel about that? How does Aaliyah feel about that?"

What a little girl, Nigel thought, unable to resist the urge to laugh. "I don't know. That talk is still, uh, lingering in the air for us. But, didn't *you* used to date Paige, too? How does *Laney* feel about her coming back, since you're asking me?"

"Ah, that was a million years ago—high school. Feels like a lifetime ago. And it was never really any official thing. We just messed around. You know, kid stuff. Believe me," Vince grinned, "I'm definitely no threat to you on that front."

"There's no threat on any front, because we've been done for years. I'm with Aaliyah now, hadn't even thought of Paige 'til she popped up and started shaking shit up."

"Shaking shit up is what she does best. But I mean, she *is* a better match for you, don't you think?" Vince sipped his water expectantly, awaiting Nigel's response. But he only offered a frown.

"A better match for me? Why would you even say that, 'specially when you know how I feel about Aaliyah?"

Vince held up his hands in mock surrender. "Hey, man, I'm just saying. Aaliyah and Laney have been friends forever. There must be something about her—I get it. But she isn't...one of us, you know. She isn't...like us."

Nigel noticed the hesitancy in Vince's voice, the pauses as he tried to step delicately. "Neither am I, man."

"Oh, but that's where you're wrong. You are. You've always been like us. You understand how the game is played; you're a climber. We're all climbers. I mean, ha! I know you like to play that round-the-way role and shit, but you know what it is. You know this is the life you want. That's why you signed those papers, Nigel. And that's why you need a woman in your life who also knows how to play the game, who also knows what it is. Aaliyah isn't that. Her entire existence moves against the grain. Will just anchor you down, slow you down. Drag you down. You know it, and I know it. And—" another mock surrender gesture to ward off the words Nigel opened his mouth to say "—I know you've convinced yourself otherwise and you don't wanna hear it. But just think on it. Paige is back. Maybe that's just God's timing, you know?"

Vince shrugged with a knowing smile and watched his fraternity brother from across the table.

"God's timing, my ass. I took this job because it was a great move for me. But I've never been interested in all that other shit that comes with it. I like the simple life, and ain't shit simple about a woman like Paige."

"Nah." Vince glanced at his menu again. "You're well past that now. You don't see it yet, but you will. And just remember I said I won't be the one to say, 'I told you so.'"

Nigel shook his head and closed his menu. Pulled his phone out. Typed out the text he'd been meaning to send to Aaliyah for hours.

Hey beautiful, what r u doing?

Somewhere along the line he'd dropped his guard and Vince had snaked his way in, pulling the conversation into a territory

Nigel hadn't bargained for, maybe even one he'd been avoiding. That feeling he'd been having. That feeling like it was all coming too easily now, like back clapping and dinner parties and evenings out on the green at their club had been the direction he'd been headed all along. Maybe he'd slipped into those shoes too easily, too willingly. But he couldn't tell if he'd lost something of himself or gained it. Vince's words rang in his ears as he typed out that text to fight them off then tried to re-find his place and redirect the conversation.

"But, uh, you said you and Delaney have been going through it. What's up with that? What's happening in *your* world?"

Vince sipped his drink, maintaining eye contact. Nodded his head slowly, recognizing the switch in conversational direction perhaps; maybe deciding if he would take the bait. After a few seconds, he did.

"Laney's got buyer's remorse."

Nigel's phone buzzed in his hand. "Excuse me?"

Headed to Laney's. Got a biz idea, need to bounce some ideas off her.

"Buyer's remorse for which part?"

"Can't be sure yet. All of it probably."

Vince nodded at the waiter who came over and greeted them, tucking the conversation away. He ordered a Porterhouse, mid-rare, and another drink. Nigel, following suit, ordering a ribeye, medium, and another round for himself as well. When they were alone again, Vince didn't pretend he'd forgotten what they were talking about, didn't wiggle out of telling Nigel what was on his mind.

Biz idea?

"Laney says she doesn't want to go down this road I've put us on, but this is the *way*. Certainly, the only way I know. This is all

I've ever thought of doing my whole life and I just—fuck, I don't know. I just thought she'd see that, that she knew that."

"That this is the life you want."

"That this is the life I *have* to lead. There's no *getting out* of this for me, even if I wanted to, which I don't. There's no out. What she's talking about—it's just not like that and it can never be like that."

Nigel peered at him from across the table, hearing something click in Vince's solemn tenor. "What part?"

"Well, I mean, there's nothing wrong with her getting a job, per say. She's been talking about getting her Ph.D., teaching, all that. And that's fine and all. That could *be* fine. But, that's just not what I envisioned for us. That's not how my pops and grandpops and grandpops before him did it. I just...didn't see us like that."

Nigel chuckled and shifted in his seat, smelling the angst in the air wafting from his old schoolmate. "Times change, man. Times change. We just gotta be ready to change with them when the moment comes."

Biz idea. I'm done sitting around here. Gonna go into bizness for myself this time. I'll tell u about it when ur back

There was little more Nigel could respond to this without crossing some sort of boundary, without pressing his nose into some new frontier, and he felt his toes on it just as he had felt his toes at so many other precarious lines since toasting with Vince at Reneé's soiree and pulling out his phone to set the meeting that'd galvanized it all. The professional line would surely be behind him if he kept on this path offering his new proprietor marital advice, and yet he sensed this was exactly what Vince expected if not wanted. Why else was he offering Nigel love advice and nosing his way into his relationships? Crossing personal lines between them that they'd never even toed before. Talking about a woman they both shared in their past whom one of them used to love and she, apparently, still loved back.

His limbs ached from the constant dance of arm's-length conversation, of standoffish maneuvers. From carrying around the heavy artillery designed to protect and defend himself against their Gold Coast institutions. He pushed those thoughts away and turned back to his phone.

Damn, babe that sounds phenomenal. But that's not all we need to talk about. When I get home, we're gonna talk about what happened Sunday night.

Yet Vince continued, "Didn't used to be this bad. I told her, 'All I'm saying is, you get a trial period with your new car and you don't take it back, can't wait seven years then start bitching and complaining to the dealer about it then,' right?"

Nigel succumbed to the laughter he tried fleetingly to withhold, and his shoulders eased downward a few degrees when Vince joined in.

That's fine, Nigel. Thought you'd pretend it didn't happen forever.

Their laughter curled and trailed away as Nigel surprised himself in spouting, "Just talk to her, Vince. Tell her what you told me—none of that chauvinist bravado you're always spewing—and I think she'll come around."

No baby not forever

"Ha, chauvinist bravado is never the goal, just...always the outcome." Vince shook his head and reached for the black napkin roll. Played with it back and forth in his hands. "I'm like a bull in a china shop when it comes to that one there. I know it, feel it. I know I haven't always done right, you know? I've done my share of bad shit and hurt people I should never have harmed. But, that one there? I've always loved her. She's always been the one, and I hate to see Laney hurting like that."

Remember what I said about the hooks Nigel

"I know. Just talk to her."

The line.

His toes.

A step.

A hesitation.

Another step.

It was all too easy, like it was right. Like this *was* his place. Like he'd been fighting inevitability trying to distance himself from that clan, a circle of folks that wanted nothing but to offer him the things he'd yearned for all his life and worked toward since he could remember. He was here now, so why was he fighting it? Why did his own eyes still view him as the other?

Nigel felt that moment when he stopped swimming against the current, that moment when the ache in his shoulders ceased and the racing of his heart slowed. That moment when it wrapped around him and it didn't feel cold and threatening as the chilly ocean depths. It felt warm and inviting like slippers warmed at a hearth. It felt like home. A new home. A bigger, roomier, cozier home, but home. And home he could explain to Aaliyah. Home is something she would want too. So, he surrendered to it, promising to himself to explain it all to her when he got back, to show her the way when he could see her face to face. He was home, and he would make it home for her too. He mentally signed the Faustian deal and felt good about it. He signed the deal, right there at that table, and knew he could take the deal but keep his soul.

"Look, Vince, if you want, we can get outta here tonight, in the morning at the latest. You can talk to Laney. I can do the same with Liyah. You know," Nigel sat back in his booth looked Vince head on. "So many offices will be closing down over the next few weeks—Christmas slows down everything. We can count this trip as a bonus—we saw four properties—and pick it up again after the holidays. Anything pops up, we're mobile."

Nigel left this to waft and vibrate in the air between them and only broke eye contact to type one last message.

No worries baby. No hooks

A leer crept across Vince's boyish face in what strangely appeared to be a smile of uncommon frankness. "See, this is what I was talking about! A four-man crew."

"Huh?"

"A four-man crew. You, me, Nate and Micah. You *are* one of us, and we gotta be like this if it's gonna work." A gesture back and forth at the two of them. "Steady whatever comes. Trust each other with it all. No secrets, no lies, no bullshitting each other."

Nigel laughed throatily but wasn't surprised to find he felt no sarcasm behind it. "Alright man, whatever. No bullshitting. I'm in."

Vince grinned back, nodding to himself. "You're in. I always knew you would be." He extended his hand across the table to Nigel. "I've been saying all along, a house is only as strong as its four sides, Nigel. And I'd say we're brick all the way around now." When they withdrew their hands, Vince nodded again. "Cool. You think we should go home? I trust your judgement. So, let's go home."

A RAISIN IN THE SUN

AALIYAH

Aaliyah washed her hands in the kitchen sink and dried them on the towel hanging over the faucet before she left the house. She'd been wrist deep in gilded papier-mâché for the better half of the morning, and gold flecks peppered her ebony skin up to her elbows, imbedded themselves under her fingernails and glinted in the light when she moved through the living room and through the kitchen archway. Her résumé—six copies of it, actually—lay in tattered shreds on the rug, some long shreds from where she'd torn the paper in half, others smaller than dime-sized and spotted with the mixture she'd toiled over for days, thought and rethought for weeks.

But that was behind her now. It was complete. And, as she stepped over the remnants of her artistic venture and grasped the finished product in her hands to hang on the wall, she admired the craftsmanship of her work. She hadn't known what she was making until she was making it, sitting on her living room floor Indian style with those meaningless words of her accomplishments in her lap. She wasn't sure of what it would be until she started stirring, but when it was finished, she knew it was just right. A four-foot-by-three-foot canvas of golden papier-mâché, framed in a heavy oak frame, peppered with the torn, shredded and mashed remains of her old resume.

Graduated from here. Honors from there.

None of it mattered anymore.

There was better use to be found for these useless, lifeless, rewardless pieces of paper than to be emailed in to the next corporate empire, considered for the next fruitless role she could easily earn and add to the futile current of empty accomplishments she'd already amassed. There was more that it could be. It could be better.

Therapy.

Growth.

She hung her creation on the newly painted wall with hooks and twine to the left of the sofa, and the sun-setting skies outside lit the piece up in a gilt haze. Aaliyah touched the canvas, running her fingers over it, feeling the roughness of it all beneath her fingertips. She pulled away when she felt the vibration of her phone in her hip pocket and heard the jaunty jingle announcing a new text message.

Hey beautiful, what r u doing?

She glanced down at it and hesitated before responding. Pulled on her coat and tied the wrap. Reached over to the end table and grabbed her little notebook of ideas. Names, concepts. Where could she rent a space?

She tossed it in her bag and slung that over her shoulder, heading out the front door.

Headed to Laney's. Got a biz idea, need to bounce some ideas off her.

II

By the time she got down to her car, there was air in her step, a smile pulling at her face. *Style Noire* had been her brainchild for endless hours over the past few days, the result of her mind running away with her as she mixed and stirred papier-mâché, molded it with her hands onto the canvas. A place where she could put her mind to work for herself, her creative talents to work for others. Her own space.

Autonomy.

No more ladders, *sans* wheels.

It had taken her this long to find her own way, to feel comfortable standing on her own two feet and trusting her own instincts. But the wait had been worth it, as most waits were. The delay had tempered her outlook on life and landed her just where she needed to be. Nigel was out with those slugs, fending off their residue as he'd always promised he would. He'd come home and look her in the eye and tell her who the blonde hellion was, and she'd forgive him. Maybe, she could forgive him. Aaliyah grinned when she heard the jingle again and paused on the street beside her car to read the message. A wry chuckle as her fingers tapped a response to him.

Remember what I said about the hooks Nigel

She didn't see them coming as she pressed send, and they didn't see her. There was the familiar whisper of cars whizzing past, the chilly December dusk surrounding her. The pressing of the Send button and the impact. A crunch and scrape of metal as the red sedan sideswiped hers, as the blow of the collision overtook her. As blackness came for her.

The gaping darkness had already swallowed her by the time the driver slammed on their brakes, started freaking out, hands to their head. The teenaged boy had dropped his own phone when he lost control of the car and it went careening to the right toward Aaliyah. Now he reached for it, forgetting the text he'd been in the middle of sending, reaching, reaching, reaching, between his legs searching for it. Pale fingers over the leather seats of the car, frantic, hunting for his phone. To what? Call the police? Call his mom? He wasn't sure. There was blood. A woman's blood. Pooling. Spreading. Deep, dark, red. Crimson. Coming toward him.

He released the brake and slammed his foot down on the other pedal, sending up a piercing screech of rubber to cement and a grey haze of smoke in his wake.

Aaliyah's phone chimed again as he rounded the corner on two wheels, but she didn't hear it.

Couldn't hear it.

The darkness had already taken her.

No worries baby. No hooks

It would have made her laugh.

MAMA'S BABY, DADDY'S MAYBE

JILLIAN

J illian lit a cigarette and slammed her textbooks closed on the coffee table. Maneuvering the smoking stick to one side of her mouth, she pinched it between her teeth and shoveled the books one by one into a duffle bag. Nora Jones' "Seven Years" played softly from her living room stereo, less so because she was in a melancholy mood and more so because her randomized playlist had decided she was. But she didn't mind. There was some kind of tranquility in a song about a little girl, though she realized she herself hadn't been one in a long time.

She ignored Xander's texts, glancing around the room deciding what more she needed for her stay, holding the vibrating phone in her hand. What was there to say to him, to this guy who'd functioned as "Exhibit A" when she needed to take her mind away from reality? To this man who'd left little impact on her life other than to prove to herself she was exactly what her mama had told her not to be. She was still the woman he'd met weeks before, but somehow her focuses had shifted. Since Thanksgiving. Since Laney. Since not being alone anymore. He was just a boy. And there would always be boys.

In theory, she needed to get her brain moving to crank out this last few months—to get her mind back on her thesis, to push forward into something she had no desire for and saw the hypocrisy in. While part of her swore to push forward, to finish what she'd started, so much more of her knew she couldn't. The silence in her place was too loud, deafening. She knew where all her secret stashes were here, hidden in bathroom cabinets and underneath beds. Little boxes shoved here, small baggies tucked there, like an Easter egg hunt she already had the map for. She needed out, even if just for a few days, even if for just long enough to restrain her mind back from tumbling over the cliff of sanity.

Jillian neither winced nor limped on her injured leg, which had already begun the healing process as if it'd already been prepared for such an assault. It never failed to dawn on her the irony of her situation, that she was the very person who should've been able to help herself: a counselor in training, a possessor of a professional eye educated to cut to the core of emotional baggage, of traumatic hurt. She knew all the words and definitions, scenarios and studies that pertained to a woman—a patient—such as herself: cutter, masochist, recreational drug user, loner. She could diagnose that on a written test in a second. And yet, it was never—could never be— so simple. Because it was too easy to casually mark on a form that someone had masochistic tendencies. Or that they'd been emotionally stunted during years of emotional abuse at the hands of their nuclear unit. Those were just words. They didn't really describe shit, did they?

'Victim' was too hard of a word to swallow for her, though she'd seen it so many times a day for the last several semesters that she liked to think she was now immune to it. It didn't fit nicely in her throat. Instead, it bulged and itched as it went down, cut and burned as she digested it. Why did they have to be that—victims, sufferers—she wondered? Why was that always the word with so few alternatives? Jill understood that she held no fault in the matter, not where her upbringing was concerned, yet that was never enough either, that simple knowledge. There was no reason for her to continue in her self-inflicted mental torture, no reason to keep up with such a thought process at all because—

Bam bam bam.

The sound at the door made her flinch but only for a second, only in surprise rather than fear. Jill turned the music off and took one last deep drag, for the millionth time thinking, *I gotta get off this shit. I'm too young for this shit*, then stubbed out the cigarette only half smoked. She held the smoke in, wanting to feel it coursing through her. And it was neither her newest sexual liaison's nor her sister-in-law's face that she exhaled her smoke into with the opening of her front door but that of her mother's.

Addison Dessommes stood on the other side of her door—for the first time in easily over a year—glaring at her second born and waving smoke from her face.

"Glad to see some things haven't changed, Jillian."

She stepped back from the door to let her mother in, pressing away the surprise that she was there on her front steps in the first place. There was no room for paralysis in Addison's presence, no excuse for losing her cool.

"I didn't even know you knew how to get here, Ma."

"I know where all my property is, Jill. You should know that. Any and everything I own, I can find in a heartbeat."

Jill shuddered, her back to her mother as Addison closed the door behind them, her heart somewhere up near her throat. If she would've somehow anticipated the impromptu reunion, she might've fluffed her hair, checked her makeup, tried to look presentable before presenting herself to the queen. Yet, her outward appearance would have to do. Her sweatpants, t-shirt and bare feet—so unceremonious for the moment, she knew—would have to be enough for the woman who'd birthed her then complained about it nearly every day after.

"Well, what's up? I'm kinda on my way back to Laney's—"

Jill turned to find her mama glaring at her and felt the strongest urge to look away, to avoid her incensed and judgmental glance. But she did not. She held her ground and looked her in the eye. Even when Addison rummaged in her Birkin bag and pulled out Jill's little tin box.

She recognized it before she even knew that she had. The little box she'd packed with her to Laney's house what felt like a lifetime ago. Really, it had only been days.

The one she'd left in the nightstand—her nightstand—in her room.

Her room.

The Wheat Room.

Her room.

Seeing that little square of tin in her mama's hands sent her thoughts tripping and jumbling all over themselves, rolling down a hill of disbelief into a gulley of uncertainty, her thoughts no more sure of where to land than her feet were sure of the very ground below them. Addison had sealed it in a large Ziploc bag and was now holding it between her thumb and forefinger like some filthy dish rag pulled from the sewer, as if she was trying to avoid being polluted by it through sheer proximity and contact.

Instinctively, Jill reached for the box. Reflexively, Addison pulled it away. Fuck, she hadn't thought Laney had it in her, going straight to the queen bee and ratting her out like that. Jill snorted to herself, shook her head. All that concern, all that care. *False. A ruse.*

Bullshit. Jillian wished in that moment that she could have been more surprised, that she could have felt a catch in her throat or a tear in her eye. But she couldn't. She didn't. She'd thought Laney was different, after the rain-surrounded heart to heart, after the shower. Like all that water had somehow washed over them like a baptism and made them clean, washed away all that ill will and disdain, jealousy and pity. But, maybe she wasn't. It hadn't. And that was just how the world fucking worked.

Standing there so close to her mother as she remained so unaffected, matching Jill's gaze, Jillian felt the armor she'd equipped herself with crumbling and falling to the floor. She could almost hear the palpable sound of it clattering down, could almost feel the vibrations as it fell into a pile around her feet. Addison had knocked the wind out of her, made her forget how to breathe. And there she was, staring at Jill as if she couldn't have cared less, as though she knew the exact buttons to push to make Jill doubt herself. She knew how to punch her right in the gut without ever even moving her loafer-clad feet.

Jillian felt the pang of shame punch her deep down in her core, winding up slowly like a vine taking hold. There were words she could have said, but she resisted. Too cliché. Too pedestrian and expected. So, she stood there waiting for the punch line to come, for the angry words, the cutting disappointment to spew from her mama's mouth. She'd take her licks and move on. Accept her verbal whooping and self-medicate to heal later, perhaps.

"Okay, Ma. Go ahead with it then."

Addison continued glaring, pinching the bag. When Jill stepped forward into her space, ready to just have done with it, Addison dropped it. It clattered to the floor, the top of the tin box popping off and sliding around in the plastic, a straight razor and baggie of coke peeking out from under the lid. A prescription bottle full of marijuana rolling around in the now-open box. Addison stepped on it, kicked it away, and neither of them winced at the sound of it skittering across the wood floor.

Addison sucked her teeth and stared back at her daughter.

Jill shook her head and sighed again. "Ma."

"Do you think I just came over here on a whim, Jillian? Is that what you think, that I just hopped in my car and said to myself, 'I wonder if I should return my daughter's drugs and—and razor blades to her? She might want those.'"

"Ma—"

"Shut your fucking mouth, Jillian."

That rang between them, Addison's finger still in the air to halt Jill's flow of words. Those five little words rattled Jill's head and heated the room around them. There was nothing about this woman standing before her that hinted at a four-lettered-word vocabulary. Nothing, because she never used them.

Jill pulled her lips in and waited. Breathed through her nose, trying to keep from making too much noise. Addison was crossing the few feet between them before she could blink again.

"Where are they? Show me!"

She grabbed Jill's arm and snatched it toward her. Pushed her sleeves up roughly and inspected her arm then reached for her other arm. Jill pulled away when she realized what her mother was after. Took a step back. Then another.

"Show me! You show me what you've been doing to yourself!"

"Ma, stop!"

Addison's hands kept reaching. Jill kept stepping back, shrugging her off, pulling away.

"Those razors still have *blood* on them, Jillian!"

Jill couldn't conceive of the edge of desperation in her mother's voice. She heard it loud and clear in the air between them. She recognized that higher octave, that breathiness. And yet, she couldn't place where it was coming from inside of her mother and why. When it had manifested, for, certainly, it hadn't always existed there. Not for Jillian. Not to be directed at her. Addison was never desperate when it came to Jill. Never so affected.

"What have you been doing to yourself?"

Jillian left her mother standing there and went into the kitchen. The added space between them helped only nominally, only in theory. She downed a glass of tap water, trying to avoid glancing at that Ziploc bag and its contents on the floor.

"Ma, please just get this over with—your lecture. I know you've got one for me."

"We're too far gone from that now, Jill. There isn't a lecture on God's green earth that would change you now. That would turn you into the woman I wanted you to be. To make you the woman you could've been."

"You have no idea what I could've been."

"That baggie proves otherwise, now doesn't it? No, I didn't come here to waste my time lecturing to your hard head again, girl. I came here to disown you."

II

There was no way her father could have known about this.

Dear, sweet, oblivious Carl would not have allowed such a thing. Not to his Little Florence. Not to his daughter, estranged though she might have been. Jillian said as much, measuring the distance between herself and her mother with her eyes, closing it between them.

"Your father wants you hospitalized. Institutionalized until you get your senses back in your head. But you and I both know you won't go. And even if you did, it wouldn't help a thing. And you'd have embarrassed us on top of it all, you—"

"Embarrassed you? *Embarrassed* you? That's what you're worried about? Where is he?"

"You know your father. He couldn't be here for this. He's not cut out for this sort of...thing. He could never do it. But you and I both know where this goes from here. I'm not going there with you, Jillian. It's not help that you need. Some fancy hospital," Addison spat, shaking her head. "Every check I write to that posh little school of yours is me helping you, girl." Addison pointed to the door like the topic of their discussion was right outside it. "All you need do is pick up any one of those damn books we've paid for to get yourself some help."

"Where did you get that box, Ma? Did Laney—"

"Laney? *Laney* knows about this?"

Jill watched her mama, unsure of anything anymore. Because, if not Laney then—

"Your brother found your little box of paraphernalia in a drawer and had the wherewithal to be concerned about your simple self. Simple as milk, I tell you! Laney wouldn't do this to herself. But you—you would."

"Vince." A tired chuckle. "Of course. Always the do-gooder. Always the hero."

There was an assassin in her home, Jillian realized, her mother on her doorstep like a mercenary to do away with her for good. There, there was the scythe in her hand, that little tin box. There was the poison in her eyes. But Jillian forced it down, that initial reaction to flee, to turn and run. She forced it down and knew there was nowhere to run. So, she didn't.

"Always the easy fix, huh? Even for Dad—that way you don't have to get your hands dirty and deal. Because it's easy to lock me up, but it's not so easy to look in the eyes of what you've made—of what you've done—and recognize it as your own, is it? That'd be too hard, even for you. Too much like right. And 'right's' never much been part of our credo, has it?"

Annoyedly, impatiently. "What are you talking about, Jill?"

"You know what I'm talking about, Ma. *Who* I'm talking about: your fucked-up son, my messiah brother."

"Oh, Jill, this again? Why do you have to do that, try to drag everyone else down with you? Bring them down into the dirt next to you? Does that make you feel better?"

"Make me feel better?"

I don't know. In some fucked-up way, it makes me feel better...

"And what if it does? Your son trying to *rape* me made *him* feel better. Hurting Laney—that made him *feel* better. Every fucked-up deal he makes and word he says is to make him *feel* better, but *I'm* the problem here?"

"He would never do that." Addison tossed her another annoyed glare, a glance with an edge of pity.

"He did. He tried. He wanted to."

"He would *never* do that," she repeated through gritted teeth, but this time her words were shakier, carried far less venom. "I know my son. He would never hurt—"

"Anyone? Were you going to say that he would never hurt anyone or just that he would never hurt me, because one thing you've never known me to be is a liar, and one thing I've never known you to be is stupid."

Addison set her jaw and slammed the palm of her hand to the counter. "How *dare* you lie like that?"

"The shit he's done to me—you've done to me. Behind my back. In front of my face. You've done the same as he has. You ignored it. Knew it. Saw it. I know you did. I know...you know I'm not lying. You know what he's capable of, don't you? The proof was all over Laney—all over me—and all you ever had to do was ask! It was all over you—hands up your skirt, Ma? Remember? All over Renée. But you didn't ask, did you? Didn't speak up—stand up. Didn't do shit for me. For any of us. Never needed to, right?"

Jill hoped she'd succeeded in punching her in her own gut, but, more so, she wanted to finally feel that feeling—that sensation of truly shirking it all away, of telling the truth, of refusing to lie, not just through silence but with action. That feeling she'd dreamed up and sensationalized for too many years. That she'd gone to bed thinking of, wiping wetness from her eyes. That feeling of finally, even just for the slightest of moments, revealing her brother for what he truly was. Them for what they were. Who they were. Darkness. A super massive black hole of darkness and depravity.

She leaned toward Addison, calmer now, her mother's composure now transferred to her because there was serenity in truth. There was composure in throwing aside the fear.

"You have to, Ma. You have to know the monster you made. That *you* made. Because to believe otherwise would be to play the fool. And you never play the fool. Help yourself if not me. *Hear* me. Vince is a true fucking monster. A lying, cheating, aggressive—but I guess," Jillian paused on second thought, "that's what we're all about, though, isn't it? That's what we're all about."

Addison reached into her purse again, swallowed, stepping over the Ziploc baggie between them as she approached her with the large envelope heavy with documents. She held it out to Jillian who glared at it but dared not touch it. Addison tossed it on the island next to them with a *thud*. Told her that it was all there, the deed to the townhouse, the title to her car. All that she owned in the world. Their gift to her. Their very last gift to her.

"You could certainly do worse, Jill. Don't do worse."

Addison stepped back from her, gave her one last glance over. The front door clicked behind her, closing with a calm and quiet sound that seemed out of place in such a scenario. A slammed door Jill would have expected. A scream, perhaps a trademark slap to sting her face and burn her skin. But there was none of that, only the soft padding of Addison's steps toward the door and the sound of it closing behind her. She heard the Boxter start up in the driveway and the sound as it faded away around the corner.

Unsteady breaths filled the air. Jill grabbed the back of the bar stool for support, felt her knees shaky and weak beneath her. Her breathing wouldn't correct itself. Her heart wouldn't stop hammering.

Hammering.

Hammering.

Is this what it felt like, to be truly free? They'd cut the cord on her instead of the other way around, instead of the way she'd envisioned it for far too many years to count. And now she was experiencing something strangely kin to panic. Her nails cut into her palms, prickling pain points exploding in her hands.

Hammering.

They were taking it all. They'd stripped it all from her. But had they? Why did she care? She shouldn't care. She'd thought she wouldn't care.

That envelope stared back at her, unmoving. She found her feet again and moved toward the couch, grabbed her bag, pulled out her wallet and let the rest fall to the floor.

Panicking.

Picked up her cell and tapped the series of numbers on the screen she'd come to memorize somewhere along the line. And yet, with each press of a button, the hammering quieted. Her breathing calmed.

Free.

Freedom.

And she acknowledged that feeling of relief she'd sought by dialing those numbers, the yawning emptiness she felt when the automated voice finally came on the line. It was all there. Every red cent that had been in her account the last time she'd checked a statement was still there. A mistake, probably. If they were disowning her, Addison would have made sure to strip away everything she could from Jill. Even the clothes on her back, the cigarette out of her mouth. Or, maybe, could it be, Carl's real final gift to her? Could it have been that he hadn't told her mother, that he'd lied to Addison, that he'd snuck Jillian one last underhanded throw of the baseball she'd never caught? Maybe.

Maybe.

Maybe he'd really left it all for her, padding the blow. Still watching out for her in that passive way of his. As she contemplated her next move, feeling herself reaching for her car keys on the island and turning toward the front door, she knew she couldn't do it. Wouldn't do it. Her first instinct was to run to the bank and claim it all before the mistake was discovered. And while that first inclination had been so strong, the rising panic so overpowering, she resisted it. She wouldn't go to the bank to claim the series of numbers preceded by a dollar sign that sat in there. She wouldn't greedily pounce down upon it, whether it was a mistake or a gift. She wouldn't go back to them. Because she finally felt it, truly, wholly. She finally felt that ever-distant thing she'd been yearning for. And she wouldn't hand that back to them.

Not to *them*.

Jill dropped the keys on the floor, metal clanging against wood. Stepped over the Ziploc baggie without so much as a glance. Grabbed the kitchen shears from the knife block. Ransacked her wallet for every piece of plastic not solely in her name. One card and then the next fell in shards, fell down, down, into the trash. Each credit card after the last left her less tethered. More weightless. Snipping and cutting. It all falling away.

The name.

The ties.

The leash.

That leash.

She cut.
She cut.
And this time...the cutting didn't hurt at all.

FAMILY IS FOREVER

DELANEY

She found it strange how the worst news always came via telephone.

That was the first thing she thought when she hung up, disconnecting her call with Addison. Somehow, that electronic middleman cheapened the exchange, stealing some of the magnitude of the moment away every time one of those calls came. The death of her parents, the demise of Aaliyah's career, the fall of Jillian Dessommes—they'd all started for her as a phone call, a simple ringing of a man-made contraption. And now, there was only the silence that came after.

At first, she'd ignored all of Addie's calls but answered Jill's. And it wasn't until she heard her sister's words on the other end of the line that she realized what all the calls filling her phone for the day had been about.

Jill.

Always Jill.

The Dessommes had gone to their attorney and blithely signed away their connection to one half of the children they had, as if a single bundle of papers could ever truly do such a thing. In their world, a single pen stroke could cut a person away and hold them at bay forever, like she was as disposable as a stranger on a late-night street.

"She's dead to us, Laney. You need to know that. She's dead to us, and that means she's dead to you, too."

"Addie, no one is dead to me unless *I* say they're dead to me. Jill is my sister."

"Oh, Laney. Laney, Laney, Laney..." Laney could hear the *tsk* in her voice, the dismissiveness of such a comment. "Sisters come and go. You'll learn that. But family is forever."

True, she'd think about Addie's words from time to time as the days slipped by and then the months slipped on, but it was Jill's calm confession before that which would stick with her forever.

"He did it, Laney. He did it."

II

Laney sipped her Merlot anxiously, feet up on the sofa in her study, until she heard the familiar sound of the lock turning in the front door. The briefcase in the hall, footsteps into the kitchen, the tab popping on a Coke. She sat up with a start that splashed wine in her lap.

Ah, there it was, the sound of his whistling. That carefree trill in time with his footsteps in the foyer.

Vince.

He did it, Laney. He did it...

That whistling. Of course, it was just another day for him. This man she'd lain next to for years. Slept beside. Learned everything about and told everything to. Stroked, loved, trusted, at some point or another if not at that very moment.

331

"Laney? Babe, you here?"

She heard his footsteps on the staircase. Heard the crumple of the Coke can in his hand. Just another day. Just the same routine. When he stuck his head around the corner of her study, he smiled.

"There you are. Did you hear me calling you? I'm so glad you're still up. I wanted to talk to you..."

Vince tossed the crumpled can into the wastepaper basket beside her desk in one fluid motion and moved her way. Laney held up a hand meant to halt her husband in his tracks and set the wine aside.

"Where'd you find it?"

"Find what?"

"Vince, don't do that. Don't. Play. Stupid."

"I told you before, Laney. I never play stupid. What are you talking about?"

"Where did you find Jill's box, Vince?"

Vince deflated, rolling his eyes and flopping down on the sofa next to her. He pulled her feet into his lap. "Are you serious right now? I came home to talk to you about something else. About us. About...you going to work and..."

"Where'd you find it?"

"What? Why do you even care—you don't even *like* Jill. This is more important."

This misjudgment didn't allude her. She heard it loud and clear, his admission to knowing absolutely nothing about her life, her feelings, her everyday going-ons. She scoffed that away, chewing the inside of her cheek.

Where was he when he was right beside her? In the car and lying in bed, holding hands at a party or at the dinner table. What did he truly think of her? That she was oblivious like him? That she harbored no other emotions outside of those he knew about—those he allowed her? That it was black and white—had always been black and white—with no need for further assessment necessary?

You don't even like Jill...

The phone hummed in her hand, but she didn't glance down at it.

You don't even like Jill...

There it was, Laney thought. That right there. *That* must've been the feeling she felt, those words she heard, right before she pulled the razor down. Right before she angled it over her skin.

You don't even like Jill...

He did it, Laney. He did it...

His casual disregard was neither shocking nor surprising to Laney, and that's what pulled at her the most. If it wasn't upsetting to her, how could it have been anything other than the norm to Jill? The way it had just fallen off his tongue—his indifference toward her feelings, for her very existence—as though it were a given, as though there was no reason to feel otherwise, itched beneath Laney's skin.

"No, *this* is more important than whatever you're about to say. She's your *sister*, Vince. Your *blood*. What did you say to them? What have you *been* saying to—"

"To what? Get them to see what they shoulda seen a long time ago? To tell the truth. Is that what you're talking about? You wanted me to lie?"

"How did you even...?"

"I slept in there Thanksgiving night. But, of course, you ran out of here like a bat out of hell. Didn't even know where I was. Didn't even care, I guess."

Again, their sturdy structure of pleasantries had failed them. Once again, they'd neglected such civilities and leapt directly into the matter, sidestepping the affection of newlyweds, heedless of the warmth that could have thawed the frost between them. There was no need for such warmth; it only burned away the truth, obscuring its charred remains that resembled trust and kinship but never quite added up to it.

"What have you been saying to them to make them only see you?"

Vince pushed himself up and away from the couch, shaking his head as though she were a silly child to be petted down into submission. When he approached her, his fingers in her hair, leaning in for a kiss, she shrugged him off.

"Vince, you're disgusting. What is *wrong* with you people? I know. Vince, I *know* what you did to Jill."

"Did to Jill? What are you talking about? I've never *done* anything to Jill."

"Really, do you touch all the women in your family between their legs, or just your sister, Vince? Grab us by our hair. Assault us." In the silence that seeped between them, Laney scoffed. "Yeah, Vince. That. *That's* what I'm talking about."

"Laney, what the fuck do you want from me, huh? What the fuck are you looking for that you do not see? Open your eyes—those pretty little things on either side of your nose." He jabbed his fingers toward her face. Laney, balking, incredulous, stood to her feet, the phone rolling out of her lap. "Open your two fucking eyes and see what I see, why don't you? See that there's no place in this picture for the likes of Jill. For a loser, a fucking quitter. She's a goner, Laney. She's gone. If you want her sniffing around your life, fucking your shit up, you're more than welcome to open your doors to her. But not these. Not the doors to my house."

"So, what? Is this the game you play? You push your sister to the sidelines, harass her, terrorize her, make her feel less than nothing so you can be everything. Pin me down between a rock and a hard place when you knew I would leave you, when you knew the jig was up. You always get what you want, Vince, don't you? And everyone else is just collateral damage. I see you now. I see you."

The moment passed where their eyes locked in determined contempt, and Laney turned away. Walked away, shaking her head, until Vince grabbed her arm roughly and pulled her back.

"You don't see shit, Laney, because if you saw me, you'd see a man who loves you. A man who's showing you the way. A man who came back here just to tell you—"

"Oh, I've seen the way, Vince. Don't you worry about that—I've seen it. But you hear *me* when I say I won't cut my feet walking that way anymore. I don't know what the hell you're expecting from me with that simple ass simper on your face—but that wide-eyed Laney you love so much? She's the one who's gone. Flown the fucking coup, because I see it all now. And it's repulsive."

She snatched her arm away and grabbed her phone from the floor. Shoved it in her back pocket. Started out of the room without another glance his way, but he intercepted her, blocking her way out of the study. Laney stepped away from him.

"I don't want to do this with you anymore, Vince. I really don't. In fact, we're *not* doing this anymore."

"Do what?"

"I said it before, and I was right. For once, what was right in front of my face really was what it seemed. I *was* delusional. Completely out-of-my-mind delusional, because I *did* think you were some other guy, Vincent. Some other man. Some man who wouldn't ambush me with some public proposal when he knew I wanted out. A man who wouldn't toss away his own sister like she was some vagrant on the street! But you're not. You're exactly who you are. Exactly who you always have been, always will be. Some man childishly standing in my way, blocking the path I want to take. And that's not enough for me anymore. It shouldn't be enough for anyone."

Vince pulled his hands into tight knots at his side, his eyes boring a hole into her, vehemence at the corners of his mouth. Laney watched him, observing the transformation beyond the petulance she'd become accustomed to and into some unknown territory of personal violence. She stepped closer to him, unable to move his solid frame from her path but approaching it. Feeling his breath from his nostrils lightly on her face, noticing those long, boyish lashes of his framing anger rather than playfulness.

"Is that where we are now, Vince? At balled fists? Do you...want to hurt me? Is that it? Is that what I mean to you now—what I've always meant to you? Something to control?" Laney stepped toward him, never pulling her eyes from his, until they were toe to toe again. "Is that what you have in that black heart of yours, Vince? Bitterness? Hostility? Violence—?"

It wasn't until he grabbed her by the shoulders that she reacted, but he'd already started shaking her, Laney's body tensing as Vince shook her back and forth, clutching her shoulders harder and harder until his nails dug into her skin, burning, biting his lip with a glint in his eyes that only flashed before her when her head rocked toward him. Laney hadn't been prepared for that, and she heard it in the small shriek that escaped her lips.

"What. The fuck. Is wrong. With you?"

His words hit her in time with each shake she withstood. Until he stopped and she crumpled against the couch, sliding down to a sit. Her legs felt like two rubbery columns beneath her, and she's lost some feeling in her left arm.

Vince grabbed the glass from the coffee table and flung it against the wall. It shattered into the smallest of pieces. Red wine rolled down the wall like blood. Laney winced and shrunk away from the flying shards of glass. She looked over at the man that she'd married as he lifted his chin in defiance and, for the first time since she'd met him, she felt fear unmasked by intentional denial.

Fear.

She'd never felt afraid of him or what he was truly capable of. Fear of his magnitude or his intent. Never truly understood the hatred in Jill's eyes or the admiration from his parents'. Never truly until it was thrust directly upon her, burning her arms and dizzying her head.

Laney pushed herself up and away from the couch, shaking with anger, laced with alarm. Her sand-filled legs threatened to give out on her at any moment. Vince rubbed his hands over his face, using his body position to thwart her chances of exiting the room at anything short of a sprint. There was a dismissive air to his action that immediately got under her skin.

"Oh, this is the man that I love, is it?"

"I *am* the man that you love."

"You think you can just snap your fingers and our problems will go away? You think the world is your playground and I am your fucking marionette? That you can do anything you want to anyone and the world will smile down on it? That's not how this goes, Vince.""

"I am your husband. And I say we should just let it be, move on from this."

"And what am I supposed to do? After this—after Jill? Trust you? Understand you—fuck, love you? Am I just supposed to love you, Vince, after what you've shown you can do to your own family. After what you've shown you could do to me?"

"Yes! You're not hurt, Laney. You're just upset."

"And your sister? Is she just upset? Should I wait to see how far it goes? Where the uphill river leads. How you *could* hurt me?"

"You should trust me. Trust me that I know what I'm doing. I know the way for us!"

"How can I ever trust you again?"

"How can you not? I'm all you have, Laney. And you're all I have. All we *can* do is trust. All we *have* is trust."

This time it was Vince who turned to leave the room and Laney who stopped him. He headed for the door, his mind already moved on to other things, away from their words, as serious as she was about them, and in that moment everything ceased to matter to her. She didn't care about the need for upheld appearances or those cutting glances from their friends. There wasn't a luxury in that house that could hold her there because everything she'd ever touched, every word she'd ever uttered since accepting him had been a lie. Indoctrinated propaganda. Sharp falsehoods that cut as she swallowed them.

The little girl was gone. Delaney Coker had been smothered away.

Sitting between her mama's knees getting her hair greased.

Gone.

Snapping green beans at the sink, laughing.

Gucci.

Prada.

The montage took her breath away, stole it and bottled it up deep inside of her.

She didn't know where that girl had gone, who that woman could've been. And what words were there to convey those feelings she held for him. Nothing she could think of would ever adequately transmit those thoughts, those feelings that tingled down to her fingertips. She pulled her rings from her finger and pitched them toward him, at him. Without those rings, she felt lighter. Unbound. Without those rings, she could do anything. They glinted in the light, as one struck his shoulder and the other slammed into the wall then skittered across the floor. Vince's feet stopped moving and his head turned back toward her.

"There are no words other than those, Vince. I want a divorce."

He twisted back around to face her as she'd known he would. There was nothing she wanted more in that moment than to kill that haughty demeanor of his. But most of all, she wanted to finally tell him the truth.

Vince scoffed at her, shaking his head, smiling just a touch. "Don't be ridiculous."

"I'm not."

"You are. You can't divorce me. I won't let you. Don't be naïve. You need me just the same as I need you. We work good together and despite some little spats, that will never change."

"I can't believe you're even this bothered. We haven't spoken two words to each other in weeks, Vincent."

"Don't be a child; that's not the point. This is marriage. This is what it's about. Those moments like this? This is what marriage is made for."

"Oh, to tie me down?"

"To get us through."

"I don't want to get through. I want to be done." Vince took his hand away from the doorknob and walked back toward her. Laney held his gaze until he was right in front of her, less than a foot away.

"You're being silly."

There it was, that slow and deliberate condescension in her husband's tone. Laney raised her hand to slap that smug expression off his face, but he was too quick for her. He caught her hand mid-air and knocked it away. When she tried again, he pushed her against the wall. Laney lost her footing and felt the back of her head connecting with the wall under the weight of his hand.

"Calm down, I said."

His hand pressed against the base of her throat, immobilizing her against the wall. All that filled her ears was Vince repeating those words as she struggled against him. It wasn't until he realized that he was choking Laney that he backed up and released her, leaving heavy breathing in the air and five purple bruises blooming at her throat.

His hands caressed her face before she could even catch her breath. Vince kissed her forehead; she tried to squirm away. He kissed her lips and she was pinned down, stunned by the contact. Laney willed herself to scream and press him away, but his tongue was halfway down her throat, muffling her protests. Laney closed her eyes, shoved him again, felt her skin tingling and ripping across her arms and down her spine.

Vince pulled away and told her he loved her.

The door slammed behind him. Laney watched it bang closed. Tried to catch her breath. Turned and took in her surroundings, her valuables. But she didn't need any of it; she realized that before she'd even taken a full survey of the room and the saliva filling her mouth disintegrated to ashes. She already knew that when she walked out the door of their home she wasn't coming back.

ASHES TO ASHES, DUST TO DUST

JILLIAN

Florence's exquisite veiled pill box hat fit perfectly on Jill's head, once she smoothed her curls back into a knot. Even in her jeans and t-shirt, it looked appropriate on her. Fitting. The heat of the flames warmed her face. Shadows leapt and danced over and across her, pooling at her feet in a way that rippled and swayed like a river at night. The trash can was on fire and her old life with it.

Just how she wanted it.

Burn it all.

Jillian stood on her upstairs balcony looking out into the wooded stretch behind her townhouse. The metal trash can enfolded the flames like hands, containing them but allowing them to dance upward if not outward. She fed those flames the crunchy winter leaves strewn across her deck for dinner, with a helping of hundreds of pages ripped from university texts as dessert. Her texts. Those old paper chains that held her down to their way of life.

One by one she dismantled them, setting entire stacks of textbook pages alight in her hand before snapping the antique lighter shut and tossing them into the embers. Jill ripped pages away and watched them flutter down until they were licked and then consumed by the growing blaze, until she'd worked herself short of breath and her arms were too weak to complete the tearing motion again. By then, the dry leaves had gone up like a haystack and the once-glossy pages were nothing more than curled sheets of fragile ash, ready to disintegrate and fly away at the slightest breath of wind. She stood on and watched, lighting a Benson & Hedges with the lick of the bonfire flames. It all smoldered, burning down into nothingness. Every essay she'd written and kept, every copy of her transcripts she still owned. Everything.

Everything.

The flames crackled and snapped, sashaying in the breeze and casting growing clouds of smoke into the night air. It smelled delicious, she thought. Better than s'mores or burning hash. She adjusted the little hat on her head, tilting it forward, feeling the delicate mesh of the black veil brushing her nose. The heat gripped her in its arms, lighting her face like a sunrise. Jillian took another drag of her cigarette and watched her old self go up in smoke.

She was no David to the Goliath. She was no freer of the chained masses, no hero, no conqueror. She was Jillian Dessommes, her back turned on her namesake as her namesake had turned on her. And that was enough for her. Finally, enough.

She heard the doorbell when it rang but moved not an inch to answer it. The door was unlocked, untouched since Addison had pulled it closed behind her and driven off into the rest of her life. Whoever it was would figure it out. And when they did, she found that it was Delaney at her door, now moving through her bedroom and coming cautiously toward her.

"Jill..."

"Shhh, just watch."

Delaney stood beside her, her hands thrust into her back pockets, elbows brushing Jill's as she took a drag and released the smoke from her lungs. Flicked the ashes toward the trash can with a light laugh, as if to herself.

"It's my funeral. What'dya think? We all wonder what it would be like to go to our own funerals, right? Tonight, I can. Crematorium style."

Delaney responded not a word but watched on, shifting her weight on her feet and settling in. Jill brought the smoking stick up to her lips again with a dry smirk, feeling her sister's presence there next to her. Not fussing, not flitting, not worrying over Jill like a nervous hen, like her mother. She just stood, watching, unquestioning. And for that, Jill was thankful. When she finally turned to her, she nudged Laney with her elbow, their new form of communication still remembered.

"Damn, girl. You look like you need a hug. And some sex." She glanced at her once more, seeing the neck bruises but not commenting. "And a cigarette."

"Gimme that."

Jill handed her the stick and watched her take a long drag. Smirked away her questions as she watched Laney pull back from it without a cough and stare down at the little stick as though it had bit her.

"Ugh, these things are disgusting."

Jillian laughed and didn't mind when Laney tossed the cigarette into the fire, because her sister was laughing, and that made her laugh too.

"Yeah, they are pretty gross. I don't know, they just give me something to hold on to, you know?"

"Looks to me like you're not holding on to anything," Laney gestured with a nod toward the fire in front of them, the shells of thick texts at their feet. "So why hold on to that?"

A snicker. "I don't think it's quite that easy."

"Neither is losing your family, but I see you're doing that in style." Laney regarded the pill box on her head, the calm in her eyes and pulled her lips into a reconciliatory smile. "I've seen that hat before, in a picture of her. It looks good on you, Jill. She'd—I think she'd be proud."

Jill chortled at the thought, hanging her head a little with her hands shoved there in her back pockets. She pulled out the pack of cigarettes and held it in her hand. Tossed Laney a look before she approached the flames and tossed the entire pack in. Laney laughed in quiet delight, clapping her hands together into a clasp. Jill rolled her eyes as she stood beside her again, grinning under the pressure of Laney's pleased regard.

"No, now she'd be proud of me."

The two stood there like that as moments slipped by. They watched the fire as it settled and felt the pre-Noel chill on their skin. They stood close enough that when one shifted, their arms brushed. And they remained like this, deep in their own thoughts, enjoying the quiet, unquestioning company of the other until Jill turned to Laney and said, "I thought your friend was coming over to your place or something. Someone you wanted me to meet?"

"Yeah, I did, too. But Vince and Nigel came back early, so...guess she's with him."

Jill gave a slow nod of recognition to this, understanding the change in plans, that she wouldn't be sleeping at her sister's home that night. She started to ask Laney why she'd come over, but she was enjoying the moment between them too much to break it, and

Laney's phone trilling loudly in the night did the job for her anyway. Laney let it ring again before she pulled it out of her pocket and checked the screen.

"Nigel." She frowned. "That's weird. He never calls me."

"Probably your friend saying she's not coming. Or something about Vince." A snort. "Fuck him."

She watched as Laney contemplated whether to answer the phone, holding it in her open palm as they both stared down at the number. In the end, she pressed the phone to her face and stared out into the flames.

Book Club Questions

1) Although Aaliyah, Delaney and Jillian have different personalities, what common threads link them and their separate narratives?

2) What are the relationships between the men in the novel, and how do these relationships affect one another?

3) How does race dictate, control or influence the actions, thoughts and interactions of all the characters, no matter their economic background?

4) How do we see the impact of Vince's assault against Jillian throughout the book? How do you think it affected how she felt about her family? Discuss her coverup of the truth in light of the #MeToo movement.

5) *The Other Americans* touches on sexual assault, skin-color racism, mental health issues, social prejudices and how historical traumas shape our present day. Discuss how these issues, and others, are handled and how effectively they mirror the same issues in real life.

6) Do you think Addison was justified in her treatment of Jillian throughout her life, and did you find Jillian's reaction to it to be understandable?

7) Do you agree with the way Aaliyah handled her corporate issues? Why or why not, and what would you have done differently or the same?

8) Discuss how you felt about Nigel's storyline in this novel and where you think he's headed next.

9) How do classism and status lines play a role in this novel for each of the characters?

10) How do you think the characters will react to finding out the news about Aaliyah?

ACKNOWLEDGMENTS

They say writing a book is no solitary feat, and that is certainly true of this novel. This book was raised by a village of supportive, dedicated women who listened to my plans, ideas and neurosis patiently, who leant an ear and a word of advice when I needed it. Thank you to Jennifer Bennie, Jessica Jackson and Tamara Spiller who read drafts of this book before anyone else and gave me their honest feedback like no one else could have. Thank you to Kimberly Lipscomb who encouraged me to "take the leap from the plane" and just go for it. I feel that flying sensation we spoke about just fine now. And thank you to my mother, Patricia Johns, who started my love for books and always pushed me to be my best in every endeavor I take on. I hope it shows in this novel.

ABOUT THE AUTHOR

Navidad Thélamour was born and raised in Austin, Texas. She received her B.A. in English, Creative Writing from Georgia State University and her M.A. in Publishing from Kingston University in London. She is a regular contributor and trend writer at *Padmore Culture* and has interviewed dozens of authors and literary names. She is also the co-host of the "Organic Chemistry" relationship podcast. Navidad is currently working on the follow up to The Other Americans and a short story collection of anti-fairy tales for women, coming soon. Visit www.thenavireview.com for more information.

33704513R00210

Made in the USA
Middletown, DE
17 January 2019